Sand Castle Bay

New York Times Bestselling Author

SHERRYL WOODS

Sand Castle Bay

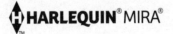

ISBN-13: 978-1-62490-271-0

SAND CASTLE BAY

Printed in U.S.A.

For all of those who've discovered the magic
of North Carolina's Outer Banks
and made happy memories there, including
my own special extended family. Thanks for the good times.

Dear friends,

My affection for living by water—be it the shores of the Potomac River in Virginia or the beaches of Key Biscayne in Florida—is well known to most of you. There's another spot that's become dear to me in more recent years: the coastal towns in North Carolina.

For the next three months I'm inviting you to share my fictional version of that special region in the new trilogy of Ocean Breeze novels that begins with *Sand Castle Bay*. You'll get to know the three Castle sisters and their wise and wonderful grandmother, to say nothing of the strong, sexy men in their lives, as they face the kind of changes and challenges many of you may have faced at one time or another.

I hope you'll embrace this new family as well as this new setting and spend the next few months imagining the sand beneath your feet and the ocean breezes on your cheeks.

All best,

Sherryl

1

The television in Emily Castle's Aspen, Colorado, hotel room was tuned to the Weather Channel, where there was minute-by-minute coverage of the hurricane aiming directly at North Carolina's coast, the place that had been like a second home to her. Childhood summers there had been slow and lazy and sweet. The beach town her grandmother called home was where she'd ultimately experienced her first heartache, yet despite those painful memories and despite everything she had on her plate at the moment, it was where she needed to be.

Even before her cell phone rang, she was checking flight schedules on her laptop. She clicked on a connecting flight between Atlanta and Raleigh, North Carolina, just as she answered the incoming call.

"Already on it," she told her sister Gabriella. "I should be able to get to Raleigh by sometime late tomorrow."

"Not a chance," Gabi argued. "Flights are going to be canceled up and down the East Coast for at least a day or two. You're better off waiting until next week and booking for Monday, maybe even Tuesday. Avoid the craziness."

"What's Samantha doing?" Emily asked, referring to their older sister.

"She's rented a car and is already on her way down from New York. She'll be here later tonight, hopefully ahead of the storm. They're predicting landfall overnight. We're already getting some of the wind and rain bands clear over here."

Of course Samantha would beat the storm! Emily couldn't seem to stop herself from frowning. Though she'd never totally understood it, the odd competitiveness she'd always felt with her oldest sister kicked in with a vengeance. She supposed with three sisters, there were bound to be rivalries, but why with Samantha and not Gabi? Gabi was the driven, successful businesswoman, the one most like her in terms of ambition.

"I'm getting on a flight out of here tonight," Emily said determinedly, motivated by Samantha's plans. "If I have to drive from Atlanta, then that's what I'll do."

Rather than admonishing her, Gabi chuckled. "Samantha said you were going to say that. From the time you understood the difference between winning and losing, you hated it when she beat you at anything. Okay, fine. Get here when you can. Just do it safely. This storm isn't looking pretty. If it wobbles even the slightest bit to the west, Sand Castle Bay will take a direct hit. You can bet the road down to Hatteras will wash out again unless they were a lot smarter when they did the repairs after the last storm."

"How's Grandmother?" Cora Jane Castle was in her mid-seventies but still going strong and determined to continue operating the beachfront restaurant opened by her late husband even though no one in the family had demonstrated any interest in running it. In Emily's view, she ought to sell it and enjoy her golden years, but the mere mention of such an idea was considered blasphemy.

"Stoic about the storm, but mad as a wet hen that Dad drove over and picked her up to bring her to Raleigh to ride out the hurricane," Gabi assessed. "She's in my kitchen cooking and muttering a few very bad words I had no idea she knew. I think that's why Dad dropped her here, then took off. He didn't want to be around when she got her hands on my knives."

"Or it could be he had no idea what to say to her. That's his way, isn't it?" Emily said with a hint of bitterness. Under the best of conditions, her father, Sam, wasn't communicative. Under the worst, he simply wasn't around. Most of the time she'd made her peace with that, but on occasion simmering resentments rose to the surface.

"He has work to do," Gabi said, immediately defensive, as always. "Important work. Do you know the kind of impact these biomedical studies at his company could have on people's lives?"

"I wonder how many times he said exactly that to Mother when he went off and left her to cope with raising us."

For once Gabi didn't overreact. "It was a constant refrain, wasn't it? Well, we're all grown-up. We should be over all those missed school plays and recitals and soccer games by now."

"Says the not-so-well-adjusted woman who's doing her best to follow in his footsteps," Emily taunted with good humor. "You know you're no better than he is,

Gabriella. You may not be a scientist, but you are a workaholic. That's why you get so uptight when I criticize him."

The silence that greeted her comment was deafening. "Gabi, I was only teasing," Emily apologized, aware that she'd crossed a line. "Seriously. You know how proud we all are of your accomplishments. You're a top executive at one of the hottest biomed companies in North Carolina, if not the entire country."

"I know. You just struck a nerve, that's all," Gabi said, then added briskly, "Let me know when you're getting in and I'll pick you up at the airport, okay?"

Before Emily could offer another apology for what she had recognized as an insensitive, ill-timed remark, Gabriella had hung up. Not with the sort of clatter that would mirror Emily's own quick flares of temper, but quietly. Somehow that was much, much worse.

Boone Dorsett had been through his share of hurricane warnings and actual hits on the coast. He had the boarding-up routine down pat. But when it came right down to it, Mother Nature was always in control of the outcome.

As a kid he'd been awed by the ferocious storms, but he'd had little real understanding of the havoc they could wreak on people's lives. These days, with a son, a home and a busy restaurant, he had a far better grasp of what could be lost to high winds, devastating storm surges and flood waters. He'd seen roads washed out, houses toppled, lives uprooted.

Thankfully, this latest storm had taken a last-minute turn east and delivered only a glancing blow. There was damage, plenty of it in fact, but so far he hadn't seen the kind of destruction he'd witnessed in the past. In fact, it had been relatively kind to him. There'd been some flooding at his waterfront restaurant, a few shingles ripped off the roof at his home, but his biggest concern after checking out his own property had been for Cora Jane's family restaurant.

Castle's by the Sea had been a constant in his life, as had Cora Jane. Both had inspired him to go into the restaurant business, not to mimic Castle's success, but to create his own welcoming ambiance. He owed Cora Jane, too, for helping him to believe in himself when no one in his own dysfunctional family had.

The biggest reason for Castle's success, other than its proximity to the ocean, good food and friendly service, was Cora Jane's devotion to it. She'd called him half a dozen times since the storm had passed to see if he'd been allowed back into Sand Castle Bay. The minute the evacuation order had been lifted, he'd crossed the bridge from the mainland to check his property and hers.

Now, standing in the middle of the damp, debris-littered dining room at Castle's by the Sea, he called her with the damage assessment she'd been anxiously awaiting.

"How bad is it?" she asked, foregoing so much as a hello. "Tell me the truth, Boone. Don't you dare sugarcoat it."

"Could have been worse," he told her. "There was some flooding, but no worse than over at my place."

"Shame on me," Cora Jane interrupted. "I never even asked how you fared in the storm. Just some flooding?"

"That was the worst of it," he confirmed. "My crew's already cleaning up. They know the drill. As for the house, it's fine. So is yours. A lot of tree limbs in the yard, a few roof shingles ripped off, but otherwise it's all good."

"Thank heavens. Now finish telling me about Castle's."

Boone complied. "A couple of storm shutters stripped away and the windows blew in. You'll have to replace a few of these waterlogged tables and chairs, treat everything for mold, and paint, but all in all, it's not as bad as it could have been."

"The deck?"

"Still standing. Looks solid enough to me, but I'll have it checked."

"And the roof?"

Boone sucked in a breath. He hated delivering bad news and had deliberately put this off till last. "Now, I won't lie to you, Cora Jane, but the roof's looking pretty bad. Once the wind gets a hold on a few shingles, you know how it goes."

"Oh, I know well enough," she said, sounding stoic. "So, is it bad, as in a goner, or bad as in a few stray shingles came loose?"

He smiled. "I'd want to get Tommy Cahill over here to check it, but I'm thinking you'd be better off just getting the whole thing done. Shall I go ahead and call him? He owes me a favor. I think I can get him here before the day's out. I can call your insurance company and see about getting a cleaning crew in here, too."

"I'd be obliged if you could get Tommy over there, but I'll call the insurance people and there's no need for a cleaning crew," Cora Jane insisted. "I'll be back first thing tomorrow with the girls. With them pitching in, we can clean the place up in no time."

Boone's heart seemed to still at her words. *The girls* could only be her granddaughters, including the one who'd dumped him ten years ago and taken off to start a better life than she thought he'd be able to give her.

"Emily, too?" he asked, holding out a faint hope that she wouldn't be back here, in his face, testing his belief that he'd long ago gotten her out of his system.

"Of course," Cora Jane said, then added a little too gently, "Is that going to be a problem, Boone?"

"Of course not. Emily and me, that's in the past. The *distant* past," he added emphatically.

"Are you so sure about that?" she pressed.

"I moved on, married someone else, didn't I?" he said defensively.

"And lost Jenny way too soon," Cora Jane said, as if he needed reminding of his wife's death just over a year ago.

"But not our son," Boone said. "I still have B.J. to think about. He's my life these days."

"I know you're devoted to that boy, but you need more," she lectured. "You deserve to have a full and happy life."

"Someday maybe I'll find the kind of happiness you're talking about," Boone said, "but I'm not looking for it, and it sure as heck isn't going to be with a woman who didn't think I'd amount to much."

Cora Jane drew in a shocked breath. "Boone, that is not what happened. Emily never judged you and found you lacking. She just had all these pie-in-the-sky dreams for herself. She needed to leave here and test herself, see what she could accomplish."

"That's your spin. I saw it a little differently," Boone

said. "Maybe we'd better not talk about Emily. We've stayed friends, you and me, by keeping her off-limits. She's family and you love her. Of course you'd defend her."

"You're family, too," Cora Jane insisted fiercely. "Or as good as."

Boone smiled. "You've always made me feel that way. Now let me make those calls and see what I can do to get this place back in working order before you get here. I know you're going to want to plug in the coffeepot and open the doors as soon as the power's back on. I should warn you that could be another couple of days. You maybe ought to consider staying with Gabi until it's fixed."

"I need to be there," Cora Jane replied determinedly. "Sitting around here and worrying isn't getting anything accomplished. I imagine we can get by on that generator you had installed after the last storm."

"I'll make sure it's working and check the refrigerators and freezer to make sure things stayed cold. Anything else you need me to do before you come home?"

"If Tommy gives you a fair estimate on the roof, tell him to get started, okay?"

"You have my word, he'll be fair," Boone assured her. "And you'll be first on his list. Like I said, he owes me."

"Then I'll see you tomorrow," Cora Jane said. "Thanks for checking on things for me."

"It's what family does," he replied, knowing it was a lesson he'd learned from Cora Jane, not from either of his own parents. Being supportive simply wasn't part of their makeup.

As he hung up, he couldn't help wondering if there

would ever come a day when he'd not regret that his ties to Cora Jane and her family weren't of a far more permanent variety.

It took Emily two frustrating days to make all the right connections from Colorado to North Carolina. More annoying than the time wasted in airports was imagining Gabi's *I-told-you-so* when she finally landed in Raleigh on a clear day that bore no lingering evidence of the nasty weather that had blown through the state two days before.

But when she emerged from the airport with her carry-on luggage, it was Samantha who awaited her. Her big sister enveloped her in a fierce hug.

Though huge, fashionable sunglasses hid most of her face, and her artfully streaked hair was swept up in a careless ponytail, there was no disguising that she was somebody famous. It had always amazed Emily how Samantha could wear faded jeans and a T-shirt and wind up looking like a cover model. She just had that celebrity look about her, even if her acting career had never taken off quite the way she'd envisioned.

"Where's Gabi?" Emily asked, glancing around.

"Three guesses."

"Gram insisted on going home," Emily said readily.

"Got it in one," Samantha confirmed. "The minute they allowed residents back out there, Gram packed her bag. Gabi stalled her for a day, then told her if she was going to be stubborn as an old mule, at least she wasn't going alone. They left this morning at dawn, so I stuck around to be your designated driver."

"Do you actually remember how to drive?" Emily

inquired skeptically. "You've been living in New York a long time."

Samantha merely lifted a brow, which told Emily what her sister thought about her sense of humor. That was the thing about having an actress in the family. Samantha could convey more with a look than most people could with an entire diatribe. Emily had been on the receiving end of a lot of those looks over the years.

"Do not start with me," Samantha warned. "I made it here, didn't I?"

Emily nodded toward the waiting car. "Is that the same car you drove from New York? Or did you have to trade in a wreck?"

"You are not amusing," Samantha retorted. She glanced at the compact carry-on Emily had brought. "That's it? That's all your luggage?"

Emily shrugged. "I'm used to traveling light. I was in Aspen on a job when I heard about the storm. I didn't have time to go back to Los Angeles to pick up more things."

"Anything in there suitable for mopping and scrubbing?" Samantha asked doubtfully. "I just don't see you mucking out the family restaurant in your designer heels. Those are Louboutins, right? You always did have expensive taste."

Heat climbed in Emily's cheeks. "I work with people who are obsessed with designer labels, but you can bet I do my share of hard labor when I'm renovating a house," she retorted defensively, then sighed. "But you're right about my wardrobe not being suitable for cleaning. This trip to Colorado was a quick meet-and-greet with a new client, so I probably need to pick up some shorts and T-shirts someplace. What about you?

You usually look like a fashion plate yourself. What's with the faded jeans and…" Her eyes widened. "Is that Ethan Cole's old football jersey?"

Samantha blushed furiously. "It was in a box of stuff in Gabi's attic. I grabbed whatever still fit."

"That shirt doesn't fit," Emily scoffed. "It's at least six sizes too big. It makes you look like a fourteen-year-old girl with a crush on the captain of the football team." She allowed a slow grin to spread. "Oh, wait, that was you, wasn't it? Sitting in the bleachers all wide-eyed and hopeful?"

"Do you realize if you keep this up, you might not live long enough to get to Sand Castle Bay?" Samantha asked tartly. "I imagine I can find some deserted section of highway where I can toss your body."

"Nice talk to your baby sister," Emily retorted. "You always swore you loved me, even when I was being a total pain."

"Back then I did," Samantha confirmed with a grin of her own. "Who could resist a cute, chubby-cheeked little thing?" She shrugged. "Now, not so much."

Once they were on the road heading east, Emily's mood sobered. "Has anyone heard how bad things are over there? What's Grandmother going to find when she walks into the restaurant?"

"Apparently Boone told her it was still standing, just badly flooded and in need of a lot of tender, loving care and, more than likely, a new roof."

Emily froze, her heart doing an unexpected stutter step. "Boone? Surely you're not talking about Boone Dorsett. What does he have to do with anything?"

"He and Cora Jane are thick as thieves these days,"

Samantha said, then gave her a quick sympathetic glance. "Didn't you know?"

"Why would I know? Nobody tells me anything." At least not anything that might matter, such as the fact that her own grandmother and the bane of her existence, Mr. Boone Dorsett, were pals.

Oh, her grandmother had always had a soft spot for Boone. She'd taken to him the minute he'd started coming around with Emily the summer they'd both turned fourteen. While Emily had fallen for a bad boy with a dangerous edge most likely headed for trouble, Cora Jane had seen a boy rebelling against parents who didn't care. She'd seen potential and, to her credit, nourished it.

Still, shouldn't she have cut her ties with Boone when Emily had, out of family solidarity or something? Even as the thought formed, Emily knew better. Grandmother wouldn't abandon Boone the way Emily had. In fact, though she'd never voiced her opinion, Emily knew Cora Jane had judged her harshly for what she'd done, choosing a career over the man everyone knew she loved.

"What's Boone after?" she asked suspiciously.

"After?" Samantha echoed with a puzzled look. "I don't think he wants anything. Cora Jane says he's been a huge help to her with the restaurant. That's all I know."

"If Boone is being a huge help, then he wants something," Emily declared with conviction. Wasn't he always after something? That had been her experience, anyway. Once upon a time he'd wanted her, and when she'd said she needed time to explore the world a bit, he'd let her go and married Jenny Farmer about ten seconds later. Last she'd heard they had a little boy. So much for that undying love he'd declared he felt for her.

Maybe she'd left, but he was the one who'd delivered a betrayal so deep she'd never really recovered.

"He probably wants the Castle's by the Sea property," Emily speculated direly. In her dark days, hadn't she entertained that thought more than once, imagining him courting her even back then with an ulterior motive? How else to explain his rapid-fire marriage to someone else after she'd gone? True love couldn't possibly have been so fickle. "I'll just bet he's hoping this hurricane will be the last straw and Grandmother will sell that prime beachfront location to him."

Samantha slanted a wry look at her. "You do know that Boone already has three very successful seafood restaurants, right?"

"Three?" Emily echoed, startled.

"Sure enough. Boone's Harbor on the bay opened first. Now he has one in Norfolk and one over in Charlotte. I think there's some guy who's like his administrative assistant who scouts out the new locations and gets them operational, but Boone's definitely in charge. Grandmother says the reviews have been great in all those cities. She has a collection of them. I'm surprised she never sent them to you."

"She probably assumed I wouldn't be interested," Emily said, oddly deflated by the news. She wanted to believe the very worst about Boone. Needed to believe it, in fact. She didn't like thinking she'd misjudged his ambition or that she might have made a terrible mistake in being so quick to let him go. She didn't believe in regrets, so what were these twinges all about?

Her sister studied her with obvious confusion. "I thought you were long over him. You did break up with

him, right? Not the other way around? I always thought
Jenny was his rebound romance."

"Over him?" Emily huffed indignantly. "Of course,
I'm over him. Haven't given him a thought since I left
here ten years ago." *Liar, liar,* her conscience shouted.

"Then why the attitude?"

"I just don't want him taking advantage of our grandmother, that's all. Cora Jane is too trusting for her own
good."

Samantha laughed at that. "Cora Jane? You must
have some other grandmother in mind. Cora Jane's as
savvy as they come where business is concerned and
sharp as a tack when it comes to judging people."

"She's not immune to a man with Boone's consider-
able charm, that's all I'm saying," Emily said irritably.
"Let's drop this. It's giving me a headache." She looked
around and frowned. They were in the jammed parking
lot of a discount store. "Why are you pulling in here?"

"To stock up on your brand-new hurricane cleanup
wardrobe," her sister said, then added, a little too cheerfully, "Let's not forget the flip-flops and sneakers."

Emily regarded her with dismay. The only flip-flops
she wore these days came from a designer shoe salon
on Rodeo Drive.

"Okay," she said sourly, "but you and Gabi better
remember that I don't scrub windows." She hesitated,
then added, "Or floors."

Samantha draped an arm over her shoulder as they
crossed the busy parking lot. "Fine, Cinderella. We'll
leave the grease trap to you. That's always fun."

Emily scowled at her. It promised to be a very long
couple of weeks, especially if Boone was likely to be
underfoot.

2

"Daddy, are we gonna help Ms. Cora Jane?" B.J. asked, his expression as excited as if they were going to the circus.

"If she'll let us," Boone told his eight-year-old son. In his experience Cora Jane never asked for help and wasn't real crazy about accepting it when offered. He'd learned to be incredibly sneaky about making sure she and the restaurant were looked after.

"Do you think she'll make me pancakes like Mickey Mouse?" B.J. asked. "The little pancakes that make the ears are the best part." A guilty expression passed over his face. "Hers are better than Jerry's, but don't tell him. I don't want to hurt his feelings."

Boone laughed, well aware of how competitive the cook and Cora Jane could be at times. "I doubt she'll have the kitchen open," Boone told him. "The storm water's barely receded. You know what a mess things are over at our place. Castle's didn't look much better when I checked it out yesterday."

He also knew that Cora Jane was the kind of woman who liked to feel in control of things. No hurricane would throw her off course for long. By tomorrow, she'd probably be cooking whatever she could on the gas grill even if she couldn't get the oven up and running.

He gave his son a warning look. "Don't be asking her for pancakes, okay? Not till we see what the situation is. We're here to help, not to make more work for her."

"But she always says making special pancakes for me isn't work," B.J. said earnestly. "She says she does it out of love."

Boone chuckled. Of course she'd tell B.J. something like that. Hadn't she always made him feel he was no trouble, too? Even when his own folks thought he was more of a nuisance than anything else. If it hadn't been for Cora Jane and the jobs she'd given him to keep him busy and out of mischief, his life would have gone in a whole different direction. He owed her. He surely did. And he counted himself fortunate that she hadn't pushed him out of her life when Emily had dumped him. Given the fierce family loyalty among the Castles, it could easily have happened.

If seeing her and listening to her brag about her three granddaughters, including the woman who'd been the love of his life, was painful, well, that was just the price he had to pay for having Cora Jane as the kind of compassionate, nonjudgmental moral compass he definitely needed.

As soon as Boone had parked beside the restaurant, B.J. was out of the car and running.

"Hold it!" Boone commanded, waiting until his son had skidded to a stop and faced him. He walked closer and put a hand on the boy's shoulder and pointed. "What have I told you about the need to be real careful right now? Just look around. There's wood all over with nails in it and who knows what kind of glass on the ground. Take your time and pay attention."

B.J. gave him an impish smile that reminded him so much of Jenny, it made his heart ache. Jenny had been the sweetest woman on the planet, and losing her to an out-of-control infection that had proven resistant to antibiotics had been devastating to him and to B.J.

With the resilience of childhood, B.J. was bouncing back, but Boone wasn't sure he'd ever get past his grief. He knew some of that was colored by guilt because he'd never loved Jenny half as much as she'd loved him. How could he when a part of his heart still belonged to Emily Castle? No matter his feelings, though, he thought he'd done the best he could by his wife. Jenny had never wanted for anything. He'd been a good husband, a devoted father. Late at night, though, he couldn't help wondering if it had been enough. It didn't help that Jenny's parents blamed him for everything from ruining Jenny's life to contributing to her death. He just knew they were looking for any excuse to try to take B.J. from him. That, he thought fiercely, would happen over his own dead body!

As for the rest, well, it was water under the bridge now, he told himself, as he took a deep breath and followed his son. Alerted by Cora Jane that all three of her granddaughters were coming home to help with the storm cleanup, he braced himself for the first glimpse of Emily after all these years.

Inside the water-ravaged restaurant, though, he spotted only Gabriella, looking frantic as Cora Jane teetered on the top rung of a stepladder. Gabi was holding it steady with a white-knuckled grip.

"Cora Jane Castle, what do you think you're doing?"

Boone demanded, wrapping an arm around her hips and lifting her down until her sneaker-clad feet were firmly on the ground.

She whirled around and glared at him. "What do you think *you're* doing, Boone Dorsett?" she inquired, her brown eyes flashing with indignation, even as he gave the obviously relieved Gabi a wink.

"Saving you from a broken hip, most likely," he said. "Didn't I tell you a long time ago that I'd take care of fixing all the lights whenever they needed it or to have Jerry or your handyman do it?"

"Well, Jerry's not here yet and my handyman's nowhere to be found," she retorted. "And since when do I need you to screw in a few lightbulbs?" Hands on her hips, she tried her best to stare him down. Given their relative size difference, she wasn't half as intimidating as she obviously hoped to be.

"You could at least have let Gabi do it," he replied.

She seemed to fight a smile at the suggestion, avoiding her granddaughter's gaze. "Bless her heart," she confided in an undertone, "Gabi is scared of heights. She got two rungs up the ladder, and I thought she was about to faint."

"It's true," Gabi replied, an embarrassed flush in her cheeks. "It was humiliating, especially when she went scampering right on up the ladder."

Thankfully, just then B.J. tugged on Cora Jane's hand. "Ms. Cora Jane, the power's back on, right?"

She smiled and ruffled his hair affectionately. "Came on about a half hour ago, as a matter of fact." She gave him a knowing look. "I imagine you asked because you're hoping for pancakes."

B.J.'s eyes lit up. "Uh-huh, but Daddy said not to ask because we're here to help."

Cora Jane rolled her eyes. "Well, since your daddy seems intent on taking over the most dangerous chores himself, I imagine I can try to rustle up some pancakes for my favorite customer. You gonna help?"

"Sure. I'll mix the batter like you showed me last time," B.J. offered, trailing after her.

Boone watched them go, shaking his head. "I don't know which of them's going to give me my first heart attack, but odds on, it's your grandmother."

Gabi laughed. "She has that effect on all of us."

"She told me you and your sisters were all coming home to help put this place back in working order," he said, hoping he sounded casual, rather than panicked, which was the way just thinking about Emily made him feel.

Gabi gave him a knowing look. "Samantha just called. Emily's flight landed about an hour ago. They stopped to pick up some things for Emily to wear. Apparently Em was in Aspen when I called her, and the clothes she had with her weren't suitable for mopping."

"Aspen, huh?" Boone said. "She gets around these days, doesn't she?"

Gabi nodded. "Her reputation as an interior designer took off after the remodel she did for some actress was featured in a magazine. Now she's working on all sorts of celebrity homes in Beverly Hills and Malibu. Last year she renovated somebody's villa in Italy, and I think this trip was to look at a ski lodge for the friend of one of her regular clients."

"Sounds glamorous," he said, a sinking sensation in the pit of his stomach.

Wasn't that what she'd always wanted, the high life with famous people? Some of their old friends accused her of being superficial and shallow, but he knew better. She'd been trying to fill some empty place in her soul with all the things she thought her simple life in North Carolina had been missing.

He wondered if she still saw that world as fascinating, if she'd gotten to know even one of those celebrities as a friend, rather than as a client. He'd learned a long time ago how much better it was to have a few people he could count on than a thousand acquaintances. The folks who'd been by his side when Jenny was sick and then stuck by him after her death had taught him the real meaning of friendship.

"I'd better go in and check on Grandmother," Gabi said. She started toward the kitchen, then came back. "I'm sorry, Boone."

He frowned at her serious tone. "Sorry for what?"

"The way Emily hurt you. She never meant to. There were just things she felt she needed to do. I think she always meant to come back, but then you married Jenny, and, well, you know how things went after that."

Boone nodded, appreciating the sentiment but determined to make sure she knew it was unnecessary. "I accepted her decision a long time ago, Gabi. And just so you know, I don't think she ever intended to come back. That's why I moved on."

Gabi glanced toward the kitchen and nodded. "Nobody blames you for that. And B.J.'s a great boy."

"The best," he agreed readily. "Probably no thanks to me. Jenny was an amazing mother. I think your grandmother's influence accounts for a lot of that, too, same as it did with me."

"Don't sell yourself short."

Boone watched her go, then sighed. Why was it that all the women in this family thought he was worth something…except the one who'd stolen his heart all those years ago?

Emily had prepared herself for seeing Boone again. At least she thought she had.

And yet the sight of him atop a ladder, his excellent butt hugged by a pair of worn jeans, his faded T-shirt stretched taut over a broad chest and outstanding biceps, was good enough to give her palpitations. A baseball cap had been pulled low, which made it hard to see his face, but she imagined his granite jaw, dark-as-onyx eyes and dimples were the same.

It had always been amazing to her that a man could be flashing fire hot as a furnace one second, flip a switch to a look as cold as the North Pole the next, and then turn right around and grin with the impish expression of a boy caught with his hand in the cookie jar. Boone Dorsett had always been something of a contradiction, in her opinion.

"Hey, Boone!" Samantha called out, when Emily just stood there, probably slack-jawed, taking in the view.

His head snapped around so fast he might have lost his balance if Emily hadn't instinctively grabbed the ladder to steady it.

"Samantha," he acknowledged solemnly before allowing his gaze to settle on Emily. "Emily."

To her annoyance there was not one tiny shred of a difference in the way he spoke her name, no hint that she was any more special than her sister, that he used to have his hands and that sweetly seductive mouth of his all over her whenever they could sneak away to be together. Seriously, shouldn't that have called for at least a hint of intimacy in the way he spoke her name?

That was then, she reminded herself sharply. *The man is married now. He belongs to someone else.*

"What are you doing here, Boone?" she asked irritably.

He held up a lightbulb. "Isn't it obvious?"

"I mean here, helping my grandmother, instead of taking care of your own business." She knew she sounded churlish and ungrateful, but she couldn't help herself. The rules had all gone and changed on her, and yet her feelings for this man apparently hadn't. That was a shocker, all right. Boone Dorsett could still stir her blood in a way that not one single man she'd met since ever had. And he'd done it from atop a ladder, without even touching her. The discovery was unsettling. She'd been so sure that the bitterness she'd felt at his betrayal would trump all those old feelings forever.

"Darlin', I know you've been away a long time, but down here, folks help each other out in a crisis. I'd say this latest hurricane qualifies. Your grandmother's in the kitchen, by the way. I'm sure she's real anxious to see you."

He turned back to his chore, essentially dismissing her. Emily just stared at him, then turned to see Samantha grinning as if she'd just witnessed a scene in some ridiculous romantic comedy.

"Oh, hush your mouth," she muttered to her sister as she headed for the kitchen at a fast clip.

"Never said a word," Samantha retorted, following along behind, still grinning. "But in case you're interested in my opinion, that was hot."

Emily blinked and stared. "Are you delusional? The man just shooed me away as if I were an annoying mosquito or something."

"Hot," Samantha repeated. "Again, in case you're interested in my opinion, I'd have to say things between you two are far from over."

"The man is married," Emily reminded her.

Her sister's grin merely spread. "Oh, didn't anyone tell you that he lost his wife?"

"Did he happen to leave her behind in the Great Dismal Swamp?" Emily asked sarcastically.

Samantha's expression instantly sobered, all hints of teasing gone. "No, sweetie. Jenny died. Just over a year ago, in fact."

Emily stopped just inside the kitchen door and stared after her sister. Oh, God, that was awful. She was suddenly assailed by more emotions than she could even begin to untangle. Sorrow for Jenny, who'd been a genuinely nice girl. Heartache for Boone and for his child, who must have been devastated.

And a completely inappropriate and unexpected flash of relief, followed all too quickly by panic. It was one thing to discover she wasn't immune to the man when he was safely off-limits, but it was something else entirely to realize he was available, after all. She had not needed to know that. She really hadn't.

Because the very last thing she needed in her very busy and tightly scheduled life was to have feelings for Boone Dorsett, the man she'd very deliberately left behind.

Cora Jane's gaze went straight to Emily when she and Samantha walked into the kitchen. In that first quick glance she saw that her granddaughter was too thin, her face bordering on gaunt. She'd been working too hard, not taking nearly enough time for herself, Cora Jane assessed.

There was also no mistaking the bright patches of color in her cheeks and the sparks in her eyes, put there by Boone, no doubt. Cora Jane turned away, hoping none of the others would see the satisfied smile she couldn't seem to stop. She wished she'd been witness to the first meeting between those two after all this time, but seeing Emily's face told her it had gone exactly as she'd hoped.

"My sweet girl," she said, then held open her arms. "It's been entirely too long since you've been home."

Emily stepped into her embrace and gave her a fierce hug. "I know. I'm sorry. I always think I'll get here, but time just flies by."

"Well, you're here now," Cora Jane said, misty-eyed as she glanced around the table where Samantha and Gabi were seated along with B.J. "You're all here. You have no idea what it means to me that you dropped everything and came."

"Well, of course we did," Emily said. "Isn't that the lesson you tried to teach us, to be there for family? Now tell me what you're doing in here cooking? Judging from the looks of things in the dining room, we should all be on our hands and knees out there scrubbing the place down."

"She's making pancakes for me," B.J. piped up, catching Emily's attention.

Cora Jane watched as it dawned on Emily who B.J. was. There could be little question he was Boone's son. The boy was the spitting image of the man. Shock registered on Emily's face for just an instant, but she managed a smile.

"And who might you be that you can convince my grandmother to make pancakes?" Emily teased, her voice unmistakably shaky.

"I'm B. J. Dorsett," he responded seriously. "Boone's my dad. I help out here a lot, don't I, Ms. Cora Jane?"

"Best helper I have," Cora Jane confirmed. "And I figured B.J. had the right idea. We all need a hearty breakfast before we tackle this mess."

"I'm betting you talked her into the Mickey Mouse pancakes, too," Emily said to B.J., whose eyes lit up.

"Uh-huh. They're the best."

"I always thought so," Emily said.

B.J. gave her a perplexed look. "How come I've never seen you before? Ms. Gabi's here sometimes, but not you or Ms. Samantha."

"Well, we both live far away," Emily said, a guilty flush in her cheeks. "Samantha lives in New York. She's a very busy actress."

B.J.'s eyes widened as he took another look at Samantha, then widened some more as recognition dawned. "I've seen you on TV. You were the mom in a commercial for my favorite cereal." He pumped a fist in the air. "I knew it. Cool! Have you been in other stuff?"

"Lots of things you probably wouldn't have seen," Samantha said. "I've been in a few plays on Broadway, a soap opera, a few other commercials."

B.J. bounced in his chair with excitement. "Wait till I tell the kids at school." He glanced at Cora Jane. "Does Dad know? I'd better tell Dad."

"In a minute," Cora Jane said, noting that Emily looked vaguely disgruntled by B.J.'s excitement over meeting a famous actress. That girl's competitive streak between her and Samantha was still alive and well, apparently. "Your breakfast's ready."

She set plates of pancakes, eggs and bacon in front of everyone, poured more coffee, then took her own place at the table. Turning to B.J. she deliberately mentioned that Emily had worked for a few movie stars.

"No way!" B.J. exclaimed, now giving Emily his full attention. "What'd you do? Who'd you work for? Did you ever meet Johnny Depp?"

Cora Jane knew that Emily didn't really like talking about her famous clients, but she also knew she needed to get the spotlight back on her. The affections of little boys could be fickle. Maybe it was ridiculous, but Cora Jane had a feeling that B.J. just might be the key to a reconciliation between Emily and Boone. The boy needed a mother. Oh, she knew that Boone was doing the best he could and would disagree with her about that, but in just the past hour she'd seen how B.J. responded to the attention of her granddaughters.

Over the years she'd been fortunate to have these three girls with her most summers. They'd been closer than many grandparents and grandchildren. She thought that was, in part, because she hadn't done a lot of meddling in their lives. Oh, she'd given advice, given the occasional nudge when called for, but in general she'd let them make their own mistakes, their own decisions.

Now, though, they were older and showing no signs of settling down. Each of them had professional successes to be proud of, but not a one of them had a life. At least that's how she saw it.

That needed to change. And though none of them had

grown up here in Sand Castle Bay, they'd spent enough time here to earn the right to call it home.

She sat back and listened as B.J. peppered Emily with excited questions about Hollywood. Her granddaughter answered patiently, a smile playing about her lips.

"What about Disneyland?" B.J. asked. "Have you been to Disneyland? I'll bet you've gone like a thousand times."

Emily laughed. "I'm sorry to disappoint you, but not even once."

B.J. looked stunned. "Not once?"

"Afraid not."

"Me and Dad will come and we'll all go," he announced excitedly. "He's been promising to take me, and Dad never breaks his promises."

Emily looked taken aback by the suggestion, as if she weren't quite sure how to respond. "I'm sure you'll have a wonderful time," she said eventually.

"You, too," B.J. reminded her insistently. "I'll go tell Dad now."

He bounded away from the table, leaving all of them grinning.

"I think you've made a conquest," Gabi said.

"Like father, like son," Samantha chimed in.

"Stop it," Emily said, blushing. "He's at that age when he loves everyone."

"You have a lot of experience with eight-year-old boys?" Gabi teased.

"No, but isn't it obvious? He was chattering away to Grandmother and you before Sam and I even walked in the room. He's comfortable here."

Gabi's expression sobered. "Be careful with him, Em. He's been through a lot."

"What are you talking about? I'm here for a few days. It's not as if there's time for him to get attached or something."

"Just keep that in mind," Gabi persisted. "You are leaving, and he might not understand that."

"Well, I think it's sweet the way he's taken a shine to you right off," Cora Jane said. "To all of you. He can use a woman's influence."

Emily chuckled. "You don't think Boone is capable of teaching him manners?"

"Boone is capable of that and much more," Cora Jane chided. "But it's not the same as having a mother's touch, that's all I'm saying."

"Grandmother, you're not harboring any illusions about Boone and me picking up where we left off, are you?" Emily asked, her gaze narrowed. "Because that's not in the cards. My life's in California."

"Such as it is," Cora Jane muttered.

Emily frowned. "What is that supposed to mean? I have an excellent life. I make a ton of money. I'm respected in my field."

"And who's there to share in all that success, I ask you?" Cora Jane retorted. "No one, that's who. Or is there someone special you haven't bothered to mention to any of us?" She glanced at Emily's sisters. "Samantha? Gabi? Have either of you heard about anyone?"

Emily ignored the sarcasm. "Plenty of women have happy, fulfilling lives without a man," she said, turning to her sisters. "Am I right?"

"Men do have their uses," Gabi said, grinning.

"Amen, sister," Samantha chimed in.

Emily just shook her head. "Thanks for the backup. Wait till she starts on the two of you."

"That's not going to happen, because our lives are perfect," Gabi said, standing up to give Cora Jane's shoulder a squeeze.

Cora Jane glanced up at her. "Well, now that you mention it..." She let her voice trail off, leaving the unspoken implication to hang in the air. It would give them something to think about. She, indeed, had plans for all of them, and, God willing, she'd been unexpectedly blessed with the perfect opportunity to see them carried out.

3

Seeing Emily had rattled Boone, no question about it. His hand was shaking as he replaced the lightbulbs that had blown when the power was knocked out and a few that had been shattered by debris blowing around inside the restaurant after a boarded-up front window had given way to the storm's fury.

He was supposed to be over her. Wasn't that what he'd told Gabriella not ten minutes before Emily had walked in the door and caught him off guard? He'd meant it, hadn't he? He was not going to allow her to stomp all over his emotions a second time, especially not with B.J. to consider.

Though he'd been out on a couple of dates since Jenny's death, he'd made it a point to keep his son out of the mix. After his own mother had paraded half a dozen men through his life before settling on a replacement for his dad, he knew the dangers of allowing a child to get too attached to someone who wouldn't be staying.

Unfortunately, that didn't seem feasible with Emily, not with the two of them in the kitchen right this second apparently whooping it up with the rest of the Castles.

With Cora Jane's undoubted encouragement, his son and Emily were probably bonding even now.

B.J. emerged just then, his face sticky with maple syrup and his eyes round with excitement. "Daddy, did you know that Emily knows movie stars?" he asked, pretty much proving Boone's point.

"Does she really?" Boone said, his tone offhand, though a perverse part of him wanted to know every detail.

"She's been in their houses and everything," B.J. reported. "She even met Johnny Depp once. Isn't that awesome?"

Boone wondered what the appropriate response was. Should he express an enthusiasm he wasn't feeling, deliver a lecture on the fact that celebrities were merely people just like everyone else, or let the moment pass and accept that Emily had impressed his son with a lifestyle he could never match?

"Hey, Daddy, how come you never told me you knew somebody famous?" B.J. asked.

"I'm not sure that working for celebrities makes Emily famous," Boone said cautiously.

"Not her," B.J. said impatiently. "Samantha. She does those soap shows on TV, and she was in a play on Broadway. She even did a commercial for that cereal I like. She was the mom, remember? I didn't recognize her right off, because she's prettier in person."

Boone recalled only that every time he'd spotted Samantha in any commercial, she'd reminded him of Emily and, out of loyalty to Jenny, he'd tried his best to wipe all those memories out of his mind.

"You gotta come in the kitchen, Dad," B.J. urged. "They're telling the best stories."

"We came here to help Ms. Cora Jane clean up, remember?"

"But she's in the kitchen, too," B.J. protested. "I think she's happy her granddaughters came home."

Boone imagined she was. He'd seen the yearning in her eyes when she'd talked about them. Oh, she'd bragged about their accomplishments, her pride showing, but he'd heard the note of wistfulness she couldn't successfully hide, at least from him. Undoubtedly she was thrilled to pieces that a hurricane had brought them running home.

Too bad none of them came around when there wasn't a crisis.

"And guess what else?" B.J. said as he dragged a reluctant Boone toward the kitchen. "Emily's never been to Disneyland, so I said we'd come to California and she could go with us. We can do that, right?"

Boone stopped in his tracks. Things were suddenly moving way too fast. He hunkered down and looked into his son's eyes. "B.J., you know Emily's just here for a visit," he cautioned.

"I know. That's why I said we'll come to see her," B.J. responded reasonably.

"Son, don't start counting on Emily, okay?"

B.J. clearly didn't comprehend the warning. "What about Disneyland, Dad? You promised we'd go there, so why can't she come with us?"

Boone counted to ten. It wasn't B.J.'s fault that this entire conversation was making him a little crazy. "Actually I promised to take you to Disney World in Florida, so we could stop by and see your grandparents, remember?" Boone said patiently, but he knew he was fighting a losing battle. B.J. had the tenacity of a pit bull, and he wasn't going to drop this, at least not right now. To his son, the two amusement parks were clearly interchangeable. And, sadly, Jenny's folks were likely no competition for the glamorous Emily. He could just imagine the outcry, though, if he chose to take B.J. to California rather than Florida. There would be hell to pay.

"Well, I want to go to Disneyland and I want her to come," B.J. said, his expression mutinous. "You promised!"

Boone sighed. "We'll talk about it later."

Was there even the faintest possibility that he was going to get through Emily's visit with his sanity intact, especially with his eight-year-old apparently as enamored with her as he'd once been?

Emily had made herself a promise not to check her cell phone for messages until she'd spent a little time with family, but ingrained habits were hard to break. When she heard the signal for yet another text message in the past half hour, she excused herself from the table.

"Sorry. I need to deal with this," she said.

"Told you she wouldn't last an hour without checking her phone," Samantha teased. "I'm just surprised you haven't been on yours yet, Gabi."

Gabi flushed guiltily. "Actually I made a few calls and sent a couple of emails right before you all got here. My very efficient assistant is on top of things at the office. She knows how to reach me if anything crops up that she can't handle."

"I wish I had one of those," Emily said. "Mine's great at taking messages and following up on details, but when it comes to taking the initiative or pacifying clients, that's all on me." She gestured with the phone. "And that's what I'm dealing with now."

"Go ahead and make your calls," Cora Jane told her.

On the deck, Emily returned a call from Sophia Grayson, a high-maintenance Beverly Hills socialite who expected everything to be done yesterday. She paid top dollar to make that happen, and her acceptance of Emily had been a huge recommendation in certain circles.

"You're up early," Emily said when she'd reached her. "It's barely eight o'clock out there."

"I'm up early because I haven't slept all night," Sophia complained with a dramatic sigh. "I've been fretting about that disastrous mix-up with the drapery fabric. You know I'm throwing a very important party in less than two weeks, Emily. You promised every last detail would be completed in plenty of time."

"And they will be," Emily assured her. "The new drapes are being made as we speak. I spoke to Enrico myself, and he's appalled by the mistake. He's put his best people on the job and he'll have the replacements ready to be installed tomorrow."

"What about the paint in the dining room?" Sophia complained. "It's just awful. I would never have chosen that color. People will feel as if they're inside a pumpkin."

"I did warn you that orange could be overwhelming," Emily felt compelled to say, "but we have the backup ready to go. I think you'll be much happier with the taupe. It's so classy, definitely much more expressive of your excellent taste and style. The crew will be there at nine and should be out by this afternoon."

"I know taupe will be just fine, but I'd hoped for

a little pop of color for a change," Sophia said with a sigh of regret.

"And we'll have that in the accessories," Emily assured her. "You have an appointment with Steve from Rodeo Gallery to look at art this afternoon. I think you'll find a lovely painting for your collection of fresh new artists that will give you exactly the splash of color you want. Once you've chosen that, we can add a few other touches to bring it all together."

"I suppose," Sophia said. "You do know I trust you, Emily. You haven't let me down yet. Where are you, though? Why aren't you here? Isn't on-site oversight part of that fee I pay for your services?"

"I'm dealing with a bit of a family emergency in North Carolina, Sophia, but you're not to worry. Everything's under control. If you need me, all you have to do is call."

A beep told her she had another call. "Sweetie, I have to run," she told Sophia. "I'll speak to you later today, make sure everything's on track. Text me if you need me before then."

She cut off the call before Sophia could come up with another crisis. Glancing at the caller ID, she saw the name of the client she'd just met with in Aspen.

"We like your ideas," Derek Young said without preamble. "How soon can you get back here to get started? We'd like to have the lodge up and running by December first to take full advantage of the ski season. Thanksgiving would be even better."

Emily hated the thought of putting him off, but she had little choice. "It'll be a couple of weeks at least," she admitted. "If there's any way to make it sooner, I will. I'll be honest with you, though, Derek. December might be optimistic even if I could be there tomorrow. You're going to have to decide if you want quality work or an expedited timetable."

"I want both," he said without hesitation. "If that means doubling up on work crews, then do it."

Emily got the message. "Of course."

"This is a big job," he reminded her, clearly intending to emphasize the stakes. "It's an entire ski lodge. I'm sure you could get some PR mileage out of that."

"I understand what a fabulous opportunity you're giving me, Derek, but I can't abandon my family right now. The hurricane's left a mess in its wake."

He hesitated, leaving her with her heart in her throat. She thought she could hear his wife murmuring in the background.

"Okay, fine, do the best you can," he said eventually. "Tricia has reminded me that, contrary to the way I live my life, family should take priority over business from time to time."

Emily smiled. "It's a lesson I'm struggling with myself," she told him. "Thank her for me."

"You'll be in touch?"

"Of course. And there are things I can get started on from here. We won't be losing much time."

When she'd disconnected the call, she allowed herself a moment of triumph over snagging the job, then sighed. She wondered if anyone in her family would be excited for her over this coup. More likely, they'd be disappointed in her for making a promise to leave before the work here was likely to be done.

Cora Jane looked around at her girls, drinking in the sight of them, and the next thing she knew there were tears gathering in her eyes. It was Gabi who caught her before she could wipe them away.

"Grandmother, are you okay?" Gabi asked quietly.

"I'm just so glad to have the three of you under this roof again, even if it is leaking in a dozen spots and the place is a disaster."

"There's nothing wrong we can't fix with a little elbow grease," Gabi assured her. "I'll make some calls about the roof, too."

"No need," Cora Jane told her. "Boone's already taken care of that. He has someone coming first thing tomorrow to replace it. Shouldn't take more than a couple of days to get it fixed up. As long as we don't have another storm between now and then, we'll be okay."

"Did I hear you mention Boone?" Emily asked, coming back inside just in time to hear Cora Jane.

"He's arranged for someone to fix the roof," Gabi told her.

Emily's expression soured. "Why don't you let me make a few calls? Negotiating with contractors is what I do."

"How many contractors do you know here who could get to the job tomorrow?" Boone asked, choosing that moment to join them in the kitchen, B.J. at his side. "But if you want to give it a try, I won't be offended."

Emily flushed pink. "She should have competitive bids, that's all I'm saying," she retorted.

"Gee, why didn't I think of that?" he asked, a hint of sarcasm in his voice.

Cora Jane looked from one of them to the other and shook her head. Hadn't it always been this way? If Boone said the sky was blue, Emily would argue it was a gloomy gray. She'd never before known two people who were happiest when they were at odds over one thing or another. She thought it was because they were so alike with high expectations of themselves and everyone around them.

"Enough, you two," she scolded. "Tommy Cahill will be here tomorrow. He gave me a price I'm happy with, so that's that. I was lucky that Boone was able to get him to take on such a small job on short notice when there's so much to be done out here. He's only doing it as a favor to Boone. I could wait for weeks for someone else to become available."

Emily sat back, her expression disgruntled. "Whatever you want."

"Thank you," Cora Jane said dryly. "Now I propose we all get busy and get this place cleaned out. I'd like to open for breakfast tomorrow morning if I can get supplies here this afternoon."

"That's crazy," Emily blurted. "The place is a mess. It's going to take days for me to get some new furniture in here, get everything painted and spruced up with a new look. I sketched out some ideas on the way from Colorado."

Cora Jane knew her granddaughter only wanted to help. And she was an expert, after all, but the last thing she wanted was to walk in the door a couple of weeks from now and not even recognize the family business started by her late husband. The decor it had—minus the debris and dampness anyway—suited her just fine. And they'd never wanted for customers. Locals and tourists packed the place. Caleb had had a knack for understanding what worked in a coastal community, and she'd merely followed the path he'd established.

"We'll look over those designs of yours tonight,"

Cora Jane promised, to take the sting out of her remark. "And you're right about a fresh coat of paint. But in the meantime there are going to be locals coming back home and workers galore, and they're all going to need someplace to grab a bite to eat. We'll make do with what we have for the time being. Maybe later we can think about making a few changes."

Emily looked as if she wanted to argue, but instead she just stood up and walked out of the kitchen and back onto the deck at the side of the restaurant.

Cora Jane turned to Boone. "Go after her."

He regarded her with predictable alarm. "Me? Why me?"

"Sweetheart, you know why as well as I do. The two of you need to talk. You might as well do it now and settle things. Arguing with you might take her mind off whatever she's stewing over right this minute."

"And you think we're going to settle things with a quick chat on the deck?" Boone inquired skeptically. "Assuming we don't fall through the damaged boards, that is?"

"Probably not," Cora Jane admitted. "But you have to start sometime. It might as well be now. Gabi, Samantha and I will get started in here. B.J. can help by washing up these dishes. You don't need to worry about him getting into mischief or in the way."

Boone gave her a resigned look, but he did head for the deck.

Cora Jane turned to see both of her other granddaughters grinning.

"Nicely done," Samantha said. "Do you have any other missions for these next couple of weeks we should know about?"

Cora Jane chuckled at the girl's impudence. Samantha might be thirty-five, but she'd always be a girl in Cora Jane's eyes.

"Guess you'll just have to wait and see," she replied. "And in case you're wondering, while I might feel I have a halfway decent relationship with Our Lord, not even I can call up a hurricane. That was His plan."

And in her view it was definitely starting to look as if it had been a blessing in disguise.

Emily was crying. Boone could tell by the dejected set of her shoulders and the soft sniffs she tried hard to disguise when she heard the door to the deck open and close.

"Go away," she muttered.

"Sorry. I'm under orders."

Her head snapped around at that. "You!"

"Who'd you think it was?"

"Samantha, Gabi, maybe even Grandmother."

He laughed. "Yeah, those would have been my first choices, too."

Surprise, then resignation registered on her face. "Of course Grandmother sent you."

Boone leaned on the railing next to her and stared at the ocean across the road. It was hard to believe that just a couple of days earlier it had been washing over the road with giant, angry, destructive waves. Today the sky was a brilliant blue, the waves were lapping gently against sand littered with boards, house siding and roof shingles.

"Cora Jane seems to think we should settle things," he explained.

"What things?"

"You and me, I'm guessing. We didn't exactly part on the best of terms. That weighs on her."

"True, but we both moved on. That's in the past," she said, a hopeful note in her voice. "Right?"

"I'd have said so until you walked in the door this morning," he said candidly. "You came in with complication written all over you."

She glanced over at him, then sighed. "That was pretty much my reaction, too, if you must know."

Boone chuckled.

"What's so funny?" she asked.

"I didn't expect you to admit it."

"I've never been a liar, Boone. That was you."

Boone frowned at the accusation. "Me? When did I lie?"

"You said you loved me. Next thing I knew you'd married Jenny."

He was startled by the level of pain he thought he heard in her voice. Had she been rewriting history? "You made it pretty clear you weren't ever coming back. What was I supposed to do? Pine for you?"

"You could have given me some time to work through things," she accused. "That's all I really asked of you."

He regarded her with surprise. "When did you ask for time? If you'd asked for it, maybe I would have. Instead, you said we were over. You made it sound pretty final." He studied her face. "Or was that the lie you had to tell yourself so you could leave town and not look back?"

She seemed to take the question to heart and actually mull it over. "Something like that," she conceded eventually. "Okay, we both made mistakes. I wasn't clear enough. You jumped to conclusions. I can admit to that much. Can you?"

He hesitated, then said, "I suppose."

"Such a heartfelt concession," she murmured dryly, then met his gaze. "But it doesn't change anything, Boone. Not really. My life still isn't here."

"Believe me, I'm well aware of that. What Cora Jane hasn't told me, B.J. has. He's very impressed with you and Samantha. You're the first real celebrities he's ever met."

Emily had the grace to chuckle at that, the tension easing slightly. "Samantha can lay claim to being a celebrity, but I just work for a few. Most of my clients aren't that famous."

"Just rich?" he queried.

"Is there something wrong with being rich? Your family wasn't exactly poor. Your father was a high-powered lawyer, and your mother married a guy who made millions on widgets or something."

He smiled at her dismissive assessment of his stepfather, who'd owned a multinational manufacturing company. "That has very little to do with me. I started from scratch and earned what I have." He gave her a lingering look. "And I wasn't making judgments. I just meant that having money calls for a certain kind of lifestyle, keeping up appearances, that sort of thing."

"No question about that." Her gaze narrowed. "Are you making a point?"

He gave her a thorough survey that put patches of bright color in her cheeks. "I just wonder what those clients of yours would make of it if they saw you in shorts and a tank top with a discount store tag hanging out the back?" He winked at her as he snapped off the tag, allowing his fingers to linger just a little too long against her bare skin before adding, "Me, I just think you look incredibly sexy."

Her breath caught, and there was no mistaking the struggle she had to keep her gaze steady.

"Let's not go there, okay?" she pleaded. "Obviously we have to find some way to get along with each other for the next couple of weeks for my grandmother's sake, but then we'll go our separate ways again. Acting crazy will only make that harder to do."

Well, that was a clear enough warning, he thought. "No craziness," Boone said. "Got it, though it might help if you defined this craziness you think we should avoid."

"No fighting," she said at once. Color climbed into her cheeks. "No touching or kissing. You know exactly what I mean, Boone. Don't pretend you don't. It doesn't take much, even now, to stir us up, apparently."

He grinned. "If you can keep a civil tongue in your head and your hands to yourself, so can I."

"Okay, then," Emily said.

He thought he detected a hint of disappointment in her eyes, but it was gone too quickly for him to be sure.

She turned to head back inside, but Boone caught her shoulder. Her skin heated beneath his touch, though he felt her shiver.

"Just one thing," he said, holding her gaze. "Why were you crying when I came out here?"

The question clearly flustered her. "Just being silly," she said, obviously not wanting to discuss it.

Boone knew better. He knew it ran deeper. The entire time they'd been together, he'd seen her struggling to find some kind of elusive acceptance from her father and even, to a degree, from Cora Jane. Her grandmother's approval had never been withheld, in his opinion, but Emily hadn't always been able to see that. And the distance between Sam Castle and his daughters had been impossible for any of them to bridge.

"You took offense when Cora Jane brushed off your offer," he guessed based on past experience. "You thought it meant she didn't need you here, didn't you? You thought that's why she didn't jump all over your advice about the renovations."

"Maybe," she conceded, the tears gathering in her eyes proving his point.

He tucked a finger under her chin. "She needs you here, Em. She needs all of you here, not because of what you can do or how much help you'll be. She needs you because she's getting older and she misses you. Remember that, okay? She loved you all enough to let you go, but that doesn't mean she doesn't want you underfoot from time to time. She needs to fuss over you, meddle a little, to feel your love again."

To his regret, more tears filled her eyes and spilled down her cheeks.

"When did you get to be so darned smart and sensitive?" she asked, her voice hitching.

"I was always smart and sensitive," he claimed, amused. "You might have missed it because back then all you cared about was my body."

Because she evidently had no response that wouldn't be a flat-out lie, Emily turned and walked away, swiping impatiently at the tears on her cheeks as she went.

Though her lack of response left him chuckling, he couldn't help staring after her and wondering just how complicated his life was about to get. Despite her declarations and his promises, he was pretty sure things between them were far from over. And that was going to cause more problems and heartache than he'd ever wanted to experience again.

4

By late morning, Cora Jane's cell phone had rung half a dozen times, and several members of her kitchen and wait staff had shown up to help with the cleanup. She had put them to work scrubbing down the kitchen, top to bottom, so it could pass the toughest health inspection ever, if need be.

The last to arrive was Jeremiah Beaudreaux, better known as Jerry. He'd been cooking at Castle's practically since the doors opened. Now in his sixties and still standing tall at well over six feet, the one-time Louisiana fisherman's face was deeply tanned and weathered, his hair white, but he still had a smile that lit his bright blue eyes.

"Well, this sure enough is a sight for sore eyes," he declared when he saw Emily, Samantha and Gabriella at work sweeping the debris in the dining room into piles to be discarded. "Looks like an ill wind blew us at least some good, Cora Jane."

"Better wait till you see how much trouble they manage to stir up, Jerry," Cora Jane retorted, but her eyes were sparkling.

"Let me give you girls a hug," he said, lifting them each off their feet in one of his massive bear hugs.

"How'd you get to be so strong?" Emily teased, just as she had the first time he'd tossed her into the air as a child. Compared to her reed-thin grandfather, Jerry had seemed like a gentle giant.

"Toting around those cast iron pots of crab soup your grandmother has me making," he responded. "Now let me get in that kitchen and see what else needs to be done. Those kids you put to work, Cora Jane, will do a slapdash job of it without my supervision."

"Some of those 'kids' are as old as you are, Jeremiah Beaudreaux," Cora Jane said. "They know what to do."

"I'll feel better if I see the results for myself." He winked at Emily and her sisters. "We'll sit down and have us a long visit once this place is set to rights. Andrew said he'd be over here in an hour, Cora Jane, soon as he helps his grandmama set a few things outside in the sun to dry out. You just put him to work whatever needs doing around here. I promised his grandmama we'd keep him out of mischief."

Jerry spotted B.J. "There's my best helper," he said exuberantly. "You gonna come with me, young man?"

B.J. beamed. "Whatever you need," he said eagerly.

Before heading into the kitchen, Jerry paused and gave Cora Jane a searching look. "You doing okay? We'll have this place shipshape in no time. You're not to fret about it, okay?"

Emily caught the tender look that passed between them. She waited until Jerry and B.J. were gone before asking, "Did anyone else happen to notice the way Jerry was looking at Grandmother just then?"

"Oh, hush! You don't know what you're talking

about," Cora Jane responded tartly, though there was a surprising blush in her cheeks. "Jerry's been my right-hand man around here for a lot of years. He was one of your grandfather's best friends."

"Looks to me as if he'd like to be more than friends with you," Samantha chimed in, her eyes alight.

"No question about it, Grandmother," Gabi added. "Is there something you'd like to tell us?"

Cora Jane regarded each of them with an impatient look. "Don't think you're going to throw me off course by trying to turn the tables and meddle in my life," she said. "Now, let's get back to work. We're setting a poor example for the girls who came in here to help out."

Emily let the subject drop as she picked up her broom and went back to work. Gabi pushed her own pile of debris over to merge with Emily's.

"You don't really think there's something going on between Jerry and Grandmother, do you?" Gabi asked. "You were just trying to rattle her, the way she said."

Emily shrugged. "I saw something. Maybe it was nothing more than two old friends exchanging a fond look, but it seemed like more to me."

"Would that be so bad?" Gabi asked, her expression thoughtful. "She must get lonely. Grandfather's been gone a long time now."

"I guess I never thought about that," Emily admitted. "I don't think kids ever give much thought to their parents being lonely, much less their grandparents."

"We're adults, not kids," Gabi said. "We should be more sensitive."

"Boone said something very much like that earlier," Emily admitted.

Gabi grinned. "You're quoting Boone now. That's quite a turnabout."

"Don't make too much of it," Emily said. "He just mentioned that, even though Cora Jane let us all go, it doesn't mean she doesn't want or need us around from time to time."

"He's right about that," Gabi admitted. "Not even I get over here half as much as I should, and I live closest. Forget about Dad. Until the other day when he drove over to pick her up, I can't recall the last time he set foot in Sand Castle Bay. He doesn't even drive crosstown in Raleigh to see me unless I force the issue."

"Did you honestly expect otherwise?" Emily asked her.

Gabi looked momentarily disconcerted by the question, then laughed self-consciously. "I suppose I did. Crazy, huh? Mom couldn't even get him to come home for dinner most nights. I guess a part of me was thinking that with Mom gone, he might need company from time to time, maybe even a home-cooked meal."

Emily regarded her with sympathy. "I'm sorry, Gabi."

"Don't be sorry for me. He's disappointed all of us, Mom included."

"But I think it affected you the most," Emily said. "Mom accepted the way things were. Samantha went her own way. So did I. We gave up expecting anything, but you're the one who's settled right there in Raleigh, followed in his footsteps, tried to become a part of his world. Now don't go and take offense at this, but we all know you did that hoping to finally get his attention."

Gabi didn't even bother trying to deny it. "I may be in the same field, but I don't sit over a microscope the way he did," she said candidly. "I write press releases about other people's discoveries."

Emily chuckled. "Worse, you do it for a competitor, who's wildly successful, in part thanks to your PR work," she said. "That must give Dad heartburn."

Gabi grinned. "It isn't nice to gloat," she chided.

"Well, it makes me smile. It's what Dad deserves for not hiring you himself. I know that's what you really wanted."

Gabi sighed. "It would have been a disaster. I can see that now. He was right to say no."

"I'll give you that," Emily said. "I'm glad you can finally see it, too. You'd have been miserable having a boss who withholds praise or is too distracted to even notice you're alive until you make a mistake."

Gabi frowned. For a minute Emily thought she might jump in and try to defend their father, but instead she let it go. That alone hinted at her disillusioned acceptance of their father's flaws.

"How'd you and Samantha get along on the ride over?" Gabi asked, deliberately changing the subject.

"Fine," Emily insisted, a defensive note immediately creeping into her voice. "Why?"

"Because she always seems to get on your last nerve without even trying."

"Not this time," Emily swore, "though she does seem to have some crazy idea about me and Boone."

Gabi laughed. "Sweetie, we all have crazy ideas about you and Boone, even you if you're being honest with yourself. Tell me you did not just about swoon when you laid eyes on him for the first time today?"

Though she'd have denied it had Samantha asked, with Gabi she admitted the truth. "Maybe just a little swoon," she said. "I told him there couldn't be any craziness between us, though."

"Did you now?" Gabi said, clearly amused. "And why did you find it necessary to say such a thing?"

"Because there was a moment out there on the deck, just a moment, when there seemed to be something sizzling between us the way it used to."

"And you're totally opposed to any sizzle?"

"Totally," she declared very firmly, as much for her own sake as to prove anything to her sister.

Gabi looked disbelieving just as Samantha had earlier. "Oh, honey, you are in a heap of trouble if you believe that."

"I can't want anything to happen between me and Boone," Emily insisted.

"Saying it won't make it so. Feelings as strong as what you two once shared don't vanish just because time has passed or because they're inconvenient."

"But we moved on," Emily protested. "Both of us."

"And now you have another chance. Seems to me what would be really crazy is not taking advantage of that."

Emily started to utter another more vehement protest, but Gabi cut her off.

"I'm just saying it's something you should consider before you get all stubborn and dig in your heels. Boone's an incredible man."

Not even Emily was fool enough to try to deny that. "But he's an incredible man who lives in North Carolina."

"Gee, last time I checked we had phone lines, airports and even Wi-Fi," Gabi said. "And from everything I hear, you have an established reputation in your field that might even follow you all the way to this mid-Atlantic wilderness outpost."

Emily laughed. "Okay, point taken."

But that didn't mean she was going to open her heart...or risk breaking Boone's for a second time.

Boone left the Castle women working inside the restaurant, while he got started cleaning up the parking lot. After his exchange with Emily earlier, he needed to work off some steam without her in his face. The physical labor of picking up boards and cutting up tree limbs, loading them into the bed of his truck, was exactly what he needed. And when Jerry's teenage neighbor showed up, he put Andrew to work at the task, too.

They'd been at it for a couple of hours and had made two trips to the dump when Cora Jane came into the parking lot with bottled water and a thick tuna salad sandwich on toasted rye, just the way he liked it.

"The others are taking a break out on the deck," she told him. "I've coaxed Andrew up there, too, but something told me you might not be interested in joining us."

"No, this is good," he said, grateful for her perceptiveness.

"You and Emily settle anything this morning?"

"We talked," he said, taking a long sip of the cold water.

"And?"

"Cora Jane, it might be best if you stayed out of the middle of this," he suggested gently.

"Your opinion," she retorted. "It's not in my genes to sit on the sidelines and watch two people I love being miserable."

He laughed at that. "Emily doesn't look all that mis-

erable to me. She's a confident, successful businesswoman."

"With no personal life to speak of," Cora Jane assured him. "I could say exactly the same about you."

"Have we not had this conversation more times than
I can count?" he asked with good-natured exasperation.
"I have exactly the amount of social life I'm interested
in having."

"Your focus is on B.J., *yada-yada-yada,*" she confirmed sarcastically.

"Well, it's true. B.J. is my top priority. And I don't
think getting involved with your granddaughter, only
to have her take off again, is in my son's best interests,
or mine, for that matter. I can only imagine what Jenny's parents would have to say. They'd find a way to
drag me into court and sue for custody of B.J. faster
than you can say disaster. I won't put any of us through
that, especially not my son."

She gave him a disgusted look. "Stubborn fool."

"I've been called worse," he said, not the least bit
offended.

"Well, we're not done yet," she told him before heading back inside.

Boone watched her go and heaved a sigh. Heaven
help him! Once Cora Jane got an idea in her head, there
was no reasoning with her. He wondered if there was
any way on God's green earth to get her to focus her attention on somebody else's love life. Sadly, he doubted
it.

"Grandmother, I swear if you don't sit down in one
of these booths and put your feet up, I'm going to have
Boone carry you out to his truck and take you home,"

Emily declared, standing before Cora Jane who looked as if she was about to collapse.

Her grandmother's eyes flashed. "You wouldn't dare."

"Try me," Emily said, staring her down.

"I think she might, Grandmother," Gabi said more gently. "If you really want to get this place open tomorrow, you can't wear yourself out today."

Cora Jane looked around the restaurant in frustration. "I think we're fighting a losing battle, girls. There's no way I can open tomorrow, no matter how badly I might want to. I suppose I might as well admit that and sit down, at least for a minute."

"Thank you," Emily said. "If you sit for ten minutes, so can the rest of us. Anybody besides me want something to drink?"

"Sweet tea," Cora Jane said at once.

"I'll have the same," Gabi said. Emily echoed her response.

"I'll get it," Samantha offered.

She came back from the kitchen with four tall glasses of sweet tea, along with a pitcher filled to the brim, as well.

She sighed as she slid into the booth next to Gabi.

"I'm not afraid to admit it," Samantha said with a groan. "I'm beat."

"And I've discovered muscles I had no idea I had," Gabi said. "I'm sore everywhere."

"We've been at this since late morning," Emily reminded them. "And it's now going on seven. I vote we call it a day." She said that last part as if it were actually a democracy, though they all knew Cora Jane had the last word.

As expected, her grandmother started to protest, but Gabi cut her off. "You wouldn't even let me stop at the house this morning. We have no idea what we'll find there. We need to go home while it's still daylight. My vote's with Emily."

"I'll third that motion," Samantha said. She reached over and squeezed Cora Jane's hand. "We'll get a lot more done when we're back here fresh in the morning. Another day isn't going to make that much difference. No one expects you to perform miracles, Grandmother."

"I just hate the thought of letting folks down," Cora Jane said.

"How about this?" Emily said. "Tommy Cahill replaced the few boards on the deck he thought were damaged and says it's solid. The kitchen's mostly functional. How about you serve a bare-bones menu out there tomorrow? Just eggs, bacon and toast in the morning and maybe burgers at lunchtime. Call in one or two of the waitresses to help and we'll keep cleaning in here."

Her grandmother's eyes brightened at the suggestion. "That could work. And the bakery is going to deliver pastries tomorrow morning, so we'll have those."

"You scheduled a bakery delivery?" Emily said. Fearing the answer, she made herself ask, "What time?"

"Five-thirty, same as always," Cora Jane said cheerfully.

"Oh, sweet heaven," Samantha muttered. "Then we definitely need to go home. I'm going to crawl from a bath straight into bed."

Cora Jane chuckled. "What has happened to the three of you? I certainly didn't raise you all to be such wimps."

"No, you didn't," Gabi agreed. "But I'm starting to recall the downside of spending summers with you."

"Me, too," Emily said.

Just then Boone, B.J. and Andrew came in from the parking lot. Boone gazed around at the four of them settled into a booth, shoes off, and shook his head.

"You all must not work for the same boss I have," he said. "She never mentioned I could quit and put up my feet."

"We rebelled and took her captive," Emily explained. "And as soon as any of us can move, we're going to take her home."

"What about dinner?" he asked. "Did you grab something to eat here, because with the power out for so long at the house, you shouldn't risk eating anything left in the refrigerator."

"I never thought of that," Gabi said with a groan, "and I'm starving."

Jerry emerged from the kitchen just in time to overhear her. "Then isn't it a good thing that I just made up a pot of crab soup. I could throw some burgers on the grill, too. With the generator here running, we didn't suffer any spoilage."

"And French fries?" B.J. asked excitedly. "Can I have a burger and fries?" He wrinkled his nose. "No soup, though. Yuck!"

"I'm with B.J.," Samantha said. "I'll take a burger and fries. No soup."

Cora Jane shook her head. "How did you come from around these parts and have such an aversion to seafood?"

Samantha shrugged. "I just know I never liked the smell, the taste or the texture."

"Or maybe it's because you had a big-time nasty re-action every time you tried it," Emily said. "You're allergic to it, you idiot."

"Don't call your sister an idiot," Cora Jane scolded automatically. "Are you sure it's an allergy?"

"Swear to God," Emily said. "Gabi, don't you remember the time Mother insisted Samantha at least taste a crab cake and the next thing we knew we were traipsing off to the emergency room? She could barely breathe."

Samantha looked momentarily taken aback. "I'd blocked that, but you're right. I was scared to death. After that even the thought of seafood turned my stomach."

"Well, I'll take the soup, the burger and the fries," Boone said. "Jerry, why don't I help with those burgers?"

Emily frowned. "I guess that means we all should be back on our feet helping out. Grandmother, you stay put. We can handle everything. B.J., can you find silverware and napkins? Do you know where they are?"

He beamed at her. "Sure. I've helped with setups before. Want me to show you?"

Emily grinned at his eagerness. "That would be great."

"I'll get the drinks," Gabi volunteered. "Are you all sticking with sweet tea? Do you want to switch to beer? Sodas?"

"I'd love a beer," Samantha said, "but tired as I am, that would knock me right out. I'll have a soda."

"Make that two," Emily said.

As soon as all the orders were in, they went about

their respective assignments, working together as smoothly as if they'd been a team for years.

When two tables had been pushed together and set, drinks had been served and Boone came around with the bowls of soup, Cora Jane regarded them all with approval.

"I don't ever want to hear any of you say you couldn't take over this place in a heartbeat," she said. "As long as it's been since you were last here, you still remember everything I taught you."

"Don't go getting any ideas," Gabi warned her. "Running a restaurant takes skill, business savvy and passion. Boone obviously has it, but I sure don't."

"Me, either," Samantha declared. "Sadly I've kept up some of my skills working in restaurants between acting gigs, but it is not my calling."

"And apparently you've forgotten my tendency to lose patience with difficult customers," Emily reminded her. "I believe you were forced to pay several cleaning bills my last summer here after I *accidentally* dropped a few things into people's laps."

Cora Jane chuckled. "A few of them would have tested my patience, too," she admitted.

"And I came close to dousing a few drunks with ice water after I heard about the unwanted passes they were making at you girls," Jerry chimed in. "Only thing that stopped me was that you took care of them yourselves."

"Actually Gabi and I didn't," Samantha said, grinning. "We turned 'em over to Emily. She really enjoyed retaliating."

"I did take a certain amount of pleasure in it," she agreed. When she noticed B.J. listening, wide-eyed, she leaned close. "What I did was not appropriate, though. Do not follow my example."

"Thank you for that," Boone said wryly. "After listening to you all, I'm probably going to have to completely deprogram him before I ever let him near a customer in any of my restaurants. We pride ourselves on impeccable, friendly service."

"Well, fortunately, the lunch crowd rarely gets that rowdy," Cora Jane said. "It's one of the reasons I'm happy we close by midafternoon and that beer's the strongest thing we have on the menu. Let the other places deal with the out-of-control drinking, loud music and such. This place is meant for families. It's rare that the real party folks wander over from the beach in the middle of the day."

"You've definitely made Castle's into something unique," Boone said. "It's a real institution in town. I hope my restaurants last even half as long."

"You run a good kitchen and have great service," Jerry told him. "Last time Cora Jane and I came by, we were both impressed. I had a conversation with your chef, and he clearly knows his stuff. He's got the whole Cajun influence going on, and you know I can appreciate that."

Emily listened to the praise with growing surprise. Coming from Jerry, those were high marks, indeed. He might be working for a seaside diner, but his own credentials in the kitchen were pretty impeccable, and his standards were high. She recalled when her grandfather had recruited him from a restaurant in Louisiana.

"Thanks," Boone said. "I paid close attention to everything you and Cora Jane taught me. If I'm succeeding, it's because I had the best possible teachers."

He stood up. "Now, let me bus these tables, help with cleanup and get B.J. home. You ladies should probably take off now. It'll be dark soon, and you still need to be cautious on the road. Most of the debris has been cleared from the highway, but there's bound to be some piled up on the side roads."

"Boone, you went by the house," Cora Jane said. "Anything we need to watch out for there?"

"There are a lot of branches in the yard, but the driveway's clear. Just watch your step going inside. I flipped on the outside light, just in case the power came back on. I called your neighbors earlier and they say the power did come on over there. You should be okay. I didn't spot any leaks in the house, but you might want to take a closer look."

Cora Jane gave him a kiss on his cheek. "Thank you."

"Not a problem. Are you still planning to open here tomorrow?"

"Just with deck seating," Emily told him. She gave a pointed look at Cora Jane. "We compromised."

"Then I'll be back here early in case you need help," he promised. "What time?"

"Grandmother scheduled the bakery delivery for five-thirty," Emily said dryly.

Boone laughed. "Of course she did. And that is why I run a restaurant that serves only dinner. I also postponed our reopening till the weekend. I wanted my employees to have time to get their own situations under control, deal with insurance issues or whatever they needed to do."

"Can we come help you out, instead?" Samantha pleaded.

"Traitors," Cora Jane said. "Family comes first, and don't you forget it. We'll all be here at five-fifteen with smiles on our faces."

Jerry chuckled at their groans. "Well, at least you and I will be, Cora Jane."

"Oh, we'll be here," Emily said. "But the smiles might be expecting too much."

Fully clothed might be the best they could promise.

5

"Bad news, boss," Pete Sanchez announced when Boone called him to check in after finally getting home from Castle's and getting an exhausted B.J. into a bath and then to bed.

Pete was Boone's manager of restaurant operations. Though Pete was a year younger than Boone, he'd come to him with ten years of solid experience. Single and eager to be on the go, he spent most of his time overseeing the restaurants in Norfolk and Charlotte, taking the burden of travel off of Boone. Even so, he'd come straight back to North Carolina the minute residents and business owners had been allowed back on the barrier islands.

"Tell me," Boone said. If the usually low-key Pete thought the news was bad, it probably rose to the level of disaster.

"Looks like the restaurant's been flooded one too many times, and the last repairs must have been made with poor quality materials. When we pulled up the carpets, we found sections of rotting floorboards all over the place."

"Blast it!" Boone muttered.

"It gets worse," Pete disclosed direly. "We discovered mold behind some of the drywall on the side closest to the bay, where the water stayed high the longest. A lot of mold. It's pretty pervasive."

"You have to be kidding me," Boone said, thoroughly frustrated. If there was extensive mold now, even as quickly as it could appear after a flooding incident, this definitely hadn't happened overnight. Nor had those sections of floor rotted since this last hurricane blew through. These were most likely things his inspectors should have caught before he bought the property.

Exhaling a sigh, he concluded he'd just have to consider this a lesson well-learned. Next time, he'd hire an actual contractor to go over any potential real estate purchase to assure that the inspection wasn't superficial or in the seller's favor.

"Why didn't you call me on my cell?" he asked Pete when he had his temper under control. "I could have gotten Tommy over there today to take a look."

"I tried, but I guess the service is still spotty," Pete responded. "One of the cell towers blew down or something. I did get through once and tried to leave a message, but it cut me off before I could explain what was going on."

Boone pulled his cell phone from his pocket and noted the call logged in early in the afternoon. It must have come in while he'd had the noisy chain saw going. "Sorry. I was tied up over at Castle's."

"I knew that, so I didn't want to make a big deal out of something that could just as easily be handled tomorrow. I thought about calling Tommy myself, but I figured he was there with you. You'd told me you wanted him to get Cora Jane's roof fixed. I know how you feel about making that a priority."

"It's okay, Pete. None of this is your fault. I'll call Tommy now. We'll both come by first thing in the morning so he can assess the damage and give me a timetable for the repairs."

"You talking daylight?"

"Or thereabouts," Boone confirmed.

"You want me there?"

"No, give yourself a break," he told the night owl. "I'll handle this one. How about meeting me there around nine and we'll come up with an action plan. Looks like I'll need you to stick around here longer than we originally talked about. Is there anything you need to get back to right away in Norfolk or Charlotte?"

"No, both restaurants are good," Pete assured him. "You have excellent management teams in place."

Boone chuckled. "You pretty much have to say that. You hired most of them."

"Doesn't make me biased, though. If they screw up, that's on me, too." He hesitated, then said, "I've been thinking we could probably start looking for that fourth location you talked about once things around here settle down."

"You getting bored, Pete?"

"Maybe just a little," he acknowledged. "You know I love doing the start-ups."

"Well, we'll get serious about the next one soon," Boone assured him. "Start compiling the market research for me, okay?"

"Will do," Pete said eagerly. "In the meantime, should I cancel the ads announcing the reopening for this weekend?"

"We'll decide that after I've been through the place with Tommy. Maybe it's not as bad as you thought at first glance."

"This is bad," Pete warned him. "If that mold has spread beyond what I saw, we're talking major renovations."

Boone thought of the compromise Cora Jane had reached to get Castle's reopened. "Is the kitchen operational?"

"Good to go and spotless," Pete confirmed.

"And we know the deck is solid," Boone said thoughtfully.

"What are you thinking?"

"That we could serve on a limited basis out there temporarily. We're at the end of the season. Tourists will be pouring in here again by the weekend, based on what I heard from the local officials earlier today. I'd hate for the wait staff to lose out on the kind of tips they get this time of year."

"You'd want to keep them all on, even with limited seating?"

"Dividing the tips more ways would be better than laying 'em all off, don't you think?"

"And you're not worried about our reputation if we can't handle the usual crowds and can only serve a couple of specialties, rather than our full menu?"

Boone chuckled. "If anyone's in a rush or out here to review the food, I imagine we can put a good public relations spin on keeping our kitchen open, our food selections limited but high quality, and our people working, despite being damaged by a hurricane." He thought of Gabi. "I know just the person to draft a press release, in fact. I imagine she can make us sound like benevolent angels."

Pete laughed. "If she can pull that off for a couple of guys like you and me, she's a magician. Get that done and I'll have it distributed. Might as well do a preemptive strike and generate some good buzz."

"Now you're getting into the spirit of this," Boone said. "Put that press release on the list of things we need to finalize when I see you in the morning."

Pete chuckled. "You are such a glass-half-full man," he praised. "I don't know how you do it. Even after Jenny, well, let's just say it's one of the reasons I love working for you. I know this was lousy news, yet you've turned it around, come up with a plan and are ready for action."

"That's why they pay me the big bucks," Boone joked, thinking of how often he'd gotten by on practically nothing just to keep the first restaurant afloat in the early days. "And making sure the action really happens on schedule is why I pay *you* the big bucks. See you in the morning, Pete."

As soon as he'd disconnected that call, he punched in the numbers for Gabi's cell phone. Other than Cora Jane's, hers was the one Castle number he'd memorized. She'd be the closest if he ever saw a need for a family member to get here in a hurry. He'd last used it just before the storm to make sure that someone was coming to get Cora Jane away from the danger zone. He'd known she'd never choose to go on her own. If she ever found out he was behind Sam Castle's appearance on her doorstep, she'd be furious, but he was willing to take the heat to keep her safe.

Now Gabi answered, her voice sleepy. "Boone? What's up?"

"Sorry, did I wake you?" he asked.

"No, just settling down."

"I promise not to keep you long." He explained about the crisis. "Any chance I could hire you to draft a press release for me on short notice? Pete's worried people will be disappointed if we're not operating at full capacity."

"And you want them to see that you're open at all just for the benefit of your employees and your customers, even though the situation isn't optimal," she summarized.

"Exactly. Can you do something with that?"

"Of course I can. Leave it to me. Is the fax machine at the restaurant operating? Or do you want me to email you the document?"

"Send it by email. That'll be more efficient for distribution, I think."

"Perfect. What time's your meeting with Pete?"

"Nine."

"You'll have it well before that. And if anything about your plan changes, just give me a call and I can do a new draft on my iPad and get it right back over to you."

"You're an angel, Gabi."

"Seems to me your halo's pretty shiny, too," she teased. "Want me to spread the word about that to anyone in particular?"

"I don't need you to talk me up to Emily," he said, grasping exactly what she was getting at.

"Why not? It couldn't hurt."

"Stick to PR, not meddling, please. Don't make me regret calling you."

"Okay, since you asked so nicely, I'll focus on the task assigned for now."

"Will you let Cora Jane know why Tommy and I are running late?"

"Don't worry about that. You did more than your share to help out today. We'll see you when you get there."

"Thanks, Gabi."

He hung up wondering what the odds were she'd keep her nose out of his personal business. Given her genetic makeup, probably not all that good.

Emily's gaze kept drifting toward the parking lot. It was midmorning, and there'd been no sign of Boone. Castle's had been swamped from the minute they'd opened the doors at six. Word seemed to have spread quickly among the locals that they were open for business, at least with deck seating. After an initial trickle, there in time to see a glorious golden sunrise, there hadn't been a vacant table the rest of the morning.

No one had complained about the limited menu, either. The coffee was strong. The eggs, bacon, toast and grits were plentiful. Everyone seemed thoroughly happy with the limited selection. The baskets of free mini-pastries Cora Jane insisted on putting at each table were a huge hit, too. And the long-time regulars had been delighted to see Emily, Gabi and Samantha working side by side with Cora Jane again.

With the help of two waitresses, Emily and her sisters had managed to keep things moving, but they hadn't had a minute to deal with any more of the cleanup inside.

Now with the customers thinned out, Emily was finally able to take a deep breath. She carried a cup of coffee to a table by the railing where she could see the ocean...and the parking lot.

"Looking for somebody?" Samantha teased when she joined her, propping her sneaker-clad feet on an adjacent chair with a sigh of relief.

"No, why?"

"You've spent a lot of time with your eyes peeled to the parking lot. I just thought you might be wondering where Boone is."

"Well, he did say he'd be here today at the crack of dawn," she said. Years of doubts and bitterness crept into her voice. "Despite Grandmother's faith in him, I guess he can't be taken at his word, after all."

"He called Cora Jane right after we got here," Samantha reported. "And he spoke to Gabi last night to explain."

Emily stiffened. "He spoke to Gabi? Why?"

"He had some work he wanted her to do for him."

"What kind of work?"

Samantha grinned. "Please do not tell me you're jealous of your own sister?"

"Don't be ridiculous. I'm just wondering when he and Gabi got to be so tight that he'd ask her for help? Why not you? Or me?"

"Maybe because Gabi's the one with public relations experience," Samantha said patiently. "If you give me two seconds, I can explain all this and put your mind at rest."

Emily knew she was overreacting, looking for excuses to judge him so she could keep him at a distance, so she drew in a deep breath and nodded. "Explain away."

Samantha described the mess they'd found on closer inspection at Boone's restaurant, Boone's solution for working around it and Gabi's role in spreading that word.

"This morning he had to meet with the people doing the cleanup over at his place, see for himself how serious the problem is and make some decisions," Samantha concluded.

"And Tommy Cahill? Where's he? Boone promised Grandmother he'd be working on the roof today. They're predicting thunderstorms later this afternoon. We'll be underwater inside, if he doesn't at least have a tarp down up there."

"Tommy's with Boone, checking to see what repairs are needed. He's meeting his crew here at eleven." Samantha glanced toward the parking lot as several pickups turned in. "And there they are now. Right on schedule."

She slanted a look at Emily. "You might want to cut Boone some slack. He spent all day here yesterday, even though he had his own worries. He put Cora Jane and Castle's first."

"You're right," Emily admitted, knowing that once more she'd misjudged him. "I know I'm just looking for reasons not to get along with him."

"Because you're scared," Samantha suggested.

"Scared of what?"

"Falling for him all over again."

"Not going to happen," Emily insisted, though Samantha had hit the nail on the head.

Samantha grinned. "We could take bets on that, little sis, but I never take money from the delusional."

After her conversation with Samantha, Emily went inside the restaurant, grabbed her laptop and slipped into one of the booths, hoping to get a little bit of her own work done before she was needed to wait tables or do more cleaning. She had a list of suppliers she wanted to check for the availability of their ski lodge furniture. With a deadline staring her in the face, she couldn't afford to deal with anyone who didn't have most things in stock in sufficient quantities. She didn't have the luxury of waiting for custom pieces.

She'd been jotting notes and scanning websites for a while when she noticed B.J. standing quietly by the table.

"Hey there," she said with a smile.

"What're you doing?" he asked, sidling closer.

"Looking for furniture."

"Can I see?"

"Sure," she said, sliding over to make room for him.

He crawled onto the bench and knelt, leaning into her. The feel of his body with its little boy smell caught her off guard. She'd never really thought much about being a mother, but suddenly what she guessed were faintly maternal instincts were coursing through her. *How about that?* she thought, surprised and not entirely dismayed by the sensation.

She observed the way his brow was knit with a frown, the tip of his tongue caught between his teeth as he studied the screen intently. She'd seen that same expression on Boone's face a time or two, when he was deep in thought. Finally B.J. turned to her.

"That stuff would look kinda weird in here," he said hesitantly.

Emily laughed at his apt assessment. "It definitely would," she agreed. "It's not for here. Tell me why you think it would be wrong, though."

"It's all dark and it's too big."

"Precisely," she said. "You have a good eye. Now, can you think of anyplace where it might look right?"

"Someplace really big," he said eventually.

"Do you think it might look good in front of a great big stone fireplace?" she asked.

His eyes lit up. "You mean like one of those places where people go in the winter to ski?"

"That's exactly it," she said, impressed once more. "It's for a new ski lodge in Colorado."

"Cool. I think it would be better if it were red, though."

"Why is that?" she asked, laughing at his boundless confidence in expressing his opinion.

"Because red's my favorite color. It's the color of fire trucks and candy apples."

"And you like both of those things."

"Uh-huh," he said, then sobered. "And it was the color of my mom's car. The one she picked out before she died." He met Emily's gaze. "Daddy bought it for her as a surprise for her birthday, but she never got to drive it. She got too sick."

Emily swallowed against the lump in her throat. "I'm sorry."

"Sometimes I miss her," B.J. confided.

"Of course you do. My mom died a while back, and I still miss her, too."

"Do you ever cry?"

"Sure. Do you?"

"Uh-huh, but I try to be brave, because I know talking about her makes my dad really, really sad."

Emily suddenly wanted to gather him close and hold him until he could shed all the tears he'd stored up. It wasn't her place, though. Instead, she said gently, "I'll bet your dad would want you to talk about your mom anytime you need to. Even when it makes us sad to talk about someone, I think it always helps if we can remember them with someone else who loved them."

B.J.'s expression brightened slightly. "You really think so?"

"I really do," she said. "Where's your dad now?"

"He's still at his restaurant. I was bored over there, so he called Ms. Cora Jane and she said it was okay if I came over here with Tommy."

"Does she know you're in here with me?"

"Uh-huh," he said, then flushed guiltily. "She sent me in to tell you to get back outside and get to work."

Emily laughed, immediately suspicious that it hadn't been Cora Jane's sole motive. "Did she really? Well, how about we don't tell her that you forgot? We'll tell her that I asked for your expert opinion on the job I'm working on. That'll make you my consultant."

"Really?" he said, his eyes wide.

"Sure thing," she said. "But I guess my break is over. I'd better do what she said and get outside."

And later she'd have a few words with her grandmother about deliberately sending B.J. inside for the sole purpose of nudging the two of them a little closer. She had a feeling there was going to come a time when she'd regret that it had worked so successfully.

* * *

Boone had arrived at Castle's and stepped inside the restaurant just in time to overhear his son's conversation with Emily. Her insight and her tenderness caught him by surprise, but it was B.J.'s fear of upsetting him that made his heart ache. He slipped back outside before they caught sight of him.

"Weren't they in there?" Cora Jane asked, looking puzzled by his quick retreat.

"They were there," he said tightly.

"Why do you sound angry about that?"

"I'm not angry," he said. He wasn't sure exactly what he was feeling, but anger wasn't part of it. Blind panic, maybe. Once again, he'd seen evidence of his boy bonding with a woman who would wind up leaving and hurting him. There were a lot of things in life he hadn't been able to protect B.J. against, but he hadn't anticipated needing to protect him from another loss quite so soon.

"I think I'd better keep him away from here for the next couple of weeks," he said, trying to figure out how he'd pull that off without a major rebellion on B.J.'s part.

"Why on earth would you do such a thing?" Cora Jane asked, clearly mystified.

"He's getting too close to Emily."

"Seems to me that's a good thing for both of them," she replied.

"She's leaving," Boone reminded her. "Me, I know how that works, how it feels. He's a kid. He's already lost his mother. What if he gets attached to Emily and she walks out of his life? How's he supposed to cope with that?"

Cora Jane regarded him impatiently. "I know you have your issues with Emily, but do you really think she'd be so cruel that she'd get close to B.J., then walk away without looking back? You're not giving her much credit."

"Why should I? She left me without a backward glance."

"And we both know why she did that," Cora Jane reminded him gently. "She was terrified that with one word, you could make her stay. Instead you didn't even try. Worse, in the blink of an eye, you turned right around and married Jenny."

He frowned at the hint of accusation he heard in her voice. "You actually think the breakup was my fault?"

She smiled at his indignation. "No, I think she broke up and your pride stopped you from trying to fix things."

"You let her go because you loved her," he accused. "How is what I did any different? I could see she'd never be happy here with me."

"Really? Even though you could have offered her something I couldn't, the future she really wants?"

"Cora Jane, she made it abundantly clear that a future with me wasn't what she wanted."

"Maybe not right that second," she conceded. "But she loved you then, and I believe she loves you now. She just has to figure out how to have it all, that choosing you doesn't mean sacrificing the career she wants. That's a lesson that comes with maturity. I think she's just about there now."

Boone scowled at her. "Too late," he said stubbornly. "What's that expression—once burned, twice shy?"

"So you don't believe in second chances? Seems to me you had a couple of them in your day. I recall sending my husband to the police station one night to bail you out when you got caught trying to buy beer with a fake ID. You called me instead of your folks."

Boone winced. "I was an idiot."

"But I didn't hold it against you, did I?" she said, not denying the truth of his assessment.

"Because you're a saint," he joked. "Or maybe because you wanted something to hold over my head for a lifetime."

"Or maybe just because I love you and know that your flaws are part of the bargain," she said.

He sighed as he met her gaze. "I hear what you're saying, Cora Jane. I really do. I just can't take another chance, not with my heart and sure as hell not with my son's."

Left unsaid was the furor he'd stir up with Jenny's parents if they got wind that Emily was back in his life. They unreasonably held her as accountable for any misery Jenny felt as they did Boone. If anything would bring them back to Sand Castle Bay on a tear, that would be it.

"There's too much at stake," he told Cora Jane. "Nothing's worth the risk of hurting B.J."

"Then I feel sorry for you," Cora Jane said quietly. "Nothing in life comes without risk. Would you have given up the chance to have B.J. if you'd known ahead of time the pain you'd face when you lost Jenny?"

"Of course not."

"That's all I'm saying. If you want to experience the highest of the highs, then you have to take a chance that you'll get the lows, as well."

"I want my life—and B.J.'s—on a nice even keel," he countered, knowing even as he said it that it was an impossible pipe dream.

"A noble goal, but an unrealistic one," Cora Jane admonished. "Life doesn't work out that way." She held his gaze. "And you know as well as I do, Boone Dorsett, you'd be bored to tears if it did."

Maybe. Maybe not. He sure would be willing to give it a try for a time.

6

B.J. burst through the door onto the deck at Castle's, caught sight of Boone and went running in his direction. Emily followed more hesitantly, regretting that she couldn't avoid the man completely. Instead, she seemed to be drawn to him like a magnet.

"Daddy, guess what? I'm Emily's consultant," B.J. announced happily.

Boone smiled at his son's excitement but gave Emily a curious look. "How'd that happen?"

She shrugged. "It turns out he's amazingly perceptive about interior design. I appreciate his insights."

Boone didn't even try to hide his skepticism. "He's eight. What kind of insights could he have?"

"He knew immediately that the furniture I was looking at online wasn't suited for here," she explained, then grinned. "He didn't hesitate to tell me that, either. That's a very good trait in a consultant."

Boone actually chuckled at that. "Yeah, there's not much he holds back. If it crosses his mind, it comes out of his mouth." He ruffled his son's hair. "You weren't pestering her, though, were you?"

B.J. regarded him impatiently. "I told you, I'm her official consultant. She *wants* my help."

"Now, if only he could wait tables for me," Emily said, anxious to get away, though not exactly enthusiastic about the prospect of dealing with what already looked like a huge lunch crowd, proving that, as usual, Cora Jane's instincts about reopening had been right.

"I could carry stuff," B.J. offered eagerly.

"Sorry, buddy, we have to get going," Boone said. "I have to get back over to my restaurant. I just wanted to make sure Tommy's guys had things under control with the roof."

"Judging from the hammering overhead when I was working inside, they must be making progress," Emily said.

Boone nodded. "Tommy says the protective sheeting will all be in place before any rain this afternoon. They'll have a good start on the new shingles, too."

"That'll be a huge relief to Grandmother. She was afraid we were going to be dealing with more water damage inside. Speaking of that, did she tell you that the cashier station is a mess?"

Boone nodded. "I'll take a look before I leave. I have an excellent cabinetmaker I use. I can get Wade over here tomorrow to build something exactly like she wants to replace it. If there's any other updating she wants in the dining room, just let Wade know."

"Updating?" Emily said, rolling her eyes. "I'm lucky she's letting me bring in the painters."

"Yeah, she is a big fan of the status quo." He gave her a searching look. "You okay with that now?"

Emily shrugged. "I'll continue nudging, but I'm not holding out a lot of hope."

"Okay, then, I'd better check out that cashier area, then hit the road. Let's go, B.J."

"But I want to stay here," B.J. protested at once.

"Not this afternoon," Boone said firmly. "It's too busy for you to be underfoot right now. Cora Jane can't keep an eye on you when it's crowded like this."

"I will," Emily blurted impulsively before she could stop herself. "If that's okay with you, that is. Between Grandmother, Gabi, Samantha and me, he'll be fine. And he can always hang out in the kitchen. Jerry loves having him around. Besides, don't you have your hands full over at your place? I heard about the damage you found."

"I do, but—"

B.J. bounced up and down. "Please, Dad."

"Sorry, pal. I made arrangements for you to spend the afternoon with Alex. His mom said you could have a sleepover tonight, too."

"I'd rather stay here," B.J. pleaded.

"We're only open until three, anyway," Emily reminded Boone. "Then we'll be cleaning some more. We can keep him busy with that. Then one of us can drop him off at your restaurant or the house later."

She wondered if the real issue was Boone wanting him out from underfoot because he had a date tonight. For all she knew, he was involved with someone. "Or if you have plans for tonight, he can stay over at our house," she suggested mildly.

"No plans," Boone said, an oddly tense note in his voice. "Usually he loves having a sleepover at Alex's house because they have all the game systems I won't let him have at home."

"But today I want to stay here and help," B.J. repeated emphatically.

"Okay, fine," Boone agreed with unmistakable reluctance. "Let me speak to Cora Jane."

"No need," Emily said. "I'll let her know."

"Then I'll pick him up at your place tonight around seven-thirty. Will that work? That way if I get held up at the restaurant, he won't have to hang around there."

"Absolutely. Knowing you're coming by will be the perfect excuse to get Grandmother out of here at a decent hour."

"Then I guess it works out well all around," he said, a wry note in his voice. He hunkered down in front of his son and held his gaze. "You do as you're told and don't give Emily or Ms. Cora Jane any trouble."

"Promise," B.J. said, and scampered quickly away as if he feared his father might change his mind.

Boone studied Emily with a narrowed gaze. "I'm not entirely happy about this."

"So I gathered. Mind telling me why?"

"I told you the other day. I'm scared to death you'll disappoint him when you leave."

His candor wasn't a total shock, but his lack of faith in her hurt more than she'd expected it to. "Boone, he's a wonderful boy. I won't let him down. I promise."

His gaze locked with hers. "I'm holding you to that, Em. That boy is the most precious thing I have in my life. He's been through enough."

"And so have you," she said, understanding the pain they'd both suffered. "I get it, Boone."

He hesitated, holding her gaze, then nodded. "I'll see you later, then."

She swallowed hard as he turned and walked away.

"Later," she whispered, wondering if she hadn't just made a huge mistake by making a promise she'd never be able to keep, no matter how good her intentions were. After all, what did she really know about protecting a little boy's heart?

It was about six-thirty, and Boone was wrapping things up for the day, preparing to head over to Cora Jane's house to pick up B.J., when his cell phone rang. He glanced at the caller ID but didn't recognize the area code or number.

"Boone, it's Emily," she said when he answered.

The shakiness in her voice put him immediately on full alert. "What's wrong? Has something happened to B.J.?"

"He fell in the parking lot and cut himself on a nail sticking out of a board," she blurted as if she had to get the words out in a hurry. She drew in a deep breath, then added, "It's a pretty deep gash, but he's fine. I swear, Boone, he really is fine. He's handling it like a real trouper."

"Where are you?" he asked, trying to temper panic and the need to lash out. He'd known leaving B.J. behind today was foolish. What had he been thinking?

"We're at Ethan Cole's Emergency Clinic," Emily told him. "Grandmother called Ethan and he met us here. B.J. needs stitches and probably a tetanus shot, unless he's already up-to-date on that. That's really why I'm calling. Ethan doesn't want to give him the shot if he doesn't need it."

"Let me speak to Ethan," Boone demanded, needing not only the insights of an expert, but his reassurance.

"Of course," Emily agreed at once.

"Hey, Boone," Ethan said, sounding calm and completely unruffled, exactly the demeanor one wanted from an emergency physician. "B.J.'s going to be just fine. Hasn't shed a tear. In fact, he's excited about having a scar. I'm numbing the area right now so I can do those stitches. He'll be good as new in a couple of weeks."

"Swear to me he's okay."

"He's okay," Ethan said. "Emily had the bleeding stopped by the time they got here. She really kept her wits about her and kept B.J. calm in the process."

"What the hell was he doing running around in the parking lot, anyway? And where'd that board come from? I cleaned the parking lot of debris myself."

"You're asking the wrong person," Ethan said. "But, if you're looking for speculation, seems to me it could have washed into the road overnight on high tide and somebody tossed it into the parking lot. Does that really matter?"

Boone sighed. "I suppose not. I knew I shouldn't have left him over at Castle's today. Emily was supposed to be keeping an eye on him."

"Sounds to me as if she and Cora Jane were both right there when he tripped and fell. It was an accident, Boone. Things like this happen, especially to little boys who don't think about the dangers that might be underfoot after a storm."

"But I warned him," Boone said in frustration.

Ethan chuckled. "Do you not recall that eight-year-old kids have the attention span of a gnat? I can't tell you how many people I've patched up this week from incidents just like this one. Where does B.J. stand on his tetanus shots?"

"He's up-to-date," Boone said.

"Then it's all good. I'll have him out of here in a half hour."

"I'm on my way."

"Why don't you just meet them at Cora Jane's as planned?" Ethan suggested. "It'll give that temper of yours time to cool down. I know you're looking to place blame, but I'm telling you it's an accident that could have happened to anyone. Don't make Emily the scape-goat. If you do, you'll just make Cora Jane feel guilty, too, and she's shaken enough."

Boone sighed. "You're probably right." He hesitated, then asked, "How are your sewing skills? He's not going to look as if he was sewn up by a butcher, is he?"

Ethan laughed. "You do recall that not that long ago I was stitching up soldiers on the battlefield in Afghanistan, right? The United States Army trusted me to know what I was doing. The scar will be real pretty, I promise."

Boone finally managed a chuckle. "Okay, okay, I get it. I'm overreacting. Thanks, Ethan."

"Any time, pal. See you soon. I'll want to see B.J. to remove the stitches in a couple of weeks. Just stop by during office hours or if that doesn't work, give me a call and I'll come by the house."

"We'll settle up the bill then, too," Boone promised.

"Just invite me over for steak next time you're grill-ing," Ethan said. "It's been a while since we've gotten together."

"Then we'll plan it," Boone promised. A guy's night was way too rare these days. He could use one, too, a night free of the complications that seemed to be piling up in his life these days.

When he'd disconnected the call, he drew in a deep breath and said a little prayer thanking God that B.J.'s injury hadn't been worse. He understood that accidents could happen anytime, anyplace to anyone. But this had been his boy, and B.J. had been in Emily's care. He wondered if he had it in him to forgive that, despite the logic that told him no forgiveness ought to be required.

"Daddy's going to be really, really mad at me," B.J. said, looking dejected as Emily drove him and Cora Jane home.

"He's just worried, that's all," Emily assured him, though he'd certainly sounded angry on the phone. She hoped that had been the fear talking and that Ethan's reassurance had settled him down. The last thing B.J. or Cora Jane needed was to have Boone storming in on a tear.

They'd barely pulled into the driveway at home when Boone turned in behind them, tires squealing as he hit his brakes. He was out of his car practically before the engine cut off. He yanked open the back door of the rental Emily was driving, his expression easing only when he saw for himself that B.J. was essentially in one piece.

B.J. held out his bandaged arm. "Dr. Cole says I'm going to have a scar," he said excitedly. "I had to have stitches. I didn't even cry."

"He was incredibly brave," Cora Jane confirmed, giving Boone a warning look.

Emily watched Boone blink back a tear as he forced himself to give his son a congratulatory high-five.

"You're not going to ground me, are you?" B.J. asked

worriedly. "Or yell at anybody? Or keep me from going to Castle's?"

"You might need to take a couple of days off till your arm's healed up," Boone said. "But, no, I'm not going to ground you."

"How about the yelling?" Emily asked quietly. "I imagine you'd like to direct a few pointed words at me."

Boone glanced up at her, his eyes filled with emotion. He looked as if there was plenty he wanted to say, but he managed to censor himself.

Cora Jane seemed to sense that the two of them needed to talk privately. She put an arm around B.J.'s shoulders. "Come on, B.J. Let's get those cookies and the milk I promised you. I'll bet Samantha has them on the table waiting for us."

"All right!" B.J. enthused, then took off running.

Boone shook his head as he watched him. "That boy never slows down. I'm sure that's how he fell in the parking lot."

"It is," Emily confirmed. "I'm really sorry, Boone."

"Intellectually, I know it wasn't your fault." He tapped his chest. "But in here, I'm looking for somebody to blame."

"I get that, and it did happen on my watch, right after I'd assured you he'd be safe with me."

"And I was standing right here when he took off running across the lawn just now, oblivious to all the branches that could trip him up. He's a rambunctious kid."

"That almost sounds as if you're letting me off the hook," Emily said.

"Trying to," he admitted, grinning. "Ethan gave me an earful. That helped to put things in perspective, too."

"You two are still good friends?"

Boone nodded. "Ethan didn't make it easy when he first got home from Afghanistan. He was angry and bitter and pretty much hated the world after he lost his lower leg."

Emily's eyes widened. "He lost his leg? I had no idea."

"He'd be delighted to hear that. The truth is that most people don't even notice. He's mastered the prosthesis, had a huge attitude adjustment and finally seems to be on track again."

"That's amazing. Good for him."

"It really is good for him," Boone said. "There's nobody around I admire more."

"Wasn't he engaged? Is he married now?"

Boone hesitated, then said, "That didn't work out. And, word of advice, don't bring it up around him."

Emily stared at him. "They broke up because of his injury?" she guessed.

Boone nodded. "Talk about being bitter where women are concerned? Ethan wrote the book on it."

"That's a shame," she said.

Boone nodded.

Emily met his gaze. "You coming in for cookies and milk? Or would you rather have something stronger? I think we have some beer."

Boone looked torn. She had a hunch if it hadn't been for B.J., he'd have taken off right then. He surprised her, though, by suggesting she get a couple of beers.

"Maybe we could sit down by the water," he said. "Catch up?"

"Sure," she said, eager to accept the olive branch he was extending.

When she went inside to retrieve the beers, she found her sisters doting on B.J., exclaiming over his bandaged arm and his bravery.

"Where's Boone?" Cora Jane asked.

"Outside. I'm going to grab a couple of beers and join him for a little while, if that's okay."

The three women at the table exchanged amused looks.

"I win!" Samantha said, holding out her hand.

"Win what?" Emily asked with a narrowed gaze.

Cora Jane and Gabi each put five dollar bills into Samantha's outstretched hand. The sight of her sister gloating grated.

"You're kidding me," Emily said. "What was the bet?"

"How long it would take for you and Boone to settle your differences," Gabi said with a grin.

Emily frowned. "Nothing's settled. We're having a beer and a conversation."

"Close enough to count," Samantha said.

"And you bet it was going to take a couple of days?" Emily asked, then looked at her grandmother. "How about you?"

"I thought you'd hold out for at least a week," Cora Jane admitted.

"And my money was on never," Gabi said. "Given how stubborn the two of you are."

Emily simply shook her head, grabbed the beers and went outside. She found Boone sitting on the dock, his jeans rolled up and his feet dangling in the warm waters of Pamlico Sound.

"How many nights do you suppose we sat out here like this, talking till Cora Jane insisted you come inside?" he asked, as he accepted his beer from her and took a swig.

Emily smiled at the memory of her grandmother's determination to make sure that nothing more than talking went on between the two of them. She'd succeeded until Boone got his driver's license. After that, they'd found plenty of places with more privacy.

"Well, I was fourteen the summer we met. We were pretty much inseparable after that. You do the math. Of course, back then we were drinking sodas, not beer."

"I thought you were the most beautiful girl I'd ever seen," he said, his voice filled with nostalgia for a change, rather than the bitterness she'd grown accustomed to the past couple of days.

"And I thought you were the most dangerous boy around, especially after I found out you'd been picked up trying to buy beer with a fake ID." She slanted a look at him. "Seriously, you thought you could pass for twenty-one? You'd just turned fifteen."

"Not one of my shining moments," he admitted. "Cora Jane reminded me of that just this morning. She claims it should have made me into a believer in second chances."

Emily regarded him closely. "You don't believe people deserve second chances?"

"Depends on the circumstances, I guess," he said with a shrug. "Some things are pretty unforgivable."

"Since you were having this conversation with my grandmother, why do I have a feeling it had to do with what I did to you?"

He slanted a look her way, a smile on his lips. "Because she thinks my attitude toward you is a little too unyielding."

"It is," Emily agreed, then grinned. "But I get it, Boone. I hurt you. And, to be honest, I haven't been cutting you much slack, either."

"To hear you tell it, though, I hurt you right back when I married Jenny."

"Yep," she confirmed. "I took it personally, no question about it."

"I thought you'd be relieved."

She stared at him incredulously. "Relieved? Why? I'd told you I loved you. I thought it was understood that you'd wait for me."

"Sweetheart, trust me. If you tell a guy you love him as you're walking out of his life, it makes it a little hard to believe. You might want to keep that in mind if the occasion ever arises again."

She recalled how devastated she'd felt when she'd learned he was marrying Jenny. "Did you have to turn to someone else so fast?"

He shrugged. "What can I say? I was lost without you, and I was hurt and angry. Jenny was right there. She made no secret of being in love with me. There were no games, no pretenses, no hidden agendas. She wanted marriage and a family. That held a lot of appeal after you telling me you weren't ready for any of that."

She forced herself to ask, "Did you love her, Boone?"

He glanced at her, his expression unreadable. "Will it make you feel better if I say no? The truth is I did love her, Emily. Otherwise I wouldn't have married her. At least I like to think I'm a better man than that."

Emily felt the unexpected sting of tears in her eyes. Somehow she'd held out hope that there'd been no love between them, but how selfish was that? Had she honestly hoped that Boone had sentenced himself to a love-less marriage?

"I'm sorry," she said, not entirely sure what she was apologizing for. Was it for his loss or for her own child-ish desire to have remained first in his heart? "Were you happy?"

He gave her another long look, then said, "Yeah, I was. And when B.J. came along, I thought I had every-thing I ever wanted."

Emily smiled. "I can understand that. He's an amaz-ing kid."

"He's certainly taken a shine to you," Boone said, still not sounding especially happy about that.

"Well, the feeling is mutual. I hope you won't keep him away because of what happened today."

"Oh, I'm tempted to do just that," he admitted, then added in a resigned tone, "but I doubt I could if I tried. B.J. is very clever about getting his way. I seem highly susceptible to his tactics. Jenny was a much tougher dis-ciplinarian than I am. And since she died, I want him to have whatever he wants or needs. That's probably going to come back and bite me in the butt one of these days."

"I don't think so. You know what I see in him? I see a boy who knows he's loved and responds to that. I don't see him taking advantage of it. He's a very re-sponsible kid."

"He's had to grow up too soon."

"You know he worries about you," Emily told him. "He doesn't like to bring up his mother because he knows it makes you sad."

Boone sighed. "I know. I heard him tell you that ear-lier. It ripped me apart. I guess we need to have a talk about that. I need to reassure him that he can talk to me about Jenny anytime he wants to."

"That's what I told him."

"I know. You were very good with him."

She slanted a look at him. "You sound surprised."

"I suppose I am, a little. I never had the sense that having kids was a big deal to you. That was another reason I thought any future for the two of us was doomed."

Emily frowned at the assessment, though she understood where it came from. "Just because I wasn't ready for kids ten years ago doesn't mean I never thought about having them. You were just ahead of me. It scared me how ready you were for everything—a wife, a family, settling down. I felt as if I was just starting out. There were so many places I wanted to see, things I wanted to achieve."

"And you thought being with me would get in the way of all that," he said.

"Sure."

"Being married and having B.J. didn't stop me from starting my restaurant, expanding into a couple of other markets."

"Obviously you turned out to be a better multitasker than I am. I thought I needed to focus a hundred percent on my dream."

"So, have you achieved everything you wanted to achieve?" he asked.

"Not everything, but I do have an amazing career."

"And a personal life?"

"I date," she hedged.

"Anybody special?"

She shook her head, reluctant somehow to admit that there was no one—other than a few clients—who'd even notice that she was away from Los Angeles for an extended period of time. It sounded too pitiful, even to her, despite the fact that she was mostly perfectly content with her life. It was as if losing the most important relationship of her life had soured her on ever trying again.

"Too busy to get serious, I guess," she said eventually. "You? Have you been dating?"

"I've been out a few times, but it's too soon for me to be bringing anyone new into B.J.'s life. I have plenty on my plate without worrying about a relationship these days. And I'm trying to be respectful of the Farmers' feelings. Jenny's death crushed them. If I got serious about someone, they'd hate me for attempting to replace her. There's enough ill will between us already."

"You don't get along with your in-laws?"

"We do okay, as long as I don't rock the boat. Dating right now would be rocking the boat big-time."

"Our reasons may be different, but it sounds as if we're pretty much in the same place."

He turned to meet her gaze, his expression vaguely startled. "That's how you see it?"

"Sure. Don't you?"

"Em, I don't think we've been on the same page since we were teenagers sitting out here on nights just like this."

"Oh," she said softly, her eyes stinging once more as the unexpected barb hit its mark.

He frowned. "Are you about to cry?"

"No, of course not," she said, swiping impatiently at a tear. "I just thought...we seemed to be getting along, maybe even making peace."

"And that's what you want? To make peace?"

"We were best friends once, Boone. Wouldn't that be a good place to start over?"

"Sure. I guess," he said with unmistakable reluctance.

"You don't think it's possible?"

"Possible? Anything's possible. Men walked on the moon, didn't they?"

"Are you putting the likelihood of us being friends again in the same category as a space walk?" she asked, not sure whether to be amused or insulted by the unlikely odds he seemed to be suggesting.

"Yeah, I think so," he said.

Emily let his doubts wash over her. Oddly enough, they stirred an unexpected reaction. She doubted he'd intended it, but he'd just uttered an irresistible challenge. For whatever time she remained in Sand Castle Bay, she suddenly found herself with a new mission— getting back the friendship they'd once shared and that she, at least, had treasured.

At least until she'd stupidly thrown it away. However she viewed his marriage to Jenny, she was the one who'd set the wheels in motion by walking away.

7

Boone realized his mistake too late. The instant he saw the glint of competitiveness in Emily's eyes, he realized that he'd just uttered a challenge she wouldn't be able to resist. While all he'd hoped to do was warn her off, keep her from chipping away at his defenses, instead he'd ensured that she'd try harder than ever to recapture what they'd once had or at least to get his attention. Either way, he was probably doomed.

"Do not start getting ideas," he warned her, his gaze narrowed.

"What sort of ideas?" she inquired innocently.

"You know exactly what I'm talking about," he accused. "Games, challenges, the whole routine. We're over, Em. We have been for a long time. It's best to leave it that way."

"Boone Dorsett, are you suggesting that I might try to work my feminine wiles on you just to prove a point?" she asked, laying on a sugary accent she'd otherwise trained out of her voice.

He barely resisted the desire to laugh at her exaggerated Southern persona. He didn't want to encourage her, not when the game spelled danger. "Maybe not to prove a point," he admitted. "But to get your way? Absolutely."

She, however, did laugh, obviously not concerned with the seriousness of the stakes. Though he'd alluded to the uneasy relationship he had with Jenny's parents, she couldn't possibly understand the threat they constantly held over his head to fight for custody of B.J.

"You know me so well," she teased. "I guess we'll just have to see how this plays out. Have you had your inoculations?"

"Inoculations?"

She batted her eyes in a very un-Emily way. "Against feminine wiles?"

"Sweetheart, trust me, I've definitely built up an immunity," he declared, wishing he were half as certain of that as he tried to sound. He regarded her with frustration. "Emily, why do you want to stir this particular pot, anyway? Wasn't breaking my heart once enough for you?"

She blinked at that, looking vaguely nonplussed for the first time since they'd headed down this particular path. "I'm not going to break your heart again, Boone," she promised with quiet sincerity.

"If you try to start something you don't intend to be around to finish, what do you think will happen?" he asked, unconvinced.

She studied him, her expression suddenly thoughtful. "Okay, I hear you," she said eventually.

"Seriously? We can go back to the original plan? No craziness while you're here?"

"Seriously," she insisted. "No craziness."

Boone held her gaze, trying to determine if she'd

taken his warning to heart or if she was just lulling him into a false sense of complacency. Unfortunately, despite what she thought, he couldn't read her quite the way he once had. Or maybe he just didn't trust his own instincts where she was concerned. After all, he'd once believed that their love was strong enough to survive anything.

Either way, he had a hunch this thing he'd inadvertently stirred up between them was far from over. And once again, if he dared to let his guard down, he'd wind up the loser, this time in ways more devastating than she could possibly imagine.

The day after her disquieting conversation with Boone, Emily walked inside Castle's, her eyes taking a couple of minutes to adjust to the dim interior. The sight that greeted her when she finally got a good look across the room was every woman's dream of a blue-collar god.

A white T-shirt stretched across a broad chest and was tucked into faded, form-fitting jeans. Sun-streaked brown hair, just a little too long, skimmed over a tanned forehead. Wide, work-roughened hands caressed the wood of the cashier's counter the way a woman dreamed of a man's hands on her body.

"Holy saints in heaven! Who is that?" she muttered to no one in particular, though she was well aware that Boone was within earshot. Though she'd intended him to hear every word, they were nonetheless heartfelt.

Boone appeared at her side, his expression amused. "That's Wade Johnson. I told you I intended to get him in here today. He does the best custom cabinet work in the region."

"I'll bet that's not the only thing he excels at doing," she murmured, watching his hands stroke that wood.

Boone slanted a look at her. "I'm suddenly very leery of introducing you. You sound a little intense."

"You probably should be jealous," she suggested. "That man could make a woman forget her own name, much less any other man in her life."

"I'm so pleased you're impressed," he said wryly. "That is exactly why I had him come around."

Just then Gabi came in, stood next to them for a moment as her eyes adjusted from the sun, then followed the direction of Emily's rapt gaze.

"Do you see what I see?" Emily asked, not taking her gaze off of Wade.

Gabi looked at her blankly. "What?"

"The god that Boone has brought to our doorstep," Emily replied.

Gabi glanced at Wade again, then shrugged. "I guess he's good-looking in that HGTV, home repair guy way."

Emily stared at her incredulously. "Are you blind?"

Just then Wade glanced up, his blue eyes glittering with amusement at his audience. "Hey, Boone, do I get paid extra for being a sideshow?"

"Only if you strip," Boone replied.

"Oh, my God," Emily whispered, stunned by the thought and deliberately exaggerating her reaction for effect.

Gabi stared at her impatiently. "Get a grip, Em." Then she seemed to grasp that more might be going on here than she'd guessed. "Oh," she said softly, then laughed. "You're wasting your time."

Emily regarded her with feigned confusion. "Meaning?"

"I know what you're up to," Gabi said.

Boone chuckled. "We *all* know what she's up to. And I'm not jealous."

Emily scowled at her sister, then gave Boone an indignant look. "As if I'd bother trying to make you jealous. Did I not promise you just yesterday that I would not play that sort of game?"

"A promise I took with a grain of salt," Boone admitted.

"Does anybody here care about my suggestions for building the new cashier station?" Wade inquired, studying the three of them curiously.

"I care," Gabi said. "And I may be the only female in the room who poses no danger to you."

Wade gave her a very thorough, appreciative once-over, then commented, "Too bad."

Gabi blinked in confusion at the flirtatious remark.

"Seems you caught his attention," Emily said, chuckling at Gabi's reaction. "Hard-to-get always works."

"But I *am* hard to get," Gabi said in an undertone, casting a worried frown in Wade's direction. "I have a boyfriend."

Emily just rolled her eyes. In her opinion, whoever this man was in Gabi's life, he couldn't be too important or he would have been here by now helping out. Instead, as far as she knew, he hadn't even been checking in that regularly.

She observed as Gabi approached Wade with unexpected caution, as if his comment really had thrown her. "Interesting," she murmured.

Beside her, Boone laughed. "Quite the little wrinkle in your plan, huh?"

"What plan?" she asked, maintaining her innocent posture, even though it had lost some of its credibility.

Rather than answering, he bent down and pressed an unexpected and way-too-brotherly kiss to her cheek. "That's okay, sweetheart. I was maybe a tiny bit jealous for about two seconds."

She frowned at his teasing. "I'm so relieved."

She should have known better, of course. Boone had always been an uncomplicated, confident guy. He'd never liked games. As far as she knew he'd never once been unsure of himself when it came to her. He'd certainly never had any reason back then to be jealous.

What had made her think that feigning an interest in a friend of his would work now? Not that Wade hadn't been interest-worthy. The man really was sexy as all get-out. She hoped Gabi noticed that. Emily thought he might be exactly what her sister needed to shake up her workaholic life. Wade obviously wasn't what Emily needed to shake up Boone.

That was going to take an entirely different plan. She'd have to give it some more thought. Because Boone had been right about one thing—she didn't have especially honorable intentions when it came to her promise to behave.

Cora Jane took a hurried step away from Jerry when Emily and Boone walked into the kitchen. A guilty blush crept into her cheeks. She had no idea why she felt that way over the fact that she and Jerry had grown closer or why she felt the need to keep her feelings from her granddaughters. Maybe she was just old-fashioned enough to believe that a late-in-life romance was a bit unseemly, that no one would understand.

Jerry glanced down at her, his amusement plain. "You don't think they've figured out that something's up with us?"

"Probably," she admitted in an undertone, "but we don't need to confirm it. I can live without the aggravation."

He merely shook his head, his expression tolerant. "Your call."

Cora Jane noted that Boone seemed oblivious, but Emily was studying the pair of them with suspicion.

"Did we interrupt something?" Emily asked.

"Not a thing," Cora Jane said brightly. "Jerry just asked me to taste his crab soup to see if he'd made it too spicy."

"And?" Jerry said, going along with her.

"Just right," she said. She turned to Boone. "How's Wade coming along in there?"

"He has some ideas for the new cabinetry," Boone said. "He's going over them now with Gabi."

"Really?" Cora Jane said, oddly pleased.

In her opinion, a laid-back, grounded man like Wade would be perfect for Gabriella, but she doubted that her granddaughter would see that without a little nudge. She tended to gravitate toward uptight professionals exactly like her father, bless him. Sam might be Cora Jane's son, but she was well-versed in his flaws. It was a wonder he'd managed to stay married as long as he had. In her opinion, the girls' mother had been a saint to put up with his late nights and frequent absences.

"Grandmother, is that a matchmaking gleam I see in your eyes?" Emily inquired.

"I have no idea what you're talking about. I'm not the

one who brought Wade over here today, am I? Boone did that all on his own."

"And I'm wondering now if it wasn't a really bad idea," Boone muttered. "There seem to be a lot of nefarious schemes afoot."

Emily laughed. "Not a lot," she corrected. "I think Grandmother and I might be on the same page about this one."

"So, you see it, too?" Cora Jane asked, eager to have an ally.

Jerry sent a commiserating look over her head in Boone's direction. "Think we should warn Wade?"

"Don't you dare," Cora Jane ordered. "He's a grown man. He can take care of himself."

"Gabi, then?" Boone suggested. "She might deserve a heads-up."

"Or maybe you should both stay out of it," Cora Jane said.

Boone held up his hands. "Okay, then. I'm out of here to safer territory."

Jerry nodded. "Can't say I blame you. I wish I could come along."

"You can walk out any time you tire of being around," Cora Jane said tersely.

Jerry lifted her off her feet and planted a kiss on her mouth. "I never tire of you. Don't you know that by now?"

Cora Jane felt her cheeks flame. "Now you've gone and done it," she muttered.

But he only laughed. "You were the only one who thought the girls weren't onto us."

"He's right," Emily confirmed. "And we may not

know exactly what's going on, but you have my approval. Gabi's and Samantha's, too."

"Did I ask for approval?" Cora Jane inquired with a little huff of indignation.

Jerry gave her a chiding look. "Just say thank you, Cora Jane. You know perfectly well you wanted their blessing."

"I might have wanted it, but I certainly didn't need it," she grumbled, then met Emily's sparkling eyes. "Okay, fine. Thank you."

Emily gave her a fierce hug, then kissed Jerry's cheek. "I'm so happy you two have each other."

Tears gathered in Cora Jane's eyes. Despite her grumbling, that was exactly what she'd hoped to hear. Maybe these feelings she had for Jeremiah weren't so crazy after all.

"That was a nice thing you did in there," Boone said when he and Emily were outside alone on the deck.

"What?"

"Giving Cora Jane your blessing. I think she was scared to death you all wouldn't approve."

"She was right about one thing. It's not really our place to approve or disapprove," Emily said.

"But the approval matters to her. She was worried sick you'd think she was behaving like an old fool."

"She talked to you about it?"

"She mentioned it," he confirmed.

"So you knew there was something going on with her and Jerry?"

He nodded. "Anyone around the two of them for more than a split second could see it."

Emily immediately got defensive. "Is that some

sort of knock about Samantha, Gabi and me not being around enough?"

"Take it however you like," he said. "Bottom line, I think Jerry has had a thing for Cora Jane for years, but there was no way he'd ever act on it while your grandfather was alive. He and Caleb were friends. He'd never have betrayed the friendship like that. He's an honorable man."

"I guess I never really thought about why there was never a woman in his life," Emily admitted. "He always seemed like part of the family. You know, the bachelor uncle who keeps his private life private."

Boone gave her an odd look. "You thought he was gay?"

Emily laughed. "Oh, please. Not even for a heartbeat. I'd seen him looking over the women customers a time or two. For all I knew, he could have been seeing a different woman every night. He just never made a big deal about it."

"My hunch is he went out just often enough to keep your grandparents from guessing about his real feelings. Once when I was helping out in the kitchen, I overheard your grandmother trying to set him up with a friend of hers. He turned her down flat, said it would be too awkward if it didn't work out. Obviously he couldn't say that the woman didn't stand a chance compared to Cora Jane."

He studied Emily's thoughtful expression. "You're really okay with this?"

"I was just thinking that it's sweet in a way, all those years of unrequited love finally paying off."

"It is reassuring, isn't it?" Boone said. "It says the universe has a way of making things right in the end."

"That's a very romantic way of looking at things," she said, sounding surprised.

He smiled at her reaction. "I have my moments."

He just couldn't allow these crazy, romantic notions to get the better of him when it came to Emily.

Emily thought about Boone's comment that night when she was sitting on the porch at Cora Jane's, her bare feet propped up on the railing, a tall glass of sweet tea in her hand.

"I thought I might find you out here," Gabi said, settling into a wicker chair next to her, her own glass of tea in hand. "You were awfully quiet during dinner tonight. Everything okay?"

"Just thinking about love and how complicated and unpredictable it is," she admitted.

"Ah, the easy stuff," Gabi said with a smile.

"Grandmother admitted earlier that she and Jerry are an item," Emily told her.

Gabi's expression lit up. "Really? How'd you wrestle that news out of her?"

"Boone and I walked in on them in the kitchen. It wasn't exactly a compromising moment, but Grandmother looked as if we'd caught them in bed. Took a couple of nudges, but she finally spilled the truth. Boone says he thinks Jerry's had feelings for her for years."

"When did Boone get to be so observant, especially when it comes to romance?"

"The same thing I wondered," Emily said. "I've been seeing a different side to him since I got back here."

"You sound surprised."

"Once upon a time, I thought I knew everything there was to know about Boone," Emily said. "It is kind of a shock to discover all these new facets. Do you suppose they were there all along or do you think Jenny brought them out in him?"

"Maybe he's just matured," Gabi said. "That can happen between the age of twenty-one and thirty-one. You're not the same woman you were when you walked out on him, are you?"

Emily thought about that. "Not really."

"How do you see the changes in yourself?" Gabi asked curiously.

"It might make more sense for you to tell me what you see. I could probably use an outside opinion."

Gabi looked oddly reluctant to answer. "Do you really want to know what I think? Uncensored?"

Her sister's reaction startled her. "Sure. Why wouldn't I want to hear the truth?"

"Maybe because you're human, just like the rest of us, and sometimes the truth hurts. Remember how you managed to upset me on the phone last week, when you were teasing me about being like Dad? It's certainly true, but I wasn't crazy about hearing it."

Emily frowned. "But we've been telling you that for years. Why did it suddenly strike a nerve?"

"Because lately I've been starting to want more. At least I think I want more than a demanding job that I obsess about 24/7."

"Seriously?" Emily said, taken aback by the admission from a woman who'd been even more goal-oriented than either Samantha or Emily herself, and they were no slouches when it came to going after what they wanted.

"Shocking, huh?"

"Is that because of this man you're seeing? Are you

in love with him? Are you thinking about a future with him?"

Gabi hesitated, then shook her head. "I don't think so. I mean we could be heading in that direction, and it's been amazing to have someone in my life who's there at the end of the day, who understands how important my job is to me and doesn't get all worked up if I have to stay late at the office. We get along, you know. It's easy and comfortable."

"You're not mentioning anything about passion," Emily noted.

Gabi flushed, but grinned. "Oh, there's plenty of that, believe me."

"Sounds like a perfect match."

"It does, doesn't it?" Gabi said with a sigh.

Emily frowned at her reaction. "Then why don't you sound happier?"

Gabi met her gaze. "I have no idea."

"Then there is something holding you back," Emily concluded. "You probably need to figure out what that is."

"Probably," Gabi agreed, then shrugged. "Enough of that. You managed to steer the conversation away from you, which suggests you weren't that anxious to hear my thoughts about how you've changed, after all."

"I should have known you wouldn't forget. Your brain's like one of those fancy new phones that has little reminders that pop up."

Gabi laughed. "A godsend, by the way. And yes, my mind is exactly like that." She studied Emily. "So, do you want to hear what I have to say or not?"

"Go ahead," Emily said, oddly reluctant, but suspecting that she needed to hear whatever her sister had observed. Since it was coming from Gabi, rather than Samantha, she could take it.

"I think you're at a turning point in your life," Gabi began. "A really important one. You can have this extraordinary career, fill every minute of your day with work the way I have, or you can try to find some balance."

"Are you sure you're not still talking about you?" Emily asked.

"Absolutely, but the same thing applies. Here's where it's different," she said, holding Emily's gaze. "You used to have this softness about you with Boone. You had the ambition, sure, but it was tempered by the crazy love you felt for him. You had the balance I'm talking about. Now, you're a hundred percent focused. You're tense, maybe even a little hard. I don't have a doubt in my mind that someone could throw a major interior design project your way, give you an impossible deadline to meet, and you'd do it without batting an eye."

"Why doesn't that sound very complimentary when you say it?" Emily grumbled.

"Oh, it is complimentary, if that's all you want out of life. Me, I'd like to see you truly happy again, laughing the way you used to with Boone, sneaking off to be with him in the middle of the night. I'm not sure I'm explaining this right, but there was a lightness about you then, a rightness, if you will. You were a complete woman."

"Are you suggesting I can't be complete without a man in my life?" Emily asked, indignation stirring.

"Absolutely not. But you—Emily Castle—can't be complete without the kind of deep-down happiness you had with Boone. Maybe you can find that in your work eventually. I don't know. But I'm not seeing it now." She shrugged. "Not any more than I've found it in mine, and, believe me, no one is more stunned by that than I am."

Emily let her sister's words sink in. Gabi had been right, they did hurt, but there was an undeniable ring of truth in them. She hadn't been happy, not a hundred percent carefree and deliriously happy, in a very long time. How had she not noticed that? How had she missed that all the successes in the world, all the demands for her talents didn't add up to real fulfillment? The jobs she took on were challenging, but not ultimately rewarding, at least not in the way she thought maybe work should be.

Gabi reached over and put a hand atop hers. "You're not furious with me, are you?"

"How could I be? You were just calling it like you see it."

"I could be wrong," Gabi said, clearly hoping to take the sting out of her words.

Emily shook her head. "You're not wrong," she admitted. "I wish you were. Unfortunately I have no idea how to change things. It's not as if I can snap my fingers and have a whole new life."

Gabi smiled at her. "You sure about that? Maybe you just have to snap them when the right person is in the vicinity."

"Meaning Boone?"

"Meaning Boone," Gabi confirmed.

"You still think he's the right man for me or that I'm the right woman for him, even after the way I hurt him, even after everything he's been through?"

"Doesn't matter what I think. Or what Grandmother

and Samantha think—and they're both on the same page, by the way. It only matters what you think."

"And Boone," Emily said. "He has a pretty big say, and he's not all that happy with me."

"You can hardly blame him," Gabi said.

"Hardly," Emily agreed. "But that would make it an uphill battle."

"The Emily I grew up with wouldn't be daunted by that."

"But the Emily you knew doesn't exist anymore. Didn't you just get through making that point?"

"Oh, I think she's still in there," Gabi said. "You just have to want to find her. You just have to remember what it felt like to fight for a relationship the way you've learned to fight for bigger and bigger jobs."

"And Boone? Do you think the man who was once head-over-heels in love with me still exists?"

"Oh, hon, anyone who sees the two of you in the same room knows he still exists. The sparks are hot enough to burn the whole town down. He's just fighting it with everything in him."

"He's probably wise to fight it," Emily said bleakly. "What if, when push comes to shove, I can't give up my career and wind up leaving again?"

"Then that would make you an idiot," Gabi said. "I don't think you're going to lose anything. Rather, you have everything to gain." She squeezed Emily's hand. "And the sister I know and love is *not* an idiot. Deep down, she knows that."

Emily wished she had as much faith in herself as Gabi had, because if she were to follow her sister's advice, there was an awful lot at stake—for her, for Boone *and* for B.J. B.J. was a critical part of the equation, after all. She and Boone were adults. They could handle whatever happened. But it would be selfish and wrong to put B.J.'s emotions at risk, especially if she weren't a hundred percent certain of what she wanted.

And wasn't that exactly what Boone had been telling her all along?

8

"You're leaving?" Cora Jane stared at Emily in shock. "Now, when there's still work to be done? I thought you'd be staying at least a couple of weeks."

"I'd intended to," Emily said, trying not to meet Gabi's dismayed gaze as she tried to explain to her Grandmother. "But this job in Los Angeles is at a critical stage. The client is incredibly demanding and she's about to have a breakdown because things aren't finished. I need to check in personally to soothe her ruffled feathers. And my client in Aspen needs to take a look at the plans I have for his ski lodge and sign off on those. This seemed like a good time, since things here are under control for the most part."

"Is this because you didn't get your way about renovations?" Cora Jane asked.

Gabi shook her head, clearly not buying her excuses for a minute. "No, Grandmother, this is really about what Emily and I discussed last night." She gave Emily a penetrating look. "Isn't it?"

"And what was that?" Cora Jane demanded. "Did you two argue?"

"No, not at all," Emily insisted, her comment directed at Cora Jane, but her gaze on Gabi, silently pleading with her not to say any more.

"I told her she ought to reach out to Boone, that she needed to find a way to make him a part of her future," Gabi said, giving her a defiant look. "And she obviously got scared, so her answer is to run."

"I'm not running because of what you said, or because of Boone," Emily retorted. "I have jobs to do. I've been neglecting them. I'll be gone a few days at most, and then I'll come back."

Cora Jane looked relieved. "So this is just a quick trip?"

"Definitely," Emily assured her, though only to get the two of them off her back.

"Unless she can dream up another half-dozen excuses for not coming back," Gabi said, her gaze on Emily unrelenting.

"You don't know what you're talking about," Emily said, annoyed that her sister obviously knew her too well. She had been considering ways to stay away and avoid all the complications that were clearly looming on the horizon. "Now, I need to run if I'm going to get over to Raleigh to catch my flight this afternoon."

"How do you intend to get there?" Gabi inquired smugly. "You don't have a car."

"Samantha told me I could drive her rental over there and turn it in. I'll get another rental when I come back. After all, you have your car here and Grandmother has hers. The rental's barely been out of the driveway."

Samantha walked into the kitchen just then and evidently sensed the tension as she gazed around the table.

"Did I do something wrong? Should I not let her take the car?"

"You've just made it easier for her to run away," Gabi said in disgust. "Not your fault, of course. She probably would have hitchhiked if there hadn't been an alternative."

Gabi stood up and walked out of the kitchen.

"Why's she so upset?" Samantha asked.

"She thinks I'm running out because I'm scared," Emily said.

Samantha shrugged. "Of course you are. It's what you do."

Emily regarded her sister with dismay. As usual, Samantha's accusation carried a weight that Gabi's did not. "I do not," she said defensively.

"That's what you did ten years ago, isn't it?" Samantha persisted. "I was already in New York, but it was pretty plain to all of us you got scared by the intensity of your feelings for Boone and took off."

"I left because I wanted a career somewhere else," Emily retorted impatiently.

"Anywhere Boone didn't happen to be," Samantha said. She looked at Cora Jane. "Am I right?"

"Seemed that way to me," Cora Jane confirmed.

"And look how well that turned out," Samantha added. "Surprise, surprise, he took you at your word and moved on, leaving you hurt and confused and bitter."

"You don't know what you're talking about," Emily said. "And I don't have time to sit around arguing with you. Samantha, where are the car keys?"

Her sister tossed them to her. "The rental papers are in the glove compartment."

"Thanks," Emily said tersely.

She leaned down to give Samantha a hug, then dropped a kiss on her grandmother's forehead. "Love you. See you soon."

"I'd better, missy, or I'll send someone after you," Cora Jane warned. "I didn't raise you to be a coward. Neither did your parents."

"I am not a coward," Emily said, but she could tell she was wasting her breath. Neither of them believed she was leaving because of work. Heck, she wasn't entirely convinced of it herself. She'd made the decision impulsively last night because, well, to be honest, she had gotten scared. Sophia's latest panic attack had given her the perfect excuse. Now she had to follow through or look like an indecisive idiot in front of her family and anyone else who might be the least bit interested.

Boone managed to keep B.J. away from Castle's until after lunch, but only by bribing him with a handheld game he'd been wanting for months. He could already tell he'd made a mistake. Just as he'd feared, B.J. hadn't put it down for a single second all morning.

As they pulled into the Castle's lot, Boone held out his hand. "Turn it over," he commanded.

"But you gave it to me," B.J. complained. "And I want to show Ms. Cora Jane and Emily."

"You can show them another time. For now, we need to put it away. We'll decide later how long you can play with it each day."

"But that's not fair," B.J. argued. "You said it was mine."

"It is yours, but there are limits, just like the ones we have for TV."

B.J. gave him a sour look, but he handed over the

game, then jumped out of the truck and went running inside the restaurant. Apparently he'd already forgotten how he wound up with those stitches in his arm, Boone thought, watching him with a sigh.

He followed B.J. more slowly, stopping to talk to Tommy about the roof repairs and how soon he'd be able to get to the work in his restaurant.

"I'll finish up here tomorrow morning at the latest," Tommy assured him. "I'll have the crew at your place after lunch."

"That'll work," Boone said. "And the bill for Cora Jane's roof? See that I get it."

Tommy looked uneasy. "Boone, she'll have a fit. You know she will."

"Just tell her you haven't had time to get to it."

"You want me to put her off?" Tommy asked incredulously. "It'll take about two days for her to get suspicious."

"Only one, more than likely," Boone conceded. "I owe her. I want to do this for her. If she puts it on her insurance claim, heaven knows what it will do to her rates. This is better. I'll battle it out with her. You won't be caught in the middle."

"If she starts lecturing me about my lax business practices for not billing her or, worse, calls my mother to complain about them, I swear to you that I will spill the beans," Tommy warned him. "I do not want to be on Cora Jane's bad side. Nor do I want my mother sticking her nose into my business. She's been itching to take over the accounting, and this would give her the perfect excuse."

Boone laughed. "Not to worry. I'll take the heat." He gave Tommy an amused look. The man was successful, thirty-seven, six foot four and, despite that, obviously still scared of his mother, who was admittedly something of a force to be reckoned with. "I won't let you get in trouble with your mama, either," he consoled Tommy.

Tommy muttered an expletive in response, then walked off.

Just then B.J. came bounding back out the door, his expression dismayed. Boone reached out and grabbed him by the shoulder, then hunkered down in front of him.

"Hey, buddy, what's the problem?"

"Emily's gone," he said with a sniff, his eyes filling with tears. "Nobody knows when she's coming back."

Blast it all! Boone thought furiously. This was exactly what he'd feared all along. "When did she leave?"

"This morning, I guess." He gave Boone a betrayed look. "I should have been here, but you made me stay with you. Maybe if I'd been here, she wouldn't have gone."

"You knew all along she'd be going back to her job, back to where she lives," Boone said, though he was as thrown by the suddenness of her departure as B.J. was.

"But not yet," B.J. protested. "It's too soon. I thought she was my friend, and she just left without even saying goodbye."

Exactly as Boone could have predicted, he thought heatedly.

"I'm sorry, pal. You said she'll be back, though, right?"

B.J.'s shoulders heaved in what could have been a shrug or a heartfelt sigh. "I guess. That's what Ms. Cora Jane said."

"Then I'm sure she will be," Boone said, though he

was certain of no such thing. Needing to do something to put a smile back on his son's face, he said, "Why don't you get your game out of the truck and show it to Jerry? I'll bet he'd like to play it with you."

There was a brief spark in B.J.'s eyes. "It'd be okay?"

"I think just this once, yes."

B.J. took off across the parking lot.

"Slow down!" Boone called after him.

B.J. obediently slowed. Once he'd retrieved the game, he walked back, exaggerating each careful footstep in a way that had Boone hiding a smile.

"Just so you don't start running the second my back's turned," he commented as his son passed him. B.J. gave him an impish grin but kept his pace slow.

As soon as B.J. was back inside, Boone pulled out his cell phone, found Emily's number still on the list of incoming calls from the other night when she'd phoned from Ethan's clinic, and called her.

"Boone?" she said when she answered.

"I warned you," he said, his voice low and furious. "I told you not to hurt my son."

"What are you talking about?" she said softly. "I didn't do anything to B.J."

"You left without even saying goodbye. He's devastated, Em. He doesn't understand. He thought the two of you were friends."

The harsh words she uttered under her breath were filled with self-derision. Aloud, she protested, "But I'm coming back, Boone. Didn't anyone tell him that?"

"He's eight. His mother left and never came back, even though I'd reassured him she'd be okay. He's not exactly trusting when it comes to that sort of thing. He's feeling abandoned. I told you it would be like this.

I begged you to keep him at arm's length." Unable to help himself, he lashed out. "If you do come back, I don't want you to have anything to do with him. Is that understood?"

"Boone, you can't mean that," she protested, sounding stricken. "What will that accomplish? He'll think he never mattered to me at all."

"And what do you think he's thinking right now?" he said angrily.

"I'll make it right. I'll call him right this minute. Are you two at Castle's?"

Boone wanted to tell her not to bother, to leave it alone, but that was his anger talking. It wasn't what was best for B.J.

"I'll go inside. Call my cell back in five minutes. I'll give him the phone. You can say goodbye, apologize, whatever. Just don't make any promises you don't intend to keep."

"I won't," she said softly. "I'm sorry, Boone. I wasn't thinking. I would never have hurt him intentionally, you know I wouldn't."

"You never mean to hurt anyone, Em. It just seems to happen." He sighed. "Five minutes, okay?"

"Absolutely," she said.

Boone disconnected the call and went inside to find his son, praying that he'd done the right thing. Maybe it would have been better to let B.J. go through this disillusionment now, rather than later, when it might be even more difficult.

Emily paced the airport, checking her watch as the five minutes Boone had requested ticked by way too slowly. What had she been thinking? After all Boone's warnings, she'd done exactly as he'd feared. She'd hurt his son. Just as he'd said, it didn't really matter that it hadn't been intentional. It had been careless.

And wasn't that exactly why she'd left, because she'd been afraid that she was going to eventually hurt both father and son? It seemed she simply hadn't taken off soon enough. Better yet, she probably should have made her excuses and stayed away, but how could she have let Cora Jane down like that?

When the last second of the five minutes had ticked by, she called Boone's cell. He answered, his tone terse, then immediately handed the phone to B.J.

"Emily?" B.J. said hesitantly.

"How's my consultant?" she asked, trying to sound upbeat.

"Okay," he said.

"I'm sorry I took off without saying goodbye. I need to go check on a couple of jobs, so I left in a hurry."

"Okay," he said, none of his usual exuberance in his voice.

"I'm going to show the client in Aspen the furniture you helped me pick out for his ski lodge," she said, thinking that would please him.

Silence greeted her words, but she waited him out, hoping his natural curiosity about her work would get the better of him.

"Will you show him the red?" B.J. asked eventually.

"I will," she promised.

"Will you tell him I helped pick it out?"

"Of course. You're my consultant, aren't you? I always give credit where it's due."

He released a little sigh then. "When are you coming back?"

"I'm not exactly sure," she said honestly. "But soon."

"Soon, like when? Tomorrow?"

"No, not that soon. A few days, more than likely."

"By the weekend?" he asked, his voice hopeful. "My soccer team's playing again on Saturday. You could come with Dad. He never misses a game."

Emily saw that for the minefield it was. Even if she should be back, she doubted Boone would want her anywhere near that soccer field.

"No promises," she said carefully. "I'll have to see how it goes."

"But you will come, if you're back?" he persisted.

Suddenly she heard Boone's voice in the background, asking for the phone.

"Emily has to catch her flight," he told B.J. "Say goodbye."

"Dad says I have to say goodbye," B.J. said, his frustration plain.

"Bye, sweetie. Be good. I'll see you."

"Bye, Emily."

"Tell me you did not promise him you'd be at his soccer game," Boone said, his voice hushed, clearly trying to keep B.J. from overhearing.

"I told him I wasn't even sure if I'd be back by then," she said. "I know you don't want me there, even if I am back."

"You've got that right."

"I'm so sorry," she apologized again, though she knew she was probably wasting her breath. In Boone's view, what she'd done was inexcusable. And to be honest, she was none too happy with herself. The only possible bright side was that it seemed B.J. had forgiven her. All that told her, though, was how easily a little boy's emotions could be sent on a devastating roller-coaster ride. She had to avoid doing that again, no matter what it cost her.

The next three days were a whirlwind of activity. She spent two of them with Sophia, making sure that every single detail of her new interior design was to her liking and ready for this weekend's gala fund-raising dinner. Though Sophia had been happy with the results, she was dismayed by the news that Emily wouldn't be there for the event.

"Don't you realize how many excellent contacts you could make?" Sophia had asked. "Everyone's going to be asking who made all these lovely changes for me."

"I could leave you some business cards," Emily said, knowing that what Sophia really wanted was to show off her latest protégé. She loved being seen as the mentor to the latest hot talent in Los Angeles, whether it was an artist, a singer, an actor or an interior designer. And she had gotten Emily the meeting with the actor who'd had her update his villa in Italy, the design that had been photographed for a major design magazine. Emily owed her.

Sophia greeted the business card suggestion with the disdain even Emily knew it deserved. "Darling, that simply isn't done," Sophia said.

"I know. I was joking," Emily assured her. "And I would be here if I could be, but I left my family in the lurch to come here to be sure everything was ready for this party of yours. And you are the one who hooked me up with Derek Young. He needs to see these ski lodge designs before *he* loses patience, too."

"Oh, all right," Sophia had said, relenting. "Your

loyalty to your other clients and to your family is admirable. I can hardly argue with that."

If only the meeting with Derek had gone half as well. Though he was pleased with what Emily had to show him, he wasn't pleased with the overall progress.

"We'll never make that deadline," he grumbled. "You need to stay right here and get on this now."

"The deadline was always unrealistic," Emily said. "I told you that in the beginning. Even so, I think you will be ready to open before Christmas."

"Can you commit to that?"

"Once you give me an okay on what I've shown you, I'll set everything in motion. Give me a week and I should be able to give you a firm date."

"That's reasonable, Derek," Tricia chimed in, giving her husband a chiding look.

Emily regarded her with gratitude. She knew if it weren't for Tricia's more reasonable expectations, Derek would probably have fired her, or perhaps never hired her in the first place.

She looked from Tricia to Derek. "You have my promise to make this a top priority."

"And you can do that from North Carolina?" Derek inquired skeptically.

"Of course she can," Tricia answered for Emily. "Look what she's already accomplished from there. It's going to be lovely, exactly what we were hoping for." She smiled at Emily. "And you tell that young man who's helping you that I am very excited about the red fabric he chose."

Emily laughed. "You do know he's only eight? He's probably going to insist that his father bring him out here so he can see for himself that you actually took his suggestion."

Tricia chuckled. "We'll give them the best room in the lodge," she said. "Bring them anytime."

Emily heard the sincerity in her voice. "I'll definitely let him know," she said, though she was doubtful that Boone would ever take advantage of the offer, not if there was even a chance they'd cross paths with her.

Emily gathered up her papers and closed her laptop. "We're all set, then? Any changes you'd like to see? If not, I'll have the contractor in here first thing tomorrow and start making the calls to order the furniture and accessories."

Tricia slid closer to her husband and tucked her arm through his. For all of his gruff demeanor with Emily, it was evident that when it came to his wife, he was putty in her hands. "Derek, everything's perfect, isn't it?"

He smiled at her, his expression indulgent. "If you say it is. There's little question that you have better taste than I do when it comes to this sort of thing."

Tricia laughed. "If we left it to him, everything would have been brown so it wouldn't show dirt," she confirmed. "You have our go-ahead, Emily."

"Fantastic. You'll have updates from me every day, and I'll be back as soon as I can manage it," she promised.

From their private quarters at the lodge, she headed straight for the airport and the connecting flight that would take her to Denver. From there she would have to fly to Atlanta and then to Raleigh. She figured that would give her just enough time to try to figure out what she could possibly say to Boone to make him relent about her spending time with B.J. Unfortunately it probably wasn't nearly enough time to imagine any scenario in which he'd forgive her for hurting his son in the first place.

Now that Tommy and his crew were working on his restaurant renovations, Boone had managed to stay away from Castle's for a few days in a row. B.J. had complained bitterly about that, and none of the activities Boone had arranged for him had gone over well. Apparently he'd been impossible when he'd spent the day with Alex, had been rude when he'd gone to a minor league ball game with another family and had sat in stubborn silence in front of the TV all day when left at home with a sitter.

"Do I have to ground you to get it through your head that being rude isn't acceptable when someone's included you in an outing?" Boone demanded in frustration. "Because if that's what it takes, I will do it. You'll spend the rest of the summer at home with a sitter, and there will be no games and no TV."

B.J. simply stared at him mutinously. "Whatever."

"That attitude is not winning you any points," Boone told him.

"Whatever," B.J. said again and stormed off to his room.

Boone stared after him in frustration. This was all Emily's fault. He didn't have a doubt in the world about that. Other than that one call, she hadn't been in touch. Not that she'd even promised to be, but B.J. had obviously been missing her and hoping for another call.

Tomorrow was B.J.'s soccer game, and Boone was torn about whether to take him or keep him home as punishment for his behavior the past few days. He finally decided to take him. The poor kid was miserable enough without losing out on the soccer game he'd been looking forward to. Maybe playing would boost his spirits.

The game was scheduled for first thing Saturday morning. Boone woke B.J. at seven.

"I'm not going," B.J. said.

"But you've been looking forward to this all week. It's the first game since the hurricane."

"I wanted Emily to see me play."

"She's not even in town," Boone said, praying that was the case.

"How do you know? Did Ms. Cora Jane tell you?"

"No, but Emily told both you and me that she probably wouldn't be back in time."

"But she might be," B.J. said hopefully. "We could call and find out. You have her number."

The hopeful expression in B.J.'s eyes tore at Boone's resolve. Still, he tried to put him off. "I'm sure Ms. Cora Jane would have let us know if Emily had come back."

"Not if she thinks you're mad at her," B.J. said reasonably. "And I'll bet she won't come to the game unless you tell her it's okay."

The kid was obviously too darn smart and overheard way too much.

"Fine. I'll call her," Boone said through gritted teeth. "But don't be surprised if she's still in California or Colorado or wherever she had to go."

Once again he found the number in his caller ID directory and connected. Emily answered almost at once. The sound of her voice set off feelings he'd really hoped were dead and buried after her latest stunt.

"Hi, it's Boone," he said tersely.

"I know."

"B.J. wondered when you'll be back in town," he said, wanting it to be clear that he personally didn't care one way or the other.

"I got in last night," she told him. "Grandmother says you haven't been around much. Is that because you don't even want B.J. around my family now?"

"No, it just seemed best. I've had a lot to do at my restaurant."

"So you were just too busy to drop him off and risk having him run into me again?"

"Okay, yes," he admitted.

"Boone, why are you calling?"

"B.J.'s soccer game is this morning," he said.

"I know."

"He wants you there."

"And you? What do you want?" she asked pointedly.

Boone lowered his voice. "I want him to be happy again," he said, knowing the response was way too telling and gave her way too much power.

"Then it's okay with you if I'm there?" she said, clearly wanting reassurance.

"I'll make it work," he said. "But Em—"

"I know, Boone. I'll do everything in my power not to be careless with his feelings again. Besides, I have big news for him."

"Big news?" he asked cautiously.

"My client loves his fabric choice for the ski lodge. In fact, they want the two of you to come to Aspen sometime as their guests."

Boone couldn't believe his ears. "You're kidding me. They took the advice of an eight-year-old? Did they know that?"

"They did, and that invitation was serious. I have to admit I wasn't nearly as sure about the red as B.J. was."

Boone recalled the day B.J. had made the suggestion, the day he'd talked to Emily about his mom and her love of red. How crazy was it that the interior of this fancy ski resort would wind up being some kind of tribute in a way to Jenny, thanks to his son?

"You're going to make him very happy," Boone said.

Of course, the real truth was that B.J. was going to be over the moon simply because Emily was back and attending his soccer game. His so-called interior design success was just going to be the icing on that cake.

9

Emily arrived at the soccer field just after the start of the game. She tried to slip into the stands unobtrusively, but during a time-out in play, B.J. caught sight of her from the field and made a mad dash in her direction. He threw his arms around her in a hug that almost knocked her off balance.

"Dad said you were back and that you were coming," he enthused. "Did you see me on that last play? I almost made a goal."

"Did you really?" she said, smiling at his excitement even over an apparent near miss. "I wish I'd been here, but it must have been when I was walking over from the parking lot."

"You're gonna stay, though, right? For the whole game?"

"I'm definitely going to be here," she assured him.

He glanced toward the field where play was about to resume. "Gotta go. I'll see you after, okay?"

"Okay," she said.

She'd barely taken a seat in the bleachers when

Boone appeared from somewhere above her in the stands and sat down beside her.

"When you weren't here at the start of the game, I assumed you couldn't make it, after all," he said.

"I told you I'd be here."

He merely lifted a brow at that.

She frowned at him, hurt by his complete lack of faith in her. "Do you really not trust me at all?"

"How can I?" he asked simply.

She held his gaze, her own look steady, until he flinched. "Okay, here's the deal," she said finally. "I will do my absolute best never to let B.J. or you down again. When I make a promise, I will keep it. If for any reason on God's green earth I can't, I will tell you ahead of time so neither of you will be disappointed. I don't know what else I can do, Boone. I really don't. Life's unpredictable. Things come up. You have a successful career. You must know that."

"The difference is that I put B.J. first, always."

She nodded. "I respect that. He's your son and it's what he deserves from his dad."

Boone frowned. "But he's no real relation to you, so you have no obligation to do the same?"

"That is not what I meant," she said impatiently. "Of course he's important to me."

"But work will always take precedence?" he persisted.

"Not always," she said, frustrated by his determination to misread her. "But sometimes, yes. Can you honestly tell me that you've never once let B.J. down because something came up at work? Not once?"

She watched the play of expressions on Boone's face

and knew she'd struck a nerve. "When Jenny was alive, you thought it was okay," she guessed.

Boone sighed. "More than I should have," he admitted eventually. "Now, though, I'm all he has. It's different. It has to be."

She touched his arm. "And I get that, Boone. I really do. You have no idea how much I admire your devotion to B.J. He's incredibly lucky to have you as his dad. Believe me, I know all about workaholic fathers who don't put their children first, or even second. That is not you."

"It could have been," he said quietly, his expression distant. He met her gaze for just a heartbeat. "I came so close to being exactly like that."

She saw the regret in his eyes, heard the pain in his voice and understood in a way she hadn't before. Boone wasn't an amazing dad because it had come to him naturally. He was, at least in part, making up for past mistakes.

And when she screwed up, on some level he saw himself in her actions, and it reminded him of a time he was trying desperately to forget.

Boone had revealed far more than he'd ever intended to about the way he'd once been, driven and ambitious, yes, but also cramming every minute of the day with activity to keep Emily out of his thoughts.

At least he hadn't given her so much as a hint about the mistakes he'd made in his marriage as well as those he'd made with his son. He never wanted Emily to know about the probably inevitable distance there'd been between him and Jenny, a gap he hadn't been able to close no matter how much he'd wanted to, all because a piece of his heart had been missing. That was a guilt he'd have to live with forever. And if he ever forgot it, the Farmers would always be there, ready to remind him.

What he had revealed was damning enough. Emily was right about one thing, for sure. She, of all people, understood what it was like to have a father who was so absorbed in his own world he neglected everyone around him.

As close as he'd been to the family for all these years, Boone barely knew Sam Castle. He could count on one hand the number of times Emily's father had put in an appearance at the beach. It had been her mother who'd dropped the girls off when they'd spent summers with Cora Jane, who'd paid visits to check up on them, who drove over for holiday meals with their grandparents. Even when Emily's mother had died and Boone had skipped school and driven across the state to be there for Emily at the funeral, it was as if Sam Castle weren't really there. Oh, he was physically present, but emotionally he'd been in some other place. It had been Cora Jane who'd comforted the girls and handled the reception.

Samantha rarely mentioned their father. Emily spoke of him mostly with disdain. Only Gabi seemed to worship him, carving out a workaholic lifestyle for herself in Raleigh in an unmistakable attempt to get his attention. From what Boone had observed and heard, it hadn't worked.

If Boone had needed a role model for the type of father *not* to be, Sam Castle would have been it. Even so, he'd wandered dangerously close to being exactly like him.

Jenny's death had shocked him into taking a closer look at the man he'd become. He hadn't liked what he'd seen. Ironically, even though she was long out of his life, on some level he'd found a way to blame Emily for that, too. After all, had he been able to throw himself heart and soul into his marriage, he wouldn't have chosen work over his family time and again.

Emily's return had raised all those complex emotions once more. Just the realization that he was still attracted to her had filled him with guilt. He'd shortchanged his wife, shortchanged his son, buried himself in work and, in the end, it had been for nothing. Emily still had a hold on his heart...and he hated that. Now she had a hold on his son, and he hated that even more.

Boone was suddenly aware that Emily was on her feet beside him, shaking his arm. All around them people were cheering.

He stared at her blankly, but instinctively stood up. "What happened?"

"B.J. just scored a goal, that's what," she said excitedly.

He looked at the field where B.J. was surrounded by his screaming teammates. B.J. looked toward the stands, a mile-wide smile on his face.

"Did you see?" he mouthed.

His words couldn't be heard, but Boone knew what he wanted to know. He gave B.J. a big thumbs-up, his own smile as big as his son's.

When play resumed, Emily regarded him curiously. "Where'd you go a few minutes ago?"

"I was right here," he equivocated.

"Physically, yes, but you sure weren't paying attention to the game."

"My mind wandered for a minute, that's all."

She looked as if she had questions she wanted to ask, but for once she kept them to herself. Good thing, he thought, since talking to her about the mistakes of his life and her role in them would open a can of worms best left sealed tight.

In the end, B.J.'s team won the game, two to one. B.J.'s goal had been the winning one, and now everyone was going out to a casual restaurant in nearby Manteo to celebrate. B.J. bounced up and down in front of Emily.

"You'll come, right? It's okay, isn't it, Dad?"

Emily saw that it was anything but okay with Boone. "Sweetie, I really should get out to Castle's and see how things are going."

"But you have to come to the celebration," B.J. insisted.

Boone interceded. "You heard her, son. She has other obligations."

"A half hour," B.J. pleaded.

Used to getting his own way, he seemed to know all the persuasive tactics required—asking, pleading. Emily suspected there'd be pouting next.

"That's not so long," he told her. "I get a prize for scoring a goal. Don't you want to see that?"

Emily glanced at Boone, who shrugged, clearly giving up the fight just as B.J. had obviously anticipated. Sadly, she wasn't made of tougher stuff.

"A half hour," she conceded. "Just till you get your prize. Cora Jane will definitely want to see a picture of that. I can take one on my cell phone."

"You can ride with us," B.J. said, dragging her toward their car.

"I really should take the rental car, so I can leave," Emily protested.

"I'll bring you back to get the car whenever you're ready," Boone said, his voice resigned.

At the restaurant, B.J. immediately bounded off to sit with his teammates. Emily glanced at Boone, who stood just inside the door looking thoroughly uncomfortable.

"You planning to ditch your unwanted date?" she asked lightly. "Maybe hang out with some single soccer moms?"

His lips twitched. "And hear about it from now till eternity from B.J.? I don't think so."

"I won't tell anyone. After all, it would be pretty humiliating. Why would I tell?"

He laughed. "You might not, but B.J. will have a lot to say. He may not have a name for what he's up to, but my son is matchmaking."

Emily was genuinely startled by that. "He is? He's only eight."

Boone nodded. "That's old enough, apparently. We can probably thank Cora Jane for planting the idea in his head. She's not even subtle about her agenda."

"No, she's not," Emily agreed. "So we're just supposed to go along with it?"

"Hardly," Boone said with heartfelt conviction.

Despite herself, Emily chuckled. "Well, that certainly tells me where you stand."

Boone looked vaguely chagrined. "Sorry. Did that sound like an insult?"

"Maybe a little."

"I only meant that we both know where things stand between us. We just have to be civil while you're here, try not to give either of them any false hopes. Isn't that what we agreed to when you first arrived? We just need to stick to the plan."

"So, we sit over there, order a couple of sodas, share a little idle conversation, then you take me back to my car, and we call it a day."

He shrugged. "Works for me."

Emily wished it worked for her. It should. In fact, after her disconcerting conversation with Gabi a few days ago, it should be exactly what she wanted, some careful chitchat with no complications. Except this was Boone, and she wanted more than anything to know where his thoughts had roamed back at the soccer field when he'd looked so lost and had missed his son's winning goal.

He took her silence for assent and led the way to a table. Emily sat across from him, then agreed to the beer and the burger he suggested ordering. She thought about the best way to find out what she wanted to know, decided to be direct, then leaned forward.

"Boone, why did you get so upset earlier?" She spoke in a low tone, even though the restaurant was so noisy she risked not being heard.

He frowned at the question. "I wasn't upset."

"Yes, you were. When you were talking about the kind of Dad you'd been before Jenny died, it obviously took you to a bad place."

"The last thing I'm going to talk to you about is my marriage," he said tightly.

She studied the tension obvious in his clenched jaw, the way he avoided looking at her. Still, she persisted. "You told me you were happy. Was that a lie?"

"Of course not," he snapped.

Emily saw the flush in his cheeks and knew he was still lying to her. "Did you love Jenny?" she asked quietly.

"Of course I did. Why are you trying to dredge all of this up? Do you want to torture me?"

She found his choice of words telling. "If you were in love with your wife, if you were happy, then thinking about those days shouldn't be torture. It would make you sad, but it wouldn't make you angry or guilty of whatever it is that's put that look on your face."

His gaze narrowed. "What look is that?"

"The one that says you're considering your options for shutting me up," she said, her tone deliberately teasing. She had a feeling lightening the mood might get her closer to the answers she wanted.

His expression did ease. There was even a faint twinkle in his eyes. "I remember how I used to do it. Do you?"

"With a kiss," she recalled, her breath hitching. "Probably not the best way to go right now."

"It was always effective, though," he reminded her, holding her gaze. "Always."

The air between them seemed to crackle with tension, as she waited to see what he would do, not entirely certain if she desperately wanted that kiss…or was terrified of it. What on earth was wrong with her that she insisted on dancing toward danger with him?

Finally when she thought she might die if he didn't do *something,* he swallowed hard and closed his eyes.

"You could drive a saint to drink," he finally said, meeting her gaze again. "We can't go back, Em. We just can't."

"I know that," she replied softly. "But every now and then, like right this minute, I can't seem to remember why."

"Yeah, I'm having that problem, too."

She pushed aside the untouched burger. "I should probably go. It doesn't seem as if they're going to hand out those prizes anytime soon."

Boone nodded at once, clearly relieved by the reprieve. "I'll take you."

"But you could miss the ceremony," she protested.

"I'll make sure one of the parents takes pictures, and I'll be back before B.J. even realizes I'm gone," he said, leading the way to the car.

"Is he going to be upset again because I missed it?" she worried.

"I'll make sure he understands. You already told him you had to get to Castle's to help out." He gave her a curious look. "I'm a little puzzled by what you're planning to do over there, though. They'll be closing for the day in an hour. Are you planning to wash dishes?"

"Very funny," she replied. "I'm going to sit Cora Jane down and have another conversation about making some updates. This time I have color swatches and sketches."

He gave her an amused look. "Maybe you ought to run those by B.J. first, since he has such good instincts and all."

She frowned at his attempt to be funny. "I think I can handle this."

"I swear, I was serious," Boone said. "Cora Jane adores B.J. You know she'd listen to him."

"She'll listen to me, too," Emily said grimly.

"Yeah, but you're going to take it personally again when she rejects your plan."

"She's not going to reject it," Emily said confidently, though she knew there was every chance that her grandmother would, indeed, turn her suggestions down flat.

"How about this?" Boone said, pulling into the Castle's lot. "After we finish up here and B.J. gets a shower, I'll bring him over to Castle's. You two can talk your ideas over, then double-team your grandmother."

She frowned at his persistence. "You really think this is doomed, don't you?"

He nodded. "Afraid so."

"But I'm good at what I do," she protested.

"I'm sure you are, but Cora Jane is stubborn as a mule, to say nothing of set in her ways. She doesn't want to change the restaurant. I'm still a little shocked that she went along with Wade's plans to update the whole cashier area."

Emily chuckled. "Of course she went along with it. She had to keep him around if her plan to set him up with Gabi was to succeed. Are you aware that she's figured out some essential change he had to make practically every day?"

Boone regarded her with surprise. "You're kidding. And Wade's gone along with it?"

"He seems to welcome it. The man hasn't taken his eyes off Gabi since that first day, at least according to Grandmother. He's no more anxious to leave than she is to let him."

"And Gabi?"

"Oblivious," Emily admitted, grinning. "It's driving Grandmother crazy. Samantha's finding the whole thing highly entertaining."

Emily slanted a look at Boone. "I know a surefire way to get her to agree to these changes I want to make."

"Oh?"

"You could agree to supervise and we could get Wade to do all the carpentry," she said, oddly pleased by the deviousness of the idea. "Two birds with one stone. She'd be in matchmaking glory."

"And we'd be exactly where?" Boone asked.

She grinned. "Deep trouble, I imagine, but it could be worth it."

"Just so you could get your way?"

She nodded. "I'm just saying, I'd certainly consider it a favor."

Boone shook his head. "Sorry, sweet pea. No can do. Not even for such a noble cause. You're on your own unless you want B.J.'s help."

"Fine," she said, as he pulled up behind her car. "Bring him over. Even a pint-size ally is better than none."

Boone laughed. "See you in an hour, then."

As Emily watched him drive away, she couldn't help wondering when he'd stopped worrying about her spending time with his son. Had he started to trust her, after all? Or had he simply accepted that B.J. would make it all but impossible for Boone to keep them apart?

As Boone had predicted, the last of the customers was leaving Castle's just as Emily arrived. With the dining room closed, Wade had arrived to work on the cabinets Cora Jane had decided she wanted behind the cashier stand.

"How's it going, Wade?" Emily asked. "How many times has Grandmother changed her mind today?"

He laughed. "So far, we're sticking with yesterday's plan. Three cabinets for storage, but now she's decided some open shelving would be good, too."

"For?"

"Souvenirs, I think. Gabi suggested it. She's been

over there poring over catalogs for a couple of days now. Says it would be great PR to have people walking around all over town wearing Castle's T-shirts and ball caps and drinking out of Castle's fancy to-go cups. I recommended she look into sand pails, the perfect thing for making sand castles on the beach, right? I thought it was an inspired tie-in."

"It actually is," Emily agreed. "What did Gabi say?"

He shrugged. "About what you'd expect. She told me to stick to carpentry." He beckoned Emily closer. "But I sneaked a peek at the catalogs she has over there today." A grin spread across his face. "Sand pails."

Emily laughed. "Good for you."

She headed for the booth where her sister had set up shop. "On a spending spree?" she asked, sliding into the booth opposite her.

Gabi looked up, the smile on her face fading as she realized who it was. "Bravely returning to the scene of the crime?" she inquired.

"What crime?"

"Running off on a little boy who was counting on you."

"B.J. and I have made peace. So have Boone and I, more or less, anyway. Didn't Grandmother tell you I'd gone to B.J.'s soccer game this morning? And where were you when I got in last night, anyway?"

"I was here late," Gabi replied. "Somebody has to keep an eye on Wade."

Emily managed to fight a grin. "Wade seems to me to know what he's doing. Does he really need supervision?"

"I don't trust him," Gabi said. "He keeps making

all these changes. I think he's trying to run up Grandmother's bill."

"And I think Grandmother is making all those changes to keep him around," Emily told her.

Gabi looked vaguely nonplussed. "Why would she do that?"

"Eye candy for you," Emily suggested.

"Be serious."

"I am serious. Grandmother's matchmaking engine is running full-throttle. Me and Boone, you and Wade. I can hardly wait to see what—or should I say who—she has in mind for Samantha."

"I have a boyfriend," Gabi reminded her yet again.

"So you keep saying. Why haven't we met him? Why doesn't he call every ten minutes to tell you he's pining for you?"

Gabi frowned. "It's not that kind of relationship. We both do the things we need to do. We understand about obligations."

"Gee, that makes me feel all warm and fuzzy. No wonder Grandmother's on a mission to find a suitable replacement."

"There is nothing suitable about Wade," Gabi protested.

"He's gorgeous. He's nice. He's funny. And he seems pretty darn eager to worship at your feet. I'd say that puts him several notches above what's-his-name." She frowned. "What is his name, anyway? And why don't you talk about him more, if he's so right for you?"

"His name is Paul, and I don't talk about him because I don't want to deal with all this attitude from you and Samantha and Grandmother. Cora Jane may have Jerry, but I don't see you or Samantha carrying on any big love affairs. Until you are, your opinions are suspect." She gave Emily a questioning look. "Unless there's something I don't know about you and Boone. You said you'd made peace. Does that mean you've accepted your destiny and crawled into his bed?"

Emily really, really wished she could confirm that she had, if only to wipe that smug look off her sister's face. Then, again, was that really the only reason she could think of for wishing things had heated up between her and Boone? Hardly. Despite every word they'd exchanged, every off-limits declaration they'd made, the break she'd taken to get her perspective back, despite all of that she seriously wanted that man's hands on her body again.

Even if it would be a huge mistake.

10

Even as he was driving B.J. over to Castle's as promised, Boone was already having misgivings. Every minute he spent with Emily grew more complicated. Back at the restaurant he'd been within seconds of tossing caution to the wind and kissing her. While he might be oblivious to a lot of the ramifications of some of his actions, he knew with absolute certainty that one kiss would doom him. Whatever willpower or restraint he'd mustered to keep her at arm's length would have dissolved like sugar in hot tea.

B.J. was clutching his little plastic soccer award as if it were a Super Bowl trophy. "This is so cool," he said. "Huh, Dad?"

"It is very cool," Boone confirmed.

"Maybe Ms. Cora Jane will want to put it on display," he said hopefully.

"Hey, what about me?" Boone protested. "Maybe I want it to be on display in my restaurant."

B.J. regarded him incredulously. "Really?"

"Why not? You're my son and it's your first sports award. It should be where people can see it and know how proud of you I am." He glanced over at B.J. "What do you think? The first award in a trophy case at Boone's Harbor?"

"Awesome!" B.J. said enthusiastically. "You can have it, but only after I show Emily and Ms. Cora Jane."

"Of course."

"Did Emily really say she wanted my help with picking out stuff for Castle's?"

Boone smiled at his excitement. "Well, I might have planted the idea in her head, but she was eager to get your input."

"How come you told her to ask me?"

"Because I happen to know how persuasive you can be and how much Ms. Cora Jane likes you," Boone admitted. "I think both of those things will help Emily make her case for redecorating. It means a lot to her."

"Yeah, and Ms. Cora Jane is really, really against it," B.J. said direly, then admitted, "I kinda get why she feels that way. Castle's is really nice the way it is."

Boone gave him a curious look. "You planning to tell Emily that?"

B.J. grinned. "Heck, no. Then she won't need my help."

"I thought what she liked best about your advice was your candor."

B.J. regarded him blankly. "Huh?"

"You tell her what you really think," Boone explained. "She counts on that."

"Yeah, I guess," B.J. said. "But I don't want to hurt her feelings."

Boone laughed. "And you have just learned man's eternal dilemma."

"Huh?" B.J. said again, looking even more bewildered.

"You'll understand when you're older. Men are always trying to find the right balance between the truth, diplomacy and what a woman really wants to hear. We get tripped up on that a lot."

B.J. shook his head. "Sounds way too complicated. I'm thinking girls might not be worth it."

"Believe me, it is complicated," Boone said. It had gotten him in trouble more times than he could count. He smiled. "But it's definitely worth the trouble. You'll see."

Cora Jane was in the kitchen going over tomorrow's specials with Jerry when B.J. came bounding in, followed at a more sedate pace by Boone. She saw the plastic prize in B.J.'s hand and beamed at him.

"What do you have there, young man?" she asked as if Emily hadn't already filled her in on B.J.'s big day on the soccer field.

"I scored the winning goal today," B.J. told her excitedly. "And they gave me a prize, and Dad's going to put it on display in his restaurant, because it's my first sports trophy."

Cora Jane chuckled. "Well, of course he is. He must be very proud."

"No question about it," Boone confirmed.

"Where's Emily?" B.J. asked, practically bouncing up and down with excitement. "She had to leave before I got my award. I want to show her."

"She's sitting in the dining room with Gabi," Cora Jane told him. "Go right on in there. I'm sure she's anxious to see it."

"And then you come back here," Jerry told him. "I want to hear all about how you scored that winning goal."

"Okay," B.J. said. "It was awesome, huh, Dad?"

"Awesome," Boone confirmed.

"You're not going in there with him?" Cora Jane asked, studying Boone intently. He was staring after his son, his expression filled with worry.

"Nope. He and Emily have things to discuss. Mind if I pour a cup of coffee and hang out with you?"

"Sounds to me like you're avoiding her. Any particular reason? I thought the two of you made peace earlier."

"We did."

Cora Jane grinned. "She's getting under your skin, isn't she? Reminding you of what the two of you used to have?"

Boone gave her an impatient look. "It's not as if I've ever forgotten what we had. She's the one who threw it away."

"And you're scared she'll do it again, and now B.J.'s feelings are involved," she guessed, feeling sorry for the mess her granddaughter had left behind all those years ago.

"Something like that," Boone conceded. "Could we not dissect this, please? It is what it is."

"Doesn't have to be," Cora Jane said. "You could do what I know you're itching to do and just give the woman another chance."

"Cora Jane, has she done one single thing to indicate that she wants a second chance? I sure haven't seen it."

"Leave it be," Jerry warned her, stepping in for the first time. "Let them work it out for themselves or you'll find yourself caught in the middle."

"I *am* in the middle," Cora Jane retorted. "I love both of them. I know they were happier together than either one of them has been apart, whether they want to admit the truth or not." She met Boone's gaze. "No disrespect to Jenny intended. She was a wonderful girl and a wonderful wife to you. Heaven knows, she was an incredible mother for B.J."

"She was," Boone said. "And I don't ever want to forget that."

Cora Jane studied this young man who'd survived Emily's abandonment, married too impulsively and in far too many ways lived to regret it. She thought she understood what was at the heart of his reluctance to move forward, at least with Emily.

"Do you intend to do penance for the rest of your life for not loving Jenny enough?" she asked him gently. "You loved her the very best you could, Boone. No husband could have been more devoted."

Boone regarded her with disbelief. "You know better."

"I know no such thing. I saw the two of you together, remember? Jenny wanted for nothing. You had this amazing son together. Jenny's face glowed with happiness."

Boone obviously remained unconvinced. "There was a part of me that was never hers."

"Well, of course not," Cora Jane said impatiently. "In a lifetime we may fall in love only once, if we're very, very lucky. Most people love twice, even more. The heart doesn't have limits on its capacity for love. A part of mine will always belong to my late husband, rest his soul, but that doesn't mean my feelings for Jerry are any less deep or sincere."

"And I wouldn't expect her to forget about Caleb," Jerry added, backing her up in this. "Of course he's still in her heart."

Cora Jane gave him a grateful look, then turned back to Boone. "And I imagine Jenny never expected you to forget entirely about Emily. Of all people, she understood what losing her cost you. Because she loved you so, that girl understood your heart in ways I'm not even sure you did."

"But I felt as if I was cheating on her every day we were married," Boone said. "Because I never entirely let go of the past. I wanted to be a good husband, the kind Jenny deserved, but I failed time after time."

"You did not fail," Cora Jane insisted. "It's only your misplaced guilt talking. You did nothing wrong, Boone. You weren't chasing after my granddaughter. As far as I know, the two of you never even spoke on the phone or kept in contact any other way. You honored your commitment to Jenny from the day you made it."

"Tell that to Jenny's parents," he said. "They knew. Her mother told me as much when Jenny died. She said I'd ruined her daughter's life and it was all my fault that she'd died, that she'd had nothing to live for."

Cora Jane stared at him in shock. "Jodie Farmer dared to say such a thing to you, especially at a time when you were dealing with the death of your wife?"

"And a lot more," Boone confirmed, thinking of her threats to take custody of B.J.

"And of course you believed her," Cora Jane said, finally understanding. "You'd already condemned yourself, so you took the words of an angry, grieving mother to heart."

"How could I not? I knew the truth. As hard as I'd tried to do right by Jenny, I'd let her down."

Cora Jane simply couldn't allow him to go on thinking like that. She had to find the right words to show him that Jodie's bitterness wasn't based in reality.

"Did Jenny even once suggest that *she* thought you'd let her down?" she asked Boone.

"No, but that was just the kind of person she was. She loved everyone. She overlooked all their faults, mine most of all."

Cora Jane shook her head. "Boy, you refuse to cut yourself even the tiniest break, don't you? Jenny was smart, right?"

"Absolutely."

"And she picked you to love?"

His gaze narrowed. "What's your point?"

"I don't think a smart woman would have chosen someone she didn't consider worthy or put up for a minute being anyone's second choice, at least not if they threw it in her face that that's all she was."

"Of course I didn't throw it in her face," Boone said indignantly.

Cora Jane smiled. "No, you didn't. And that's precisely my point. Once you made the commitment to that girl, you gave your marriage everything you had to give. However much that was, it was enough to keep a sunny smile on Jenny's face and joy in her heart. She was happy, Boone. I'd stake my life on that. And that was because of you." She gave him a hard look. "And I won't hear another word from you saying otherwise."

Boone's smile was a long time coming. When it came eventually, it was accompanied by a sigh. "What did I ever do to deserve someone like you in my corner?"

Cora Jane stood up and put her hands on his cheeks. "You became part of my family the very first day you walked in here with Emily. Nothing, not one thing you could ever do, will change that." She gave him a little shake. "And you need to remember that I'm nobody's patsy. When it comes to people, I can spot a fake or a cheat or a jerk quicker than most. You are none of those things, Boone Dorsett. You're a decent, strong, loving man or I wouldn't want you for my granddaughter. Understood?"

His smile finally spread. "Understood." He planted a kiss on her cheek. "But I think I'd better get B.J. and head home."

"Now?" Cora Jane said incredulously. "Did I just waste my breath here?"

Boone laughed. "I heard you. Doesn't mean I'm going to jump off the deep end just because it's what you want."

She shook her head. "I might have to take it all back," she warned him.

"Up to you," he said, giving Jerry a wink. "See you soon."

"Maybe you will. Maybe you won't," Cora Jane replied. "I really don't like it much when my advice is ignored."

"Keep that in mind when Emily comes to you with her latest plans for this place," he suggested. "She's not crazy about being ignored, either. The two of you are a lot alike in that regard."

"Well, I never," she muttered as he walked out. She turned to Jerry. "I honestly thought I'd finally made some progress with that man."

Jerry chuckled. "Maybe you ought to think about

sitting back and letting nature take its course. Neither one of them is going to stand a chance against those sparks that fly whenever they're in the same place, not for long, anyway."

"I don't like leaving the important stuff to chance," Cora Jane said in frustration.

"Think of it this way," Jerry suggested. "You're putting it in God's hands. Last time I checked, He was even better than you at making sure things turn out the way they're supposed to."

Cora Jane could hardly deny that, but she sure as heck didn't have to like it.

Boone had heard every word Cora Jane said to him on Saturday. He even believed some of it. That didn't mean he was quite ready to let go of the guilt that had wrapped itself around him like a cloak ever since Jenny's death. That being the case, he tried to give Castle's a wide berth at least until Emily left town for good. He managed to steer clear on Sunday and Monday, but by Tuesday B.J. was having none of it. Boone dropped him off that morning and returned only to pick him up. He didn't set foot inside.

On Wednesday he tried yet again to convince B.J. to spend the day with him. Unfortunately B.J.'s attachment to Emily was growing. Boone might not consider it healthy, but he understood why his son was basking in her attention. He missed his mother and needed a woman's tender touch.

"How about hanging out at my restaurant today?" Boone suggested when they left the house.

B.J. immediately shook his head. "It's boring there. Everybody's too busy to pay any attention to me.

Tommy won't let me help with anything. He says I might get hurt."

Boone could hardly argue with Tommy's instincts, though they certainly didn't help him out of this particular jam. "I'll find something for you to do," Boone promised. "Or maybe you could help Pete with something."

B.J. didn't look convinced. "Like what?"

"We'll ask him when we get there," Boone said, since no immediate ideas came to mind.

"No way," B.J. protested. "Once you get there, you won't want to leave, no matter how boring it is."

"But you have that game you insisted was the best thing ever," Boone said in frustration. "This is exactly the reason I bought it for you, so you'd have something to keep you from being bored."

"It's not as much fun as real work, like the kind they give me at Castle's," B.J. argued. "And Emily needs my help. You said so yourself."

Boone conceded defeat, drove right on by his restaurant and headed north to Castle's.

"What exactly did Emily let you do yesterday to help her?" he asked his son, curious to know what B.J. found so fascinating.

"She showed me this cool computer program she uses to decide on paint colors and stuff," B.J. explained. "She thinks Castle's should be a sky blue color with sunshine yellow trim, instead of all dark and dreary the way it is now."

Boone hid a smile. "I assume that's a direct quote, the dark and dreary part?"

B.J. nodded. "She called it something else, too. Rus...something."

"Rustic?" Boone suggested.

"That's it," B.J. confirmed. "I wasn't sure what it meant, so that's when she said dark and dreary, kinda like a cave."

Boone could only imagine how Cora Jane would react to *that* comparison. "And did you happen to hear what Ms. Cora Jane said when Emily proposed that idea?" Boone asked. Despite his own less-than-subtle attempts to get Cora Jane to at least listen to Emily, he had a feeling Cora Jane still wasn't going to be open to such a dramatic change from basic beige walls and all that dark brown wood she thought gave the restaurant its beachside character.

"She says it'll be all prettified over her dead body," B.J. mimicked, grinning. "What's prettified mean?"

"Something a girl would pick out," Boone assumed. "And how did Emily handle that remark?"

"She called her a stubborn old coot," B.J. reported. "Ms. Cora Jane just laughed. She said it took one to know one."

Wasn't that the truth? Boone thought as he made the turn into the Castle's parking lot. With the main dining room back open, the restaurant appeared to be jammed. Apparently people didn't care that there there'd been water damage and a layer of sand on the floor a few days before or that there was a hint of damp mustiness lingering in the air. The air-conditioning was back on, the place was drying out, the burgers were as good as always and the beer cold.

He was about to open the door, when Emily nearly knocked him down with it. "You talk some sense into her," she said as she sailed past. "I give up."

Boone instructed B.J. to go inside and went after

Emily, who was crossing the road and heading for the dunes. Two cars had to hit their brakes to avoid her.

With no death wish of his own, Boone allowed the traffic to pass, then caught up with her at the water's edge. He was half surprised she hadn't walked right out in it, clothes and all. Maybe she should have. It might have cooled her temper.

"Want to talk about it?" he asked, keeping his hands shoved in his pockets to avoid reaching for her. She looked as if she might shatter completely at any offer of comfort.

"What's to talk about? I've shown her a dozen different ways to bring the restaurant up-to-date, to give it a little style, and she's blown off every one of them. She doesn't seem to realize I actually know what I'm doing. People pay me big money for my ideas."

"Maybe she thinks those ideas are just right for a fancy restaurant in Beverly Hills, but not so great for a casual place on the beach in North Carolina," he suggested carefully. "It's not as if Castle's needs to boost business. There's a standing-room-only crowd in there right this second."

The look she gave him cut right through him, probably damaging a couple of vital organs.

"Don't you think that perhaps the reason I'm successful is because I know how to research customer expectations, how to create the right atmosphere for the right place?" she asked irritably. "And who knows this restaurant and these customers even half as well as I do? I started waiting tables here as soon as I could carry a tray."

"Hated every minute of it, as I recall," he said with a smile.

"That's beside the point." She gave him a look filled with frustration. "I'm not telling her to bring in leather settees and mood lighting, for heaven's sake. I'm just trying to give the place some beachfront charm. It's depressing in there."

"Rustic?" Boone suggested.

She gave him another of those piercing looks. He shrugged. "B.J. mentioned it."

"Okay, yes. Rustic. Would you tell me why she couldn't keep that dining room closed another couple of days until it aired out? I'm sure it's only because she didn't want to lose the business."

"Maybe it's because she knew there would be folks in town counting on her," Boone suggested gently. "Emily, you know how many regulars that place has. It's not even about the tourists, though they keep us all going. It's about the locals who like to gather there to see their neighbors, catch up on what's going on around here. Far more than my restaurant, Castle's is an important part of the community."

She frowned. "Okay, maybe. But what is so wrong about sprucing the place up?"

"Maybe it's more about the timing," he suggested, though he was convinced of no such thing.

Emily rolled her eyes. "If I thought that's all it was, I could get this in motion and she could have the work done when the tourist season slows down, but trust me, she'll have none of that, either."

Boone allowed himself a small smile at the annoyance in her voice. He actually understood the point she was trying to make about bringing Castle's interior up-to-date. He'd paid an expert much like Emily to design the ambiance for the interiors of the Boone's

Harbor restaurants to be inviting and classy. He hadn't wanted stuffed fish and decoys hanging on the walls. He'd wanted a look that would work as well in a city like Charlotte as it would here on the coast.

"Maybe you should give Cora Jane a little credit," he suggested mildly. "She seems to know what her customers want. She's been in business here a lot of years."

"I'm just saying I think they'd like it even better if we brought some of that sunshine inside," she grumbled.

"Thus the blue paint and sunshine yellow trim," he said. "B.J. mentioned that, too."

"Did he also tell you Grandmother's reaction?"

Boone barely managed to hide a grin. "He did."

"Yeah, well, she could get her wish. Maybe I will do it over her dead body. Maybe one of these days, if she hasn't already driven *me* into an early grave, I'll come back here after she's gone and paint the whole place in the wildest colors imaginable. A brilliant flamingo pink and blazing fire engine red come to mind. How's that for a shocker of a combination?"

It took everything in him to bite back the chuckle that threatened. "It'll be an attention-getter, all right. And then what? You harboring some desire to run a restaurant that'll keep you tied to this place?"

"Hardly. Samantha, Gabi and I will sell it for top dollar." She glanced at him. "Maybe even to you. That is what you're angling for, isn't it? To get your hands on this location?"

The camaraderie of the moment disappeared in a heartbeat. Boone froze at her words. That she could think such a thing, even for a single second, stunned him.

"Since I know you're upset, I'll let that ridiculous remark pass." He leveled a look into her eyes. "You should know me better than that, Em. You really should."

He turned on his heel and walked away, seething. Once in a while, he felt a hint of the old connection between the two of them, a suggestion of the *us-against-the-world* mentality that had kept them together as teens. Right this second, though, he realized they'd never been further apart.

Emily stared after Boone, feeling small and spiteful and mean. She'd hurt him just then. Maybe she'd meant to do it, even, but when her barb had struck its mark, she'd immediately wanted to take it back. He'd come after her just now, listened to her complaints, tried to offer comfort, and how had she returned the favor? By suggesting he had underhanded motives for helping out her grandmother. Even now, after seeing the bond between the two of them, she'd been suspicious and unreasonable.

Sure, it had been a stupid, knee-jerk remark because she was hurt and angry, a suggestion she honestly didn't believe, but thinking it, much less saying it aloud, had been uncalled for. Boone didn't deserve that from her.

Of course, admitting the mistake to herself was one thing. Apologizing to Boone was quite another. She needed to do that, and sooner rather than later.

Uttering a sigh of resignation, she put her sneakers back on and crossed the street, hoping to make amends. Instead, she was just in time to see Boone and B.J. leaving the parking lot. Boone didn't even glance her way, though B.J. waved excitedly and called her name.

She gave B.J. a wave in return and stared after Boone

with regret, then slipped into the restaurant kitchen through a side door. She found her grandmother at the stove dishing up bowls of crab soup. Cora Jane glanced up at her.

"I could use your help in there," her grandmother said as if they hadn't been arguing less than an hour ago. "We're swamped, inside and out. Gabi and Samantha are trying to keep up with the regular wait staff, but we could use another pair of hands."

Emily nodded and grabbed an apron and an order book. Though waiting tables was only a distant memory, she'd spent enough summers helping out here to know the drill. As Boone had said, she hadn't liked it, but she had mastered it, because it was her nature to do everything well or not do it at all.

Even as that thought struck her, it occurred to her that maybe that's why she'd left Boone, because she'd feared that a real, lasting relationship was something she'd never do well. She'd have to give that some thought later. Right now there were customers waiting. She headed for the dining room.

"When things quiet down, you and I will talk," her grandmother said as she passed by.

"About my ideas?" Emily asked, unable to hide the hopeful note in her voice.

"About Boone," Cora Jane retorted.

Emily stilled. "Not up for discussion."

"We'll just see about that," Cora Jane said stubbornly, then she sashayed by and disappeared into the dining room where the noise level defied further conversation.

Just as well, Emily thought as she followed. She

doubted there was one single thing Cora Jane could say about Boone Dorsett that she had any desire to hear. And whatever lecture Cora Jane had in mind was nothing compared to the one already echoing in Emily's head.

11

For once B.J. was silent as Boone sped away from Castle's. Boone couldn't recall ever being quite so angry and disillusioned, not even when Emily had walked out of his life ten years ago.

When his cell phone rang just after he sped out of the Castle's parking lot, he hit the connection for the hands-free device. "What?" he snapped.

"You sound cheery," Ethan Cole said.

"It's not the best time."

"Then I'm really glad I called. I wanted to remind you to bring B.J. by the clinic so I can take a look at those stitches. Maybe I can cure whatever ails you at the same time."

"I doubt there's a medicine on the market strong enough for that," Boone said. "We're only a few blocks away. Is now a good time?"

"Sure. If you're close, swing on by."

"Thanks, Ethan."

B.J. sat up a little straighter. "Was that Dr. Cole?"

Boone nodded.

"Is he going to take my stitches out?"

"More than likely," Boone confirmed.

"Is it going to hurt?"

"Maybe just a little," Boone told him..

"Then I want Emily to be there," B.J. said, his eyes filling with tears.

Boone stared at him in shock. "You were so brave when Dr. Cole put them in. Everybody told me so. Why would you be scared to have them taken out?"

"You said it might hurt."

"Not as much as when he put them in," Boone assured him.

More tears spilled down B.J.'s cheeks. "I want Emily."

Boone fought to hide his frustration. This was one time he just couldn't give in, no matter how much B.J. thought he needed Emily. He told himself B.J. would be fine. Even if Boone happened to be a mess at the moment, Ethan surely knew how to comfort a scared kid.

"Not this time, buddy."

"Why not?" B.J. cried. "Are you mad at her? Is that why we had to leave Castle's?"

"B.J., you and I were doing just fine before Emily came to town. We're a team, right?"

"I want Emily," B.J. repeated, crying in earnest now.

His tears tore at Boone's heart, but this time he refused to give in. He pulled into the lot at the emergency clinic, then opened the door for B.J., who refused to budge.

"To the count of three, buddy," Boone warned. "If you don't get out on your own, I'll have to carry you inside like a baby."

B.J. regarded him with shock, but he did get out. "I hate you," he said as he stormed past.

Boone stared after him, his heart aching. It wasn't the first time those words had been thrown in Boone's face, but they never failed to devastate him.

Inside the clinic, Ethan gave Boone a curious look, but followed B.J. into the examining room. Boone joined them, standing just inside the door as B.J. scowled at both of them, his arms folded across his heaving chest.

"How you doing, B.J.?" Ethan asked, his voice calm and steady.

"Okay."

"Ready for these stitches to come out?"

"No."

Ethan looked startled, then glanced at Boone.

"I warned him it might hurt a little," Boone admitted.

Ethan smiled. "What do dads know?" he said. "Yours was probably a wimp, but I know how brave you are. You didn't even shed a tear when I put the stitches in. I'm betting you won't even feel this."

B.J. watched him suspiciously but didn't put up a fuss as Ethan went to work.

"See, I told you so," Ethan said when he was done. "And the scar is hardly noticeable. A nice job, if I do say so myself."

B.J. studied his forearm. "Will the scar go away before school starts?"

"Probably not entirely," Ethan said, smiling. "You planning to show it off to your friends?"

"Uh-huh," B.J. said. "Stitches would have been even better."

"Yeah, well, leaving those in longer might have been a bad idea," Ethan told him. "Why don't you go out to the front desk and ask for a piece of candy? Your dad will be right out."

B.J. ran out of the examining room without looking back.

Boone shifted his weight as Ethan studied him.

"Mind telling me why you were in such a mood when I called? And why you managed to scare B.J. to death before you brought him in here?"

"I was just trying to be honest with him about the chances that it would hurt to have the stitches removed," Boone said defensively. "Ever since Jenny didn't come home after I promised him she'd get better, total honesty is my new policy."

"An excellent theory, but as you've just seen, it can be tough on an eight-year-old."

"Yeah, I get that now," Boone said.

"Was there something else?" Ethan asked with the perceptiveness of an old friend.

"He insisted I call Emily to meet us here and I refused."

Ethan smiled. "How did I know Emily had something to do with it? You two have a fight?"

"I wouldn't call it a fight," Boone said. "She said something completely uncalled for about my motives for being around Cora Jane, and I walked out."

Ethan shook his head. "When are you two going to stop pretending that you've moved on and just accept that you'll never be totally happy unless you get back together?"

"When hell freezes over comes to mind," Boone said. "You're wrong, Ethan. I have moved on. Aren't this wedding ring I'm wearing and B.J. proof of that?"

"The wedding ring is a defense mechanism, in my opinion," Ethan said. "Jenny's been gone awhile. You could take it off and no one would think less of you. Not that I'm an expert in these things."

Boone regarded him with disdain. "Since you won't even date because the last woman you cared about left you emotionally scared for life, you'll have to pardon me if I don't take your advice seriously."

"Actually not dating has left me a lot of time to observe other couples," Ethan countered, essentially confirming Boone's accusation that he wasn't in the game himself. "I've picked up some useful information about the stupid things people do in the name of love. I'm more than happy to share them with you, if you're in the mood to toss a couple of steaks on the grill tonight."

Boone wasn't sure he was in the mood for advice, well-meant or not, but he wasn't looking forward to his own company, either.

"Six o'clock okay?" he asked his friend.

"I'll be there," Ethan said. "I'll bring a six-pack or would you rather have something stronger?"

"An occasional beer's pretty much my limit," Boone said. "Much as I might like to drown my sorrows, I can't do it when I'm responsible for B.J."

"Fair enough," Ethan said. "See you this evening."

Boone went into the reception area, paid for B.J.'s treatment, then gestured for B.J. to go outside.

After they were in the car, Boone turned to his son. "I'm sorry about before," he said quietly. "I never meant to upset you."

A single tear tracked down B.J.'s cheek. "And I don't really hate you."

Boone smiled and opened his arms. B.J. crawled over the console and scrambled into them. "I know, buddy.

Sometimes we're both going to say things we regret. We always need to find a way to forgive each other, okay?"

"What about Emily?" B.J. asked, proving that his mind had a single track. "Are you going to forgive her? She must have said something really bad for you to be so mad at her."

"You don't need to worry about that," Boone said.

"But she's my friend."

"I know. And we'll work things out. I promise." He just wished he had the first clue how they might do that if she truly believed what she'd said to him earlier.

Emily was filled with trepidation as she followed her grandmother's directions to Boone's house. She wasn't sure what she'd expected, but it wasn't the charming little white bungalow on an inlet with a screened-in side porch and a yard full of deep blue hydrangeas. The flowers were a little the worse for wear after the storm, but enough of the huge blooms remained to add just the right touch of old-fashioned summer color.

As she pulled to a stop, she spotted B.J. sitting at the end of a pier with a fishing pole. Because she was in no hurry for an uncomfortable confrontation with Boone, she walked out on the pier.

B.J. regarded her with surprise and a little caution. "How come you're here? I thought you and Dad were fighting."

"Is that what he said?"

B.J. nodded.

"Well, the truth is that I said something I never should have said," she admitted. "I came to apologize. Is he inside?"

B.J. nodded, then held out his arm. "I had my stitches taken out and I didn't cry," he said proudly.

She grinned at him. "Wow! That's really great. I knew you were brave."

"I wanted you to be there, but Dad wouldn't call you."

"I'm sorry, but you obviously did just fine without me." She hunkered down beside him. "So, are you catching anything?"

"Not really. I'm just staying out of the way while Daddy does some business before dinner."

"I see."

B.J.'s expression brightened. "Maybe you could stay for dinner. Dr. Cole's coming, too."

"I don't think so," Emily said. "I just came to talk to your dad for a few minutes. I won't be here long."

"But Dad's grilling steak. It'll be really good," B.J. said enthusiastically. "We're having corn on the cob, too. Dad says it might be the end of it for the summer because the hurricane hurt the farmers real bad around here."

Just then the back door opened and Boone stepped outside, surprise and caution registering on his face when he saw her with his son.

Emily stood up, took a step in his direction, then paused. "Could we talk?" she asked. "It won't take long."

He hesitated, then nodded. "Come on inside. B.J., you have fifteen minutes, then you need to come in and wash up, okay? Ethan will be here soon."

"Okay. I asked Emily to stay for dinner, but she said no. Maybe you should ask her."

"We'll see," Boone said, committing to nothing. "Maybe she has plans."

Emily followed him into a bright, airy open kitchen with granite countertops, stainless-steel appliances and windows everywhere. She couldn't have designed a more welcoming room herself.

"I love what you've done with the kitchen," she told him. "I imagine it wasn't like this when you bought the house."

"Not even close," he confirmed. "I think the white appliances it had were original to the house and barely functioning."

He gestured across the room. "There was a wall in here, too, right about there. It created a formal dining room not much bigger than a closet. Jenny saw the possibilities before I did. She knew exactly what she wanted in here down to the handles on the cabinets," he said. "All I did was tell the contractor to follow her directions."

"She had a good eye." She met his gaze. "I know I've said it before, but I really am sorry you lost her."

"So am I. She was a wonderful person. She didn't deserve what happened."

"What did happen?" she asked, curious to know the real story. If Cora Jane knew, she'd been very circumspect about filling in the blanks. Maybe she'd figured it was Boone's story to tell if and when Emily was ready to hear it.

"A massive infection," he said. "She thought she'd caught some kind of a bug, no big deal, but then it got into her lungs. It was late by the time she saw a doctor, and it turned out to be resistant to every antibiotic they tried. There was nothing they could do to save her."

"How horrible," she said. "I really am sorry."

Boone nodded. "Thanks." He held her gaze, then asked, "Why are you here, Em?"

She took a deep breath, then admitted, "Because what I said to you earlier was insensitive and rude."

"You mean accusing me of having ulterior motives for being friends with your grandmother?"

She regarded him earnestly. "I know better, Boone. I really do."

"Then why did you say it?"

"I've been thinking about that. I think it's partly because seeing how you are with her, how you are with B.J. and everyone for that matter, reminds me of how much I lost when I let you go. All these years it's suited me to paint you as another type of man, someone unworthy, a man with no sense of loyalty. I guess I needed that to justify what I did. In a way, you marrying Jenny made it easier. It was proof you'd never loved me at all."

"Did I have to be a bad guy all those years ago in order for you to claim what you wanted for yourself?"

"I thought it might make it easier to leave," she conceded, then shrugged. "It didn't."

Boone faced her, his frustration evident. "I knew you had dreams, Emily. How often did we sit on the beach at night talking about all you wanted to accomplish? Did you think I didn't hear you? I might have wanted like crazy to hold on to you, but I never expected to do it." He held her gaze, his expression sad. "I just hoped you'd come back eventually, that what we had would be important enough to bring you back."

"I don't think I could handle the pressure of knowing you were waiting for me, so, yes, I probably did make my leaving sound final," she told him. "And I needed to make you the bad guy, because I didn't like myself for hurting you. Grandmother was already completely out of patience with me for mistreating you. Samantha and Gabi thought I was crazy for walking out on what we had." She shrugged. "I couldn't let myself even consider the possibility they could be right. I needed a clean break, even if it turned out to be uglier than it should have been."

"Is that what today was about, too? You got scared that some of those old feelings are still there between us, so you needed to put me in my place, put that distance between us again?" he asked.

"No, today I was frustrated with Grandmother," she admitted. "I just needed to lash out at someone, and I couldn't yell at her. You were right smack in the path of my foul mood."

Boone shook his head. "Not buying that. On some level, you had to believe the words that came out of your mouth."

"I swear to you that I know better," she said. "That's not the kind of man you are. In a way, that's the trouble. The kind of man you are is too blasted appealing."

His lips curved at that. "Irresistible, perhaps?"

"Don't be smug."

He just laughed at that.

Emily picked up a mug that said World's Best Mom, smiled at it, then tried to imagine how much Boone's heart must ache when he saw it. And yet he kept it out, kept his son's memories alive. That was the kind of man with whom she'd been so careless. She'd tried to tell herself he was reckless and irresponsible, but he wasn't then and he certainly wasn't now. He was an incredible father, a good friend, a decent man.

"Grandmother's furious with me," she confessed, giving him a wry look. "Not that it's the first time or anything, but now that I'm all grown up, it actually feels rotten to have her look at me as if I kicked her cat or something."

Boone had the audacity to grin at that. "I'm the cat, then?"

She chuckled. "Something like that. You should have heard her going on and on about what a paragon you are. I don't think she's ever spoken that highly of me."

"Of course she has," Boone corrected. "That woman thinks you three girls practically walk on water. She has an album with pictures and news clippings right at the cash register. If anyone asks how you all are doing, she whips it out and makes them look at every page. It's one of the first things she asked about when I called her to fill her in on the storm damage. She needed to know it hadn't been ruined. That album means the world to her."

On one level, Emily had trouble believing that. For whatever reason, she'd never thought of Cora Jane as especially sentimental. On another level, it was obvious that she was deeply sentimental. That was one reason she was fighting so hard against the changes Emily wanted to make at Castle's.

"Seriously?" she asked Boone, wanting to believe that her grandmother was proud of her in ways her father had never been.

"Cross my heart."

"And the customers keep coming back?" Emily asked incredulously, not sure if she really believed that her grandmother would boast so openly about her granddaughters, especially when they exasperated her so regularly. There'd been nothing sentimental or affectionate in the lecture she'd delivered earlier. She'd been disappointed in Emily and had let her know it.

"Of course they come back," Boone said. "That sense of being part of the family is what makes Castle's by the Sea special. It's something you can't re-create with paint and fabric and pretty pictures on the walls."

Emily sighed, reluctant to accept the truth of what he was telling her. It would make her plans for sprucing up the restaurant impossible. Unfortunately, it was hard to deny what was in front of her face.

"I'm starting to get that," she conceded.

"Will you stick around long enough to really understand what that place means to this community, what your grandmother means to me and everyone else?"

"I have a couple of pressing jobs to get back to," she equivocated. "You know that, Boone. I can't stay much longer, especially with the restaurant up and running again. I'm not really needed here."

Boone nodded stiffly. He obviously wasn't surprised. It was probably exactly the answer he'd expected. "I'm sure Cora Jane understands how busy you are."

She frowned at the edge in his voice. "But you don't. You think I should stay, even though she doesn't need or want my input."

"I think you'll do whatever feels right to you," he said. "No question you have obligations to your clients. I can hardly argue with that."

"You're saying the right words, but the tone's off. You're disappointed in me." He'd just made it plain without saying it that he thought she was acting selfishly...again.

He held her gaze, let the moment simmer, then said softly, "Maybe I'm just disappointed, Em."

Her heart hammered at the unexpected admission. *"You* want me to stay?"

"We'll never know what could have been if you don't," he said.

He stepped closer, tucked a finger under her chin, then slowly leaned in and kissed her. It wasn't the kind of hot, demanding kiss she remembered, the kind that had kept her awake at night wanting more. Instead, it was a sweet kiss, full of promise.

"Think about it," he said softly, walking her to the door.

There was no further mention of dinner, no plea to keep her in town, just the lingering memory of that kiss to hold her here.

She had the most astonishing feeling it might be enough.

Boone had the steaks on the grill and a couple of beers already on ice when Ethan arrived. B.J. bounded out to meet the doctor.

"Emily was here, but she had to go," he announced. "I showed her my scar."

"Was she impressed?" Ethan inquired, glancing curiously at Boone over B.J.'s head.

"Sure. I gotta go take a shower now, 'cause I accidentally fell in the water while I was fishing."

"Accidentally?" Ethan said, grinning.

"Uh-huh. Swear to God. I tripped."

"Over his own feet, more than likely," Boone said. "Hurry up, kiddo. The steaks are almost ready."

As soon as they were alone, Boone glowered at Ethan. "Leave it alone, okay?"

"Leave what alone?" Ethan asked innocently. "You

mean the fact that Emily apparently drove over here and you let her get away?"

"It wasn't like that," Boone said stiffly. "She came to apologize, said her piece, then left. That's all."

"What's next?"

"She'll leave town. Life will return to normal, and peace will reign over all the land," Boone said wryly.

"If you believe that, you're dumber than dirt," Ethan said succinctly. "Letting her go once, you could chalk that up to youthful ignorance. Letting her go again would be just plain stupid."

"Thank you so much for your insightful observation," Boone grumbled. "Want to talk about why you let a woman who obviously had the sensitivity of a storm trooper turn you into a recluse?"

"I'm not a recluse," Ethan said defensively. "And we weren't talking about me. You're the one with the immediate problem. Want to hear what I think?"

"I can't come up with a single way to stop you short of gagging you, and that would probably set a bad example for my son," Boone said with frustration.

"Probably," Ethan confirmed, grinning. "So, here's what I think. I think you should take advantage of my presence here right now, leave B.J. with me and go after her."

"And do what exactly? I've already told her we'll never know what we could have if she doesn't stick around to find out."

Ethan regarded him with amusement. "Did you say it with exactly that much passion? Gee, I can't imagine why she wouldn't fall right into your arms, abandoning her life's work to be with such a poet."

Boone scowled at him. "Bite me."

"Just calling it like I see it. You love this woman, right? Always have."

"That doesn't mean we were meant to be. She has to want this as much as I do."

"And you have absolutely no powers of persuasion at your disposal?" Ethan asked. "Couldn't maybe kiss her senseless, haul her off to your bed, even talk a blue streak about the future you could have together?"

"I did kiss her," Boone said irritably. "She left anyway."

Ethan hooted at that. "Then you sure as heck didn't do it right, not with the finesse of which we both know you're capable. Could she still think? Was she still standing?"

Boone chuckled. "I think you might be overestimating my talents."

"Nah. I heard all the talk back in high school. Every girl you ever kissed swooned. Not a one of them ever forgot you. Tell me that you haven't been approached by a couple of the available ones since Jenny died, all eager to get back what you once had."

"Okay, yes," Boone conceded. "And a few who aren't available, to be perfectly honest. I'm not interested."

"Because your heart belongs to Emily," Ethan concluded.

"Okay, yes, but it's not that simple. It wasn't simple ten years ago, and it's even more complicated now."

"It's only as complicated as the two of you want it to be," Ethan said. "Take away all the doubts and the angst and listen to your heart. That's my advice."

It was pretty much the same advice Cora Jane had been throwing his way, so Boone couldn't dismiss it as readily as he wanted to.

"Well," Ethan prodded. "Are you going after her or not?"

"Now?"

"No time like the present. How much longer is she going to be around, anyway? Or are you hoping she'll leave, and the decision will be taken out of your hands? Then you'll get to sit around and pine for her and try to convince yourself you did all you could."

Maybe that was exactly what he was hoping, Boone thought. And maybe Ethan was right. Maybe he was a damn fool.

"You'll stay here with B.J.?"

"Absolutely," Ethan confirmed, then grinned. "I can spend the night, too, in case things take a turn for the better."

"I doubt that's going to be necessary," Boone said, though his pulse sped up at the thought.

"Just saying the offer's there," Ethan said. "A smart man would take advantage of it."

Boone wished he were half as certain of that as Ethan was. He had a feeling a really smart man wouldn't be putting his heart on the line with this particular woman yet again. There was, however, only one surefire way to find out.

12

Emily took a long, hot shower after leaving Boone's, left her hair damp to curl at will, pulled on a pair of shorts and a tank top, then headed for the porch where her sisters had gathered after dinner. Cora Jane, it seemed, had gone to the movies with Jerry.

"You and Boone make peace?" Gabi asked as Emily settled on the chaise longue with one of the fancy rum drinks Samantha had made. Samantha seemed to have developed a fascination with improving her bartending skills.

"I apologized," Emily said. "I guess we're okay, though he wasn't very happy when I told him I'd be leaving soon." To keep them from seizing on that, she quickly asked, "What about you two? Have you made plans to go home yet? Everything at the restaurant seems pretty much back to normal."

"I'll probably head back on Sunday," Gabi said. "I'm getting some rumblings that my boss isn't very happy that I've been gone this long. Amanda doesn't consider being available via phone, fax and email every second to be sufficient dedication."

"Any rumblings from the boyfriend?" Emily asked.

Gabi frowned at her. "He'll be glad to have me home again, of course."

"Of course," Emily echoed dryly.

"Leave it alone," Samantha advised. "You and I might not get why this guy has been AWOL the whole time we've been here, but it doesn't seem to bother Gabi, and that's all that matters."

Reluctantly, Emily let it be. "What about you, Samantha? You heading back to New York?"

Her sister shrugged. "Not right away. My agent will call if something comes up, and it's not as if I'm vital at that restaurant where I fill in as hostess from time to time. August is usually pretty dead in New York. Everyone who can takes vacation this month. I might as well hang out here a little longer."

"That'll make Grandmother happy," Emily said. "Be careful she doesn't figure out a way to talk you into staying for good."

Samantha smiled. "Not likely. I may not be working as much as I'd like, but what work there is happens to be in New York." She studied Emily. "But you intend to leave soon even though things between you and Boone aren't resolved? Why would you do that?"

"What's unresolved?" Emily asked. "His life is here. Mine's on the West Coast. How are we supposed to find middle ground? Settle in Kansas?"

Gabi chuckled. "I think you could probably find a better alternative," she said, then added diplomatically, "Not that there's a thing wrong with Kansas if the man you love is willing to meet you halfway across the country."

"I don't think Boone is interested in compromise," Emily said.

"And you?" Gabi pressed. "Are you willing to compromise?"

Emily was about to make some flip remark, but instead she actually gave the question some thought. Was there a compromise? Were her feelings for Boone still strong enough to be worth exploring? And how on earth was she supposed to find out if she kept running away? It was one thing to take off in search of some elusive goal at twenty-one. It was quite another to do it ten years later, when she should be smart enough to see that a successful career wasn't quite as fulfilling as she'd imagined, that maybe there was more to life.

She was still thinking about that when the sound of a car engine drew closer, then cut off.

"Oh, boy," Samantha muttered as they saw Boone turn the corner of the house and amble in their direction. "I'll be inside if anyone needs me."

"Me, too," Gabi said, leaping to her feet with surprising agility given the two potent drinks she'd consumed. "Hey, Boone."

Boone stood at the bottom of the steps, his gaze on Emily. "You going to run off, too?"

She smiled. "I think I've been rude enough for one day. Besides, this is my home. No one gets to run me off."

"In that case, mind if I join you?"

"Why not? You want a drink?" She held up her half-empty glass. "I'm not entirely sure what Samantha put in this concoction, but it definitely takes the edge off."

He shook his head. "That's okay. Probably better if I keep a clear head for this conversation."

He took a seat on the glider at the side of the porch, then set it in motion. To be honest, watching him made Emily a little dizzy. She frowned at her glass. "What the devil did Samantha put in here?" she murmured.

Boone chuckled. "Maybe I should make coffee."

"It might be a good idea," she conceded, "especially if you intend to say anything you want me to remember."

"I'll be right back," he told her, then held out his hand for her glass. "You should probably be done with that."

"Probably," she conceded, handing it over, though with some reluctance.

Boone wasn't gone long, just long enough for her nerves to quicken as she considered all the possibilities behind his unexpected appearance here tonight. When he came back with two cups of coffee, he set hers on the table beside her.

"You'd better let it cool off a little," he advised, then went back to the glider.

"I'm surprised you're here," she blurted. "Wasn't Ethan coming for dinner?"

"He came," Boone confirmed. "One thing about having a really good friend who's known you just about forever, they say stuff and you generally have to listen."

"What kind of stuff?"

"In this case, about you and me," he admitted.

Emily smiled. "Yeah, I've been getting a lot of that, too."

"I have a feeling there's some consensus on this," Boone said. "What I keep hearing is that we'd be idiots not to give our relationship another try."

"Pretty much what I've been hearing, too," she confirmed. "Ethan said that, as well?"

"And a lot more," Boone said. He finally looked her directly in the eyes. "I wish I honestly knew what we should do next, Em. From the minute you left town, I told myself not to look back. Then there was Jenny, and she made it easier to look forward. So did B.J. Now, Jenny's gone, and here you are again."

"And you see taking a chance on me as taking a step backward?" she suggested.

He nodded. "It might not be fair, but, yes."

"Then why are you here, Boone? Seriously. Not even Ethan could persuade you to do something you didn't feel right about."

He shrugged, looking genuinely bewildered and surprisingly vulnerable. "Because I can't seem to stay away," he admitted with unmistakable reluctance. "You're still in my blood, apparently, and I know I'll kick myself from now till doomsday if I don't seize this chance to see if anything's left between us. Anything real, I mean, not just my memories and a few solid-gold fantasies."

Despite all the positives in that response, Emily heard only the unspoken misgivings. "You don't sound happy about this decision."

He smiled. "Can't say that I am. I always thought I was supposed to learn from my mistakes, not repeat them."

Though she could have taken offense, she saw his point. Would it be a painful mistake to try to rekindle what once was?

"Maybe we should do this one day at a time," she suggested, looking for that middle ground Gabi had mentioned earlier. "No pressure. No huge expectations."

"But there *is* pressure," he said. "You announced earlier that you're leaving, and suddenly I feel as if we have to settle this in the next fifteen minutes or something."

He gave her a sad look. "It'd be funny if it weren't so tragic. Falling in love with you back then was so easy. I never once gave it a second thought. It just was, like the beat of my heart or breathing."

"And now?"

"You tell me," he said. "Does anything about this feel easy? The way I see it there are complications galore, maybe even more than last time. Now we both have careers, we have established lives." He gave her a wry look. "And I have in-laws who are just waiting for me to screw up."

Emily frowned at that. "Meaning?"

"Jenny's parents—well, her mother, anyway—would love nothing more than to find an excuse to sue me for custody of B.J. I'm trying really hard to avoid that. Not that Jodie could win, but she could make my life and B.J.'s hell for a while."

Emily didn't even try to hide her dismay. "Do you honestly think she'd be so vindictive?" she asked, finding it almost impossible to believe anyone would hold that sort of threat over a father's head.

"I'd rather not find out," he said.

"Then maybe being scared and cautious is smart." she conceded. "Why rattle her cage for no good reason? And maybe most important, there's B.J. to take into account. If we tried and it didn't work and he got hurt, I know it would rip your heart out, but it would kill me, too."

"Then what the heck are we supposed to do, Em?" he asked in frustration. "Give up?"

That would surely be the easy, safe choice, she

thought. But was it what she wanted? She studied this man who'd once been the most important thing in her world, until her horizons had broadened. Here he was again, putting his feelings on the line. Had her horizons reached a more inclusive stage, one where there would be room for love and marriage and family? Or would she only wind up letting him down? Was she crazy for even considering starting over? Or was he the crazy one for giving her an opening to break his heart for a second time, especially if that custody threat was real?

Unfortunately there was no way to answer those questions without taking a chance. Life was full of risks. Avoiding them might be comfortable, but was it really living?

She stood up and took a tentative step in his direction, then gestured to the seat next to him on the glider. "Is it okay?"

He chuckled at her hesitation. "You afraid I might try to have my way with you?"

"More afraid that you won't," she admitted, settling next to him. He put his arm around her then, and she released a sigh. It felt exactly as she'd remembered. More than coming back to this house, this community, sitting here with Boone's arm around her shoulders felt like coming home. He still smelled of the same citrus-scented aftershave, still felt solid and safe.

Now, if only he'd kiss her as if he meant it, the kind of kiss that had always been a prelude to much, much more. She turned to face him, only to see an amused glint in his eyes.

"Not the answer," he murmured, touching a finger to her lips.

Only the apparent disappointment in his eyes made the firm response easier to bear.

"You sure about that?" she asked, not even trying to hide her frustration. "We could go for a drive, park someplace where it's secluded and dark the way we used to."

"I'm not sure of a lot," he responded, "but I am sure of that. Making love to you would be easy and memorable, just the way it always was, but it doesn't hold the answers."

"Then what does?"

"You said it earlier," he told her. "Time. We need to agree to give this a chance, see where it leads."

It all sounded reasonable and sensible, except for one thing. "Boone, I *am* leaving. I can put it off a day or two, but I will have to go. What happens then?"

He held her gaze, then released a sigh. "I guess if we intend to pursue this, then we'd both better sign up for one of those unlimited calling and data plans. We might end up racking up a lot of frequent flier miles, too."

She regarded him with surprise. It was an offer he'd never made back then, not that she'd have agreed to it. She'd been stubborn and so sure that a clean break was for the best.

"You could live with that? The whole long-distance thing?"

"Apparently I can't live without you, so, yes, I'm willing to give it a try. How about you?"

She took a deep breath, then nodded. "I'm in."

"And we give it our all, no looking for excuses to bail?" he prodded.

"Absolutely."

"Okay, then," he said softly, sounding relieved. "This might be for the best."

"How so?"

"If this is a long-distance thing, we can keep B.J. out of the mix for now. And, by extension, the Farmers."

Emily frowned. "I get it about the Farmers, but B.J.? You don't want him to know we're involved?"

"Not yet," Boone said, then added earnestly, "We need to agree on that, Em. I have to protect him."

She pulled away. "That sounds as if you're already convinced we'll fail."

"No," he said hurriedly. "Not at all. I swear to you I won't hold back anything."

"Except your son."

"You know why," Boone said. "It would be wrong to let him get his hopes up. When we're sure it's going to work out, of course he'll know what's going on. He'll be thrilled to pieces. You know how crazy he is about you. And when we're solid, I'll find a way to deal with Jenny's parents, a way to make them understand that being with you isn't a slap in their face."

Even though a part of her felt Boone was demonstrating a lack of faith in this relationship they intended to build, she couldn't honestly deny that he was probably right to protect his son. After all, Boone had seen too many potential parents come and go. He knew firsthand the toll that could take on a boy's emotions.

"You're right," she conceded. "What about my family? Are we keeping them out of the loop, too?"

"It could limit the meddling," he suggested. "But I doubt we can pull it off. Besides, Cora Jane for one would be absolutely furious if she found out we'd been sneaking around behind her back. I don't think I can hide it from her. How about you?"

"Are you kidding me? She'll figure out the truth the first time she gets a good look at my face when you're in the room."

He laughed at that. "You could always claim it's just wishful thinking on her part."

"And deny her the satisfaction of knowing that her meddling might be paying off? That would be cruel. Let's not make a big deal about it, though. If they figure it out, we'll confirm it and leave it at that."

"Given the fact that your sisters are probably hanging out the bedroom window over our heads right now, it's probably a wise choice," Boone said, raising his voice just a little.

"Blast it, Samantha. I told you that window squeaked," Gabi complained.

"Congratulations, you guys," Samantha called out, laughing, then made a point of slamming the window closed.

Emily gave Boone a wry look. "Want to take that drive now? Obviously privacy is not possible here."

"Nah," Boone said, pulling her close. "If I have my way, there won't be any talking for them to overhear."

She regarded him hopefully. "Is that so?"

He tucked a finger under her chin, leaned in and sealed his mouth over hers. This time there was no holding back. He kissed her as if there was no tomorrow.

"Oh, wow!" she murmured against his lips. "I remember this."

"How about this?" he asked, slipping his hand inside her tank top.

"Oh, yes," she said, her breath coming faster, her

pulse scrambling. "Why do I feel like I'm seventeen again and panicky that we're going to get caught?"

"Maybe because Jerry's car just pulled into the driveway and I can hear your grandmother getting out now," Boone suggested, laughing as he straightened her shirt. He winked at her. "We'll definitely pick this up another time."

For the first time since she'd arrived in Sand Castle Bay, Emily suddenly wasn't quite as anxious to leave. Not with that promise on the table.

Boone walked into his house after midnight to find Ethan settled on the couch, his shirt and prosthesis off, a blanket draped low and a ball game on the TV.

"You look comfortable," Boone commented, sitting down and reaching into the bowl of popcorn on the coffee table and taking a handful. "How's B.J.?"

"Down for the count a couple of hours ago. What are you doing home? Things didn't go the way you'd hoped?"

Boone laughed. "They didn't go the way *you'd* hoped. Me and Emily, we're on the same page for the first time in years."

"Together?"

"We're hopeful," Boone confirmed. "But we're going to move slowly."

"Is she sticking around?"

"No."

Ethan frowned. "How's that going to work exactly?"

"People have long-distance relationships all the time," Boone replied.

"So I've heard. You ever heard of one that lasted?"

"It won't be forever," Boone said optimistically.

"We'll work it out. If it's meant to be, that is." He stood up. "I'm beat. I'm going to head up to bed. The guest room's yours if you want it."

Ethan gestured to the nearby prosthesis. "I'm good here, but I will stay the night if you don't mind. Probably not smart to hit the road after that last beer."

"Stay wherever you want. Need anything?"

"Not unless you can figure out a way for the Braves to pull this game out in the bottom of the twelfth. They've blown a lead four times tonight."

"They'll break your heart, all right."

He left his friend to the game, stopped to look in on B.J., then went to his own room. He sat on the edge of the bed and picked up the snapshot of him, B.J. and Jenny taken the summer before she'd died. He looked at her face and thought he saw some of that joy Cora Jane had insisted was there.

"I did love you, Jenny, and I hope I did right by you," he whispered, then sighed. "I just hope I'm not betraying you now."

To his shock he thought he felt the whisper soft touch of a breeze on his cheek just then. He glanced across the room, but the windows were closed. His gaze returned to the photo.

"Thanks," he said, putting a finger to his lips and then to hers.

When he crawled between the sheets, he fell right to sleep. For the first time in what seemed to be forever, he wasn't tormented by nightmares and regret.

Emily sighed when she saw the message from Sophia on her cell phone Thursday morning. She'd already spoken to her twice since the successful fund-raiser. It was hard to imagine what more she could have to say. Because she was an important client, Emily called her back.

"Good morning," she said cheerfully when she reached her. "Are you still basking in all the glory of that fortune you raised at your dinner?"

"That women's shelter needs all the help it can get," Sophia told her. "What I raised was just a pittance compared to what they could use. I was over there yesterday and they said they're running out of room. It just breaks my heart to think that there are women out there in need of a safe place to stay and the shelter can't accommodate them."

"But you have a plan," Emily guessed. "I know that tone of voice, Sophia. It hasn't been twenty-four hours since you were over there, and you already have something in mind." It was Sophia's generous spirit that made all the petty annoyances of working with her easier to take.

"Well, of course, I do," Sophia said. "But I'm going to need your help with this, Emily. How soon can you get here?"

Emily thought of her promise to Boone. She couldn't go running off today, or even tomorrow, not even for Sophia.

"The beginning of next week," she told her.

"Not soon enough," her number one client said. "Make it Monday. I already have an appointment scheduled for us."

"That's only a few days from now," Emily protested, thinking of her promise to Boone. "I don't know that I can wrap things up here that quickly."

"Monday," Sophia repeated, unrelenting. "It's not for me. It's for these women who need our help."

"Why don't you fill me in now?" Emily suggested, knowing that she was already hooked. If Sophia wanted her there Monday, she'd find a way. Not only was this woman her top client, they were slowly becoming friends, as well. Either status might be enough to lure Emily back, but combined, they assured it.

"I found another potential safe house," Sophia said, sounding pleased. "I've already spoken to the board, and we're ready to move on this. The problem is that it needs a little work. That's where you come in. I'm hoping you can call in some favors, get us a break on some materials and furnishings. We won't have a lot of time to make this happen, not if we want some of these women to have a place to stay before Thanksgiving."

"Sophia," Emily protested with a groan. "Thanksgiving? That's impossible."

"Nothing is impossible if you want it badly enough," Sophia contradicted. "Everyone should have a safe place to spend Thanksgiving. Especially single mothers with kids. I'm already working on turkey donations, and my caterer has agreed to provide an absolute feast."

"Of course he has," Emily said. It was rare for anyone to deny Sophia whatever she wanted, Emily included.

"What about you? Are you in?" Sophia pressed.

"Of course I am," Emily said. "What time is the appointment?"

"Ten o'clock, but I could push it back to the afternoon. That's the best I can do."

Emily thought of the flight schedules she'd looked over before her last trip. "Try to set it up for three," she said. "That should give me time to get in and get to your house. If I'm running late, I'll call and you can give me the address and I'll meet you there."

"You're an angel, Emily."

"Hardly that, but I owe you for all the business you've sent my way. If this is important to you, it's important to me."

Sophia hesitated, then said, "You know, Emily, I honestly thought you'd seize the chance to get back out here with a little more enthusiasm. Is there something back there that has a hold on you, besides the whole family thing, that is?"

It was the most personal question Sophia had ever asked. Usually she was all business, even though she obviously had a soft spot for Emily. It was one more hint at their evolving friendship.

"Just a few things I'll need to juggle," Emily replied evasively, thinking that it was best to keep this discussion on a professional footing. Or maybe just not wanting one more person chiming in with an opinion about her personal life. "I'll work it out."

"Then I'll see you at my place around two on Monday," Sophia said. "With traffic the way it is out here, it could take us an hour to get to this house. You do know that the address can't become public information, right?"

"Understood," Emily assured her. She knew that for some of these women their lives and even their children's lives depended on being someplace where no one could find them. The consequences of a slip could be tragic.

She thought of the women who'd gotten their lives back, thanks to Sophia's efforts with this particular cause, and it reminded her yet again that all the parties, the galas, the dinners weren't just a frivolous exercise by someone with too much time and money.

"Sophia, what you're doing here? It's pretty amazing," Emily told her. "Thank you for letting me have a small part in it."

"Oh, honey, your part won't be that small," Sophia said with a laugh. "I'm counting on you to donate your time and to save us a bundle. I expect you to work your magic and create something warm and wonderful on a shoestring. There's this one room, it's a mess now, but it will make the most amazing playroom for the children. I can already envision it."

"I'll do my best," Emily promised.

She sighed as she disconnected the call. Now she just had to find the right words to persuade Boone that she wasn't already going back on her promise to give the two of them a real chance.

13

Boone was about to call Emily to invite her on a formal date when his cell phone rang. He glanced at the caller ID and saw she'd beat him to it.

"Great minds," he commented when he answered. "I was about to call you."

"Really? Then you go first."

"How about dinner tonight? I'm thinking it's about time you tried my restaurant. You've never even set foot inside. Of course, the inside's a construction zone, but you'll get the idea. And it should be a nice night for eating on the deck. What do you say?"

"I'd love it," she agreed at once.

"And you won't start telling me how to redecorate?" he teased. "I know that's an ingrained habit of yours."

"Very funny. I'm sure it's lovely already, even with the repairs you're having to make. And Grandmother and Jerry certainly give it high marks for the food. I'm anxious to see what's on the menu."

"Why don't I pick you up at the house around six-thirty? That'll give me time to get B.J. settled over at Alex's for the night."

"A sleepover?" she asked, an unmistakably breathless note in her voice.

Boone chuckled. "For him," he confirmed.

"And us?"

"I suppose we'll have to see how things go."

"Way to dangle a carrot, Dorsett."

Boone chuckled at the frustration she didn't even try to disguise. "You called me, by the way. Anything in particular on your mind, or were you just calling to hear the sound of my voice?"

She hesitated, then said, "Why don't we talk about it tonight? It's something we should probably discuss face-to-face."

Boone felt his heart still. "That doesn't sound good. Maybe you should tell me now."

"Tonight's soon enough," she insisted. "I'll see you at six-thirty. I'll wear something pretty and knock your socks off."

Boone was not about to tell her that it wouldn't take much to knock off his socks and anything else he was wearing. Just looking at her made him want to strip down and haul her off to bed. How he'd resisted this long was beyond him.

"See you tonight. Since you have this big plan, I won't bother wearing socks. It'll save time."

She was laughing when he disconnected the call. Despite the teasing note he'd managed to pull off, he wished this feeling of dread hadn't just settled in his stomach.

Samantha looked over Emily's shoulder at her computer screen, then frowned.

"You're leaving Sunday?" she asked when she saw the ticket Emily was booking for Los Angeles.

Emily nodded. "I have to be in L.A. for a meeting Monday afternoon. As it is, I'll be cutting it close. One missed connection and I'm doomed."

"What about all those promises you made to Boone about giving your relationship a chance? Gabi and I heard you make them."

"Because you eavesdropped," Emily accused as Samantha slid into the booth across from her. "It's not as if it's any of your business."

"Okay, forget my reaction. What's Boone going to think? Did you consider that?"

"Of course I did. He's going to think we're starting this long-distance stuff a little sooner than we planned," Emily said. "At least I hope he'll be able to see it that way."

"Good luck with that," Samantha said, her tone dire.

"Thanks for the support," Emily told her with a scowl. "Aren't you supposed to be on my side?"

"I am, which is why it kills me to see you shooting yourself in the foot already. You want this thing with Boone. I know you do, but you're not willing to give it even half a chance."

Emily described the offer Sophia had made to her that morning. "It's not as if I'm rushing back just to make big bucks on something," she told her sister. "This shelter matters, Samantha. It's a chance for me to make a real difference for some people who need it. I'm finally at a stage where I can do a *pro bono* job like this."

"Would you have agreed if this Sophia weren't one of your best clients?"

"I'd like to think I would have," Emily said. "I know

you, Gabi and Grandmother all think I'm just in this for the money and the fancy celebrity clients, and maybe that's what it's been up to now. This shelter is a way for me to give back, to find a whole different level of professional fulfillment."

Samantha nodded slowly. "Okay, I can see why you couldn't turn it down."

Emily regarded her hopefully. "Do you think Boone will see it that way?"

"Only one way to find out," Samantha said. "But I don't envy you having to tell him."

"Yeah, I'm not exactly looking forward to that myself. I'm hoping a dress that shows a lot of cleavage will distract him enough that he'll hardly hear a word I say."

"A sneaky but sometimes effective tactic," Samantha agreed. "But when the words do sink in, I still think it's going to bite you in the butt."

"What if I suggested he and B.J. come to Los Angeles? B.J.'s dying to go to Disneyland."

"Boone wants to leave B.J. out of this for now," Samantha reminded her.

The comment proved just how intently she and Gabi had been paying attention the night before. The pair of them must have taken notes.

"Well, I have to do something so he understands that I'm not just ditching him," Emily responded.

Samantha seemed to be giving the matter some thought, so Emily waited to see what her sister would come up with. She certainly hadn't thought of an effective approach. Samantha admittedly had more experience with men, even if she was flying solo lately.

"Asking him to follow you to the West Coast before you've even gotten started might be a tactical mistake,"

Samantha said slowly. "Maybe it would be better to give him a concrete date when you'll be back here. Or suggest he meet you someplace a little more neutral. Do you have to go back to Aspen on this trip?"

Emily brightened. "That's a thought. A couple of days in Aspen could be pretty romantic, almost like a honeymoon. I like that." She gave Samantha a hug. "Sometimes you're not half bad."

Samantha just arched a brow. "What a glowing review! I think I'll add that to my resume."

Emily laughed. "Have Gabi spin it for you," she suggested. "That's what she does. Now I'm bailing on you to go home to get pretty. It's been a while since I've taken the time to get buffed up and polished for a date."

"And what do I tell Grandmother if she wants to know where you've gone off to right before the lunch crowd gets here?"

"Tell her I have an official date with Boone. She'll be so thrilled, she'll probably send over a hairdresser and a manicurist."

"She probably will," Samantha said, chuckling. "You may have found the magic formula for getting out of working around here. Gabi and I both need boyfriends."

"Gabi claims to have one."

"And we both know she's deluding herself," Samantha said. "I just hope she's not devastated when she figures it out."

Emily sighed. "Yeah, me, too."

Boone couldn't recall ever seeing Emily as perfectly put together and sexy as she looked when he arrived to pick her up.

He swallowed hard and worked to keep his jaw from dropping.

"You clean up nice," he said approvingly. He'd gotten used to seeing her in shorts and a tank top that showed off quite a lot of her assets, but that was nothing compared to the designer sundress that made her look utterly feminine and sophisticated.

She wore it with a pair of strappy, high-heeled sandals that he suspected cost more than his weekly take-home pay. He was pretty sure he'd seen something similar in a *Sex and the City* movie that one of his less-than-stellar dates had dragged him to.

Emily smiled at his reaction, amusement sparkling in her eyes, and suddenly the woman he'd known forever was back.

"I knew those shorts were a mistake," she said. "If I'd worn this a lot sooner, you and I would have been in bed long before now."

"I'd like to think my resistance is stronger than that," he responded, but he wasn't so sure of it. Right now the idea of wasting time on dinner didn't hold a lot of appeal.

As if she'd read his thoughts, she tucked an arm through his. "Come on. I'm dying to see your restaurant. Don't even think about skipping that."

He glanced sideways at her. "Don't try to tell me that blowing off dinner didn't cross your mind."

"Well, of course it did, but *you're* supposed to be made of tougher stuff."

Boone had a hard time keeping his eyes on the road as he drove to the restaurant, but he did try. His frequent glances in her direction seemed to amuse her.

"There's something different about you tonight," he said.

"It's the dress and shoes," she said. "You're used to seeing me looking as if I've just come off the beach."

"That's the obvious answer, but it's more than that. I guess in those other clothes you seem like the girl I used to know. Now, you're this sexy, sophisticated woman. I'm not sure I know this Emily at all."

She looked dismayed by his words. "I'm just me, Boone. What I'm wearing doesn't change anything."

"Doesn't it? Those shoes probably cost a fortune."

"So what if they did? I was doing just fine in cheap flip-flops and sneakers." She studied him with a narrowed gaze. "Please tell me you're not going to get all bent out of shape over which of us makes more money. You have three successful restaurants. You're obviously doing okay. I'm not interested in your bank balance, Boone. Why should you care about mine?"

"I don't," he said with frustration. "At least I shouldn't. It just hit me that we're not exactly in the same league."

"Oh, please. I buy expensive clothes because my image matters with potential clients, not because I love throwing away a lot of money on a blouse. You dress to meet customer expectations, too." She frowned at him. "Do you realize this could be the most ridiculous conversation we've ever had?"

It was, Boone thought to himself. He forced a smile. "Only one way I can think of to put it behind us."

"Oh?"

"Get rid of the clothes," he said with a wink.

Emily chuckled. "Feed me first, then we'll talk."

"So, it's open for negotiation?"

She met his gaze, her expression sobering. "It's definitely open for negotiation."

That was the best news Boone had had since he'd picked her up.

Emily had put off her big announcement as long as she possibly could. They'd toured the restaurant, which was even nicer than she'd imagined. There was no beach kitsch, just a warm, inviting atmosphere that surely made diners comfortable and took full advantage of the water views from almost every window.

The smells emanating from the kitchen had been tantalizing, so she'd been more than ready to let Boone order all the specialties for her to try. The Cajun influence was evident, but not overwhelming. The fish and jambalaya had been seasoned to perfection.

She'd pushed aside an incredible crème brûlée after just a few bites. "No more," she'd murmured with a groan. "I'm stuffed."

"Want to take a walk before coffee?" Boone suggested.

She met his gaze. *This is it,* she thought. "Why don't we have that coffee at your place?"

"Why don't we?" he agreed softly.

If it had been up to her, they'd have fled from the restaurant, sped across the bridge back to Boone's and raced across the lawn to the house, but there was no way the owner could make a quick escape. Regular customers wanted to speak to Boone, the chef had a few questions, even Boone's second in command, Pete Sanchez, seemed to have a few burning issues that had to be resolved. By then even Boone had lost patience.

"Tomorrow," he told Pete with a warning look.

"But—"

"Will this place fall apart if we don't discuss this before morning?" Boone inquired impatiently.

Pete glanced at Emily, then grinned. "Nope. Enjoy yourselves."

"No question about it," Boone muttered as they walked away.

"Obviously he's not used to you being on a real date," Emily said, oddly pleased by the knowledge.

"He's never seen me with any woman other than Jenny," Boone confirmed. "It finally dawned on him just then that you must be special and that I had much better things to do tonight than going over one of his lists."

"He's good at lists?" Emily asked.

"He's excellent at lists. Normally I consider that a plus. Tonight, not so much."

"We're free now," Emily reminded him as they reached his car.

"Yes, we are," Boone said, backing her up against it. "And I've been waiting all night for this." He lowered his mouth to cover hers.

Emily felt his desire in that kiss and in his arousal. She gave him a gentle shove, tempering it with a grin. "Don't you think it would be better not to start this till we can finish it?"

"My house?" Boone said, sounding dazed. "Definitely. Let's go."

He helped her into the car, practically raced around to jump behind the wheel, then peeled out of the parking lot.

"This takes me back," Emily said.

"To?"

"A time when you couldn't wait to get your hands on me."

"Seems that hasn't changed," he said with a heated glance in her direction.

"Do you wish it had?" she asked, needing to know if there was regret blended with the anticipation.

He blinked at the question. "Seriously?"

"I really want to know. Are you sorry that these feelings aren't dead and buried?"

Boone sighed. "Are you going to make me sorry?"

"I'm going to try like crazy not to," she said, knowing that tonight when she told him her plans would be the first test. She also knew she probably ought to give him that information before they took this next step.

"Boone, wait," she said as they pulled into his driveway, stopping him before he could exit the car. "There's something you need to know."

He regarded her incredulously. "Now?"

She nodded. "I have to go back to Los Angeles sooner than I'd expected."

The light seemed to drain from his eyes at that. "How soon?"

"Sunday. I have an important meeting Monday."

"I see."

"I'll be back, though," she said hurriedly. "Probably by the middle of next week. Next weekend at the latest."

"Okay."

She reached out and put a hand on the tense muscle in his arm. "Can I explain why this is important? Will you listen?"

"I said I was going to give this a chance, so I suppose I have to," he said, though he didn't sound happy about it.

She told him all about Sophia and about this passion of hers for helping women escaping abusive relationships and in need of shelter. "This is the first time she's asked me to be a part of one of her projects, Boone. I suppose I could have turned her down. I know she wouldn't have held it against me, at least not for long."

She met his gaze, willed him to understand. "I got to thinking about those women, about the fear that must haunt them, about the kids who have maybe never known a safe place to live, and I couldn't say no. I just couldn't."

Boone closed his eyes, sighing. "No, you couldn't," he agreed. "I think if you were going back for any other reason, it would be different, but how can I object to you agreeing to something like this? It proves what a huge heart you have."

Tears stung her eyes. "I was so afraid you wouldn't see it that way, that you'd think I was being selfish and already going back on my word."

"Oh, believe me, I wish I could think that," he admitted. "It would make letting you leave a lot easier if I were furious with you."

She nudged him in the ribs. "But now you're maybe just a little eager for me to go and get back?"

He smiled at that. "Now I'm eager to get you inside and make the most of the time we do have."

"I don't suppose you'd want to meet me in Aspen in a few days?" she suggested lightly. "I'll have to check in there and make sure things are progressing on schedule for the ski lodge. We could have some time together away from here."

He smiled at that. "As appealing as that sounds,

there's B.J. to consider. I wouldn't be comfortable leaving him with anyone here."

"Not even Cora Jane? You know she'd love having him to herself, and Samantha will be around."

He gave her hand a squeeze. "Next time, okay? When I've had a little more time to plan for a getaway with you. Anticipation's part of the fun, right?"

"True," she agreed. "But we're good?"

"We're good," he assured her, then got out of the car.

When he'd opened her door, she stepped out and put her hand on his cheek. "Thank you for being so understanding."

"Something tells me I'm going to get a lot of practice at that," he said, a wry note in his voice.

She laughed. "As if you won't test my patience from time to time."

"I'll do my best," he said. "It ought to keep things interesting."

She looked deep into his eyes as they stood on the lawn with moonlight streaming through the trees. "I don't think interesting is ever going to be a problem for us. In fact, we may start to crave dull."

"Not me," Boone assured her, his mouth finding hers. When the kiss ended on a sigh, he added, "I'm just starting to realize that this is exactly the sort of excitement that's been missing from my life."

She leaned back into him, lifted her lips to his. "Happy to oblige," she murmured.

And even happier that they'd weathered this first potential tempest. Since it struck at the very core of their past conflict, the resolution tonight seemed to bode well for the long haul.

* * *

Inside Boone noticed that the message light was blinking on the answering machine. Even though most important calls should have come to his cell phone, he couldn't ignore it, not with B.J. at a friend's house.

"Em, let me check this," he said, already reaching for the play button. He gestured toward his wine rack. "Why don't you open a bottle of wine?"

"Sure," she said. "Red or white?"

"You choose," he said distractedly, listening to a couple of annoying calls before a familiar voice came on in the third message.

"Boone," his former mother-in-law said, an indignant huff in her voice. "I just got off the phone with Caroline Watson. She was at your restaurant tonight and called me to tell me you were there with *that* woman."

Boone muttered a curse under his breath. Behind him, he sensed Emily going perfectly still. He was about to shut off the machine, but Emily stepped up and put her hand on his.

"You might as well listen to all of it," she said quietly.

"I don't need to," he said, cutting off the message. "Jodie's just in one of her impossible moods. You certainly don't need to hear what she has to say. I should have known when we stopped to say hello to Caroline that she'd be on the phone to Jodie before we hit the parking lot. There's not a lot I do that doesn't make its way to Jodie. Some people seem to enjoy feeding the animosity she feels toward me. I'm used to it."

"But this is a first for me," Emily said quietly. "I've never thought of myself as the other woman."

"Because you're not," Boone said, thoroughly frustrated. "And Jodie has no right to make you feel that way. It's not even about you. It's about me. She never thought I was good enough for Jenny. She hated that we got married and made no pretense about her belief that I'd wind up hurting her daughter."

"Why would she feel that way?" Emily asked. "You weren't exactly some disreputable bum."

Boone smiled at that. "By her standards, anyone who looked twice at her precious daughter was a disreputable bum."

"But in your case, it was worse because of me somehow," Emily guessed.

Boone saw no point in denying it. "Everyone around here knew how I felt about you. It was hardly a secret that I was devastated when you dumped me. Jenny and I had always been friends in a casual kind of way. We started hanging out after you left. I knew she was crazy about me. I probably should have kept her at arm's length, but she made it almost impossible to do that. And, I'll admit, I needed someone like her, someone uncomplicated and undemanding."

"So, Jodie thinks you took advantage of Jenny's vulnerability?"

He nodded. "And I did. She's not wrong about that."

Emily gave him a long look. "Did you ever stop to consider that maybe Jenny took advantage of you?"

Boone frowned. "What? Of course not."

"Why? Because she was a sweet woman and you're the devious guy?"

"That sums it up, yeah."

Emily shook her head. "Boone, women know what they're doing, too. They can recognize when a man's in pain, when he needs someone around who's easy and uncomplicated. I'm not saying Jenny wasn't a wonderful woman, because she was. At least the girl I remember was. I'm just saying she knew exactly what she was getting into when she came after you. If anyone took advantage of the situation, I'd say she did."

Though what she said made a crazy kind of sense, Boone wasn't buying it. "It wasn't like that."

"In what way?"

"Jenny was…"

"A woman in love?" Emily suggested. "We've been known to do some crazy things in the name of love, probably even crazier than most men would ever consider. Look, I'm just saying that Jodie's being unfair to lay all this guilt on you. You and Jenny were two consenting adults. Whatever happened was as much Jenny's responsibility as it was yours."

She regarded him with a narrowed gaze obviously intended to warn him to give careful thought to his response. "Unless you somehow believe women don't know their own minds and can't be held accountable for their own actions?"

Boone saw that for the trap it was. "Okay, point taken."

She gestured toward the answering machine. "Do you need to call her back?"

"And listen to more of the same?" he asked. "I'll pass for tonight. Tomorrow will be soon enough. At least now you know firsthand what we're up against."

"Duly warned," she said and took a step closer. "Can we get back to our original plans now, please?"

Boone slid one spaghetti strap of her dress off of her shoulder, then kissed her bare skin. "Looking forward to it," he murmured.

"Me, too," she said, swaying into him.

He scooped her into his arms and headed for the master bedroom, hesitating only for a heartbeat in the doorway as a tide of misgivings about the past washed through him. Then he drew in a deep breath and stepped into what he hoped like crazy would be his future.

14

On Sunday morning, Emily made a call to B.J. to say goodbye, knowing that this time he needed to know her plans in advance. Then she sought out her grandmother before leaving for the airport. She found her in the kitchen at Castle's helping Jerry keep up with the breakfast orders. Cora Jane glanced up from the eggs she was scrambling.

"You about ready to take off?" she asked, her disapproval plain.

"In a few minutes," Emily said. "Could we talk before I go?"

"Cora Jane, I've got it covered," Jerry said at once. "Go on. Spend a little time with Emily."

Cora Jane nodded, then led the way to a booth in the back corner that was usually reserved for staff breaks unless the restaurant was mobbed.

"How does Boone feel about you running off again?" Cora Jane asked directly.

"He understands," Emily said. "And I'll be back by next weekend at the latest."

Cora Jane's eyes lit up at the news. "Nobody mentioned that to me."

"Maybe because Gabi and Samantha don't entirely believe it," Emily said dryly. "Listen, what I really wanted to ask you about is Jodie Farmer."

Cora Jane's eyes widened. "What's she done now?"

"You sound as if nothing she did would surprise you," Emily said.

"She's a perfectly nice woman when it comes to everything except Boone," her grandmother said. "She's held a grudge against him since the day he married Jenny. And when Jenny died, well, that's when she made it her business to heap as much guilt on that man's shoulders as she possibly could. Somebody ought to shake some sense into her, but her husband doesn't have the gumption." She regarded Emily curiously. "Why are you asking about her?"

"Apparently one of her friends saw me with Boone the other night and couldn't wait to fill her in. By the time Boone and I got to his place, Jodie had left a message berating him for being with me. He cut the machine off before she'd finished, but she clearly wasn't happy about the news."

"No, I don't suppose she was," Cora Jane said. "If it were up to her, he'd have thrown himself straight into Jenny's grave with her. Or preferably instead of her."

"Grieving mother talking?" Emily asked.

Cora Jane shrugged. "That's been my assessment, but sometimes I have to wonder if I'm not being too kind. Maybe she's just a vindictive woman. My advice to you, stay out of her path if you can. And pay no attention to anything she has to say."

"But Boone does, doesn't he? He takes every word to heart?"

"Unfortunately, yes. Her words do have the power to hurt him and make him question himself," Cora Jane admitted. "I've tried to give him some perspective on her behavior, but she feeds right into the guilt he feels about Jenny."

Emily nodded slowly. "That's what I thought, too. Any suggestions for what I could do to help?"

"She's in Florida, thanks be to heaven, so you shouldn't have to do anything. There's only so much poison she can spew from down there."

Emily wondered about that. If there was a pipeline feeding Jodie news from North Carolina, it had to work in reverse, as well. Still, for the moment, there was no point in borrowing trouble. There'd be time enough to figure out a strategy—if one was even needed—when she got back to town.

"One last question. Do you really think she'd sue Boone for custody of B.J.? Am I giving her the perfect excuse to do that?"

Cora Jane looked shocked by the suggestion. "She wouldn't dare!"

"Boone thinks she might," Emily said. "Just the thought of it is killing him."

"She'd lose," Cora Jane said confidently.

"But it would be ugly while she tried," Emily assessed.

Though Cora Jane looked suitably shaken, she touched Emily's cheek. "Don't let her be the reason the two of you don't try, okay?"

"I just don't want to be responsible for her stirring up trouble for Boone," Emily told her.

"There will be plenty of us in Boone's corner if she tries," Cora Jane told her with feeling.

"Thanks," Emily said to her grandmother, relieved by Cora Jane's conviction that things would work out. "Now I'd better get on the road."

When Cora Jane stood up, she gave Emily a fierce hug. "You come back soon," she ordered. "You have people here who love you."

Emily smiled at her. "That goes both ways."

"And is Boone one of those people?" Cora Jane inquired slyly. "Is that what's really behind this whole conversation? You're finally ready to admit you still love him?"

"Could be," Emily admitted.

Her grandmother's eyes lit up. "Well, praise be. It's about time the two of you came to your senses."

"We have a lot to work out," Emily cautioned.

"That's the nature of relationships," her grandmother said. "There are always things that need to be worked out. Life is never static. Or if it is, I guarantee you'll be bored to tears."

"I think Boone and I are agreed that boring doesn't enter into what we have," Emily said with a chuckle.

"Some details you can keep to yourself, young lady," Cora Jane scolded.

Emily laughed. "I'm definitely not planning to discuss my sex life with you. You might be inclined to turn around and tell me about yours."

For an instant her grandmother looked shocked, but then a grin spread across her face. "As if I'd do such a thing," she muttered indignantly.

But Emily noticed she didn't deny that there was a

sex life to be discussed. Just thinking about that kept a smile on her face all the way to the airport.

Boone leaned back in the chair in his office, closed his eyes and thought about all the information Pete had just given him about potential locations for new restaurants. Expansion could be a dicey business. If he intended to keep food quality and service consistent, someone had to keep an eye on each location. With Pete primarily responsible for travel, Boone didn't want his second-in-command to be spread too thin to do the job well.

Sometimes instinct kicked in and sent him in a particular direction. Norfolk had made sense because of its proximity to the North Carolina coast and its seaside location. Charlotte had been attractive because he'd wanted to experiment with a different type of market. Both additions had proven as successful as the original right here in Sand Castle Bay.

He sensed Pete watching him, opened his eyes and chuckled. "I'm not going to decide right this second. You could go and do something else, instead of sitting there staring at me."

"I thought you might want to bat around the pros and cons," Pete said. He held up a sheaf of papers. "I have all this market research if you want it."

"No, I trust you not to bring me anything that you haven't thoroughly explored." He studied the eager expression on Pete's face. "But you have a preference. I can tell from that glint in your eyes. Go ahead. Tell me."

Pete nodded. "I'd like to see us take a crack at New York," he admitted. "I know it's a crazy, unpredictable, ridiculously expensive market, but I think we're ready for it. What's that expression? Go big or go home, something like that?"

Boone regarded him skeptically. "Tell me your thinking," he suggested, rather than immediately blowing the idea out of the water based on costs alone.

"I think we could find our niche there, I really do," Pete said, clearly excited by Boone's willingness to listen. "Nobody's doing exactly what we do."

"Okay, let's go with that premise," Boone said, though he didn't entirely buy that there weren't plenty of seafood restaurants in a city the size of New York. "The cost for real estate is much higher than it is here, whether we lease or buy. Employee costs are going to be higher, too. So are food prices. That means we couldn't serve a meal for anything like the prices on our menu here."

"No," Pete agreed, "but New Yorkers are used to paying more for quality."

Boone continued to play devil's advocate. He wanted Pete to realize the downside on his own. "And what happens when one of our regulars from here or one of the other cities goes to New York, decides to order one of our signature dishes they're used to getting for under twenty bucks and sees a bill for twice that? Maybe even more?"

"How often would that happen?" Pete argued, though he seemed less sure of himself.

"More than I'd like, I'm afraid," Boone said. "A lot of people who discover us here travel to other cities, Pete. I've had quite a few customers mention to me that they've been to our Norfolk location or to Charlotte. I don't want them to walk into a restaurant of ours in New

York and walk out feeling as if they've been cheated. And I don't see any way around that happening."

"But making it big in New York could establish us on the national playing field," Pete said. "We'd have people begging us to open in other cities."

"If it happened that way, it would be incredible," Boone agreed. "I'm more worried that a failure could destroy our reputation."

"We wouldn't fail," Pete said confidently.

Boone shook his head. "Sorry, Pete, I think we need to focus on these other options where we can provide quality food for reasonable prices."

There was no mistaking Pete's disappointment. Boone even understood it. Pete was eager to make his mark in the restaurant business, and he clearly believed the place to do that was New York where celebrity chefs abounded and fine dining was an art form.

"Pete, will you be satisfied with anything other than New York?" Boone asked pointedly. "One of the reasons you and I have always worked so well together is that we've been on the same page."

"I have to admit it throws me that you're questioning my judgment like this," Pete admitted, then sighed. "But to be honest, I can see your point. I don't like it, but I can see it."

Boone studied his friend. He sensed there was something else behind this desire to tackle New York. "Is there some reason you're so anxious to get to New York, other than the challenge of that competitive environment?"

For a moment Pete looked so startled by the question that Boone almost took pity on him and let it go.

"A woman?" Boone guessed.

Pete stared at him as if he'd suddenly displayed a previously unknown talent for ESP. "How the heck did you figure that out? I haven't said a word about her."

Boone grinned. "I recognized the symptoms. So, what's the scoop? Are you serious about her?"

"There hasn't been time to get serious," Pete said with frustration. "We met in Norfolk when she was there to welcome her brother home when his navy ship got back into port after being at sea for a year. She's been back a couple of times. I flew up to New York for a few days right before this whole hurricane thing came up and I had to get back here. She got me excited about the possibility of living up there."

Boone thought of his own complicated long-distance situation. "And is living in New York the only way you can see this relationship working out?"

"Of course not," Pete said. "I just got caught up in the idea, that's all. Who knows if it will even work with this woman? She's a high-powered attorney. We've had a lot of fun together. She likes good food and great wine, so we hit some excellent restaurants in New York. That's when I started sizing up the competition."

"And?"

"I think we're as good as, if not better than, most. Lexie—that's her name, short for Alexandra—agreed. I figure she's pretty savvy." He shook his head. "I have to admit, after seeing her on her home turf, I started wondering what she saw in me."

"Even without a New York restaurant you can point to, you're pretty successful in this field," Boone reminded him. "You certainly know food and wine, which you said matter to her. Don't sell yourself short."

Pete grinned. "She seems to think I have a few other

things going for me," he admitted. "And thank goodness we can both afford the airfare."

"Maybe I'll even throw in a couple of tickets to New
York with your bonus this year," Boone said. "Now,
let's get serious about these other possibilities. Which
one was at the top of the list if we leave your libido out
of the mix?"

Pete laughed, clearly not taking offense. "I'd have
to say Charleston, especially if we can find the right
location in the historic district. I gave you my notes on
a couple of properties that would work."

Boone nodded. "I've always liked Charleston. Let's
take a trip down there in the next couple of days. I'll
have to bring B.J. along, but we should be able to get the
lay of the land. See about setting up the usual appointments with a Realtor, the Chamber of Commerce, the
mayor, maybe a couple of other key players."

"Got it," Pete said, his good mood restored. "When
do you want to go?"

With Emily out of town, Boone figured now would
be a good time. It would provide just the distraction he
needed. Since he wasn't counting on Emily's quick return despite her promise, he suggested, "Monday, the
day after, if you can pull it together."

"I'll make it happen," Pete promised.

And with luck, Boone thought, by the time they were
back, Emily would be home.

Naturally Emily's flight connections hadn't gone
as smoothly as she'd hoped, so she arrived Monday at
mid-day, too late to meet Sophia at home. She had to go
directly to the property under consideration for the safe
house. In a way, it was probably better. Sophia hadn't

been able to color her expectations about the property. She would see it with fresh eyes.

"I'm so sorry," she apologized to Sophia and the two women with her, one from the board of directors of the shelter, the other a Realtor. "The flight from Atlanta was cancelled. I had to wait till this morning for another one."

She glanced past the women to the house. Built on a sizable corner lot, she could immediately imagine its potential, but it required a real stretch of her imagination. Right now the yard was overgrown and littered with trash. The paint on the stucco exterior was peeling, so that patches of an original turquoise color showed through a more recent faded pink. The downstairs windows were behind bars and mostly broken. The concrete porch steps were crumbling and dangerous.

Emily glanced at Sophia and lifted a brow. "Seriously?"

Sophia only grinned at her. "Oh, don't even try to pretend you're not intrigued," Sophia chided. "You know you can't resist a challenge like this, Emily."

Emily tried to keep her expression dismayed, but couldn't. Sophia knew her too well. "How's the interior?"

"Worse than the outside," the board chairman said direly. Marilyn Jennings, the wife of a major movie studio president, didn't look hopeful.

"But promising," Taylor Lockhart argued, spinning it as only an excellent Realtor possibly could. "Right, Sophia?"

"Beyond promising," Sophia insisted optimistically. "Emily, you're going to love it. I know it."

"Then let's take a look," Emily said, following them inside.

Almost immediately, she saw the room that Sophia had envisioned as a children's playroom. The kitchen, though a disaster of outdated appliances, peeling linoleum and obviously rusty plumbing, was roomy enough for a large communal table.

In fact the biggest recommendation for the entire house was its size. All of the downstairs rooms could accommodate multiple adults with children underfoot. The drawback was the lack of a downstairs bathroom.

Upstairs there were a half-dozen bedrooms large enough for a mother and child to live comfortably, or perhaps two children with the use of bunk beds. One sunny room was large enough for, perhaps, a mother with three smaller children. Emily could already envision trying to make maximum use of the space and turning each room into something homey and comfortable with simple furniture, bright colors and textures. That, she knew, would be a godsend for many of these single-mom families fleeing bad situations. They needed a safe, clean, comfortable environment, not luxury. The bedrooms would give them privacy. The playroom, living room and yard would give them much-needed space.

"There are only two bathrooms," she noted. "That's a problem. With this many people, we should have at least three, and four would be better. I'm not sure how we can do that without giving up one of the bedrooms. I'll have to check into code requirements."

"Come with me," Sophia said, leading the way to a door at the end of the hall. She opened it to reveal a sizable storage closet. "Could you work with this? It's right next to one of the existing bathrooms, so the plumbing wouldn't be a nightmare, right?"

Emily studied it thoughtfully. The space wasn't huge, but it would certainly accommodate a sink, toilet and walk-in shower. "I'll get with the plumber and see what he thinks," she said, making a note on her phone, where she'd already stored other observations and preliminary measurements, along with photos of every room they'd been in.

"Want to see the attic?" the Realtor asked.

Emily's excitement stirred. "There's an attic?"

Taylor grinned. "Wait till you see."

Though access now was through a pull-down staircase, that could easily be changed to something more permanent, Emily thought, making another note. As she climbed the steps and emerged into a huge room filled with sunlight, she gasped.

"Two more bedrooms, at least," she said at once.

"Or a dormitory style room with a bath for the older kids," Sophia suggested. "A room with beds and desks, so they can study. It would give the moms and the teens both a little more privacy."

Emily nodded. "Not coed, of course."

"Of course," Sophia agreed.

"Some moms won't be comfortable being separated from their kids," Marilyn commented. "They need to know they're close and safe."

"The little ones, for sure," Sophia said. "But the teens? I think they need this tiny little taste of independence." She regarded her friend with a coaxing smile. "We'll talk about it some more, okay?"

"And you'll win," Marilyn responded with an air of resignation. "You always do."

"Only because I'm so often right," Sophia joked. "Okay, Emily, you've seen it all. What do you think? Can you pull off a miracle?"

"Do you still want this open by Thanksgiving?"

"Absolutely," Sophia said, her expression unyielding.

Emily hadn't expected any equivocation, and she'd prepared herself for an impossible schedule. "What fun is ordinary when we have a chance to perform a miracle? Let me spend tonight and tomorrow making some calls." She glanced at the Realtor. "Can I have access again, maybe late tomorrow afternoon, if I can line up some people to take a look and get started?"

The woman chuckled. "You're asking the wrong person. If the board signs the papers this afternoon, they'll be able to give you all the access you want."

"You're moving that quickly?" Emily asked, her gaze on Sophia.

"We don't have time to waste. I'll have a set of keys sent over by courier as soon as these papers are signed. My attorney has been on this for several days now, getting the paperwork taken care of. I've called in every favor in my arsenal, and we'll have the title by tomorrow. He's already started the process for building and zoning permits."

"That could take forever," Emily warned.

"Not with Sophia on the case," Marilyn commented. "The mayor swoons when she walks into the room and sees to it that she gets whatever she wants. I've never known anyone who could cut through bureaucratic red tape the way she can."

Emily regarded Sophia with admiration. "Is there anything you can't accomplish when you set your mind to it?"

Sophia winked at her. "Not so far. And I'm counting on you to live up to my standards."

"I'll do my best," Emily promised her.

But even as she spoke, she wondered how on earth she was going to pull it off and still keep her promise to get back home to Boone later in the week.

"Oh, Boone, you should see this place," she said, when she finally spoke to him that evening. It was already past eleven in North Carolina, but it was the first chance she'd had to call after contacting all of her most reliable contractors and vendors. She'd used every persuasive power she possessed to get several of them to agree to meet her at the house tomorrow.

She described the house and all the work it was going to require. "But when it's finished, it's going to be so perfect," she said. "I can practically hear the echo of happy children in those rooms."

"It sounds like there's going to be an incredible amount of work involved," he said. "Are you going to have to stick around to oversee it all, especially with such a tight deadline?"

"Maybe a little more than I'd originally thought," she admitted. "But the people I'm hiring are good. They can be left on their own. I'll definitely make it back next week, if only for a couple of days."

"I hope you're talking about the end of the week," Boone said. "I didn't expect you so soon. Pete and I are going to Charleston at the beginning of the week to check into opening a new restaurant there."

"Oh," she said, taken aback. She hadn't envisioned any sort of conflict arising because of his schedule. "I'd hoped to come earlier, then get back here before things kick into high gear. I want workmen on the job by the end of next week and I need to be here to oversee that, at least the first few days."

"I see." He fell silent.

"This is going to be harder than we thought, isn't it?" she asked, not even trying to hide her disappointment. "Could you maybe reschedule, just this once?"

"Pete's spent the whole day setting up meetings with important officials down there. We can hardly call back and ask them to change the appointments. We're trying to get off on the right foot."

"I know. You're right. I shouldn't have asked."

"And obviously you can't juggle what's on your plate," Boone said. "Not with those families counting on you."

"Okay, look, this is the first shot we've taken at this," Emily said. "We're bound to hit a few kinks. Let's compare notes now for the following week. That way we'll be locked in when we're both free."

"Sure," Boone said. "I'll be back. No travel on the schedule for that week. The only thing pressing will be getting B.J. ready to go back to school."

"Maybe we can take him shopping," Emily suggested. "That would be fun. I can remember going with my mom to buy new school clothes every fall."

Boone laughed. "You were a girl. Trust me, B.J. does not get excited about clothes shopping or picking out notebooks and pencils and a lunch box. He prefers to complain about whatever I bring home."

"Which is why he should be along when you shop," she argued, then hesitated. "Is this really about me coming along? Is that crossing that line we talked about?"

Boone's hesitation was answer enough.

"Okay, it is," she said briskly. "Still, I'll be there for a few days and we'll get to spend some time together, just you and me."

"And you'll see B.J.," Boone promised. "Just not when he'll get any ideas about the two of us."

"Okay, then," she said, managing to hide her disappointment. "I should let you get some sleep. It's late there, and I still have work to do tonight."

"Em?" Boone said when she was about to hang up.

"What?"

"I miss you already."

"I miss you, too. And we are going to make this work, Boone. It's too important for us to screw it up."

"We'll give it our best shot, that's for sure," he promised.

"Talk to you tomorrow?"

"Absolutely. I'll catch up with you on your cell, since it sounds as if you're going to be on the go from morning till night."

"Good night, then."

"Wish you were here," he said. "You have no idea how much."

"Oh, I have some idea," she said with feeling.

Being back in his bed even once had left her wanting more. A whole lifetime, in fact.

But today had complicated the likelihood of smooth sailing for the two of them. While her work had always been satisfying and challenging, today, for the very first time, she'd felt she was doing something important. She liked the way that felt. It added an element of fulfillment she'd never anticipated.

But to do work like this shelter, she would have to accept even more paying jobs, which would lead to being busier than ever. How would the addition of a relation-ship work, especially with Boone on the opposite coast?

She sighed and pushed that worry out of her head. It wasn't a problem she could solve, not tonight and not alone, but there were plenty of other things she could tackle. Better to concentrate on those, at least for now.

15

"What's with her?" Emily asked, gesturing in the direction Gabi had taken. She'd fled the room right after Emily walked into her grandmother's house on her return from California and Colorado.

"She says she has the flu," Samantha said. "I have to tell you, though, I'm a little worried about her. It's not like her to miss more work, not when she was so anxious to get back over there. I think she's more stressed out about that job than she's been letting on."

Emily stared at her sister in surprise. "She never went back to Raleigh? I thought she was heading home the same day I left."

"That was the plan, but then she came down with this bug and hasn't been able to shake it."

"Has she seen a doctor?"

Samantha shook her head, her frustration plain. "Grandmother wanted her to stop by Ethan's clinic, but she refused. She insisted she'd be fine and would be heading home by the end of last week. When she blew off that deadline, too, I was tempted to drag her to the clinic myself."

Emily grinned. "Not that you're looking for an excuse to get a glimpse of Ethan, I'm sure."

"Bite me," Samantha replied, probably unaware that the color in her cheeks betrayed her interest in the old high school football hero.

"Still can't take the teasing, huh? Then you should stop wearing that old football jersey of his around the house."

"It's comfortable," Samantha insisted. "So, how was your trip? You were gone longer than I'd expected."

"I was gone longer than *I'd* expected," Emily said. "But the work is so exciting, Samantha. It's going to take a miracle to pull this off by Thanksgiving, but I really want to do it. I think everyone working on the project understands how important it is to have this place ready by then. What a blessing it will be for some of these women and their kids to be in a safe environment for the holiday."

Samantha smiled. "I love seeing you excited about something so worthwhile, rather than indulging the whims of all these wealthy clients of yours."

Emily took offense at the comment. "Those wealthy clients make it possible for me to take on a project like this."

"I suppose," Samantha conceded, letting the subject drop and moving on to what she obviously considered to be safer territory. "How soon can we expect to see Boone? I imagine he's anxious to get over here now that you're back."

Emily frowned. "Not till tomorrow, I'm afraid. B.J. had asked a friend to spend the night before Boone knew when I'd be getting back into town."

"I could go over and give him a break," Samantha

offered. "Or you could go over yourself and help chaperone."

Emily shook her head. "We agreed it's best that we not spend too much time together around B.J. And if Boone took off, even for an hour, B.J. would know something's up."

"So all this caution around B.J. is just in case things don't work out," Samantha guessed. "I suppose that makes sense, but how do you feel about it?"

"Not great, to be honest," Emily admitted. "Still, the last thing I want is for B.J. to get hurt. So, Boone will shoo B.J.'s friend out as early as humanly possible, then come by here for a quick visit before he takes B.J. out to shop for school."

Samantha's gaze narrowed. "You're not going with them?"

"Nope." She tried to keep her expression neutral, but she was sure it was plain how much that grated, too.

"Emily, this isn't good," her sister protested.

"Boone's son. Boone's rules," Emily said tersely. "And after hearing how Jodie Farmer reacted when Boone and I were spotted by one of her friends, I can understand his caution on that front, too."

"Well, I don't," Samantha said, her indignation rising. "I think this stinks. I'm not seeing a lot of respect for your feelings. When exactly are you supposed to spend time together, or do you plan to sneak out for a quickie in the driveway while B.J. sleeps?"

Emily frowned. "Come on," she protested. "It's not going to be like that."

"You sure about that? Because it sounds to me as if at least one of you believes that what you're doing is wrong or, at the very least, doesn't want to rock any boats in case it doesn't last. Is that you?"

"No," Emily admitted, knowing that Samantha had a point. The situation had been bugging her, too. For now, though, she was determined to be understanding. She knew Boone's attitude had almost as much to do with his feelings of betrayal and abandonment when she'd left the first time as it did with protecting B.J. Whether he'd admit it or not, he was keeping his guard up. And with the Farmers' threats looming, he had added incentive for being cautious.

Samantha, however, made no pretense of understanding. "You need to change the rules, Emily. Right now, they're not fair to anybody, and certainly not to you. You shouldn't have to sneak around to be with the man you love, not at this stage of your life. And Boone shouldn't ask it of you."

"I know you're right," Emily said, her own misgivings confirmed by her sister. "I thought it was too soon to make an issue about this, but I will talk to Boone when I see him. There has to be a better plan."

Unfortunately, if she was being totally honest, she couldn't imagine what it might be, not with the past weighing so heavily on the present.

Boone was thoroughly frustrated by having to waste a whole night of what would likely be a very brief stay by Emily. He just hadn't been able to think of an alternative. Alex's mother would have been happy to have the boys at her house, but he'd been asking a lot of her recently. He just couldn't ask again, not after the invitation had already been issued. By now Kim probably had plans of her own. As a single mom, he was sure she must crave a social life that didn't include a couple of rambunctious eight-year-old boys.

With the boys upstairs playing video games, Boone went into the kitchen and called Emily's cell phone.

"Hey," he said, his heart skipping a beat at the sound of her voice.

"Hey yourself."

"Any problems getting here?"

"Nope. Smooth flights all the way and an easy drive over."

"I wish I could have been at Cora Jane's when you got there," he said.

"You could have been," she said, her tone mildly accusatory.

Her attitude caught him by surprise. "Come on, Emily. I explained about this sleepover."

"You did, but I've been giving that some thought. Would it have been so awful for you to bring both boys over here for a couple of hours? We could have grilled some burgers or something. B.J. wouldn't have made anything out of that."

"Probably not," he admitted. "I just didn't want to chance it."

"Because B.J.'s so intuitive or because you're afraid word will get back to Jodie?" she pressed.

Boone was taken aback by the unexpectedly bitter note in her voice. "Both," he said. "But I thought you understood. What's changed? Did somebody say something to upset you? Cora Jane, for instance?"

"It's not about what anyone else thinks. I'm the one who's frustrated," she admitted. "I came all this way. I have only a couple of days here, and we're going to spend, what, maybe a few hours together? That's not going to work, Boone. We can't build a relationship that way."

"Sweetheart, believe me, I am every bit as frustrated as you are. This sleepover came up before I knew your schedule. Next time I won't let anything interfere. I'll make plans for B.J. so we can have every minute together. Don't you think that's what I want, too?"

She sighed. "Yes, of course."

"Come shopping with us tomorrow," he said impulsively. "I know you wanted to."

"But you said it was a bad idea," she countered, clearly surprised by his change of heart.

"It may be, but it's not as if anybody can make anything of us being caught together buying school supplies or eating lunch in a mall food court."

"Are you sure?"

"Yes," he said before he could change his mind. He couldn't allow Jodie's hostility to rule his life. If she got wind of him being with Emily, so be it. She needed to get used to the idea sooner or later and it might as well start now.

Of course, if him being with Emily infuriated his former mother-in-law, it was likely to be nothing compared to what she'd have to say about B.J. being along. Still, B.J. was his son, and a shopping trip was about as innocuous an outing as the three of them could possibly take.

"I'll pick you up at ten, as soon as I drop Alex off. We'll make a day of it. You game?"

"For shopping?" she asked with a laugh. "Hon, you are talking my language."

Boone had a feeling he'd opened more than one can

of worms with his invitation. Giving his credit card a serious workout was probably the least of it.

B.J. flew across the yard when he spotted Emily and threw his arms around her. "You're back!" he announced happily. "Dad, look who's here."

Boone grinned. "I heard. I figured you'd want to stop by and say hello."

"Are you back for good?" B.J. asked hopefully.

"Only for a couple of days," she said, hugging him tightly. "Now, stand back and let me get a good look at you. I think you've grown at least an inch since I left."

"Dad says it's at least two inches this summer. All my school pants are too short."

"Then you definitely need new ones," Emily said. "Ready to do some serious shopping?"

B.J.'s eyes widened excitedly. "You're coming, too?"

"I am," she confirmed, her gaze on Boone, who was smiling, even though she thought she could detect a hint of worry in his eyes.

"Awesome!" B.J. said with a first pump. "Dad says we can eat in the food court and I can have pizza *and* tacos."

Emily feigned surprise. "Really? That's a lot of food. Think you can handle it?"

"Sure," B.J. said confidently. "I'm a growing boy. I need lots and lots of food. That's what Grandma Jodie says. But she thinks I should only eat vegetables and fruit and stuff like that. She's a veggie..." He glanced at Boone. "What is she, Dad?"

"A vegetarian," Boone explained.

"Ah," Emily said. "That can be a very healthy lifestyle." Just a little tough on a kid, whose friends were eating pepperoni pizza, burgers and fries. Still, she wasn't about to criticize his grandmother's choices. That was a surefire way to stir up trouble with Jodie Farmer.

"Son, why don't you run inside and say hello to Cora Jane?" He glanced hopefully at Emily. "She's home, right? Doesn't she go in a little later on Saturdays?"

"She's here," Emily confirmed. "She claimed she took the morning off to spend a little time with me, but the truth is, I think she's worn herself out the past few weeks getting the restaurant back into full operation."

B.J. dutifully scampered off, leaving them alone. Boone took a few steps toward her. "I want to kiss you," he murmured with only inches between them. His breath fanned across her cheek.

"Then do it," she said, her gaze locked with his. "We have maybe five minutes before B.J.'s back. Grandmother will keep him occupied for at least that long."

Boone grinned. "Five minutes, huh? It will have to be some kiss."

"I'm sure you're up to it."

"I guess we'll find out," he said, pulling her into his arms and sealing his mouth over hers.

Emily swayed into his embrace, letting everything go except the sensations he stirred in her—the desire, the heat, the familiar scent of citrus and pure male.

"Much better," she murmured as the kiss ended. "I was so afraid we weren't going to sneak in even one kiss on this trip."

"It's going to get better," Boone promised. "We won't always have to sneak around."

"I hope not, because I'm not sure I can do that," Emily told him candidly. "It feels too sleazy, as if we're ashamed or something."

Boone touched her cheek. "Maybe you're just looking at it all wrong. Sneaking around could be kind of exciting. It used to be. Remember when we were afraid of getting caught?"

"We were teenagers," she said, though she smiled at the memory. "Adults shouldn't have to do that, especially not single adults. We shouldn't need to explain ourselves to anyone."

"I'm just trying to be respectful of Jodie's feelings," Boone said, "as out of line as they might be. Why stir up trouble if we don't have to? And there's B.J. to consider."

"I'm not suggesting we start making out in front of him," Emily said. "I just think we could hang out together."

"And that's what we're going to do today," Boone said.

She heard the frustration in his voice and touched his cheek. "But it's making you a little crazy, isn't it? You're worried he's going to jump to some sort of conclusion and wind up being hurt or maybe blab about this shopping trip to his grandmother."

"Either one is a possibility," he retorted.

"Stop anticipating problems. I promise to be on my best behavior. I won't jump your bones in front of your son."

He finally smiled. "And now you've gone and planted that idea in my head," he said. "I'll be thinking about it all day."

"Good," she said with a wink. "Maybe it'll motivate you to find some alone time with me before I head back to Los Angeles."

He grinned. "Already working on it, so don't tease unless you mean it."

"Oh, I mean it," she said, her tone heartfelt.

The outlook for this visit had just gotten a whole lot more interesting.

Boone, like most men he knew, would rather be tortured than spend time in a mall. Somehow, though, Emily's enthusiasm was contagious. Even B.J. didn't complain about trying on half a dozen different pairs of jeans and enough shirts and sweaters to outfit his entire class. He did balk when she tried to persuade him to try on dress shoes as well as the expensive sneakers he swore he couldn't possibly live without.

"You can't wear sneakers to church," she argued.

"I already have fancy shoes," he protested. "They pinch my feet."

"Which is exactly why you need new ones," she said as Boone smothered a smile. She frowned at him. "You could back me up here."

"Son, Emily's right. As long as we're here, you should get new dress shoes. Your old ones are too small."

B.J. scowled at him. "Only if you do, too."

Emily's face lit up. "Oh, what a great idea! Boone, have you ever tried these Italian leather loafers?" She picked up a pair from the display and handed them to him. "Feel how soft they are."

"Soft," he muttered, unimpressed. At those prices they ought to whisk him through the air like a blasted magic carpet.

"You have to try them," she insisted, corralling a

sales clerk and giving him a list of shoes to bring out for him and for B.J.

A dozen boxes appeared a few minutes later. Boone regarded them incredulously. "Come on, Em. Really?"

"You'll thank me later." She beamed at the two of them. "Isn't this fun?"

Boone exchanged a tortured look with his son, but she was having so much fun, he could hardly bolt from the shoe department and spoil it for her.

Several hundred dollars later, they left with loafers for him, sneakers and dress shoes for B.J. and a pair of three-inch heels that Emily hadn't been able to take her eyes off of the entire time they'd been in the shoe department. Boone had insisted she try them on, taken one look at the effect they had on her gorgeous legs and told the clerk to wrap them up.

"Boone, you don't have to buy me shoes. I can buy my own."

"It's the least I can do after all the time you've spent helping us shop today," he said, then leaned in to whisper, "Besides, I can't wait to see you wearing those and nothing else."

Her cheeks had flamed at that, but she'd stopped arguing.

Unfortunately, the comment had also left him wanting a whole lot more than he was likely to get this afternoon. He wondered if they could skip the food court and head back to Sand Castle Bay, but B.J. was already dragging them in that direction, his mind set on pizza, tacos and heaven knew what else.

Boone glanced over at Emily. "Nothing like a little frustration to keep things interesting, huh?"

She gave him an innocent look. "Frustration? I have no idea what you mean."

"Then you're a stronger person than I am," he commented.

Either that, or she was getting a kick out of knowing that he was regretting all those blasted rules he'd insisted they abide by.

"And then I had two slices of pizza and a beef taco," B.J. was telling Cora Jane excitedly. "And a large soda." He frowned. "That might have been a bad idea, because Dad had to stop twice on the way home so I could pee."

Cora Jane chuckled, then glanced pointedly at Boone. "Don't you need to go over and check on things at your restaurant?" she inquired innocently.

Boone nodded at once. "I do like to make sure things are under control on the weekends when it's especially busy," he confirmed.

"Maybe Emily could ride along," Cora Jane said. "B.J. can stay here with me and show me everything he bought today for school."

"Are you sure?" Boone asked, though she'd just offered him the chance he'd been dying for all day to be alone with Emily.

"Absolutely," Cora Jane said. "And after all this excitement, I imagine he's pretty tired. If he falls asleep, he might as well spend the night. Jerry's coming by later, so I'll have plenty of backup."

Boone grinned at her, then bent down and kissed her cheek. "You are an angel."

"She's a meddling matchmaker," Emily muttered under her breath, but she was smiling. She certainly didn't argue with her grandmother.

"Watch your tongue," Cora Jane told her. "I could take back my offer."

"No, please," Boone pleaded. "Come on, Emily. Let's get over to the restaurant so I can see if everything's under control."

"We won't be too late," she told her grandmother.

"Don't count on that," Boone said, nudging her in the direction of the door. "Son, listen to Ms. Cora Jane. Do what she tells you."

"You don't need to worry about B.J.," Cora Jane said. "He and I will get along just fine. No need to call if you're running late. You'll just wake us up."

Boone grinned at her. "Thanks."

Outside, he pulled Emily across the lawn, and all but shoved her into his car.

"Trying to make a quick getaway?" she asked, laughing.

"I don't want her changing her mind or B.J. asking questions about why you're coming with me. This is a gift horse, and I'm not questioning it. You shouldn't be, either."

He drove to the end of the driveway until they were out of view from the house, then stopped the car. "Come here," he commanded softly.

Emily swayed toward him.

Boone cupped her face in his hands, looked deep into her eyes, then sighed. "I hope to heaven we left those shoes you bought in the trunk. I've had that image in my head all afternoon."

"I have to admit, I couldn't envision how you were going to pull off any time alone tonight, but they're there," Emily assured him. "I should have known Cora Jane would conspire to give you what you want."

He kissed her long and deep, then smiled. "I never said a word to Cora Jane. Didn't have to plant the idea, beg, nothing."

"Because she's a sneaky woman," Emily concluded.

"And you disapprove of that?"

A slow grin spread across her face. "Right this second? Can't say that I do. Hit the gas, Dorsett. We're wasting time."

"Now you're getting into the spirit of this," he said, pulling onto the road and turning toward his place. He figured he could cut the fifteen minute drive down to ten minutes. There were plenty of interesting things he could do with an extra five minutes, especially once he had Emily out of her clothes.

It was after midnight by the time they grew hungry for something other than each other. Boone led the way so they could raid the refrigerator.

"For a man who owns three restaurants, your refrigerator sure isn't stocked very well," Emily commented as she surveyed the contents.

"I haven't had time to shop this week. Besides, other than breakfast, B.J. and I have had most of our meals out. Last night he and Alex ordered pizza, made popcorn and topped it off with ice cream." He poked around in a cupboard and triumphantly retrieved a package of popcorn. "I thought there might be some of this left."

Emily lifted a brow. "You expect popcorn to give us enough energy to make it through a couple more rounds upstairs?" she asked skeptically. "Personally I need protein."

"How about a couple of omelets? There are eggs and cheese and..." He peered into the vegetable drawer and emerged with an onion and a green pepper. "What do you think?"

"That should do it," she agreed. "Any of that ice cream left from last night?"

Boone checked the freezer, pulled out the half-empty container of rocky road and held it up. "Dessert," he announced.

Emily was already shaking her head and wiggling her fingers. "Gimme," she said. "Spoons?"

Boone gestured. "That drawer right there. While you're in there, grab a couple of forks and knives, okay?"

"After dessert," she said, grinning as she spooned a healthy serving of rocky road into her mouth, closing her eyes in apparent ecstasy.

Boone chuckled. "I'm not sure you looked that thrilled when I was making love to you."

She grinned at him. "Believe me, I was," she assured him. "But this is pretty heavenly. Want some?"

"I think I'll stick with the omelet," he said, though he couldn't seem to tear his gaze away from the sight of her face as she moaned with pleasure over each bite.

"You keep that up and I'm taking you right back upstairs," he warned. "You're turning me on."

"Not really. You're just feeling oddly competitive, wondering if you can make me moan like this."

"Sweetheart, you did your fair share of moaning upstairs. A little begging, too, as I recall."

"Hmm. I don't seem to remember that."

"Trust me."

"You might have to prove it," she taunted.

When Boone took a step toward her, she held up a hand. "After the omelets."

He laughed. "I swear I don't remember you being such a tease."

"Because we were never really together," she said, her expression suddenly serious. "Not like this, with a whole house to ourselves and no curfew we have to meet. This is what it's like to be together as adults."

"And?" Boone asked, his heart in his throat.

She set down the ice cream container and stepped into his embrace, her arms circling his waist, her head resting against his shoulder. "It's pretty darn amazing."

Over her head, Boone allowed himself a relieved smile. It *was* amazing. And to think they were just getting started.

16

Boone was clearly anxious to get back over to Cora Jane's before B.J. awoke. Even though it was barely daylight, he was pacing the whole time Emily was showering and dressing.

"I guess I was wrong last night," she said eventually, frowning at him. "It seems we do have a curfew."

"I just don't want B.J. to wake up and start asking a lot of questions. He might not make anything of me not being there when he gets up, but if you're nowhere around, either, what's he going to think?"

"That I've gone for a walk?" she suggested mildly. "Or run to the store? I'm sure Cora Jane will have the perfect cover story."

"And when you walk in wearing the same clothes you had on yesterday, don't you think he'll wonder about that?"

"Not unless he's a lot more observant that most eight-year-old boys," Emily said, but she did her best to hurry, because Boone was clearly freaking out.

In the car, she looked over at his set jaw and knew

they had to deal with this. "Wait," she commanded before he could start the engine.

He glanced at her. "What?"

"Boone, sneaking around when we were a couple of teenagers was one thing. Now, it's not as much fun. I feel as if you don't have a lot of respect for me or for what I thought we were trying to build here."

Her words seemed to shake him, just as she'd intended.

"Em, you can't believe I don't respect you."

"Right this second, this feels a whole lot like a casual, meaningless fling," she countered. "The kind you wouldn't want anyone to find out about."

He looked genuinely upset by her words. "You couldn't be further from the truth. You know I want us to have a future. There are just things we have to work out before we take this thing public, especially with my son. We agreed—"

"I'm reconsidering," she said, cutting him off. "I don't like the way this makes me feel. You just hustled me out of your house as if you'd hired me for the night and didn't want a cost overrun."

"That's a little dramatic, don't you think?" he said, his temper obviously stirring.

"Okay, maybe that is going too far," she conceded, "but I'm telling you how it made me feel."

He sighed and rubbed a hand across his face. "What do you want from me, Em?"

"No more sneaking around," she said firmly. "That's my bottom line. We don't have to throw this in anyone's face, but I want to be able to have a cup of coffee or a drink with you in public without seeing a look of

panic on your face every time we're spotted by someone who knows us."

"And B.J.? How do you see this working where he's
concerned?"

Because she understood Boone's desire to protect his
son, she softened her stance in that regard. "We won't
make a big deal of seeing each other in front of him.
We'll hang out with the family, go on an occasional outing with the three of us, stuff like that. No kissing, no
touching, nothing too intimate that might cause him to
ask questions. How about that? It's a fair compromise,
Boone. Fair to B.J., to you and to me."

He sighed heavily. "I can't argue with that."

"But can you live with it?"

"What if he does start asking questions or getting
ideas about the two of us?" he asked, still clinging to
his worry.

She tossed the question right back at him. "What if
he does?"

"I suppose we'd have to tell him the truth then, that
we're trying to work things out as a couple," he said as
if testing an idea he wasn't entirely happy about.

"That seems like a good way to handle it," she
agreed. "No more information than he asks for or needs
to have."

"There's just one problem with this sane, rational
plan of yours," Boone said, an unexpected twinkle ap-
pearing in his eyes. "Suddenly I want to throw you right
back into my bed and spend a couple more hours rolling around naked with you."

Emily laughed at the unmistakable frustration in
his voice. "Good. That'll keep you highly motivated

to find a way for us to have some more alone time before I leave."

"Sweetheart, you can count on it."

And *that* was exactly the response she'd been hoping for.

Boone drove B.J. to his first day of school on Monday and was back at Cora Jane's by eight-thirty. When he walked into the kitchen, only Emily was there.

"Where is everybody?"

"Grandmother and Samantha left before dawn for Castle's. Gabi drove back to Raleigh yesterday." A slow smile spread across her face. "That leaves me. I got out of going to Castle's by pleading a full day of phone calls to stay on top of the work at the shelter and at the ski lodge."

Boone pulled her out of her chair and into his arms. "So you're going to be tied up all day long?" he murmured, kissing her neck. "The whole day?"

"The whole day," she confirmed, snuggling closer.

"Too bad," he said.

"Why is that?"

"I had some interesting ideas about what we could do to keep ourselves occupied with a whole house to ourselves."

She kissed him then, a long, slow, deep kiss that encouraged whatever plans he had in mind. "Such as?" she murmured against his lips.

"Well, this is definitely a good starting point," he told her. "You know, Em, it's been a very long time since I've seen your room."

"You *never* saw my room," she protested. "Grandmother would have shot us both."

"Probably true," he said. "I just imagined every detail, so I could think of you there at night. I had some very vivid fantasies back then."

Emily smiled. "Want to come upstairs and tell me about them, maybe see if we can make one or two come true?"

"What if Cora Jane catches us?" he asked, knowing there was little likelihood of that. She'd be at Castle's for most of the day.

"I don't think we have to worry about that," Emily said. "If she were here right now, she'd probably be shooing us along in that direction with a broom. She is very anxious for the two of us to figure this out. All those rules she once had have definitely been set aside in favor of reaching her latest goal."

"I'm thinking we shouldn't let her down," Boone said. "How about you? Or did you really want to make all those calls?"

Emily glanced toward the clock on the wall. "It's not even six o'clock in the morning in Los Angeles, not yet seven in Aspen. We have time."

"Certainly enough to get started," Boone agreed, scooping her into his arms.

She grinned at him. "Aren't you optimistic?"

"What can I say? You inspire me." He winked at her. "And I did have a lot of fantasies we need to get caught up on."

Emily also made him just a little bit reckless and crazy, traits he hadn't allowed himself to express in years. One of these days he'd have to figure out if rediscovering that side of his personality was a good thing... or dangerously bad.

* * *

Emily rolled over and groaned. "Go home," she murmured emphatically, giving Boone a halfhearted shove.

He regarded her incredulously. "You're kicking me out of your bed? After I worked so hard to make sure you were totally satisfied?"

"I am," she confirmed. "You have to pick your son up from school. I have to make at least some of those business calls. And, despite my earlier comments, I really don't think Grandmother should come home from Castle's and find us in my bed. It might make her happy, but I guarantee, we'd never hear the end of it. She'll have her calendar out and the church booked before we make it downstairs."

"Would that be so bad?" Boone asked, glancing over his shoulder as he sat on the side of the bed.

As the offhand comment sank in, Emily stared at him. "What?"

"I asked if it would be so bad if we set a wedding date."

She had a very hard time comprehending this sudden about-face, this desire to leap into the future. "Seriously?" she asked.

For an instant he looked as if he might take it back, but then he nodded. "Seriously."

Stunned by the out-of-the-blue suggestion, Emily yanked the sheet up to her chin. Though she tried to choose her words carefully, the ones that came out of her mouth were anything but diplomatic.

"Boone, have you suddenly lost your mind? We've barely started seeing each other again. Sure, it's been good. Excellent, in fact, but we're not ready to go to the next level, much less take a leap over the next five levels to marriage."

He frowned at her quick-tempered response. "How do you see this progressing?"

"A lot more slowly than you do, apparently. Earlier today you didn't even want the world to know we were together. This turnaround of yours is giving me whiplash."

"It was just an idea," he said defensively. "If this is the outcome we're hoping for, why wait? Let's just do it, then deal with the fallout."

"Now that's a romantic notion," she said.

"Okay, if you're so dead set against it, tell me your objections."

"There are a lot of things we haven't even begun to work out, like how our lives would fit together," she reminded him. "That's a biggie, don't you think?"

"Maybe we're making it too complicated, that's all I'm saying." He regarded her earnestly. "I love you, Em. I always have. I fought it when you first showed up, but that was about me being angry and guilty about holding back a piece of my heart from Jenny. Now it just seems as if we're back where we used to be and we ought to grab this before a million other things get in the way again."

"And how do you see this marriage working?" she asked, genuinely perplexed by this crazy idea of his. She could tell from the bewildered expression on his face that he had no clue how it might work.

"You're being a total guy," she accused lightly when he didn't respond. "You want what you want when you want it, never mind that the other person hasn't even climbed on this runaway bus of yours yet."

He stared at her for a minute, then chuckled. "You think I'm a runaway bus?"

"Something like that. Maybe I didn't want us hiding from the world, but I sure wasn't suggesting we just throw caution to the wind. These issues we have are real. Jodie Farmer's going to be a problem. B.J. has to get used to the idea. We have work schedules that are going to have to be coordinated. I could be tied up in California for a couple of months at least on this shelter project. The deadline for the ski lodge renovation is just as crazy. And a lot of my regular clients have little spruce-up jobs that they insist be done before the holidays. I have four queries about those on that list of calls I need to return."

As her recitation went on, she saw the muscles in Boone's shoulders visibly tighten.

"So, what?" he asked. "This was hello and goodbye all in one. You'll be back, when? Sometime after the first of the year?"

"I'm sure it won't be that long," she said, though she honestly couldn't promise how much sooner it might be. "I'm hoping to get back at least once a month. I was also thinking maybe you and B.J. could come to California, so we could take him to Disneyland, or that you could meet me in Aspen for a quick getaway, just the two of us."

"I'm beginning to see what you meant," Boone said, his tone filled with disappointment and resignation. "Your priorities are still all screwed up, aren't they? You're not willing to put this relationship ahead of much."

"These are commitments I've already made, Boone."

She regarded him with frustration. "Should I slack off, not give the jobs the attention they deserve?"

"Of course not," he said, his own frustration just as plain. "What about after these jobs? Will you slow down? Take less work? Maybe even relocate your business to North Carolina?"

"I honestly haven't thought that far into the future," she admitted. "There wasn't any reason to. I thought we were just starting to test the waters, find out if we had anything left."

"Do you at least agree that we do?" he asked.

She walked around the bed and sat down beside him. "How could I possibly deny that? The sex has been amazing."

The frown on his face only deepened at her words. "That's all this has been for you? Great sex? I thought we were reconnecting on a whole lot of levels."

Now she was frowning. "Why are you deliberately misunderstanding me? Do you want this to turn into a fight? Are you hoping we'll break up here and now, then go back to the way things were, not speaking or seeing each other? It would make your life less complicated, wouldn't it? No problems with Jodie. No worries about B.J. getting hurt."

"Don't be ridiculous," he said irritably. "Didn't I just suggest marriage?"

"But when I didn't leap at the suggestion, you started picking at things, Boone. You're trying to make me feel guilty because I need time to see how this can work. There are a dozen practicalities we need to consider."

"And I think if you were really in love with me, you'd commit to marrying me, and we'd figure out how to make it work."

"Isn't that the same thing?"

"No," he said flatly. "I'm saying I love you enough to take a huge leap of faith into the future. You're saying you'll see how you feel once all the details are ironed out. This is exactly the way it was ten years ago."

"It is not the same thing at all," she said emphatically. "And I'm being reasonable," she added, though her voice rose to a very unreasonable pitch when she said it.

"I guess that's one perspective," he said, yanking on his shirt and shoving his feet into his shoes. "I've got to pick up B.J. If I don't see you before you leave, have a safe trip."

Emily stared at him incredulously as he headed for the door. "That's it. You're just walking out?"

"I have to pick up B.J.," he repeated. "And it wouldn't hurt for me to cool down. I'd say I'll have that accomplished by New Year's, which ought to fit into your schedule perfectly."

"You're being a stubborn idiot," she called after him.

"Pot, kettle," he retorted, his voice fading as he went downstairs.

She heard his car start, then peel out of the driveway, spewing gravel undoubtedly.

"What just happened here?" she muttered under her breath, clutching a pillow in her arms.

She and Boone had gotten back together, had a few hours of being closer than she'd been to anyone in years, he'd proposed, they'd fought and now they were broken up? Not likely, she thought angrily.

Though how on earth she was going to fix things, or why it was even up to her to try, was pretty much beyond her right this second.

* * *

"Daddy, you look mad," B.J. said hesitantly when he crawled into the car after school.

Boone forced a smile. "Not mad, just preoccupied," he told his son.

"Did somebody mess up?"

That was one way of putting it, Boone thought. Now that his temper had cooled ever-so-slightly, it was hard to say if Emily was the one who'd messed up, or if he had. He had an uncomfortable feeling that at least a share of the responsibility belonged to him. He'd pushed too hard. He could see that so clearly now without the leftover glow of mind-blowing sex clouding his judgment.

"It's nothing for you to worry about," he assured B.J. "Want to stop for ice cream to celebrate your first day back at school? I want to hear all about your new teacher and the kids in your class."

"Can Emily come, too?" B.J. asked. "I have to tell her what the other kids said about all the cool stuff we bought on Saturday."

"She's working this afternoon," Boone said automatically, not eager for another confrontation quite so soon.

"But I bet she'll take a break if we call her," B.J. said, clearly not interested in being put off.

"I said no," Boone snapped, then sighed at the immediate rise of tears in B.J.'s eyes. "Sorry. I just know she's busy, son. Maybe you can give her a call later on and fill her in. I know she'll want to hear all about your day."

"When's she leaving?"

"I'm not sure," Boone admitted. "Tomorrow, I think."

"Then I want to see her to say goodbye," B.J. said stubbornly. "And she told me yesterday she has pictures of the ski lodge on her laptop. I want to see them. Forget ice cream. Let's go to her house."

Boone knew he could dig in his heels, play the parental card, insist it was ice cream or home, and end the conversation right now. A part of him recognized, though, that this might be the opportunity he needed to make amends for everything that had gone so horribly wrong earlier.

"We'll stop by," he relented. "But five minutes, that's it. Understood? We can't interrupt her when she needs to work."

"Uh-huh," B.J. said in an agreeable way that told Boone very clearly that he didn't expect that five-minute rule to stick.

"Five minutes," Boone repeated, as if the repetition would get his point across.

As soon as he pulled into Cora Jane's driveway, B.J. was out of the car and racing across the lawn, yelling for Emily as he ran. The backdoor opened and B.J. threw his arms around her as if it had been weeks, rather than little more than a day since he'd last seen her. They'd all had Sunday morning breakfast together after Emily and Boone had come back here from their own sleepover.

Emily glanced in Boone's direction, a questioning look in her eyes.

"Might as well face the music," he muttered under his breath, getting out of the car.

"I didn't expect to see you again this afternoon," she said, her voice cool.

"B.J. insisted. He was afraid you might be leaving tomorrow."

"That's the plan," she confirmed. "B.J., why don't you go inside and look on the kitchen table? Grandmother brought home some cookies from the restaurant. She thought you might be coming by."

"All right!" B.J. enthused with a fist pump.

Emily waited until he was safely out of earshot before lifting her gaze to meet Boone's. "Cooled down?" she inquired mildly.

"Some."

"Want to try that earlier conversation again?"

Boone shook his head. "Now's not a good time. Why don't I give you a call a little later?"

"Don't you think we're going to have to rely on too many phone calls when I'm out of town to be wasting precious face time now?"

He heard the intractable note in her voice and sighed. "Let me see if Cora Jane can keep an eye on him again," he said, despite his reluctance to keep imposing on her.

"If you don't want to ask her, Samantha's in the kitchen, too. She'd be happy to spend some time with him. I can leave him with my laptop so he can look at the progress we're making on the ski lodge. He's really excited about that."

Boone nodded. "I'll take care of it."

When he came back, he gestured toward the water. "Want to go sit on the pier?"

"Sure."

Boone led the way, trying to figure out what he was going to say to make things right. At the very end of the pier, the afternoon sun spilled onto the faded wood, leaving it warm. He held out his hand and Emily took it as she lowered herself to sit on the edge. He dropped down beside her.

"It's so peaceful out here," she murmured, her eyes closed as she turned her face up to the sun. "I'd forgotten what it was like just to sit here and listen to the sound of the water lapping against the shore and the breeze whispering through the trees. I'm sure there are plenty of places like this in Los Angeles, but I never get there. When I think of L.A., the sound that comes to mind is traffic, horns honking, car stereos blaring. Not exactly serene."

"And yet you can't wait to rush back there," he said, unable to keep a bitter note from his voice.

She glanced at him. "It has its good sides, too, not the least of which is that I have work there."

Boone studied her. "Do you really love what you do, Emily?"

"I'm good at it," she said simply.

"That's not really an answer, is it? People can be wildly successful and realize that something's missing."

She frowned at the comment, then sighed. "Okay, the regular jobs are creatively challenging, but I've recently realized that I need more than that from my work. That's why this shelter means so much to me. It combines the things I love to do with something that is genuinely meaningful. It's an amazing experience, Boone, and I think it's exactly the kind of thing that's been missing from my other jobs."

He saw the way her eyes lit up when she talked about it and felt his stomach sink. He thought he could have competed with a plain old professional challenge and financial success, but how was he supposed to compete with something that had clearly touched her on another level? Was it time to cut his losses, after all? Just let her go? Admit that they'd tried again and failed?

When he considered the stakes—losing her for a second time in his life, at least in part because of stubborn pride—he knew he couldn't do it. This time he had to fight, just not by the almost desperate means he'd used earlier, trying to snag a premature commitment from her.

"Em, I'm sorry," he said quietly. "I got carried away earlier. I'm not giving you time to catch up."

She finally faced him then. "It's not that I don't want marriage," she said, her tone earnest. "Boone, I do love you. If I'm being honest, I can even admit I never stopped loving you. But if we're even going to consider this, we have to take our time. We want to get it right, for B.J.'s sake and for ours. Jumping in before we're ready?" She shook her head. "I'm so afraid it could doom us."

He nudged her in the ribs. "So sensible," he teased. "All these years I've thought of you as the impulsive one. I've been the mature, responsible adult with a kid. I think I just lost it a little when we were together earlier. I saw marriage as a quick way to seal the deal, maybe even to thumb my nose at Jodie and force her to deal with reality."

Her lips curved slightly. "Now there's a romantic reason to walk down the aisle."

"How about I take a couple of steps back, try to remind myself how the whole courting thing is supposed to work, and we deal with our issues bit by bit until we're both comfortable with the solutions?"

She leaned into his side. "An excellent plan," she agreed. "Very rational and mature."

When she met his gaze, her eyes flashed with humor. "I guess that rules out all that impulsive kissing we had going on earlier."

Boone laughed. "What rules that out is B.J. being less than fifty yards away in the house."

"There is that," she said with unmistakable disappointment.

"We had most of the day," he reminded her. "Seemed pretty memorable to me. It might hold me till you get back to town."

"If it doesn't, say the word and I'll try to get back sooner," she offered. "And that invitation to Aspen is still on the table. It's a beautiful place for a romantic rendezvous."

Boone finally allowed himself a smile, satisfied that they were back on track. "I'll definitely keep that in mind."

But as appealing as the thought of a tryst in the Colorado mountains might be, it was nothing compared to a lifetime of having this woman back in his life, maybe having a kid or two of their own. It was hardly the same sort of fantasy he'd been talking about earlier, but it was the one he suddenly wanted more than anything. For the first time in a lot of years, he thought it just might be within reach.

17

"Daddy, Grandma Jodie wants to talk to you," B.J. said, holding out the phone.

Boone sucked in a deep breath. He'd managed to avoid Jodie's calls—God bless caller ID—ever since she'd left her message ranting about Emily, but B.J. always spoke to her each week. Boone tried his best to be out of the room, but today his evasion was clearly impossible. He took the phone and tried to inject an upbeat note into his greeting. "How are you, Jodie?"

"Doing well enough," she said, but there was an angry edge to her voice that belied the statement.

"How's Frank?" Boone asked, hoping to drag out the pleasantries as long as possible.

"Playing more golf than any human being needs to play," she said. "Boone, there are things on my mind, as I'm sure you know."

"I listened to your messages," he confirmed. The last one had been left the night before. She'd apparently heard about Emily's most recent visit and the school shopping trip and found both objectionable.

"Then would you care to explain why you didn't have the courtesy to call me back?"

"Because I had nothing to say you were likely to want to hear," he admitted candidly. "Jodie, you don't have a say in whether Emily's back in my life or not."

"I most certainly do," she retorted with a huff. "If you intend to bring her around my grandson, then I definitely have something to say. Maybe we can start with how B.J. managed to cut himself so badly he needed stitches while he was in her care. What kind of reckless person allows that to happen? She's obviously not responsible enough to be left in charge of a boy."

Boone wondered how she'd found out about Emily's involvement in that incident, but that was hardly the point. He drew in a deep breath and prayed for patience.

"You know how it is around here after a storm," he replied. "There were boards with nails all over the place. B.J. never slows down, no matter how many times he's told to be careful. It was an accident, and he's perfectly fine."

"He had to have stitches, Boone. That is not fine in my book."

"Then let's just say the stitches are out," he replied. "There were no complications. We can leave it at that."

"Is he going to have a scar?"

"A very minor one," Boone admitted, then added, "Much to his disappointment." He tried for a more soothing tone, knowing she was truly worried about her grandson. "Jodie, I promise you he's fine."

She wasn't placated. "But it happened when he was with *that* woman. And then you go and take her along on a school shopping trip. What is wrong with you? Does she have some sort of bizarre hold on you?"

"Jodie, this conversation isn't productive."

She heaved a heavy, put-upon sigh. "Boone, I simply don't understand how you could be that inconsiderate of our feelings and that disrespectful of Jenny's memory."

"Excuse me?" Boone said, his temper finally stirring, which was never good when dealing with his in-laws. Trying to be mindful of their importance in B.J.'s life while ignoring their disapproval of every choice he made was a tightwire act.

Jodie was either oblivious to his annoyance or didn't care. She kept right on going. "You heard me. What is that woman doing back in Sand Castle Bay, anyway? Did she hear that Jenny's gone and come back for you?"

Boone was trying his best to make allowances for her grief, but she was getting pretty darn close to crossing a line. "Jodie, you need to stop this," he said quietly.

His warning fell on deaf ears.

"Why would you allow Jenny's son to be around her?" she asked, her voice catching. "That's completely inappropriate and you know it."

"There's nothing inappropriate about B.J. getting to know an old friend of mine," Boone replied. "Emily came back here to help Cora Jane after the hurricane. She and I hadn't been in touch in years. When she got here, she assumed I was married."

"She must have been thrilled to learn otherwise," Jodie said sourly, not convinced that Emily wasn't plotting to grab him.

"Actually she was very sorry to hear about Jenny. And she's been wonderfully supportive with B.J. about his mom. He's able to talk to her about Jenny in ways he hasn't with me."

"I don't believe that for a minute. I know how those West Coast women operate."

From reading too many tabloids, he suspected. "Emily's from North Carolina, Jodie."

"Well, she doesn't live here now, does she? I'm sure she's just like all those women who jump in and out of beds whenever the mood strikes them."

"Jodie," he said harshly, "we're not going to continue this conversation if you're going to make ridiculous judgments about a woman you don't even know."

"I know her type," she said, not relenting. "She probably couldn't wait to get her clutches into B.J., either."

Boone was growing tired of the whole topic, but he kept trying to get through to her. He knew his life would be a whole lot easier if the two of them could manage to get along. It would be best for B.J., too, not to have his father and his grandparents feuding.

"Jodie, you know how B.J. loves Cora Jane. Of course he and Emily were bound to cross paths. Don't make a big deal out of it."

"Well, it is a big deal. What do you think Jenny would have to say about your old girlfriend getting close to her son?"

"I think she'd be more open-minded than you're being," he said candidly. "I think she'd be pleased that he has someone he's comfortable talking to about his mom."

"Why is it he can't talk to you? Does it make you feel too guilty when Jenny's brought up?"

"No, it makes me very sad, the same way it reminds you of your loss. B.J.'s picked up on that." He bit back a sigh. "Look, I really don't want to fight with you, but you need to keep in mind that B.J. is my son, too. I'm the one here raising him. It's not something I would have chosen to do alone, but this is the way it is."

"So my feelings don't count?"

"Not when you're being unreasonable," he said, trying to keep his tone gentle. "B.J. loves you, Jodie. I want you and Frank to play an important role in his life, but I won't let you question my decisions, especially when you're not around."

"Fine," she said tightly. "Then I guess we'll just have to make a trip up there next week. I want to see what's going on with my own eyes."

Boone bit back his annoyance. Out of respect for Jenny, he didn't want to make this visit any more awkward than it was destined to be. "B.J. will be thrilled to see you," he said. "Let me know what day you're coming. Will you stay with us?"

"If you're sure we won't be in the way," she said, not even trying to keep the sarcasm out of her voice.

"You're family," Boone forced himself to say. "You're always welcome."

He just prayed that his open-door policy with his in-laws wouldn't turn out to be a huge mistake.

"I'll bet you're glad I'm out of town, after all," Emily said when Boone told her about Jodie's impending arrival. Heaven knows, *she* was glad not to be there.

"I won't lie to you, it'll make things easier," he said. "I know this is about her missing Jenny and blaming me for everything from ruining her life to her death, but one of these days I'm going to snap and say some things that will cause an irreparable rift. I came awfully close to doing just that today. The only thing stopping me was remembering what's best for my son."

"You're too kind to do that, anyway," Emily said. "You might be thoroughly and justifiably exasperated with Jodie, but you'd never intentionally hurt her."

"Even I have my limits," he contradicted. "If it weren't for B.J., I'd have spoken my mind long before now. With my parents off going their separate ways all over the world, I want him to have at least one set of grandparents in his life. Frankly, though, Cora Jane fits that role better than the whole lot of them combined. Not that Frank is so bad, but he won't go against Jodie."

Emily chuckled. "Well, Cora Jane is the ultimate grandmother," she confirmed. "Quick with the cookies and hugs. Of course, that comes with a fair amount of unsolicited advice."

"Maybe so, but the advice is usually right on target," he said. "And it doesn't disparage everything I do."

"And what does she say about this upcoming visit from the Farmers?"

"To watch my step," he said with a sigh.

Emily didn't like the sound of that. "Any idea why she'd say something like that?"

"I think she's concerned that Jodie might do something completely irrational and try to make trouble for me," Boone said. "I really don't think it'll come to that, though."

"Boone, you need to pay attention to Grandmother," Emily said. "She's got really good instincts about this sort of thing. What sort of trouble is she picturing? Did she say? Is she talking about the whole custody thing?"

Boone didn't answer immediately, which sent a chill down her spine. "More than likely," he said eventually.

"No!" Emily protested, aware of the toll such a fight would take on Boone and B.J. and on her relationship with Boone, as well. "There's no way she could do something like that."

"Of course she could," Boone said. "I told you that she threatened it before, right after Jenny died, but Frank put a stop to it then. I think that's why he pushed for the move to Florida, to put some distance between us, in the hope that things would settle down. It's the only time he's drawn a line against her behavior, but if she's really insistent, I doubt he can stop her."

"No court would take that boy from you," Emily said with feeling. "You're an amazing father and B.J. adores you. If she tries something that crazy, she'll lose for sure. B.J. won't forgive her for trying, either."

"I'm just praying it never comes to that," Boone said. "I'm going to do my best to keep the peace while she's here."

"Will she do her part?"

"Doubtful," he said wryly. "But it takes two to have a real fight, and I'm determined not to give her any ammunition."

"You mean you don't plan to tell her all about me and how we spent my last day in town?" she teased, hoping to lighten the mood.

Boone chuckled, as she'd intended. "That is definitely not going to come up," he assured her. "And I do have a weapon in my arsenal, if Jodie gets too far out of line."

"What weapon is that?"

"Cora Jane. She is very eager to take her on, not just to defend you, but she seems to be pretty provoked over the way Jodie's been treating me."

"I imagine she is," Emily said. "Nobody picks on Cora Jane's family and gets away with it. I saw her stand toe-to-toe with some bully who towered over her to get him to stop bothering Gabi one time when Gabi was waiting tables. Grandmother threw him out of Castle's without a qualm. I imagine she'd consider Jodie Farmer nothing but a nuisance."

"I certainly keep trying to think of her that way," Boone said, "but that woman can get under my skin quicker than poison ivy."

"Then I recommend you keep a giant bottle of calamine lotion handy," Emily teased.

"I was thinking bourbon," Boone replied.

To Emily, it didn't sound as if he was kidding.

Boone was in his office at the restaurant when Pete came in to announce that Jodie and Frank were out front.

"You all having some kind of a problem?" Pete asked. "When Jodie asked for you, she looked as if she'd just sucked a lemon."

Boone laughed. "The mere mention of my name does tend to turn her stomach sour," he told Pete. "I'd better get out there. Did you seat them?"

"They told me in no uncertain terms that they'd already eaten. I got the impression that they were a little leery of our food. They're standing by the front door, probably scaring off the other customers."

Boone walked quickly to the foyer and found his in-laws were indeed right by the door, looking as if they might flee at any second.

"Jodie, Frank," he said, being determinedly cheerful. He dropped a quick kiss on Jodie's cheek before she could jerk away, then shook Frank's hand. "How was the trip?"

"Long," Frank said. "Jodie insisted we do the whole drive in a day. She was anxious to get up here."

Boone frowned. "You left this morning? What time? You must be exhausted."

"Too early, in my opinion," Frank said. "I thought the whole reason for people to retire was so they could lead a leisurely life, but Jodie gets a bit in her mouth and we're off to the races."

"I'm anxious to see my grandson," she said. "I want to see for myself that he's not maimed for life."

Boone glanced at his watch. "He'll be home from school in an hour. Why don't we go to the house and get you settled? You might even be able to put your feet up for a few minutes before he gets there."

"You could just give us a key," Jodie said stiffly. "We don't want to take you away from your work."

"It's not a problem," Boone said, knowing that what she really wanted was a chance to snoop around the house. "The guest room's all set, but I want to be there in case there's anything you need to feel comfortable."

"We'll meet you there, then," Frank said, his tone jovial.

When Jodie set off for their car without a backward glance, Frank stayed back.

"I'm sorry about this, son. Jodie gets her mind set, and there's not a thing I can do or say to change it. It's best just to let her get all this out of her system. Once she spends a little time with B.J., I imagine she'll settle down."

Boone nodded. "I appreciate you saying that, Frank. I know Jenny's death has been real hard on her."

"It's been pure hell for all of us," Frank said. "But Jodie most of all, I think."

"B.J. and I miss her, too," Boone said. "More than you can imagine."

"I know." Frank gave him an awkward pat on the shoulder. "See you at the house."

An hour later B.J. raced into the house and jumped onto the sofa between his grandparents, giving them both big hugs. Jodie's eyes immediately filled with tears.

"Do you know how much you remind me of your mommy?" she said, her voice a whisper. "You have her eyes, her hair."

B.J. frowned. "But everybody says I look just like Daddy did when he was my age."

Frank stepped in. "You've inherited the good looks of both of them, B.J.," he said diplomatically. "Isn't that right, Jodie?"

"Of course it is," she said with an obviously forced smile. "Now tell me everything you're doing these days. How's school so far this year?"

Boone listened as B.J. filled her in on every kid in his class, on all his assignments and the part he'd been given for an upcoming school play. "It's for Halloween and I'm going to be a ghost," he said.

"Do you have your costume?" Jodie asked.

"Not yet. I have to get it made."

"Why don't I do that?" Jodie offered. "I used to make all of your mom's Halloween costumes."

B.J.'s eyes lit up. "Cool. Will you be here to see the play?"

"I doubt that," Jodie said. "Halloween's a long way off. Your grandfather and I will go back to Florida before then."

"But you could come back," B.J. said enthusiastically. "I asked Emily to come and she said she might."

The light in Jodie's eyes died at that, and Boone cursed himself for not suggesting to B.J. that he try to keep Emily's name out of the conversation. Then, again, he didn't think it was right to censor his son just to keep the peace.

"Is that so?" Jodie said tightly. "I think I'll go lie down for a little while before dinner. I'm awfully tired all of a sudden."

She stood up and left the room, leaving B.J. staring after her in confusion.

"Did I say something wrong?"

"Of course not," Frank told him. "But I'd better go check on her. I'll take her a cup of tea, if that's okay."

"Help yourself," Boone told him. "You know where everything is."

When he was alone with his son, B.J. regarded him with a troubled expression. "I made her mad, didn't I?"

"Absolutely not," Boone said, wondering just how much he should reveal about the situation. The less said, the better, he thought. B.J. could hardly be expected to understand the dynamics among the grown-ups. "You know how much your grandmother loves you, right?"

"Sure."

"And she loved your mom, too."

"Well, yeah," B.J. said.

"I think it's hard for her to hear you mention Emily as if she's real important to you. It may make her think you're forgetting about your mom."

"But I could never forget mom," B.J. said, looking puzzled. "I miss her every day."

"Then you should mention that to your grandmother sometime. It might make her feel better."

B.J. fell silent, clearly trying to take in what Boone had told him. "Okay," he said eventually. "Should I go tell her now?"

"No, let her rest now. You'll have plenty of time to tell her while she's here visiting."

"It's cool that they came, isn't it?" B.J. said, though his eyes were shadowed with worry over the apparent misstep he'd made.

"It's cool," Boone said. "They love you very much. I might know what a pest you are, but they think you're the best kid ever."

"Hey," B.J. protested, grinning, "I *am* the best kid ever."

Boone chuckled at his son's confidence. He figured he must be doing something right if his boy had that much faith in himself. Didn't that prove that B.J. was surrounded by people who encouraged and loved him? If it hadn't been tempting fate, he'd have dared Jodie right then to try to suggest otherwise.

Cora Jane was in a booth, her feet up, going over the day's receipts, when Boone came into Castle's.

"Uh-oh, I know that look," she said as he poured himself a glass of iced tea before joining her. "What's happened?"

"Nothing really," he admitted. "I'm just afraid I'm not going to get Jodie back out of town before I lose it with her attitude toward me. She never misses an opportunity to take a jab about all the wrongs I committed against Jenny. She's gotten in a couple of jabs at Emily, too, though, to give her credit, she's been careful about those in front of B.J. I think she's figured out that I wasn't lying when I told her there's a growing bond between B.J. and Emily. She doesn't like it, but she's smart enough not to take it on with him. She reserves that for veiled comments to me."

"You knew it was going to be like this," Cora Jane reminded him. "I give you credit, though, for inviting her and Frank to stay with you. If it had been me under these circumstances, I'd have sent them to a hotel. No way would I let them stay under my roof and pick away at everything I do."

"You talk tough," Boone accused, "but I know better. You'd have put B.J. first, the same way I did."

"What's Frank doing while Jodie's trying to stir up trouble?"

"Apologizing for her," Boone said. "And trying to keep B.J. out of it. They've gone fishing every afternoon this week. He even took him to the driving range to hit golf balls one day and to play miniature golf the other evening after dinner."

Cora Jane nodded approvingly. "Frank always was a sensible man. He knows the relationship with his grandson will be forever damaged if Jodie keeps up this nonsense."

"He's said as much to me," Boone acknowledged. He gave Cora Jane a frustrated look. "I know the woman is grieving. I know she'll always be convinced I wasn't right for Jenny. I am trying to make allowances for all that."

"But she keeps pushing," Cora Jane guessed. "Why don't you bring 'em over to my house for dinner tonight? I'll put a bug in her ear. Maybe she'll listen to me."

Boone immediately shook his head. "She'd consider

that consorting with the enemy. Anything remotely tied to Emily sets her off these days. B.J. makes these innocent comments about Emily that send her straight to her room with a headache. It's happened enough that he's finally figured out it's better not to mention Emily at all. Instead, he doesn't say much to Jodie at all for fear of upsetting her. I don't think she has any idea how she's pushing him away, which is exactly the opposite of what she wants, of course."

"That's a crying shame," Cora Jane said, wishing she could shake some sense into Jodie before she lost her grandson, the only real tie she had left to the daughter she'd lost. "I feel sorry for her."

"So do I," Boone said, then finished his last swallow of tea. "Thanks for listening to me vent."

Cora Jane smiled at him. "You're welcome here anytime to tell me anything that's on your mind."

"Thanks," he said, dropping a kiss on her cheek. "Everything okay at the restaurant?"

"We're back to operating at full capacity. I thought after Labor Day, the crowds would die back some, but it hasn't happened. All the people who don't like the crowded summers come now." She grinned. "Because of that, it ends up being just as crowded. Sure is good for business, though, to have the season extended through fall."

"It's the same at my place. Tommy was able to finish our renovations last week and we're booked solid for the next few weekends, and a few week nights, too."

"You and Emily been in touch?" she asked, throwing the question in casually.

He grinned. "Every day."

"Good."

He looked at her with surprise. "That's it? No more probing questions, subtle suggestions?"

Cora Jane laughed. "Not a one. You'll hear from me, though, if I think things are getting off track."

"I'm sure," Boone said dryly. "I suppose I should head over to the school to get B.J. He was practicing for the Halloween play this afternoon. It's been a few days since I've been able to have any quality time with him alone."

"Give him a hug for me," Cora Jane said. "And Boone?"

"Yes."

"The Farmers aren't the only family you and B.J. have," she reminded him.

She thought she saw some of the tension in his shoulders ease at her words.

"You have no idea how much I count on that," he said.

She grinned at him. "Doesn't need to be legal to be real," she told him. "But I sure am hoping that one of these days it will be."

"If that is your gentle way of nudging me into marrying your granddaughter, I think you can rest easy on that score. I think we're heading in that direction."

"How soon?" Cora Jane demanded eagerly, all pretense of disinterest vanishing.

Boone laughed. "When we're ready," he said. "And no amount of meddling from you will make it happen one minute sooner."

"Duly noted," she replied. "But don't think that'll stop me if I think you two are taking too long."

"Never doubted that for a minute," he said.

Cora Jane watched him leave, then allowed herself

a full-blown satisfied smile. Things were progressing very nicely, indeed. Now she just had to find some way to make sure that Jodie Farmer didn't get in the way.

18

Emily was standing in the middle of the construction chaos at the safe house, trying to convince the foreman that the deadline for completion wasn't a joke, when her cell phone rang.

"Excuse me," she told him. "I have to take this. Look over your schedule and see what you can do to meet that deadline. There are women with kids who need to be in here before Thanksgiving. Do you really want to tell them they'll have no roof over their heads for the holiday?"

Andy Crawford gave her a hard look, then walked away shaking his head.

"Gabi, hey," Emily said. "Sorry to take so long, but I was in the middle of something. How's everything in the world of public relations?"

"Insane," Gabi said. "But I called to check on you."

"Why?"

"You don't seem to be back in Sand Castle Bay yet. I thought you and Boone were working things out, but it's been a while since you've shown your face. And, yes, you can thank Grandmother for passing along that tidbit of information. She's getting anxious, and I'm supposed to ferret out the information she wants."

Emily explained about the deadline pressure on the safe house. "Plus Boone's in-laws are there raising a ruckus about him letting me anywhere near B.J. I figured it's best for me to lay low until they go back to Florida."

"It might be better for them to spend some time with you so they can conclude you're not the devil," Gabi suggested.

"I doubt I have enough charm to pull that off," Emily said candidly. "Given how they treat Boone, I'm more likely to say the wrong thing and cause even more trouble."

"When are they going home?" Gabi asked.

"That seems to be the question of the year," Emily admitted. "They haven't given Boone a date. It's making him a little crazy. Having them underfoot isn't easy, but he feels he owes it to B.J. to make an effort."

"Well, whatever you do, don't let them keep you away indefinitely," Gabi advised. "If they realize their presence has chased you off, they might never go back to Florida."

"That is not going to happen," Emily insisted. "Not that I intend to admit this to Boone, but in a way, it's been a relief to have the extra time here. The deadline on this renovation is a killer. If I take off, it's going to be a lot harder to convince all the people working on the project that the deadline is written in stone."

"I'm just saying, don't let the Farmers ruin this for the two of you," Gabi said.

"We won't. Now tell me about you. Everything okay at work?"

"Same old craziness," Gabi said.

"And your guy?"

Emily thought she detected a faint hesitation before Gabi finally said, "Paul's okay."

"Gabi, is something wrong? Have you broken up? Was he upset about you being gone so long?"

"No, nothing like that," Gabi said.

Despite her sister's reassurances, Emily didn't like the way she sounded. "Gabriella, what aren't you saying?"

Gabi laughed, though it sounded forced. "You only use my whole name when you're annoyed with me, just like Mom."

"It always got answers for her, so I thought I'd try it," Emily admitted.

"There are no answers," Gabi insisted. "Not even any questions. I guess I'm just a little down. I miss being with you and Samantha."

"It was fun being together again," Emily agreed. "Like old times."

"But in other ways I realized you can't go back again," Gabi said, a mournful note in her voice. "We're adults now, with all the complications that go with that."

"Gabi," Emily began, determined to get to the bottom of her sister's odd mood.

"Gotta run, sweetie. Take care. We'll talk again soon."

Before Emily could protest, Gabi had hung up. "What on earth?" Emily murmured, staring at her phone. She was about to make a call to Samantha to see if she had any insights, but Andy Crawford was in front of her, his displeasure evident. She forced a smile.

"What have you worked out?" she asked.

"If I bring in a few guys on overtime for a couple of days, we can maybe pull this off," he said.

"Maybe's not good enough."

"Four days of overtime and I can guarantee it."

"Then four days it is."

He eyed her suspiciously. "You got the budget for that? I thought we were doing this on a shoestring."

"And out of the goodness of our hearts," she confirmed.

"I can't pay my men with a lot of holiday cheer," he groused.

"I'll see that they're paid," she promised. Even if it came out of her own pocket. "Want me to put it in writing?"

For an instant she thought Andy was going to pull out a pen and a scrap of paper, but then he shrugged. "Nah. I trust you."

She nudged him in the ribs. "Thanks so much for that ringing endorsement."

That finally drew a smile from him. "I've never seen you so worked up about a project before. You usually just roll with the punches and use a little smooth talk to pacify the clients."

"This job really matters, that's why," she explained. "Think about it, Andy. This could be the first time in who knows how long that some of these families have had a Thanksgiving meal without worrying about being slapped around or worse."

He blinked at her words, clearly shaken. An angry glint appeared in his eyes. "It's been that bad for them? I guess I didn't realize that. I mean I knew this is supposed to be a safe house, but for some reason it hadn't sunk in what that meant."

"Well, it has been that bad and that's why we're going to make this deadline, no matter what," she told him.

He nodded, clearly on board a hundred percent now. "With maybe a few days to spare," he promised. "Leave it to me."

She grinned. "I knew I could count on you."

He blushed furiously. "Well, just don't get any ideas about taking advantage of my good nature with any sob stories for your usual clients, you hear?"

Impulsively, she gave him a hug. "Wouldn't dream of it."

"Stop that," he grumbled. "You're messing with my tough image."

Emily chuckled as he walked off barking orders at his men, as if to contradict the scene some of them might have witnessed.

"This is going to work," she said to herself as he went. This place was going to be finished, and it was going to be beautiful and, far more important, a place where at least a few more battered women would be safe from harm.

Boone walked into his house after work and found a pile of luggage in the foyer and Jodie and Frank waiting for him in the living room. They were side by side on the sofa, clearly anxious to make some sort of announcement.

"You're leaving?" he asked, working hard to hide his elation.

"Not exactly," Frank said, casting a resigned look at his wife.

"We've leased a house for the winter," Jodie said. "We want to be here for B.J.'s school play and for the holidays. In the spring we'll decide if we want to come back permanently."

"I see," Boone said, his spirits sinking. "Where's the house?"

"Just a few blocks away. B.J. will be able to come to our house after school now," Jodie said, a triumphant note in her voice. "You won't have to worry about where he is or what he's doing."

"I haven't been worried about it," Boone said tightly. "He comes to the restaurant with me some afternoons, goes home with his friends some of the time, and is involved in after-school activities a couple of times a week. I don't see that pattern changing."

Jodie frowned at his response. "You intend to keep him from spending time with us?"

"Of course not. It just won't always be right after school," he responded, determined to keep control of his son's activities and whereabouts.

"How can you be so inconsiderate and ungrateful?" she demanded. "After we did this to help you out?"

"If you were really doing it to help me out, you'd have discussed it with me first," Boone replied mildly. "Don't get me wrong, Jodie. B.J. will love having you here through the holidays. It's great that you're going to stick around. We'll just have to work out the details about when he's going to spend time with you. Even at his age, he has things he's committed to doing, things he enjoys."

Of course, they all knew that the real goal was to ensure that none of those things involved time with Emily. And with this plan in place, there was little chance they wouldn't cross paths with Emily and find an opportunity to make things more difficult for her and Boone.

Still, in an attempt to pacify them, he said, "As soon as you get settled in the rental, we'll sit down and work out a schedule of times you can have with B.J. Since things come up, we'll probably have to do it on a week-by-week basis."

Jodie opened her mouth to argue, but Frank put a hand on her arm. "That'll be great, Boone. Come on, Jodie. We'd better take our things over to the new place and get settled. Since we didn't come prepared for a long stay, we're going to need to spend a little time shopping for warmer clothes than we brought, too."

"Don't forget you left a few boxes of winter things here just in case you came back up here this time of year," Boone reminded him. "They're in the garage."

For an instant Jodie's eyes lit up. "That's right, we did do that. Frank, put those boxes in the car right now. I'd like to have another word with Boone."

"Jodie, now's not the time," Frank said, his expression distressed.

"There's never going to be a good time," she argued. "I might as well get this out there now."

Frank looked as if he wanted to argue, then shrugged and gave Boone an apologetic look before heading out to load up the car.

"What is it, Jodie?" Boone asked, his stomach in knots and his antenna on full alert.

"You should know that if we don't like how things look the next few months, Frank and I are considering legal action," she announced.

"So, that's what this is really about," Boone said flatly. "You want custody of B.J., and you intend to snoop around looking for excuses to file for it, is that it?"

She nodded, not even bothering with a phony attempt to deny it. "I think it's what Jenny would want," she said piously.

He gave her a pitying look. "Then you didn't know Jenny at all," he said quietly. "Jenny would want our son to be right here with me. She would want you to play an important role in his life, which is what I've been trying my best to allow."

He held her gaze. "But if you insist on making threats like this, I will keep you away from him, Jodie. And I'll happily go to court to make that nice and legal, too. I doubt your threats to rip him away from his only remaining parent just because you're being spiteful will sit well with a judge, not when it's balanced against my efforts to make sure his grandparents remained in his life."

She blinked at his quiet resolve. Apparently she'd expected a different reaction, perhaps an explosive one she could use against him. Tears welled up in her eyes.

"I can't lose that boy, Boone. He's all that's left of Jenny," she whispered brokenly.

"Neither of us needs to lose him, Jodie," he said more gently. "It's up to you how ugly this gets."

She stood up shakily and started for the door. Boone followed. He saw then just how much she'd aged since Jenny's death and for the first time really understood the toll that death had taken on her. It allowed him to feel sorry for her, rather than focusing on his anger over her threat.

Outside, he touched her shoulder. She glanced up at him.

"What?" she asked.

"I loved her, too," he said softly. "No matter what you think, I did, and I tried to make sure every day I had her that she knew that." He knew he'd failed some days, but it was never for want of commitment.

Jodie merely nodded. When she was in the car, Frank glanced over at her, then back at Boone. He lifted his hand in a wave.

"Talk to you soon," he called out.

"If you need any help over at the new place, let me know," Boone said.

Frank nodded, then pulled out of the driveway.

Boone watched them go, wishing he could breathe a sigh of relief, but something told him there were plenty of problems ahead. First on the list was how on earth he was going to tell Emily about their decision to stay in town.

"Oh, boy," Emily said when Boone informed her that the Farmers intended to stick around for a few months. "How's that going to work, for you and me, I mean? Am I banished?"

"Absolutely not," he said at once.

"Then what? You want to rub their noses in our relationship? That's a surefire way to make trouble for yourself."

"I was thinking once they got to know you, they'd see that you're not a threat."

"Oh, you wonderful, sweet man! You're as naive as Gabi," she said. "She said the same thing, that I should show them I'm not the devil."

"Exactly," Boone said.

"But I *am* a threat to life as they knew it," she said.

"But life as they knew it is no more," he argued. "Jenny's gone. That can't be changed."

"No, but right now there's no other woman in her

place. Jodie can think of herself as the most important woman in B.J.'s life, stepping in for her daughter. Maybe she'd be able to accept some other woman in that role eventually, but me? Not a chance, at least if what you've told me about her disapproval of our past is true."

"Oh, it's true," he admitted with obvious reluctance. "I'm not going to let them ruin this for us, Em. We'll all have to find a way to coexist. And I think the sooner we do, the better."

"Meaning?"

"B.J. wants you here for his Halloween play. I think you should come."

"That's next week," she said, trying to envision how she could juggle her schedule to make it work. She owed it to Boone to try. To B.J., too.

"Can you do it?" he pressed. "Maybe I can keep the peace by offering them a chance to keep B.J. over the weekend and you and I can have some time alone."

Emily laughed. "There's that optimism I love. You're using B.J. as a consolation prize."

"No, I'm not," he protested. "We'll all be getting exactly what we want. It's a win-win."

"And you don't think Jodie will store that away as fodder for her suit if she ever files one against you? She'll tell the court you couldn't wait to get rid of your son so you could spend time with me."

Boone sighed. "I see your point. Okay, no sleepovers for B.J. or for you and me, while you're here," he said, sounding resigned. "Please, Em, come anyway. I need to see you. I need to remind myself that what we have is worth fighting for."

She heard the frustration in his voice and knew she

needed to find a way to be there, if only to be supportive. "Let me see what I can work out."

"But you will find a way?" he pressed.

"I will find a way," she assured him. "But I am going
to expect one very big reward, even if we have to hide
in the walk-in freezer at Castle's."

Boone finally chuckled. "I'll keep you warm."

"Never doubted that for a second," she said. "I'll have
my schedule by the time we talk tomorrow."

"Love you."

"I love you, too," she said, even though there were
times, especially lately, when she was having more and
more trouble figuring out if love was nearly enough to
make their complicated relationship work, especially
with one person so intent on sabotaging it.

B.J. was bouncing up and down with excitement.
"Grandma Jodie, are you sure I really look like a ghost?"

She chuckled. "You're the most impressive, scary
ghost I've ever seen," she assured him. "Don't you think
so, Frank?"

"Absolutely," Frank confirmed.

"Have you thanked Grandma Jodie for making the
costume?" Boone asked. "And for helping out with the
others for some of your classmates?" He had to give
Jodie credit. She had pitched in to make the play a success by taking on a task that too many mothers hadn't
had time for.

"Thanks, Grandma Jodie," B.J. said dutifully. "Mrs.
Barnes said thanks, too. I gotta go. She's waving for us
to take our places. I'll see you after, right?"

"Yes, and we're all going out to celebrate," Boone

reminded him. "Keep your costume on. We're going to take lots and lots of pictures."

He hadn't told him or anyone else about Emily joining them. Maybe that was a mistake, but he figured a surprise was the only way he was going to pull this off without a major upheaval. He was praying that B.J.'s presence would keep Jodie from doing or saying anything crazy.

Back in the auditorium, he spotted Cora Jane and Emily saving them seats on the aisle. "There are three seats over there," he told Jodie, steering them across the room.

When Jodie spotted Cora Jane, she obviously guessed the identity of the woman beside her. She froze in place.

"Absolutely not," she said, scowling at Boone. "How could you ruin this night for me?"

"Tonight isn't about you," Boone reminded her. "It's about B.J., and he wanted Emily and Cora Jane to be here. He wants you and Frank here, too. Can we all manage to get along for his sake for just this one night?"

"Of course we can," Frank said, casting a warning look at his wife. "I, for one, do not intend to miss my grandson's play for any reason. Jodie?"

She sucked in a deep breath and followed him into the row of seats, placing herself as far from Emily as possible. Boone sat between Frank and Emily. His father-in-law leaned forward.

"Nice to see you, Cora Jane," he said. "It's been a long time."

"It has been," she replied. "Jodie, you're looking good."

Jodie remained stonily silent.

"I don't think you've met my granddaughter, Emily," Cora Jane continued as if nothing was amiss.

Frank nodded an acknowledgment of the introduction. Jodie stared straight ahead.

Boone glanced at Emily. "You okay?"

"Sure, but that deep freeze at Castle's is sounding better and better. It has to be warmer than here."

"It's going to get better," Boone said with a confidence he was far from feeling. "Whatever her feelings about you and me, Jodie won't spoil this for B.J. I'm counting on that."

"I'll do my part," she promised.

The lights went down then and the play began. Despite the scary, taped music, there were more laughs than terror generated by the performances. B.J. played the best ghost ever, in Boone's opinion. Pictures were snapped every few seconds with cell phones around the auditorium. Even Jodie got into the spirit of things and took a few when B.J. was onstage.

The audience applauded loudly at the end, giving the kids a standing ovation, despite the chuckles none of them could hide.

"I don't suppose it was meant to be a comedy," Frank said, unable to hide the mirth in his eyes.

"Frank, stop that," Jodie chided. "They're just children. I thought they were wonderful. I can't wait to post some of these adorable pictures online so our friends in Florida can see them."

"I agree with you about them being wonderful," Emily said. "And B.J. looked fantastic. Mrs. Farmer, I understand you made his costume."

Jodie looked nonplussed at being addressed directly, but she managed to utter a tight, "I did. Thank you."

"Well, let's get our budding star and head over to the restaurant," Boone said, being determinedly jovial. "I've reserved one of the private rooms for our party."

Jodie immediately shook her head, but Frank said, "We're not going to miss this, Jodie. We can't disappoint B.J. And you know you're going to want our pictures taken with him wearing his costume."

She looked as if she might argue, then backed down. "No, you're right."

Frank gave her an approving look. "We'll meet you there," he told Boone.

Emily gave Boone's hand a squeeze. "I'll ride over with Grandmother."

Boone was tempted to tell her to come with him, but it made sense for her to accompany Cora Jane. "See you there, then."

So far, the evening had gone according to plan. There had been no bloodshed. The combatants had been civil. It gave him hope that the party would go off just as well, especially if everybody there focused on B.J. and making it the perfect night for him.

And there, he thought dryly, was some of that optimism Emily seemed to think was going to be his downfall.

19

B.J. was wired up on too much excitement, probably combined with too much soda, Emily concluded as he tore around the private dining room at Boone's Harbor with a couple of his cast mates who'd been invited to join the party. She had a hunch the outsiders were part of Boone's plan to keep Jodie in line. His mother-in-law would never misbehave and air personal family feuds around strangers.

"At least she's being civil," Cora Jane acknowledged from her seat beside Emily. "I was ready to pop her one if she tried to take you on."

Emily smiled at her grandmother's feisty comment. "I really don't think popping her one would help my case," she said. "Civility is the goal for now."

"Maybe I should spend a little time chatting with Frank," Cora Jane suggested. "He's a reasonable man."

Emily shook her head. "Stay out of it, Grandmother. Boone needs to handle this. One wrong word and things could go terribly wrong. Who knows what might trigger an overreaction from Jodie? The last thing we want is to put B.J. through some ugly custody battle."

Cora Jane sighed and sat back. "You're right, of course."

Just then B.J. came bouncing up to them. "Ms. Cora Jane, did you like the play?"

"I thought the play was excellent," she told him. "And you didn't miss a single line. I was very proud of you."

B.J. grinned broadly. "Did you like it, Emily?" he asked, leaning into her side.

Instinctively, Emily put her arm around him to give him a squeeze. "You bet I did. I'm so glad I was able to come back to see it."

"And, guess what?" B.J. said excitedly. "I'm going to be in the Christmas pageant, too." He looked at her worriedly. "You won't miss that, will you?"

"Absolutely not," Emily assured him, though even as the words came out of her mouth, she wondered if she shouldn't have been more cautious. She had a lot of small jobs lined up with regular clients to help them ready their homes for the holidays. That work often took her right up to Christmas Eve. Still, B.J. was clearly satisfied with her answer, so why spoil tonight by casting doubt on her own promise?

"See you later," B.J. said. He started to run off, then came back and gave Emily a fierce hug.

After he'd gone, she noticed that Jodie had her gaze peeled on B.J., which meant that more than likely she'd witnessed the entire scene. From the tight expression on her face, she clearly disapproved. She headed in Emily's direction.

"Uh-oh," Cora Jane murmured. "Red alert!"

Emily chuckled, despite the impending confrontation. "Leave her to me, okay? Why don't you check the desserts on the buffet table? Bring us back the most decadent things they have over there, preferably with chocolate. Something tells me we're going to need it."

Cora Jane looked uneasy. "And leave you alone with Jodie?" she asked worriedly. "Is that a good idea? I could keep my mouth shut. At least you'd have a witness, if she gets out of line."

"It'll be okay," Emily assured her. "Please, Grandmother. She and I need to settle things."

When Jodie reached her, Emily gestured to a chair, determined to be on her best behavior. Killing the woman with kindness was her mantra for the night. "Have a seat," she said graciously. "I'm so anxious to get to know you better. I know how happy it's made B.J. having you back home again."

"Why do you care?" Jodie said, ignoring the olive branch. "You won't be around long."

Emily frowned at the confidence in her voice. "Why is that?"

"Because if you persist in this effort to get your clutches into my grandson, I will go to court," she said as mildly as if she were talking about the weather. The threat was all the more potent because of her complete calm and her unwavering spite and determination.

Even though Emily didn't have a doubt in her mind that no court would take B.J. from Boone, she didn't want them to have to face the ordeal of a custody battle.

"Why would you do that, Mrs. Farmer? Do you really hate Boone that much? Or is all your anger directed at me? Or is it B.J.'s life you're hoping to ruin? I'm just trying to understand your motivation here."

"Oh, please. I wouldn't waste my energy on you or Boone. I'm trying to protect my grandson," Jodie responded with a huff of indignation. "Everything I do is for that boy."

"Really?" Emily asked skeptically. "What exactly is the threat you think I pose? You don't know me, though you do know my grandmother. I doubt there's a soul in this community who could find fault with her or her influence on B.J."

"Cora Jane's an upstanding woman," Jodie agreed grudgingly. "That has nothing to do with you. Because of you, my daughter was locked into a loveless marriage."

Though the accusation didn't come as a complete shock, Emily was surprised to hear it spoken aloud. "Loveless? I don't think so. Boone would never have married Jenny if he hadn't loved her. As you know perfectly well, they didn't have to get married. There was no unplanned pregnancy pushing them into making the decision to walk down the aisle. Clearly, getting married was something they both wanted."

"Maybe so," Jodie conceded, though she didn't look happy about it. "But his heart always belonged to you. Everyone around here knew that, including Jenny."

"And yet she loved him, anyway," Emily said.

Jodie waved off the reminder as if her daughter's feelings were of no consequence. "She was a foolish girl. She thought she could eventually make him love her. That's a terrible basis for marriage."

"I don't entirely disagree," Emily admitted, drawing a shocked look. "But it wasn't your decision to make, and I wasn't even in the picture. Until recently, Boone and I hadn't been in touch for ten years. Jenny and Boone were adults who made a decision that worked for them. And just so you know, I've never heard Boone express a single regret about having made it. If he has any regrets at all, it's because he lost Jenny too soon."

Jodie looked taken aback by her candor. "You actually believe he loved her?"

"I do," Emily said simply. She looked Jodie in the eyes, determined to find some way to give her a different perspective on the past, if not to reconcile her to Emily's inevitable future with Boone and her grandson. "May I ask you a question?"

Jodie shrugged.

"Did Jenny strike you as miserable after she and Boone married? Did she ever express any regrets?"

"She'd hardly say anything to me," Jodie said defensively. "She knew I was against the marriage."

"How about her father? Did she ever suggest such a thing to him?"

"Not that I know of," Jodie admitted with obvious reluctance.

"So, she never said anything to suggest she wasn't happy?" Emily pressed. "Not to you, not to Mr. Farmer, not to anyone you know?"

"No."

"Interesting," Emily said, hoping that if she gave her a minute Jodie would grasp her point. When she eventually did speak, she said, "My grandmother told me that Jenny positively glowed, especially after B.J. was born."

"That child was a blessing, no question about it," Jodie admitted. "I figured she got pregnant to keep Boone from leaving her."

Emily was startled that Jodie could think so little of her own daughter's intelligence or of her appeal to the man she'd married. "Do you honestly believe that the woman you'd raised would need to resort to that kind of trickery to keep her husband? The Jenny I knew was smart, kind and generous. She was worthy of Boone's love, and I doubt she'd have stayed with him if he hadn't made her happy."

Again, Jodie looked shaken by the straight talk that suggested she was blind to her own daughter's attributes. "No, she'd never have tried to trap Boone into staying, but..." Her voice trailed off.

"But what?"

"I guess I never looked at it quite like that."

"Because you were so locked into your own perceptions of what their marriage was like," Emily suggested. "Maybe you couldn't be objective about how real their feelings were. Outsiders seldom truly know what's going on inside a marriage."

"I can't believe you'd sit here and try to convince me that Boone loved my daughter so much," Jodie said, looking bemused.

"Why? It doesn't lessen his feelings for me now. When I left, I was totally unfair to him. I'm glad he found a woman like Jenny. He deserved to be happy. As for B.J., he's an incredible gift from your daughter. Maybe you should think of him that way, too, rather than looking at him as a pawn in your battle with Boone or with me."

Jodie gave her a long, hard look, then stood up and walked away without another word. After a moment with Frank, the two of them spoke to Boone and B.J., then left.

Boone immediately headed in Emily's direction, his expression filled with worry. He pulled a chair close and circled an arm around her shoulders. "I started to come over sooner, but it looked as if you had things under control. Everything okay?"

Emily leaned against him for a minute. "I hope so, but I don't know. She wasn't yelling when she left or making any more threats."

Boone frowned. "She started out with threats?"

"Nothing you haven't heard before, just the custody issue. I think she was hoping to scare me off. For all I know she'll consider my refusal to be scared as a sure-fire sign that I don't care about B.J.'s well-being."

"That's twisted," Boone said, then sighed. "And just like Jodie."

"I tried to put in a lot of good words for you," Emily told him. "I just about went hoarse from singing your praises and trying to get her to see your marriage to Jenny through her daughter's eyes, rather than her own."

Boone shook his head. "I'm sorry you got caught up in this. It's not up to you to heal my relationship with Jenny's parents."

"But it is up to me not to make it any worse." She looked into his eyes. "I hope I did okay. I don't want this to turn into all-out warfare or something. If it does, I'll step away, Boone. You won't lose your son because of me."

"I won't lose my son, period," he said firmly, then cupped her face in his hands and held her gaze. "And *you're* not going anywhere. Not ever again."

For several days after the Halloween play, Boone waited for any fallout from Emily's conversation with Jodie. Instead, he thought he detected the faintest thaw in his relationship with his mother-in-law. Frank certainly was no barometer because he continued to spend time with B.J. without a word of criticism for Boone or for his ties to Emily.

It was two weeks later, when he was trying to get by on a few late-night calls from the West Coast to keep his spirits up, that Jodie's new strategy surfaced.

Boone was driving B.J. over to visit with Cora Jane, when his son regarded him sorrowfully. "Grandma Jodie says I probably shouldn't count on Emily being around too much anymore," B.J. said. "She says Emily's so busy she'll probably forget all about me."

Boone had to take a deep breath to keep a check on his anger. "When did Grandma Jodie say that?"

"Yesterday," B.J. admitted.

So that explained B.J.'s dark mood the night before when he'd gone to bed early and told Boone he didn't want to hear a story or read from one of his favorite books.

"Is that the only time she's mentioned something like that?" Boone asked.

B.J. shook his head. "I didn't believe her at first, but Emily hasn't called me for a while now, so I figured Grandma Jodie must be right."

"You know Emily is really, really busy trying to get this house ready. She told you about that, right?"

"It's for some moms and little kids who need to be in a safe place," B.J. said. "She said it's really, really important."

"It is. Just think about how it would feel not to be in a safe place for Thanksgiving or any other day."

B.J. nodded his understanding. "It would be bad," he said.

"So if Emily hasn't called you as much, it's more than likely because she's working really hard to finish this work so these families will have a happy Thanksgiving. Can you understand that?"

B.J. nodded.

Boone made a decision. "Why don't we call her as soon as we get to Castle's? We can say hello and see how the house is coming along, okay?"

His son beamed at him. "Awesome."

"And would you like me to write down Emily's number, so you can call her anytime you're missing her?"

"Sure," B.J. said enthusiastically. "And I won't be a pest, I promise."

Boone grinned. "I'm counting on that." He cursed himself for not thinking of any of this sooner. He'd known how distracted Emily had been the past couple of weeks. He'd felt neglected himself, so it was understandable that B.J. would feel that way. It simply hadn't occurred to him that Jodie would be feeding into B.J.'s insecurities.

That was a problem he'd have to resolve at the very first opportunity.

Inside Castle's Boone sent B.J. in search of Cora Jane while he placed the call to Emily. Though she sounded harried when she answered, her mood brightened at the sound of his voice.

"Busy?" he asked.

"Crazy," she admitted. "But I can take a minute. How are you?"

He explained about B.J. and Jodie's spin on Emily's recent lack of attentiveness.

"Oh, sweet heaven," Emily murmured. "I should have realized."

"Realized what? That Jodie would seize on this

and run with it?" Boone said. "Nobody thinks like she does."

"Is B.J. there now?"

"He's with Cora Jane in the kitchen. I'll get him."

"I'll make this right, Boone. I promise."

"Never doubted it. Is it okay with you if I give him your number, so he can call when he starts to miss you? He's already promised me he won't be a pest."

"That's a great idea," she assured him. "And I'll always be able to find a couple of minutes to talk to him when he calls. I'll try to be better about calling him, as well."

"Thanks. I really appreciate that. He's very attached to you. So am I, by the way. Do you think you're going to be here for Thanksgiving?"

"That's my plan," she told him. "We're almost on schedule for the opening of this place on Monday. The families should be in here by Wednesday. Unless there's a glitch of some kind, I'll fly out Wednesday night and be there in time for Thanksgiving dinner. You will be at Cora Jane's, right?"

"We'll be there," he confirmed. "Though we'll probably have to stop by Jodie's first to keep the peace."

"Even if you only make it in time for pie, it'll be great," she told him.

"And miss Cora Jane's turkey and cornbread stuffing? Not a chance. She's planning a late dinner for that very reason."

Boone had walked into the kitchen as they talked and now B.J. was in front of him, his expression wary, as if he was half afraid Emily wouldn't have time to talk to him after all.

"Here he is," Boone told Emily. "See you next week."

"I'm counting on it," she said fervently.

Boone handed the phone to his son, then stepped away. Cora Jane gave him a quizzical look, but didn't ask the question that was obviously on the tip of her tongue. Unlike some people, she would never try to stir up trouble, especially in front of B.J. Boone had come to appreciate that trait more than he could possibly express.

Emily had been on her own for so long, not accountable to anyone except her clients, that the realization that she needed to consider Boone and B.J. caught her off guard. Once she'd hung up after speaking to the two of them, she sighed.

"Problems?" Sophia asked, joining her on the porch of the house. It was the only place quiet enough to talk on the phone, much less think.

"I've just realized how many adjustments I'm going to have to make if I'm going to have a relationship with someone."

"Someone in particular?" Sophia asked. "Maybe this man who has you running back to North Carolina every few weeks?"

Emily nodded.

"Tell me about him," Sophia suggested. "Is it serious?"

"It's been serious since we were teenagers," Emily admitted. "But I took off to make my way in the world and he stayed behind, got married and had a child."

Sophia lifted a brow. "And exactly how do you fit in now?"

Emily gave her a chiding look. "It's not like that. He's a widower, a single dad. Because of what happened before, he has a lot of trust issues about me actually making a commitment. He's also scared his son is going to get hurt if I bail again."

"Are you planning to bail?" Sophia asked.

"It's not my intention, but there are days when I wonder how we're going to pull this off, especially after a call like the one I just had."

"Was he on your case for not being around?"

"No, he does understand how much this project matters to me." She smiled at Sophia. "Thanks to you, I've finally found a way to combine work I love with something worthwhile. I've never felt this way about a job before."

"Something told me it was going to be a perfect fit," Sophia said. "You've always done an outstanding job for me and for everyone I've recommended you to, but I sensed there was something missing."

Emily frowned. "You didn't think I gave the work my all?"

"Oh, heavens no!" Sophia protested. "In case you haven't noticed, there seem to be two extremes out here, at least in the circle of people with whom I associate. There are those who are sincerely passionate about the work and those who are in it to make a quick buck. While I'd certainly never lump you in with the latter, you didn't have the sort of passion for the work that takes something from being a job to being something more. I like to be around people who can't wait to get out of bed to start the day. I wanted that for you, too."

Emily grasped what Sophia was telling her. "And you're right. I think I've found that now."

"But you think that's going to ruin your future with this man?" Sophia guessed.

"I hope not," Emily said, "but it does mean I need to consider people other than myself when I make decisions. B.J., that's Boone's son, started worrying that I'd forgotten about him. His grandmother, who's not a big fan of mine, started feeding that insecurity. So while I was here, all caught up in the job, I was inadvertently hurting that little boy. How selfish is that?"

Sophia smiled. "And now that you know about this, what do you intend to do? Go on ignoring him until it's convenient to make a call?"

"Absolutely not," Emily said.

"Then lesson learned," Sophia concluded. "Sweetie, it is not all that unusual for people who've only had to think of themselves to need a little time to get used to what's necessary when there are others in their life. Now that you've been reminded of that, you'll make every adjustment necessary. I have complete confidence in you."

"What if the adjustments or sacrifices are too great?" Emily asked, voicing her greatest fear.

Sophia's gaze was filled with compassion. "Then you'll have made a choice, won't you? You'll have chosen work over a relationship."

"But I don't want to be that woman," Emily complained. "I want it all."

Sophia laughed. "Then find a way," she said. "You're a smart woman."

"What about Boone?" she asked in frustration. "Do all the adjustments and sacrifices have to be mine?"

"Not in my book," Sophia said. "But then I lost a couple of husbands because of my refusal to compromise. I don't really recommend that, not if you're hoping that things will work out. There's always a middle ground, Emily. Find it."

Emily nodded, praying that her friend was right and that she and Boone could find a solution that worked for both of them. They certainly weren't there quite yet. Emily was starting to feel pulled in two different directions. And, she admitted, she was starting to resent Boone for not having to give up a single thing thus far. To be fair, though, had she even once sat down with him and asked him to meet her halfway on something? No.

She sighed just thinking about the emotional heavy lifting still ahead for them. Sophia smiled.

"Just sinking in how complicated this is going to be?" she teased lightly.

Emily nodded.

"At least the crisis has been averted for now," Sophia said. "I'm going to take off and try to sweet-talk a couple of corporate tycoons out of some big bucks."

Emily chuckled. "They don't stand a chance. I've never known you not to get exactly what you set out to get."

"Remember that the next time I'm trying to wheedle something out of you," Sophia advised her. "Give it up graciously."

"For you, anything, anytime," Emily said.

"Oh, boy, I have you now," Sophia exulted. "I wish I'd gotten that on tape."

"My word's good enough," Emily said. "I won't forget I gave it."

And now that she had given her word, she just hoped it wouldn't come back to haunt her.

As Sophia took off, Emily's cell phone rang. She

glanced at the caller ID as she answered. "Hey, Samantha."

"How are things in Tinseltown?" Samantha inquired.

"Chaotic. How about New York?"

"Way too quiet," Samantha said, an odd edge to her voice. "Are you getting to Grandmother's for Thanksgiving?"

"I'm hoping to. You?"

"I'll head down on Tuesday most likely. Have you spoken to Gabi recently?"

Emily thought of the call she'd gotten in which she'd sensed something wasn't right with their sister. "I spoke to her a couple of weeks ago. I meant to call you then. She wouldn't admit to anything, but I felt like something was wrong."

"That's what I thought when I spoke to her last night. I was going to go by there on my way to Sand Castle Bay, but she told me not to bother, that she'd probably see me over there."

"Probably?" Emily repeated with a frown. "What does that mean? Surely she'll show up for Thanksgiving. Even Dad usually drags himself away from the office for the holiday."

"I'm not convinced Gabi will this year. I do know if she doesn't, we might need to drive over to Raleigh and see for ourselves what's going on."

"Why don't I run by her place from the airport?" Emily suggested. "Maybe I can drag her with me, if she's balking at coming."

"Even better," Samantha said. "See you next week, Em."

"Travel safe."

"You, too."

Emily sighed when she disconnected the call. If she'd learned nothing else this morning, it was that once family or anyone else was in your life, it was all but certain to get very complicated.

20

Boone had given Pete a long holiday break to spend with the new woman in his life in New York. The fact that his top executive was actually excited about seeing the annual Macy's Thanksgiving parade in person had come as a shock.

"You're just a kid at heart, after all," Boone had teased him.

Pete had responded with an expletive that was definitely not very childlike.

Now with Pete out of town, Boone had to deal with the calls coming in from various contacts in Charleston as they moved forward on opening their fourth restaurant, hopefully by spring.

"I really need you down here as soon as possible to sign the papers if you want that location you liked in the historic district," his Realtor announced when Boone returned his call. "There's another bidder, but the owner's eaten at your restaurants and he liked your plans. He wants to get the deal in place now before his people start insisting on taking the higher offer."

"You do realize this is Thanksgiving week," Boone said. "How about next Monday?"

"How about Friday?" Caldwell Marshall countered.

"Nobody works on the day after Thanksgiving," Boone protested.

"Sorry. He insisted it be by the end of the week. Even Friday's pushing it. I think he was hoping for Wednesday."

Boone sighed heavily. "I'll try to make it work. I'll get back to you before the end of the day."

He hung up and called Emily. "How would you like to take a trip to Charleston on Friday?" he asked when she answered.

"It's a very romantic city," she responded cautiously. "Are you suggesting a private tryst, just the two of us?"

"I wish," he said and explained what had come up. "I can't call Pete back from New York to handle this, so it's up to me."

"Then you have to go."

"Not without you," he replied flatly. "I am not going to lose a whole day with you for business. Our time together is limited enough as it is."

"While it's very nice to know that I'm so high on your priority list," she said, "things like this are going to come up for both of us. We're going to have to be flexible."

"So, be flexible," he encouraged her. "Come with me."

"B.J., too?"

"I could leave him with Jodie," he said, though he didn't even try to hide his hesitation.

"Only heaven knows what she'd make of it," Emily

concluded. "Samantha will be here. He could stay with her and Cora Jane, I'm sure."

Boone considered that option but dismissed it as well. "It's his school vacation. I want to spend time with him, too. And you know he'll be over the moon to have a whole day with you."

"Then we'll all go," she said. "He and I can wander around and sightsee while you do your business."

"I'll take you out for a great meal afterward," he promised, relieved that she'd agreed to this.

"On the day after Thanksgiving?" she said with a laugh. "A couple of lettuce leaves will probably be all I can stuff down. You know how Cora Jane overdoes it."

"Then we'll play the meal by ear," he compromised. "Thank you for going along with this. I know it's not what you had in mind for your Thanksgiving break."

"Hey, give and take is what life is all about, or so I'm told. And I'll be with you. What's the downside of that?"

"Any good at give and take?" he asked. "Because I have to tell you, I'm a work in progress on that front."

"Me, too."

"Well, so far you get an A-plus in my book."

"Watch out. I may have to come up with a test of my own to see how you score."

"Whatever it takes to make this work," he said readily. "See you in a few days. Love you."

"Love you back."

He was smiling when he hung up. Crisis averted, and as a bonus he'd just negotiated for an entire day with Emily far from Jodie's prying eyes.

Because of the necessity for secrecy surrounding the location of the safe house, there was no media invited to the grand opening. Only members of the board, key contractors and Emily were there as the first women moved in with their children.

Sophie had assigned Emily to show them to their rooms and explain about the amenities the house offered. The first woman, whose name was Lisa, regarded Emily with understandable caution as they climbed the steps to the second floor. Her two girls, who were so thin it was hard to tell their ages, looked to be no more than six and eight, though it was possible they were older. Their eyes held a world-weary exhaustion no child should ever know. They hung back behind their mother as they climbed the stairs and avoided making eye contact. Emily didn't like thinking about the kind of life that had made them so timid and fearful.

Emily opened the door to their room, which had been painted a buttery yellow trimmed in white. Sunshine poured through the windows and splashed across the polished wood floor. Though it was a little tight, Emily had managed to fit a full-size bed in the room, just right for cuddling, she thought. She'd also squeezed in a small dresser, bunk beds and a comfortable chair. She held her breath as they saw it for the first time.

"This is for us?" the youngest one exclaimed, her eyes wide. "The whole room?"

"It looks brand-new," her sister said.

"It is," Emily confirmed. "Every single thing in here is new." She glanced at the mother and saw tears welling up in the woman's eyes. "I hope you'll be comfortable here."

As the tears spilled over, dampening her cheeks, the woman said, "You can't know..." She blinked and tried again. "You can't possibly know what this means to us."

Until that moment, Emily hadn't realized. Not really. Seeing the relief on the mother's face, the excitement in her children's eyes, she felt the kind of gut-deep satisfaction that could only come from doing something special for people who truly deserved it. For this family to be so thrilled with a small room of their own with simple furnishings, she knew they must have survived on so little before.

Choked up herself, she managed to say, "Girls, would you like to take a look upstairs? There are desks and lockers to store your books. You can study up there if you have homework from school."

Predictably, both girls made faces that had Emily laughing. "Then how about we go back downstairs and you can take a look at the playroom? Would that be more to your liking?"

"Yes, please," the older girl said politely.

"An honest-to-goodness playroom?" the mother breathed as if she couldn't quite believe it.

Emily nodded. "We tried to think of everything that would make it comfortable. If there's anything we didn't think of, though, please be sure to let us know."

For the first time, a smile teased at the woman's lips. "If you understood where we've been and even half of what we've been through, you'd know that bare walls and a blanket on the floor would be a thousand times better as long as we're safe. This is heaven."

To Emily's surprise, the woman embraced her in a hug. "Thank you."

"I'm just the designer. The people you really need to thank are downstairs."

"Believe me, I'll be thanking them every day of my life. And once I get on my feet and I can provide a safe place for myself and my kids, I will come back here and return the favor. I promise you that."

The whole day was like that, with women who had so little showing boundless gratitude for what was being provided and promising to give back when they could. By the end of the day they'd already worked out a rotation among themselves for cooking and child care.

The experience left Emily with a full heart. She could hardly wait to get to Sand Castle Bay to share everything that had happened today with Boone. *This,* she thought as she flew across the country, was what she'd been meant to do.

Emily pounded on Gabi's door to no avail. Either her sister had gone to Grandmother's for the holiday, was off somewhere with friends, or—and this was what Emily feared—was hiding out.

She called Cora Jane's first. It was Samantha who picked up. "Any sign of Gabi over there?" she asked Samantha.

"Nope. Grandmother said Gabi insisted she had other things to do."

"Well, she's not home, or at least she's not answering the door," Emily reported.

"Did you look in the garage? Is her car there?"

Walking with her cell phone in hand, Emily crossed the small patch of lawn in front of the brick town house and tried to get a glimpse inside the garage, but the windows were too high. "I can't tell," she said in frustration. "Maybe I should call Dad. It's possible she's spoken to him."

"Afraid not," Samantha said. "He arrived here an

hour ago. He said he hasn't talked to her for a couple of weeks."

"Off with the boyfriend?" Emily speculated.

"I suppose that's possible," Samantha said. "But I don't like this, Em."

"Neither do I," Emily admitted.

"If she were spending the holiday with that man, don't you think she'd have been so excited, she'd have mentioned it?"

"Absolutely," Emily agreed.

"Well, if she doesn't call at some point today to wish us all a happy Thanksgiving, then I say we need to go back tomorrow and do a thorough search for her," Samantha said. "I'm really worried."

Emily thought of her plans with Boone for tomorrow. If they had to be sacrificed in order to make sure her sister was okay, well, that's just the way it had to be.

"I'm taking off from here now," she told Samantha. "See you later. Don't you dare eat all the turkey before I get there."

"Trust me, that bird won't come out of the oven until you and Boone are on the premises, even though Dad's already grumbling about needing to leave to get back to Raleigh. Grandmother's dug in her heels this time."

Emily laughed. "Good for her. Once in a while it's good for Dad to discover that the whole world doesn't revolve around him."

After she'd disconnected the call, Emily walked around the town house one last time, looking for signs of life, but it appeared eerily quiet. She was tempted to knock on a couple of the neighbors' doors but knew Gabi would never forgive her for stirring up talk. She'd also admitted more than once that she barely even knew the people who lived around her. With the hours Gabi worked, she never saw them.

Emily fretted over her sister's whereabouts and her odd behavior all during the drive to Cora Jane's. She was convinced it had something to do with this man none of them had met, but with Gabi determinedly mum on that subject, she couldn't prove it.

At least worrying about her sister kept her from analyzing her situation with Boone to death. She knew as they got closer and closer, the complications were going to get increasingly difficult to resolve. She didn't think he saw that. He seemed to be living in some dream world in which love conquered all...or in which she gave up everything to be with him. She wasn't sure which. Either way, it threatened to be a problem.

When she finally pulled into the driveway at her grandmother's, she saw that Boone and B.J. had just arrived, as well. Unaware that she was there, B.J. was already racing toward the house. Boone, however, spotted her and crossed the lawn to meet her.

"Good timing," he said, pulling her into his arms and kissing her.

"Here? Now?" she said, startled.

He grinned. "Lost my head," he said. "Are you complaining?"

"No, but I think you might have some explaining to do," she said, gesturing behind him.

Boone turned around to see B.J. standing there, a puzzled expression on his face.

"Hey, buddy, look who's here," Boone called out, his too-cheerful tone a sign of his nervousness.

Rather than running to meet them, B.J. remained where he was.

"Oh, boy," Boone murmured under his breath. He took Emily's hand. "Let's go face the music."

"Hey, B.J., don't I get a hug?" Emily asked.

After a moment's hesitation, B.J. flew into her arms. When he released her, though, he gave his father a quizzical look. "Dad, how come you were kissing Emily?"

"For the same reason you just hugged her," Boone said. "I'm happy to see her."

"You were happy to see Aunt Cheryl the other day, but you didn't kiss her like that." B.J. said, proving once more that he took in everything.

Emily had to swallow a chuckle at Boone's blushing reaction. "Yeah, Boone, why didn't you kiss Aunt Cheryl like that? And who, by the way, is Aunt Cheryl?"

"She was my mom's friend, not a real aunt," B.J. chimed in helpfully. "She doesn't live here anymore, but she came home for Thanksgiving."

Emily lifted a brow. "Is that so?"

"And she's married to an ex-football player who's built like a truck and she has five children," Boone supplied. "And *that* is why I didn't kiss her the way I just kissed Emily."

"Yeah, I guess Uncle Dave wouldn't like it, huh?" B.J. said.

"No, he wouldn't," Boone confirmed. "Any other questions?"

Emily and Boone waited as B.J.'s expression turned thoughtful.

"You used to kiss Mommy like that," B.J. said, his tone wistful.

Boone sighed and hunkered down in front of him. "Yes, I did," he said softly. "Because your mom was the most important woman in my life for a very long time."

"Does that mean Emily's important now?" B.J. asked.

Boone glanced up at Emily, then nodded, looking his son in the eyes. "It does. Is that okay with you?"

"Is she going to live with us?" B.J. asked.

"Maybe someday," Boone told him. "But right now we're really good friends."

B.J. seemed to absorb that news, nodding eventually. "I'm hungry. Let's go eat."

"Yes, let's go eat," Boone said eagerly. "Go on in and let Ms. Cora Jane know we're here."

"Oh, she knows," B.J. said. "She's been watching out the window."

Of course she was, Emily thought, barely containing a laugh. If they thought B.J.'s cross-examination had been awkward, it was probably nothing compared to what was in store.

Boone watched closely as Sam Castle greeted Emily as if she were a business colleague, rather than his youngest daughter. His hug was superficial, his words little more than the expected "Hello. How are you?"

Emily's response was just as restrained, though Boone thought he saw the longing in her eyes for more. The hug she received from Jerry was far more exuberant and heartfelt. Surely Sam Castle had to see that and recognize what genuine affection looked like.

"Mother, can we eat now?" Sam asked with a touch of impatience. "Or are we waiting for Gabriella, too?"

"Gabi won't be here," Cora Jane said. "It might be nice, though, if we gave Emily and Boone a minute to have a glass of wine and an appetizer before we rush them in to the meal."

Emily gave her grandmother's hand a squeeze. "It's okay. I know Dad wants to get back home. He gets palpitations or something if he's away from work too long."

Cora Jane didn't seem impressed. She scowled at her son. "This is Thanksgiving, a time for family to be together and to count our blessings. It is not a day to rush through a meal on a time clock."

To Boone's surprise, Sam looked vaguely chagrined by the criticism. "Sorry, Mother."

Samantha and Emily exchanged a stunned look that Boone interpreted to mean his apology had to be a first.

Just then the phone rang and Cora Jane reached for it at once, her eyes filled with worry. "Gabi, is that you?"

Boone glanced at Emily, who appeared to be hanging on every word of her grandmother's end of the conversation. She held out her hand.

"Let me speak to her," she commanded.

Cora Jane waved her off. "Your sisters are here. They send their love. We all miss you. And I expect you here for Christmas. No excuses. Is that understood?"

Boone gave Emily a quizzical look. "What's going on with Gabi?"

"We have no idea, but Samantha and I are convinced something is. I stopped by her place before driving over here and there was no sign of her. She didn't offer any real explanation for not being with us today, at least not to Samantha or me."

Cora Jane disconnected the call just then. "Well, she told me she had to be at work first thing tomorrow, so the drive over here for the day just didn't make a lot of sense."

"Then she is at home?" Emily said. "Why didn't she come to the door when I knocked?"

"I didn't question her about where she was spending the day," Cora Jane said. "She's a grown woman. I assume she's with friends."

"Gabi doesn't have friends," Samantha said. "She has coworkers. I don't think they're close."

"Like somebody else I know," Emily said with a pointed look at her father.

Boone saw the scene deteriorating rapidly. Apparently Jerry did, too, because he stood up. "Cora Jane, let's get that turkey on the table. You've outdone yourself this year. We don't want the meal spoiled."

"Good idea," she said at once, following him into the kitchen.

"Let us help," Boone said.

Emily and Samantha were on his heels.

"We'll all help," Emily said.

The only person who hung back was Sam Castle. Boone saw the lost expression on his face and almost felt sorry for him. Whatever his reasons for distancing himself from his family over the years, he had a hunch Sam had come to regret it but had no idea how to go about fixing it. Since Boone had the same sort of dysfunctional relationship with his parents, he recognized the signs.

"Give your father something to do," Boone encouraged Emily, nodding in her father's direction.

She seemed startled by the suggestion, but after taking a look at her father, she apparently saw what Boone had seen.

"Dad, come on. Nobody gets to eat without helping to get everything onto the table."

For an instant, Sam looked startled, but then his lips curved slightly. "I'll carry the mashed potatoes and gravy," he offered. "That is, if you trust me not to make off with them. It's my favorite part of the meal."

Cora Jane gave him a startled look. "I never knew that."

Sam actually winked at her. "See, even at your age and as wise as you are, you haven't learned all there is to know about me."

After an instant of stunned silence, Cora Jane chuckled. "And that's another thing I'd forgotten, you actually do have a sense of humor."

"I'll try to show some evidence of it more often," Sam promised.

When the moment had passed, Boone claimed the bowl of stuffing. "This is mine," he announced, heading for the dining room.

"I can carry the cranberry sauce," B.J. offered.

The turkey was left to Jerry, who brought the golden bird to the table and presented it as if it were the crown jewels.

"My best ever," Cora Jane said, standing at Jerry's elbow. "If I do say so myself."

"Hey, I had a little bit to do with it," he grumbled. "I was the one in here basting it."

"With me looking over your shoulder to make sure you did it right," Cora Jane retorted. "Other than that, you lifted the turkey off the counter, put it in the oven, then took it out at the end."

"And if I hadn't, it would have been on the floor," he insisted, giving them a wink.

She gave him an indulgent look. "That's what you think. The man is starting to think he's indispensable to me."

"I know I am," he corrected.

Boone watched as Sam took in the exchange with dawning understanding. He waited to see if he would comment, but he didn't. There was no denying, though, the smile that settled on his lips.

Cora Jane just shook her head. "Okay, enough of this. Let's take our places, thank the Lord for our blessings and enjoy sharing this meal together."

During the prayer, Boone glanced around the table and realized it was the first time all day he'd truly felt like part of a family. The meal he'd shared earlier at Jodie's had been tense, and there'd been none of the teasing and laughter that were commonplace with the Castles. Sure, a few issues had come up, but in the end, Cora Jane somehow brought them all together as a family.

He gave Emily's hand a squeeze before releasing it. She smiled at him.

"Do you realize this is the first Thanksgiving we've been together since we were in college?" he said.

"It's the first time I've been back for the holiday," she admitted.

He held her gaze. "What was the draw this year? The huge turkey?"

"No way."

"Me?" he asked hopefully.

"You, B.J., the whole family," she said, her tone heartfelt. "Suddenly I have a whole new appreciation of the importance of family and the kind of love that Grandmother has always shared with us."

"Oh?"

She nodded. "It's been quite a week. Helping with the opening at the safe house opened my eyes to a lot of things, Boone. I can't wait to tell you about them. These women and kids…" Her voice trailed off and her eyes filled with tears. "You have no idea what they've been through and how blessed we are in our lives."

"I think I have some idea," he corrected. "Being here right now with your family has brought that home to me."

"Even with all the fussing and fighting?"

"Even with that," he confirmed. "You want to know why?"

"Why?"

"Because underneath it all, there was no mistaking the love."

And that's what he wanted for B.J., and for himself.

21

Emily felt as if she'd stolen a moment out of time when she, Boone and B.J. were in Charleston. For the first time since she and Boone had started seriously seeing each other, she didn't feel as if they were under disapproving scrutiny...or even her own grandmother's hopeful gaze.

She and B.J. had wandered along the Battery and then past the row of "painted ladies"—brightly colored houses along the waterfront called Rainbow Row. They'd bought souvenirs and Christmas gifts in a few shops, then gone back to the restaurant where they were to meet Boone after he'd concluded his meeting.

B.J. was happily sipping a soda, and Emily had a glass of sweet tea as they waited for Boone's arrival. When he finally joined them, a half hour late, he looked harried.

"Everything go okay?" Emily asked after they'd ordered.

"It could have gone better," he admitted. "The seller wanted me to up my offer to meet a competing bid. I told him it was out of line. We've been haggling over it ever since. I finally had to tell him to forget it. We'll find another location."

Emily frowned. "Oh, no. I thought the deal was all set, that you were just here to sign paperwork."

"That's what I thought, too." He shrugged. "Pete'll be disappointed, but things like this happen. If we can't find another great location in Charleston by spring, we'll opt for another city. Sometimes things just aren't meant to be."

Emily didn't believe for a second that he was that philosophical. He was just trying to keep his disappointment from casting a pall on the day. She gave his hand an understanding squeeze.

"Okay, tell me what you two have been up to," Boone said. "I see a lot of packages. Have you spent all your money?"

B.J. nodded. "I spent my whole allowance," he confirmed. "And Emily and I bought a Christmas present for you, but we're not telling. It's a surprise."

Boone laughed. "I love surprises."

"I'm not sure how thrilled you're going to be with this one," she said, thinking of the print they'd found of the historic old building he'd been planning to buy. As lovely as the image was, it would be a bittersweet gift now. She doubted B.J. understood the significance of what Boone had just told them about losing the property he'd wanted.

B.J. tugged on his father's sleeve. "Dad, guess what? I know what I want for Christmas. I was gonna tell Santa, but Emily thinks I should tell you, too."

Boone looked amused. "Oh?"

"A puppy!" B.J. announced, bouncing up and down.

"Emily says we should find one at a shelter, because those puppies really, really need homes."

Boone lifted a brow. "Something tells me this is about more than puppies," he said, holding her gaze.

She shrugged. "Okay, yes. I seem to be feeling especially sentimental about puppies and people who need homes these days. When B.J. mentioned wanting a dog, I thought of the shelter."

"It's a great idea," Boone said. "And since this is going to be your dog, B.J., you should get to pick him out. First, though, you have to assure me that you're going to take full responsibility for him. You'll train him, feed him, walk him and play with him."

"Yes, yes, yes," B.J. responded excitedly. "I'll take excellent care of him."

"Then maybe we should go back home right after our meal and stop by the shelter," Boone suggested as their food was served. "I think since Emily encouraged this, she ought to have a say in the final choice, too."

"Do I have to share in the responsibility, as well?" she asked, a teasing note in her voice.

"You bet," Boone said. "Which means you might want to consider at least a month off over the holidays. I imagine it'll take at least that long to train a dog properly."

"An interesting plan," she said. "But you do know that some of the older dogs at the shelter are already trained. I think we should try to find one of those. How about it, B.J.? Older dogs definitely need good homes and a family who will love them. And it'll be less work for us."

Boone gave her an amused look. "Not anxious to stick around for so long?"

Though his tone was light, she thought she heard a critical note in his voice. "Boone, you know I can't. A month is a long time, especially with the ski lodge opening coming up next week. There will be a lot of fine-tuning after the doors open. I'll try for a couple of weeks, maybe from Christmas through the first week in January. How's that?"

Another thought occurred to her. "Or, if you wait on getting the dog till after Christmas, you and B.J. could come to Aspen. We could spend a week there, then come back here. That would give us more time together." She met Boone's gaze. "What do you think?"

"I think it's a terrible time for me to be away from the restaurant," he responded without giving the idea even a moment's consideration. "We're booked solid for holiday parties."

"And you don't have a catering manager who's in charge of those?" she asked, sensing not for the first time that all of the flexibility, all of the concessions in this relationship were going to have to be on her side.

"I do, but ultimately the responsibility for things running smoothly is mine," Boone replied tightly.

Emily was about to push harder for compromise, but she spotted the bewildered expression on B.J.'s face and sensed their disagreement, mild as it was, was upsetting him.

"We'll figure it out later," she said briskly, giving a slight nod in B.J.'s direction.

Boone agreed at once.

"Okay, buddy, what else did you and Emily see when you were shopping? Is there anything else on your list for Santa?"

When B.J. didn't immediately answer, Emily said,

"What about the train we saw in that store window? Maybe we should take your dad to look at that. He used to talk about having a train under the tree when he was a little boy."

B.J. stared at his dad. "You did? Awesome."

Boone nodded, his expression turning nostalgic. "I wonder what happened to that train? It's probably a collector's item by now. I think it belonged to my dad when he was a kid."

"Isn't it funny how people who've never even ridden on a train in real life feel as if the holiday isn't complete without a train and village under the Christmas tree?" Emily said. "It conjures up all sorts of images of an old-fashioned Christmas. I'm thinking of suggesting Derek put one up under the tree at the ski lodge. I think it will make the cozy, welcoming atmosphere he wants to create there absolutely perfect."

"Well, all this talk about trains has convinced me," Boone said. "Let's go take a look at the one you two saw. Anybody want dessert before we go?"

Since they'd barely touched their food, both Emily and B.J. shook their heads.

"Then let's do it," Boone said. He paid the bill and led the way back to the street. "Come on, B.J., show me the way."

B.J. ran ahead on the crowded streets, then stopped in front of a store window with a fabulous Christmas village on display. People were jammed in close to watch the train as it wove through the village. Lights sparkled over the snowy landscape the shop owner had created. B.J. had his nose pressed to the glass as Emily and Boone hung back.

"That does bring back memories," Boone said, giving her hand a squeeze. "I hadn't thought about that train for years. Thanks for reminding me."

"You used to talk about it every Christmas," she recalled. "When I saw this one, I thought it might make the perfect gift for B.J. He's obviously as enchanted with this one as you were with the one you used to have."

Boone turned her to face him. He tucked a wayward curl behind her ear as he looked into her eyes. "I know what upset you earlier," he said quietly. "You don't think there's going to be any real give-and-take in this relationship, at least not on my part."

"Sounded that way to me," she conceded, surprised that he'd caught on so readily.

"Not so. I may not be able to change all of my commitments, especially at the last minute, but I'll do my fair share. By next year, I'll make sure that the catering manager can handle things completely on her own. This year she's new and untested. I just need to be here. Can you try to understand that?"

Emily sighed. "Of course, I can. And I'll put it on that list of mine for the day when I need you to understand that I have no choice but to honor a commitment I've made."

"Fair enough," he said. "As long as we remember the big picture, you and me together, we can figure this out, Em. We have to."

She nodded, holding his gaze. "I want that more than anything, Boone. I really do."

When Emily showed up at Sophia's a few days after her Thanksgiving break for what she'd assumed would be a consultation on yet another of her client's redecorating projects, she was surprised to find Marilyn Jennings there, as well.

The shelter's board chairman smiled as she kissed Emily's cheek. "Sophia didn't mention I'd be here, did she?"

"No, but it's always lovely to see you," Emily said. "If I'd realized you were going to be here, I'd have brought along the latest information on the safe house. We came in under budget. A lot of the subcontractors wrote off all or a portion of their bills. Once they actually met some of the women and kids and understood how important this was, they all wanted to do their part."

"That's marvelous," Marilyn said, just as Sophia joined them and added, "I expected nothing less of you, Emily."

"That isn't why we're here, though," Marilyn said, giving Sophia a chiding look. "Didn't you give her so much as a clue?"

"Not necessary," Sophia said, winking at Emily. "She always comes when I call."

Emily laughed at her arrogance, but she couldn't deny it. "What can I say? She's one of my best clients."

"And one of your most demanding, no doubt," Marilyn suggested.

"No comment," Emily responded tactfully.

Sophia gave her an approving look. "See how smart and tactful she is? I told you she'd be the perfect person for this."

Emily gave them a puzzled look. "Perfect person for what?"

Marilyn glanced at Sophia, who shook her head. "I'll defer to you on this."

"Okay, then," Marilyn said briskly. "Emily, we'd like to hire you full-time."

Emily regarded her with confusion. "To do what?"

"Patience," Sophia chided.

Emily dutifully fell silent. Clearly these two had some sort of dog-and-pony show for her and planned to draw out the suspense as long as possible. They were too rich and powerful for her not to go along with their timetable.

"We've recently received several very sizable donations, thanks to Sophia's persistence," Marilyn explained.

"And your connections," Sophia added, then turned to Emily and added, "Her husband's studio spearheaded an industry campaign to raise ten million dollars. Some of that will go toward day-to-day operations, but at least half of it will be for capital improvements."

Marilyn nodded. "Meaning we'll be able to buy more properties, renovate them and make the spaces available to families in need of temporary protection and housing. The work you've done on this current project has persuaded all of us that you're the person we want to oversee this."

Stunned and speechless, Emily sat back, trying to absorb the magnitude of the opportunity.

"You'll be paid, of course, and I'm sure if you have the time, we'd have no objections to you taking on individual clients, but we'd need to be your first priority," Marilyn continued, filling in the silence left by Emily's shocked reaction.

"We'd want your help in choosing properties," Sophia added. "You'd have to budget for the renovations, trying to get the best possible prices, of course. The more donations you could arrange, the better, but you will have funds at your disposal."

"When?" Emily finally managed to ask, still not entirely able to form coherent sentences.

"We're all agreed that we'd like to get started right after the first of the year," Marilyn said.

"That should give you time to finish Derek's ski lodge," Sophia added. "And anything else that's on your plate."

An image of Boone and B.J. came to mind. They were most definitely on her plate. How on earth would she be able to juggle those relationships with what these two women were proposing? Clearly this new opportunity wasn't something she could handle from thousands of miles away. It had been difficult enough to get this one safe house completed with her time divided between two coasts. She'd felt pressured no matter where she happened to be.

And yet she desperately wanted to say yes. She'd found the kind of professional fulfillment working on the safe house that had been missing from her other work. She wanted to contribute more, and this was her chance. She'd just had no idea how soon she might need to call in all those chits she'd told Boone he owed her for being the more accommodating partner up to now.

Could she make Boone see how important this work was to her? she wondered. Intellectually, he would probably grasp it immediately. When it came time to translate it into reality, into longer separations, how could she even ask that of him, no matter what she might think he owed her?

"I have to think about this," she said.

"What's to think about?" Sophia asked, regarding

her with a touch of impatience. "How many times have you told me how much it's meant to you to work on this project? We're offering you a chance to do the same thing on a much larger scale. You can make a difference in hundreds of lives, Emily."

Sophia frowned at her continued silence. "This isn't about those obligations of yours in North Carolina, is it?"

"They're more than obligations," Emily replied, trying to keep her own annoyance out of her voice. "I finally have a chance to work things out with the man I've loved since we were teenagers. His life is there."

"Is it more important than yours?" Sophia asked tartly.

Marilyn held up a hand. "Spoken exactly like a woman who's ditched more than one husband because he didn't suit your mood of the moment," she said mildly, then gave Emily a sympathetic look. "You take your time. This is clearly a big commitment. You need to weigh it with the other priorities in your life and see how you can make it work. We want you for this job, Emily. I promise you we'll do whatever we can to make it manageable for you."

Emily gave her a grateful look. "I appreciate that. I really do. And I do understand the enormity of this opportunity. If there were no other considerations, I'd say yes in a heartbeat."

Marilyn smiled. "So, it'll take a few heartbeats before you have your answer. Talk it over with this man of yours. We can wait."

"For a week," Sophia said determinedly. "Not forever."

"Then you'll have my answer in a week," Emily assured them.

That would give her time to think this through and to talk it over with Boone, though the phone was not the best way to do it. This conversation ought to be taking place face-to-face. Maybe she could squeeze in an overnight visit to North Carolina before she was due in Aspen to finish up the last-minute details at the ski lodge.

She and Boone had been meandering along, feeling their way as they explored the various paths that they could take to make this new relationship work. Maybe this was the push they needed to take that final leap into the future, she thought optimistically.

Or maybe, despite all his promises, it would be the thing that tore them apart forever.

Boone was on his cell phone pacing the dock outside of his restaurant when he saw Emily crossing the parking lot. Startled, he wrapped up his call and started her way.

"Hey, you," he said, pulling her into his arms and holding her tightly. "Was I supposed to be expecting you?"

She laughed. "You mean my schedule hasn't been programmed into your calendar?"

"Actually it has been, but I could swear you're not due back until after that ski lodge opens."

"Disappointed I'm here early?" she teased. "Don't tell me you're juggling me with another girl. Have I spoiled your plans?"

"Not a chance," he said, then studied her closely. Despite the teasing note in her voice, her eyes seemed to be filled with worry. "Is something wrong? Cora Jane's okay, isn't she? I haven't seen her for a couple of days, but I spoke to her yesterday. She didn't mention any problems. Nor did she say a word about you coming home."

"Grandmother's fine and she didn't know about this trip, either. I just had an unexpected break, so I decided to take advantage of it. I have to fly to Aspen tomorrow, though."

"I thought you were down to the wire on the ski lodge," he said, surprised that she'd been able to get away with that deadline so close. "What's so important that you needed to fly in for one night?"

"Maybe I just missed you," she said, a defensive note in her voice that warned him something serious was on the agenda.

"Everything's on schedule for the lodge opening? Derek's not freaking out?"

She laughed. "Of course he's freaking out. It's what he does. But it's all good. I made sure of that before I came here."

He still sensed something was wrong. "You're happy with how it's turned out?"

She smiled. "It's going to be fabulous. I have pictures on my laptop. I'll give you the ten-cent tour later, complete with before and after shots. You won't believe the transformation."

"I can't wait."

"You seemed pretty distracted when I got here. Is there a crisis of some kind that needs your attention?"

Since she didn't seem inclined to reveal the reason for this unexpected visit, he accepted the change of subject. "I was on the phone with Pete. He's been determined to fix that snag we ran into on the Charleston property. He's handling it, but I probably should give him a call back. I'm not sure why he's got his mind set on opening there, but if I don't stay on top of this, he's liable to make concessions I won't be able to live with."

"Then I'll head on over to Grandmother's and get settled."

"Dinner tonight? I'll throw some chicken on the grill, maybe see if Ethan wants to stop by."

Emily frowned. "Do you really want Ethan around when we have so little time? Surely you aren't still trying to keep B.J. from figuring out how serious things are between us. I thought that cat was out of the bag when he saw us kissing?"

"I was just thinking it would be nice to get together with Ethan," Boone said defensively.

"Not this time, okay? We need to talk about something."

Boone sucked in a breath. So, there was something on her mind, something that had brought her clear across the country. "Fine. I'll invite him over another time," he said. "But maybe you should tell me what's going on."

"Tonight will be soon enough. I'll be over around six-thirty, if that's good."

Boone had a feeling he ought to keep her here now, settle this once and for all, but Pete's call was still weighing on his mind. He also knew they weren't likely to settle a single thing until they had more time together to explore their options and discuss how they each saw the future working out. Just as he had when he'd impulsively suggested they get married, he wondered if they weren't going to spend so much time thinking things through that they never actually moved forward.

He also had a gut-deep feeling that Emily's unexpected appearance here today was about a whole lot more than taking advantage of a break in her schedule. She was unmistakably tense, and if he knew her at all, that couldn't mean anything good.

Cora Jane regarded her granddaughter with surprise. "Well, look who the cat dragged in. Thought you weren't coming till closer to Christmas."

Emily shook her head. "You and Boone!" she muttered. "Obviously not big on surprises. I'll have to remember that."

"Boone didn't know you were coming, either?"

"I had an unexpected break," Emily told her irritably. "I decided to take advantage of it."

"Given the tension I'm hearing in your voice, a break is just what you need," Cora Jane said. "You might want to start with a nap."

Emily blinked at her, then winced. "Sorry. I am on edge."

"Any particular reason?"

Emily's hesitation was telling.

"You have bad news and you're trying to figure out how to break it to Boone," Cora Jane guessed.

"Are you a mind reader or something?" Emily grumbled.

"No, just someone who's known you your whole life. You've always shied away from confrontation. Why don't we have a cup of tea, and you can tell me about this news you don't want to share with Boone."

"Do you have time?"

"As long as I can put my feet up, I have all the time in the world. Now that both of your sisters have gone home, this house is way too quiet most of the time. It'll be good to have a little conversation at the end of the day."

"I'm surprised Jerry's not over here every night, now that you don't have a houseful of women underfoot."

"Oh, we see each other plenty," Cora Jane said, color in her cheeks. "Now, let me change my clothes, and I'll make that tea. I think it's warm enough to sit on the porch, don't you? It's rare for it to be this nice in early December. We should take advantage of it."

Twenty minutes later, she was stretched out on the chaise longue with her feet up, a cup of Earl Grey tea beside her along with a plate of shortbread cookies she'd baked the night before. She'd thrown an afghan over her legs and was wearing a sweater she'd knitted. Emily was in a rocker she'd pulled into a patch of warm sunlight.

For a while, they sat there in companionable silence, but Cora Jane knew better than to let it drag on. Emily was probably sitting there right now dreaming up excuses to keep her problems to herself.

"Okay, young lady, tell me what's going on," Cora Jane encouraged.

She listened as her youngest granddaughter poured out her heart over the amazing job opportunity she'd been offered.

"I see," Cora Jane said when she was finished.

"You're disappointed in me for even considering it," Emily said, her voice resigned.

"Of course not," Cora Jane told her. "I'm not blind to the importance of that kind of work. And it says a lot about you that they want you for this job. They're showing a tremendous amount of faith in you."

"Doing these homes could make such a difference for so many families and women in trouble," Emily said, her passion for the work unmistakable. "Working on this first house was the most fulfilling thing I've done in my entire career."

"I know that," Cora Jane said. "I could hear the excitement in your voice every time we talked."

"I meant to tell you over Thanksgiving that I met several of the families when they moved in. There was one in particular that really got to me. They'd been housed in a run-down hotel, a mom and two little girls, waiting for this safe house to open. The girls are so excited that there's a huge playroom and that everything in their room is new. And their mother?" She met Cora Jane's gaze. "You should have seen the relief in her eyes just thinking about finally being someplace safe until she can get on her feet again."

"Seems to me the answer's plain as day," Cora Jane said. "This means a chance for you to do something meaningful. You can't turn it down."

She saw the surprise in Emily's eyes and smiled. "Not the reaction you expected, is it?"

"Far from it," Emily admitted. "You didn't mention Boone once."

"Neither did you," Cora Jane pointed out.

Emily frowned at the implication. "Are you suggesting he shouldn't matter?"

"Absolutely not. You know how much I want the two of you to work things out, but it will only be right if you're both content with your work as well as your relationship. You can't build a life if one person resents the other for keeping them from something important."

"He's going to hate this, though," Emily said. "It won't be like what I'm doing now. I'll have to be in Los Angeles practically full-time. That's no way to build a real relationship."

"Maybe not," Cora Jane conceded. "You won't know unless you try." She gave her granddaughter a pointed look. "You realize I'm not the one you should be talking to about this."

"I'm seeing Boone tonight, though I doubt we'll have much time alone with B.J. underfoot," Emily said, her frustration plain. "Boone wanted to invite Ethan over, too, but at least I think I convinced him not to do that."

"No matter who's around, you'll find a way to make some time," Cora Jane said. "If you have to stay up all night and lose sleep, then do it. I'll have someone drive you over to Raleigh tomorrow to catch your flight so you don't fall asleep behind the wheel. This is too important to be put off until it's convenient."

"Agreed," Emily said, then sighed. "But I'm not looking forward to it."

"Honey bun, life is always easier when it's smooth sailing, but these waves are what keep it interesting. They make us stronger and help us figure out what's really worthwhile."

She was surprised when Emily moved to sit beside her on the chaise longue and pulled her into a tight hug. "It's times like this when I really miss Mom, but having you in my life to talk to makes that a little more bearable. Do you have any idea how much I love you?"

"Sure I do," Cora Jane said with a smile. "But it never hurts to be reminded."

"Wish me luck tonight."

"I wish you luck every single day of your life," Cora
Jane reminded her. "More than that, though, I want you
to find the love and joy you deserve."

She sat back with a sigh as her granddaughter left,
hoping she'd given her the right advice, praying even
harder that Boone would have the wisdom to listen not
just to what Emily had to say, but to the unspoken longing that was plain, at least to Cora Jane.

22

"I can't believe Emily's home," B.J. said excitedly. "She promised to play my new video game with me next time she came. Do you think she'll have time tonight?"

"Maybe after dinner," Boone told him. "Maybe you can teach Ethan, too."

In the end, he'd gone ahead and invited his friend, convinced that it would be good to have a buffer between him and whatever was brewing with Emily. He wasn't entirely sure why he was convinced tonight was going to go badly, but the feeling in his stomach hadn't gone away. Knowing it was cowardly, he'd called Ethan and all but insisted he join them, at least for dinner.

"What's going on?" Ethan had asked suspiciously.

"Why do you assume something's going on? It's been a while since you've been by for a meal."

"And you have so much time with Emily these days that, what? She's boring you?"

"Don't be ridiculous. Are you coming over or not?" Boone asked irritably.

"I'll be there, if only to try to solve the riddle of the

man who doesn't want to be alone with the woman he loves."

In retrospect, Boone knew Ethan had been right. Inviting him had been ridiculous, especially since Emily had made her feelings about it plain.

As he was bemoaning his stupidity, he felt an impatient tug on his sleeve.

"Dad, are you listening to me?" B.J. demanded.

"I'm sorry. What did you say?"

"I *said* I already taught Ethan," B.J. said, then confided, "He's not very good. I don't think he pays attention."

Boone smiled. He could see Ethan being a little too intense these days to get involved with a video game challenge, even though there'd once been a time when he'd accepted any dare. In Boone's opinion, a little fun from time to time wouldn't hurt his friend one bit. What Ethan really needed was a woman in his life, but every time Boone tried to broach that subject, Ethan shot him down. Emphatically!

Maybe Emily would have some ideas, assuming she planned to be around. That was Boone's greatest fear, that she was about to announce that she wouldn't be back for months, if ever. He fretted over the possibility that the complications were simply too much.

No matter how hard he tried to convince himself she wouldn't make that sort of decision without discussing it with him, he couldn't shake the dread that had settled over him when she'd appeared so unexpectedly this afternoon. What if she was here to talk over exactly that, an extended absence of some kind?

"Dad, Ethan's here," B.J. hollered, racing across the lawn, then slowing suddenly as he remembered that despite Ethan's agility with his prosthesis, it wasn't a good idea to hurtle himself at the Afghanistan war veteran. It was a lesson learned after they'd taken a few good-natured tumbles to the ground.

Ethan crossed the lawn, listening to B.J.'s chatter, but his gaze fixed on Boone.

"Buddy, go into the house and get Ethan a soda," Boone suggested. "Or would you rather have a beer?"

"Soda's good," Ethan said. When B.J. was gone, he gave Boone a hard look. "Mind telling me again what I'm doing here? You have one night with Emily and you want to spend it with me? Are you planning to break up with her?"

"In front of you? I don't think so," Boone said, though his laugh sounded forced. "Okay. Here's the truth. I think she's about to deliver bad news, and you're here to postpone it."

Ethan stared at him incredulously, then shook his head. "Oh no, you don't, pal. I am not getting mixed up in this drama."

"But there will be no drama if you're here," Boone protested.

"And if there's going to be drama *ever,* you need to get it over with," Ethan said. "I'm leaving, and what I will do is take B.J. with me. He can spend the night at my place. I'll even let him beat me again at that video game he loves."

Boone grinned despite himself. "You've been letting him win?"

"Of course. You didn't really think that little kid of yours could beat me, did you?" he asked indignantly.

"Actually, I did. He thinks you're pretty bad."

"Well, sure. I work at stinking, so he'll build up his

confidence. I thought that's what you're supposed to do with kids."

Boone shook his head. "You might want to kick your game up a notch. Something tells me he'll still be able to take you. He whips my butt every night, and, believe me, I'm trying."

"Yes, but you're you," Ethan said, then raised his voice. "Hey, B.J., forget that soda! We're going out for burgers."

B.J. came running out the back door. "All of us?"

"Nope, just you and me," Ethan said. "Your dad and Emily have grown-up stuff to discuss." He glanced across the yard at the sound of a car. "And there she is now. Run and give her a hug, then hop in my car. We'll play miniature golf after dinner, then go back to my place. I've been practicing that video game. I might be able to take you now."

"No way," B.J. responded. He glanced at Boone. "Is it okay, Dad?"

"Sure. Have fun. Grab your toothbrush and a change of clothes. Ethan says you can stay over and he'll get you to school in the morning."

There was no mistaking Emily's frown when she spotted Ethan.

His friend didn't miss the look, either.

"Not to worry," Ethan told her, giving her a kiss on the cheek. "I'm just here to pick up the kid, so you two can have some time alone."

"I see," she said, her expression brightening.

Ethan leaned down and whispered something in her ear that Boone couldn't hear. Then B.J. emerged from the house, gave her a hug and raced off to join Ethan.

"What did Ethan say to you?" Boone asked as Emily joined him.

"He told me to go easy on you," she said. "Any idea what he meant?"

"He meant that I've had it in mind all day that you've shown up with bad news." He scanned her face. "Have you?"

Unfortunately she didn't immediately deny it. Instead, she stood on tiptoe and pressed a kiss to his lips before taking a step back. "You may see it that way," she admitted. "But I hope you won't."

This time the feeling of dread didn't settle in Boone's stomach. It stole through his heart.

Though Emily suggested they wait until after dinner to talk, she was so fidgety through the meal, Boone had to wonder why he'd even bothered cooking. She'd shredded the chicken on her plate but hadn't touched a bite. He'd automatically shoveled the food in, but it had been tasteless.

"Obviously putting this off was a bad idea," he said, as he took everything inside. He left the dishes piled in the sink, poured them each another glass of wine and gestured toward the living room.

"Inside or out?"

"Let's sit in here. It's starting to get chilly outside," she said. "Maybe the weather's finally turning. It is December, after all."

She wanted to talk about the weather, he thought impatiently. No way. They needed to get this over with. Boone waited until she chose a place on the sofa before dropping down beside her. He set his wineglass on the coffee table.

"Okay, let's dive right in. Are you calling it quits?" he asked, then held his breath as he awaited her reply.

She looked genuinely startled by the direct question. "What? No. Absolutely not."

Boone released a sigh of relief. Anything short of breaking up couldn't possibly be so bad. "Then fill me in. What's going on?"

He listened closely as she described the opportunity being offered to her in Los Angeles and knew at once it would demand her presence on the West Coast pretty close to full-time.

"And you're going to accept the offer, aren't you?" he said, resigned.

"How can I not? It's the most meaningful work I've ever had." She regarded him earnestly. "Boone, I wish I could make you understand what it was like working on this safe house and then seeing those women and children when they saw it for the first time. If you'd been there, you'd know how I felt."

Much as he regretted it, he was forced to admit that he did understand. And as desperately as he wanted her to be here, with him and B.J., he also knew she'd resent him if he insisted that she give up this opportunity. He wondered what she'd do if he even dared to utter such a selfish ultimatum. She'd probably throw it back in his face and walk out. Her career was something she could hang on to. Their love was untested.

It was already clear to him that her mind was made up. This whole conversation was little more than a polite exercise. He had several choices, all of them flawed. He could walk away and live the rest of his life with regrets. He could fight her and wind up losing in the long run when she came to resent him. Or he could man up and try to work through this.

When he looked into her eyes, he saw the shadows of worry there. She was obviously scared that he was going to react badly. That look made him desperately want to find the right words. He just had no idea what those words might be.

He reached over and touched her cheek, felt the dampness of a tear that had escaped. "I know you want my blessing, Em."

She nodded. "I do, more than anything."

"And if I say no, that a long separation just isn't going to work for me, what happens then?"

Another tear leaked out. "I don't know," she whispered miserably. "I see your point. I know this will be hard." She looked into his eyes. "But will it be harder than never seeing each other again, not being in each other's lives?"

When she put it that way, it shook Boone. He'd been without her for years. And despite having a loving wife and son during that time, a part of his soul had been missing. He didn't see things being a whole lot better if he lost her again, especially after they'd come so close to getting it right this time.

"Boone, say something," she pleaded. "Tell me what you're thinking."

"I'm thinking that no matter what I say, it's going to be wrong. If I tell you to turn this down, that our relationship needs to be your first priority and it simply won't work with such a long separation, then I'm being selfish and unreasonable."

"No, you wouldn't be," she insisted. "Believe me,

there's a part of me that totally gets that what I'm asking of you is too huge."

"But you want this job," he said. "It's given you something you felt was missing. How can I deny you that and still claim to love you?"

Now her tears flowed unchecked. "This whole thing stinks, doesn't it?"

He smiled, dabbing at her tears with a napkin. "I think I can safely say that if we were talking about a lousy idea that truly stank, we wouldn't be having this problem. You wouldn't be torn up over whether to take this job, and I wouldn't be torn up over letting you go."

Alarm immediately filled her eyes. "Letting me go? That's your solution?"

He needed to feel his way through this, try to get it right. "Em, you need to be free to do this. With B.J. and me in the picture, even with my blessing, I know you're going to feel torn every minute. You'll be sure you're shortchanging the job or us, no matter what you do. Can you deny that?"

Though she clearly hated making the admission, she shook her head. "No."

"Then you need to do this without worrying about me. You need to throw yourself into it a hundred percent. Once the project is off the ground and you've had some time to see how the work needs to be juggled, we can take another look at us."

Offering to let her go—even temporarily—was the hardest thing he'd ever done, but he knew it was for the best. She couldn't give this her all while looking over her shoulder and worrying about letting him down.

She sat back, her expression stunned. "I thought you might be mad, that you might tell me to make a choice—you or the job—but I didn't expect you to break up with me. Am I supposed to be thrilled that you didn't give me an ultimatum?"

Boone frowned at her anger. "I'm doing this for you, so you're free to do something you obviously want to do."

"No, you're telling me to go and do this, but to count you out. You're picking up your marbles and going home. How manipulative is that?"

Talk about an unfair accusation. "I am not trying to manipulate you," Boone argued. "I'm trying to be fair."

"What's fair about losing you before we even give this a try?" she demanded, on her feet and pacing. "Were you just looking for a way to end this? Is it too complicated for you? Well, guess what, Boone? Life gets complicated from time to time. You don't manage it by making some fake magnanimous gesture."

He regarded her with confusion. Okay, he was merely a man, but he'd thought he was doing the right thing here. Breaking up sure as hell wasn't what he wanted. He'd figured he'd give her a few months, let her tackle this new job with her full attention, then they'd give their relationship another shot. Obviously she didn't see it that way—exactly as he hadn't seen her departure as temporary years ago. Clearly, though, this had gone way off the tracks, and he needed to get the conversation pointed in the right direction.

"Okay, sweetheart, settle down," he pleaded. "Let's back up the train a minute. Obviously I got off at the wrong station, the same way I did ten years ago. Let's try to be real clear. How did you see this working?"

"Not like this!" she practically shouted as she paced

past him yet again, then whirled around and marched in the other direction, the color in her cheeks high.

Boone managed to grab her hand. "Sit, please. Let's figure this out."

"What's left to figure out?" she inquired sarcastically. "Things weren't going your way, I wasn't giving up my life to come here, so you bailed."

Boone closed his eyes, wishing there were some sort of script he could follow. Wasn't this exactly what had happened ten years ago? They'd come at their situation from different directions, misunderstood things and wound up with a permanent separation, rather than the temporary break she thought she'd requested.

"I swear I didn't mean it like that," he told her. "No more than you meant that ten years ago. It's as if we've switched roles. I'm only suggesting a time-out. You're apparently envisioning an ending."

"Well, that's what I heard," she replied.

"Then let's try again. Tell me how you saw this working," he requested.

She gave him a helpless look that tore at his heart.

"I don't know," she whispered. "Phone calls, getting together on weekends, whatever. It's what we'd talked about when we first got back together."

Boone nodded. "It was," he agreed. "I guess what we hadn't talked about was how long that was going to last or how it would eventually be resolved. Did you think it would go on that way forever?"

She sighed, then sat next to him. "I honestly didn't realize it, but apparently that's exactly what I was thinking." She met his gaze. "But you didn't?"

"I didn't," he admitted. "I thought our timetables would start to mesh better, not get worse."

"And we'd live here," she guessed.

Even as he nodded, he saw that it was a selfish assumption to have made.

She looked into his eyes. "So, what happens now, Boone?"

"I think we both need to think this through some more, figure out what we're willing to sacrifice to make this work." He touched her cheek again. "But not this job, Emily. No matter what, I don't want you to give up this chance to do something you care so much about. Maybe it's a good thing that we'll be apart for a while. I don't think so clearly when you're around. All I can focus on is how much I want to make love to you, to keep you right here with me forever."

She drew in a deep breath, then settled closer to him, leaning against his shoulder. "Yeah, being close does muddy up rational thought, doesn't it?" She fell silent, then glanced at him. "Of course, not everything in life should be entirely rational."

He smiled. "My thought exactly. I think a moment exactly like this one was in the back of my mind when I pushed so hard for a quick marriage. If you'd gone along with that, we'd have had no choice but to work through this."

"Oh, you dreamer," she accused lightly. "That's precisely when too many people wind up divorced when things get hard."

"Not us," he said with conviction.

"And yet you were the one who ten minutes ago wanted to call it quits."

"Not quits," he protested. "Just a break to figure things out."

"No breaks," she said with determination. "We work

on this one day at a time. I am going to take that job, Boone, because I feel I absolutely have to do it, but that doesn't mean for a single second that I'm giving up on us."

"Then I guess I can't give up, either," he said. "Not even temporarily. When will you start?"

"After the first of the year."

"And you'll be back here for Christmas?"

"Absolutely. I intend to try to make it for B.J.'s Christmas pageant, then stick around through New Year's."

"Then we'll make the most of every day we have," he promised.

He still wasn't a hundred percent convinced they could weather the kind of separation she was anticipating with this new job, but plenty of other couples did it, like those in the military. He just had to keep reminding himself what it had been like when he'd thought she was out of his life for good. Surely, compared to that empty time in his life, knowing she'd be coming home, that she'd eventually be in his arms, would be enough.

As Emily flew to Denver and then on to Aspen, she wished she felt more relieved at having resolved things with Boone. She knew, though, that underneath their agreement was a mountain of doubt. Boone might be willing to try to make this work, but he didn't entirely believe that it would.

Maybe she was being unfair to insist on trying. Maybe a clean break would have been wiser.

Just like last time, she thought, wincing. That had certainly been disastrous.

No, there would be no break. They were going to

make a real effort to work things out. For the first time in years, she had balance in her life—a job she was genuinely excited about and a man she loved with everything in her.

The next few days were a whirlwind of activity as something seemed to go wrong with every single detail at the ski lodge. A major furniture delivery was delayed. The snow they'd been anticipating hadn't made an appearance until exactly the wrong moment, when deliveries were finally scheduled. Roads were temporarily impassable. Tempers were short. And permits for occupancy hinged on contractors correcting a seemingly endless list of thankfully minor last-minute glitches.

Emily was working from dawn until late at night trying to make sure everything came together on schedule. After a week of nonstop worry and activity, she finally took a deep breath, sat back with Derek and his wife in front of a blazing fire and smiled.

"We're going to pull this off," she said triumphantly.

"I was beginning to have my doubts," Derek said.

"Not me," Tricia claimed. "I knew Emily had it all under control. And for my part, the caterer for the grand opening party is the best around, the chef I hired is fabulous, the wait staff is well-trained and our ski instructors are excellent. I predict a huge success."

"I'll second that," Emily said, lifting her glass in a toast.

Derek glanced toward the giant fir tree in the lobby that had been decorated with hundreds of twinkling colored lights and shiny, oversize balls in red, gold and green. A train ran through a snow-covered village beneath it. Mountains had been created with tiny skiers on the slopes.

"I love that train," he said, smiling. "I don't know why I didn't think of that. My brothers and I had one just like that, only not quite as elaborate."

Emily watched the train circle under the tree and thought of Boone. She'd barely spoken to him in the past week. They'd played phone tag a few times, connected once or twice for completely unsatisfying chats. She couldn't help wondering if he wasn't pulling away from her after all, especially since her calls yesterday and today had gone directly to voice mail. The fact that he hadn't called back was even more worrisome.

She'd find out what was going on with him next week, though, when she got back to North Carolina. If he'd had second thoughts after she'd left, that was soon enough to find out. She couldn't allow anything to distract from getting the lodge open and running. She'd made a promise to Derek, and she didn't intend to break it.

"Emily, is something on your mind?" Tricia asked, a worried frown on her face.

"Just thinking about all we have left to do tomorrow," she claimed.

"That wasn't the look of a woman worried about details," Tricia chided. "That was a woman thinking about the man in her life."

Emily smiled. "Okay, you got me. I have to admit I am anxious to get back to North Carolina next week. It will be the first time I've spent the holidays there in a while. B.J.'s in a Christmas pageant the night I get back. He's so excited about it. I can't wait to see it."

At least B.J. had been in touch with her almost every day, his excitement over Christmas and Santa's approaching arrival making her smile every time they talked. She was starting to understand why people talked about the best part of the holidays being the chance to see Christmas through the eyes of a child.

"I predict you will have a very merry Christmas," her friend said. "And I am never wrong about these things."

Derek rolled his eyes. "If something doesn't seem to be going her way, Tricia nudges it along until it does. Watch out for her, Emily. She's a meddler."

"Meddlers don't bother me," Emily claimed. "I have a whole family full of them."

"Not like her," he said. "I guarantee it. Now, if you will excuse me, I need to check on a few things and then get some rest. Tomorrow's going to be a busy day, making sure everything's under control for the event tomorrow night."

"That's my cue, too," his wife said. She bent and gave Emily a kiss on the cheek. "Sleep well. You've done a wonderful job."

Emily looked around as they left and gave a little nod of satisfaction. She had done all she'd promised and then some, but it didn't have the same thrill that she'd gotten from opening that modest little safe house for the women in such desperate need of it. Just this morning, Sophia had sent pictures of their modest tree, decorated with paper ornaments made by the children. To Emily's eyes *that* had been the most beautiful tree ever.

23

After tossing and turning every night for days after Emily had left, Boone reached a decision. He couldn't lose her again, not out of stubbornness, not without trying everything possible to pull this relationship together.

"Pete, in my office," he commanded as he passed his friend in the restaurant.

"Sure, boss," Pete said, following him at once. "What's up?"

Boone sat behind his desk. "I want you to forget about Charleston. You've been jumping through hoops. They're obviously not going to come around, at least not on our terms."

Pete nodded. "I know you're right. I just hate giving up. Should I get those other options so we can look them over?"

Boone shook his head. "I want new options, this time in southern California."

Pete's jaw dropped. "Los Angeles? San Diego? Where?"

"L.A.," Boone said. "Beverly Hills, Santa Monica, Redondo Beach, whatever."

"You know real estate there's going to be as bad as New York, and the market's just as competitive," Pete said, frowning. "You were totally against that. I don't get it."

"Emily's going to need to be in Los Angeles nonstop for quite a while. She's not going to be there without me. You'll take over East Coast operations. You can hire an assistant. I'll fly in from time to time."

Again, Pete's jaw dropped. "Did I hear a promotion in there?"

Boone chuckled. "You did. I'll give you a raise, too, so you can afford those tickets you'll need for New York on a regular basis."

Pete shrugged. "I don't think that's going to work out, but the promotion is great. How soon do you want the information on Los Angeles? After the first of the year?"

Boone shook his head. "I want it yesterday. There's a bonus in it, if you can find me the perfect property by the end of the day today, so I can fly out to take a look at it tomorrow. And, by the way, I'll be in Colorado for a couple of days after that."

Pete looked as if his head were reeling. Boone had never done anything this impulsively before.

"You're full of surprises," Pete said, sounding concerned. "Are you sure you're okay?"

"Never better," Boone said with conviction. He fingered the thick vellum invitation to the opening of the Aspen ski lodge and smiled. "It's taken me a very long time to have what I want within reach. This time I'm not letting go."

* * *

Though Emily had been repeatedly told that she had no official duties at the grand opening party, that her role in readying the ski lodge had been successfully completed and that she was simply a very valued guest, she couldn't help wandering through the crowded event and looking for any problems she might not have noticed earlier. Was there adequate seating for a large crowd? Were there sufficient conveniently located end tables so guests could set down their drinks? Was there any risk of tripping at carpet edges?

"You're working," Tricia accused when she ran into her. "I thought I told you to enjoy yourself tonight. You've earned it."

"Force of habit," Emily said with a chuckle. "Sophia's stopped inviting me to her events, because she says all my obvious fretting makes her guests nervous."

Derek's wife grinned at her. "I am not going to banish you from this amazing party, but I will order you to take a walk outside, breathe in the incredible scent of that mountain air until you feel completely relaxed, then come back in here and drink this outrageously expensive champagne."

Emily laughed. "Okay, I can do that." She hugged her friend. "Thank you."

"I should be thanking you. You performed a miracle here in record time, and you did it without killing my demanding husband."

"I'll take a client who knows what he wants anytime over those who keep changing their minds," Emily said. "Now, go. Enjoy your success. I'll step outside and look at that amazing, clear sky and the fairyland of trees along the driveway."

She went to her room, grabbed her coat, scarf and gloves, then walked out onto the lodge's wide front porch, captivated by the scene spread out before her. It was like a picture postcard of the ideal Christmas setting. With snow-covered mountains as a backdrop, white lights twinkled in majestic firs as far as the eye could see. Derek had wanted the entrance to the lodge to be magical, and it was.

"It's beautiful," a voice from the shadows commented.

Stunned and not quite believing her ears, Emily whirled around. "Boone?"

He stepped into the light and walked toward her.

"It really is you," she said, her heart lifting as she flew into his arms. "When? How?"

"I received an invitation," he told her. "Didn't it come from you?"

"No, but I think I know exactly who's responsible," she said. Derek had said his wife was a meddler. Obviously Tricia had seen the perfect chance for nudging Emily's romance along. "And this explains why I haven't been able to reach you for days now. Either you were scared you'd spoil the surprise or you were en route."

"Something like that," he said, his tone oddly mysterious.

He put his arm around her and pulled her close to his side. "I'm not sure I've ever seen anything this beautiful," he said.

When Emily glanced up, she realized he was looking at her, not the glorious scene spread out in front of them.

"I've missed you," she said. "And I've been worrying myself sick that you'd changed your mind."

"Never," he said succinctly. "Not about us. What we have is a done deal."

"Thank God," she said, snuggling closer. "Do you want to come inside? See the rest of the lodge? Put your bags in my room?"

He laughed. "I think we need to avoid your room for now. We might never get out of there. And I'm content to stay right here for a few more minutes, unless you're cold. Are you?"

"Not since you showed up," she said. "Did you bring B.J.? I spoke to him earlier. He talked on and on about his school play, but he certainly didn't give me a single hint about what was going on with you."

"He doesn't know I'm here. I told him I had to go out of town on business. He's staying with Jodie and Frank. We'll bring him with us next time. He's going to love this place. And he's going to want to learn to ski."

"You sound as if that's the worst thing he could possibly want to learn," she teased. "Are you scared of skiing?"

"Of skiing? No. Of running into a tree, yeah."

Emily laughed.

Boone frowned. "I suppose you're an expert."

"Not me," she said. "There's no way to go up the mountain that I find acceptable. I'm content right here in the lodge."

"And yet you were making fun of me," he said. "How is that fair?"

"What does fair have to do with it?" she inquired, feeling amazingly carefree and giddy all of a sudden. Boone was here. He'd surprised her. He'd been adamant about being with her. Surely that meant everything was going to work out, even if there were a few bumps along the way.

It seemed as if there was every chance this would be the merriest Christmas ever.

Boone woke with Emily in his arms and all seemingly right with his world. This was exactly the way it had been meant to be, the two of them together, sharing magical moments.

When his cell phone rang, he glanced at the caller ID, then frowned when he saw Jodie's number. Holding back a sigh, he answered.

"Good morning, Jodie. How are you?"

"I've been better," she said, a familiar tight tone to her voice.

"What's wrong? Is B.J. okay?"

"B.J.'s with us," she said, then added irritably, "Of course he's fine."

"Then what's the problem?"

"I thought you were going out of town on business. Instead, I find out that you're off on some tryst with that woman."

Boone winced. He'd told her only that he was going to California and then Colorado. He'd deliberately left Emily's name out of the conversation. Someone, however, apparently hadn't. Since he doubted Jodie had been talking to Cora Jane, it had to have been Pete. He hadn't thought to swear him to secrecy.

Jodie continued, "Since she's obviously more important to you than your son, Frank and I intend to take B.J. down to Florida with us for the holidays. That way you'll be free to do, well, whatever it is you insist on doing with that woman."

Boone sat up on the side of the bed, barely smothering a curse before he responded. Yelling wasn't going to accomplish a thing. Unfortunately, he doubted reason would, either.

"Jodie, you really don't want to do that," he said quietly.

"It's exactly what I want to do," she corrected. "She's obviously more important to you than your son."

"No, Jodie. The only thing this proves is that I should never have made the mistake of giving you a chance to have your grandson with you for a few days. If I'd had any idea at all that you would try to twist this situation to your advantage, I'd have brought B.J. with me. Believe me, I won't make that mistake again. If you want all-out war, then that's exactly what you'll get."

"I should have known you'd resort to threats," she said with a huff.

"Let me talk to Frank," he commanded.

"Sorry, he's not available. He's loading up the car."

Since he was getting nowhere with Jodie, anyway, Boone disconnected the call and dialed his father-in-law's cell number. Frank picked up on the first ring.

"I'm sorry, Boone," he said before Boone could utter a word. "I've tried to get through to her, but Jodie's determined to do this. If I hadn't agreed, she'd be taking B.J. and heading off on her own. At least this way, I'll be around to keep an eye on things."

"Frank, you know I have no beef with you. I even understand what Jodie is going through, but you all do not have my permission to take B.J. to Florida. Don't make me call the authorities. I don't want to do that, not for B.J.'s sake or for yours. Talk some sense into her before this gets out of hand. Please."

"I'll do what I can," Frank promised. "But you know where we'll be if I don't have any luck in changing her mind. And you know B.J. will be safe. I'll see to that."

Boone disconnected the call and started calling the airlines. By then, Emily was awake and had obviously grasped some of what was happening.

"This is because of me, isn't it?" she said, her tone flat. "Jodie's flipped out because you're here with me."

"Jodie's just flipped out, if you ask me," he retorted, though he knew she was driven by grief and anger. He'd been as understanding as he possibly could be, but this was absolutely the last straw.

"They're heading for Florida?" Emily asked.

"Unless Frank can talk sense into her," Boone confirmed.

"Then why fly to North Carolina?" she asked. "Fly directly to Florida. I'll come with you."

Boone shook his head. As desperately as he wanted Emily by his side, he didn't want to inflame the situation. Who knew what Jodie would do if they both showed up?

"You're right about going to Florida," he said, "but I need to go alone."

Emily's expression immediately shut down. "Sure. I understand. Why make things worse?"

"I'll pick up B.J. and we'll be back in North Carolina

in time for Christmas," Boone promised. He pretended not to notice the tears gathering in her eyes. If he acknowledged them, it would be his undoing. He knew she was being made to feel like an outsider, when all she'd done was love him and his son.

An hour later, he'd made his reservations, and Emily dropped him off at the airport. "You're not flying out today?" he'd asked when he noticed she hadn't brought her bags.

"Not until later," she told him.

Boone kissed her hard. "I love you," he reminded her. "We're not letting anything keep us apart, okay? I'll be back in North Carolina in a couple of days at most. We're going to have an amazing Christmas."

She smiled, though it was clearly forced. "Sure," she said. She stayed there until he was through security, then waved one last time. Something in her forlorn expression cut straight through Boone, but he simply couldn't deal with that now. All he could think about was getting his son safely back home.

Thanks to a phone call to Frank to alert him of his plans, Boone actually managed to arrive at the Farmers' house ahead of them. Frank had dawdled on the road, taking a slew of side trips ostensibly to show B.J. the sights. Apparently Jodie hadn't caught on, or if she had, it had been too late. She looked genuinely stunned when she saw him and his rental car in their driveway.

B.J. ran straight to him. "Dad, I didn't know you were going to be here already!"

"I came as soon as I heard about your trip," he said mildly.

Jodie whirled on her husband. "You knew about this," she accused.

"I did," Frank said. "When you wouldn't listen to reason, I saw no other choice. I wasn't going to let you land the two of us in legal hot water because you were being irrational."

Jodie regarded him incredulously. "Irrational? You think it's irrational to want to keep our grandson away from the woman who ruined our daughter's life?"

"Enough!" Frank commanded, giving a pointed look at B.J. "We'll discuss this later, Jodie."

B.J. was looking from one adult to the next in confusion.

"Okay, buddy," Boone said with forced cheer. "Thank your grandparents for taking you on a cool road trip, then grab your suitcase. We need to head back home, so we can be there for Christmas."

"But I thought Grandpa and Grandma Jodie were going to have Christmas with us," B.J. said. "They said we were all going to be here."

"Not this year," Frank told him. "We'll come back in a few weeks and you can show us all your presents. You and I will do some more fishing, okay?"

"Okay," B.J. said, throwing his arms around his grandfather's waist. "I love you."

"Love you, too," Frank said.

When B.J. went to hug Jodie, tears streamed down her cheeks. She squeezed him tightly.

"Never forget how much we love you," she whispered brokenly.

"I know," B.J. said.

As they drove away, Boone glanced in the rearview

mirror and saw that Frank had gathered Jodie into his arms. She was openly sobbing now. While the scene tore at his heart, he knew there had been no other way to handle the situation. Eventually they would work things out, but only when Jodie could let go of her irrational determination to get even with Boone.

Though he should have been relieved to have his son safely beside him and to be on the way home, he couldn't stop thinking about the expression he'd last seen on Emily's face. He had a hunch the crises weren't entirely behind him.

After the long cross-country trip to California, the overnight stop in Colorado, the emergency flight to Florida, then the drive to North Carolina, Boone was exhausted by the time he got home. He'd have preferred to make the drive from Florida in a long day, but he'd known better than to push it, as tired as he was. Once home, he decided he and B.J. needed a good night's sleep before going in search of Emily.

Over breakfast, B.J. regarded him with disappointment. "I missed the school pageant last night," he told Boone. "Grandma Jodie said it was just a play and that there would be other ones, but I really wanted to be in it. Do you think Emily got home in time to see it?"

"She was supposed to be here," Boone said. "But she knew you weren't back, so I'm not sure if she went. We'll find out this morning."

But when they walked into Castle's by the Sea a few hours later, there was no sign of Emily. Cora Jane met them halfway across the dining room. She pulled Boone aside.

"I don't know what happened," she told him. "But Emily called yesterday. She's not coming for Christmas. She said it's for the best. What on earth is she talking about?"

Boone's shoulders sagged. "Dammit. I was afraid of that."

"Did something happen in Colorado?"

"Yes, but not anything you're thinking. This is Jodie again." He explained about having to leave Emily to go after B.J.

Cora Jane shook her head. "No wonder she sounded so upset. I'm sorry, Boone. I really thought things were going to work out this time, especially after you went all that way to Colorado to see her."

"They are going to work out," he said with determination. "I just need to see her, straighten out a few things."

Cora Jane regarded him hopefully. "Can you do that?"

"I *have* to do that," he said.

"Well, all I know is that her heart is here, even if she's not," Cora Jane told him. "The girl loves you, Boone. It ought to be enough."

He hugged her, noting that she felt more frail than usual. "You always were my biggest fan. Why don't you come to my place tonight? Have dinner with B.J. and me. Let me cook for you for a change. Maybe you can help me come up with a good strategy for straightening out this mess."

"I'm a poor substitute for my granddaughter," she said.

He touched her weathered cheek. "You're nobody's

substitute," he said fiercely. "In my book, you're family. You always will be, no matter what happens between Emily and me."

And that, thank God, was true.

The grill was ready for the fish. The vegetables had been brushed with oil and sprinkled with salt and pepper, then wrapped in foil. With yet more unseasonably warm weather, he'd set the table on the patio, and B.J. had actually been coaxed into taking a shower. Cora Jane was due any minute.

Through the open windows, he heard the crunch of gravel in the driveway and walked into the living room to let her in. To his shock, though, it was Emily who stepped out of the driver's side of the car.

Across the yard, he could see the hint of nervousness in her eyes, saw the hesitation in her step.

"Do you have food for one more?" she called out as she helped Cora Jane from the car.

"Around here there's always food enough for one more," Boone said. "It's a lesson I learned from Cora Jane. Unexpected guests are always welcome."

They reached him then. Cora Jane gave his hand a squeeze. "Is B.J. inside? I've been dying for him to teach me one of those games he's so fond of."

Boone merely nodded, unable to tear his gaze away from Emily.

When they were alone, he said, "I thought you'd decided against coming for Christmas."

"That's what I thought, too," she confessed. "But then I got back to my big, lonely house in California and started thinking about where I wanted to be. I'd been imagining this holiday for so long, all of us here together. I knew there was only one way to make that happen. I had to swallow my pride and come back."

He frowned. "Your pride?"

"It kicked in when you didn't want me to come with you to get B.J. I started thinking that was the way it was going to be forever, that Jodie would keep finding ways to interfere and cause problems. I figured sooner or later you'd get tired of it and I'd be the one who'd lose."

"Never!" Boone said adamantly. "This thing with Jodie will get resolved. I may have to initiate legal action, even guarantee her some visiting rights, so she'll know B.J. will always be in her life. Maybe that will be enough to make her see reason."

"And if it doesn't?"

"Then she'll be the loser."

Emily shook her head. "B.J. will be the loser, Boone. You don't want that."

He sighed heavily, aware that she was right. "No, I don't want that." He pulled her closer, touched his lips to hers. "This is my problem, though. I will figure it out."

Though he'd meant to be reassuring, he saw a shadow pass across her face at his words.

"Shouldn't we be figuring things out together?" she asked quietly, pulling away from him. "Especially the important things like this?"

Boone backpedaled at once. "Of course. You're right. I just meant that I'm the one bringing the Jodie situation into the mix, so it's my responsibility."

She didn't look a hundred percent satisfied by his explanation, but she let it go, tucking her arm through his and leaning into his side. "It's hard to believe just a couple of days ago we were freezing on a porch in Aspen, and now here we are outside without a jacket. It's even chilly in Los Angeles right now, much more like Christmas."

Boone smiled. "Well, I've never known anything else at Christmas, so when people talk about wanting snow and cold for the holidays, I don't quite get it." He looked into her eyes, thinking that maybe now was the time to tell her about what he'd decided. "But if you want cooler air, how about next Christmas in L.A.? I imagine I'll be pretty busy out there around that time of year."

She stared at him in confusion. "What are you talking about?"

"We're opening our next restaurant in Santa Monica next summer. That means I'm going to be spending a lot of time out there for the foreseeable future. Can you think of anyplace I could stay?" he inquired casually. "It would need to be in a good school district for B.J."

Emily was apparently left speechless.

"Em, what do you think?" he coaxed.

She regarded him with wide-eyed wonder. "You're serious? You're coming to Los Angeles?"

"Well, you do have a lot of work to do out there, and I'm not interested in a long separation," he said. "It seemed like a reasonable solution."

"But the other restaurants?"

"Pete's going to be in charge of the East Coast side of things, at least for now." He looked deep into her eyes. "You haven't given me an answer yet."

A smile tugged at her lips. "The only question I actually heard in there was something about a place to live. Obviously I know of a lot of excellent hotels."

Boone chuckled. "Okay, I suppose I did gloss over the obvious question. Would you consider marrying me, putting a roof over my head and helping me find a school for my son? I'm thinking this would need to be a very long-term arrangement. Forever, even."

"Yes," she said with satisfying enthusiasm, as she threw her arms around his neck and kissed him. "Yes, yes, yes!"

When the kiss ended, Boone discovered they had an audience. Cora Jane was watching, her eyes shining. B.J. looked confused.

"You and Emily are getting married?" he asked, as if wanting to be sure.

Emily knelt in front of him. "If it's okay with you, we are," she said. "What do you think?"

"Will you be my mom?"

Emily glanced up at Boone as if seeking guidance, but he said nothing. He knew she'd find the right words.

"I will never, ever try to take your mom's place," she told him softly. "But I will love you with all my heart just as if you were my son."

"What would I call you?"

"Whatever feels right," she said. "You can keep calling me Emily, if that's what you want."

B.J. shook his head, then looked at his dad. "I want to call you Mom," he said. "Dad, do you think my real mom would be okay with that?"

Tears stung Boone's eyes. "I think she'd approve of anything that makes you happy."

"She won't think I've forgotten her?" B.J. asked, clearly worried.

"She *knows* you haven't forgotten her," Boone assured him. "She'll always be in your heart."

"And in yours," Emily said to Boone. "There's room enough in there for all of us."

"Amen to that," Cora Jane said, joining them.

B.J. grinned. "This is going to be the best Christmas ever," he said, then added excitedly, "And once we live in California, I'm going to Disneyland all the time."

"Maybe not all the time," Boone corrected. "And this will still be our home, too." He pulled Cora Jane close. "We have family here, after all."

Emily had tears streaming down her cheeks. "Why do I feel as if one of us should be saying, 'God bless us, everyone'?"

"Because you're sentimental," Cora Jane said, giving her hand a squeeze. "I have to say I'm feeling a bit sentimental myself. When I started out trying to nudge the two of you back together, it never occurred to me you'd wind up in California and I'd lose my best helper." She tousled B.J.'s hair when she said it.

"You're not losing any of us," Boone said. "Sand Castle Bay is in my blood."

"Mine, too," Emily said. "These past few months have reminded me of that. We'll be here so much, you'll get sick of us."

"It could never happen," Cora Jane said.

"And I think we'll have a wedding to plan here," Emily added, smiling up at Boone. "I can't imagine it being anywhere else. Can you?"

He grinned. "I was thinking we could gather together a few people, get married on the beach next week, maybe do a barbecue at Castle's afterward. What do you think?"

Emily exchanged a skeptical look with her grandmother.

"Absolutely not," Cora Jane said firmly. "We're having a big whoop-de-do, and that's final. After waiting this long, my girl deserves a proper wedding gown, flowers, the whole nine yards."

Emily laughed. "I couldn't have said it better myself."

Since all Boone really cared about was claiming this woman for the rest of his life, he wasn't about to argue about how that came to be. If she and Cora Jane wanted a whoop-de-do, then he'd see that they had it.

"Sooner, rather than later," he requested.

"Later," Cora Jane corrected firmly. "Big weddings take planning, and with you two in California, that'll take time. You want it done right, don't you?"

"I just want it done," Boone countered, but he knew it was a losing stance. Their minds were obviously made up.

"Early summer," Emily said. "That's a reasonable compromise."

Boone nodded, albeit reluctantly. "I suppose I can live with that."

Cora Jane looked hesitant, then she, too, nodded. "But we'll need to start right now." She grabbed Emily's hand and dragged her toward the house. "We should make some lists."

"Tonight?" Boone asked, He'd had a few other ideas in mind for tonight.

Cora Jane turned and gave him a chiding look.

"You'll have a whole bunch of time to celebrate in private," she scolded. "Do you want this wedding to happen this summer or not?"

He shook his head, laughing. "Go. Make your lists. You have a half hour. B.J. and I will get dinner on the table."

But he was talking to their backs. He glanced at his son. "Looks like we're on our own."

B.J. shook his head. "No way, Dad. We're getting married! How cool is that?"

Pretty darn cool in Boone's opinion. And way too long in coming!